Praise for **SARAH GRAZEBROOK**

NOT WAVING
'Eager, observant, zestful and funny ... agile and alert, Sarah Grazebrook earns a place next to Alice Thomas Ellis, and for comedy she knocks spots off Kingsley Amis'

Evening Standard

THE CIRCLE DANCE
'Wonderful book. A very entertaining, witty, outrageous novel about human relationships and feelings'

South Wales Argus

A CAMEO ROLE
'Fresh, funny, sparkly satirical – and close to the truth'

The Good Food Guide

PAGE TWO
'Poignant, inventive ... A sure touch and neat wit ... The most attractive and resourceful underdog since Shirley Valentine'

Belgrade Weekly

Also by Sarah Grazebrook

A Cameo Role
Page Two

Foreign Parts

Sarah Grazebrook

FLAME
Hodder & Stoughton

First published in Great Britain in 1999
by Hodder and Stoughton
First published in paperback in 1999
by Hodder and Stoughton
A division of Hodder Headline PLC

A Flame Paperback

10 9 8 7 6 5 4 3 2 1

ISBN 0340 70805 0

Printed and bound in Great Britain by
Caledonian International Book Manufacturing Ltd.

Hodder and Stoughton
A division of Hodder Headline PLC
338 Euston Road
London NW1 3BH

For understudies everywhere

Chapter One

Alice Hemingway studied her hand. She scrutinised it critically, trying to work out why Madame Evelyn of Colwyn Bay (discount for Equity members and clerics), had seen so much that dusty afternoon two years ago when Alice had sat before her in the clammy little cabin on the seafront, and why none of it had come true.

A cynic could have told her that the palm of a twenty-one year old is not sufficiently lined to furnish the sort of life plan Madame Evelyn had set out for her, but Alice was not a cynic. She was an aspiring actress and, in a profession where straws are clung to, vice-like, the perception that 'fame, romance and untold wealth' lay ahead of her had done much to lighten that stifling summer of two-line parts at the end of the pier.

From Colwyn Bay Alice had moved on to fringe theatre, a season in panto, an episode of *The Bill* and, latterly, filing and general office work for an architectural partnership in Shepherd's Bush. Three years out of drama school and the first of Madame Evelyn's predictions looked as far away as ever, with its inevitable toll on the third.

But it was in terms of the second, romance, that Alice had suffered the cruellest knocks. Although at twenty-three she felt she had finally learned to identify those men whose interest lay solely with her body or her bank balance, she had come seriously unstuck in the matter of Jay Bowden, a Canadian screenwriter she had met at a literary seminar the summer after Colwyn Bay.

He was tall and golden – a god among men. Or so he had seemed to Alice that hazy August night on the terrace of the faded country mansion where the seminar was taking place. His eyes were liquid brown and his voice a honeyed purr; his corn-coloured hair flopped boyishly over his forehead which was high and creased with intellectual rigour. He wore a dark blue shirt, designer jeans, and when Alice saw him, was leaning against a balustrade, a quizzical smile playing at his lips while an earnest young woman with wild black hair, who seemed to be in the latter stages of orgasm, hurled her body around for his inspection. Alice recognised her as the woman who had been asking stupid questions all evening and made it her mission to rescue the god before he evaporated in a thunder-cloud of boredom.

Flaunting her privilege as a committee member's friend, she had commandeered a tray of wine from a waitress and made a bee-line for the pair, snapping dismissively at anyone who tried to grab a drink on the way. The god had been suitably grateful, and the scene set for the most miserable two years of Alice's life.

Jay Bowden had been ruthlessly truthful with her throughout their affair, telling her he would never get a divorce, that he was too old (thirty-five), she too young, his writing uppermost – in fact all the truths that ageing Lotharios shower upon their victims in the first flush of seduction, so that when the time comes to move on they can leave in a warm glow of righteousness, confident they have been 'honest' from the first predatory fumble.

Jay had now moved on, or so it seemed. He had returned to his estranged wife, Francesca, even sending Alice a note expressing his gratitude for the help she had supplied during 'this difficult period in my life' and detailing his plans to take said wife on a cruise along the Nile in celebration of their reconciliation.

Alice had kept this note, blotched with her helpless uncomprehending tears, along with other tokens of their time together: a programme from the seminar, a sock which had slipped behind the radiator, a hideous chunk of chrysolite Jay had assured her was a symbol of enduring passion but which her horoscope manual said was popular with fantasists. She in turn had bought him a tiny chip of amethyst (fidelity and true love) which he had dropped down a drain while searching for his car keys.

Actors are, by nature, superstitious and Alice more than most. There was no sound reason for this. Her parents were agnostic, her upbringing liberal, yet her whole existence was packed with hostages to fortune. Shrivelled twigs of heather lay crumbling in her pockets, ladders were avoided, black cats pounced upon. Pointless to tell her it was stupid. She knew that. No one who had laid a trail of teal tail feathers round their bed in the hope of landing the lead in *The Wild Duck* and ended up as Third Villager needed persuading that magic was no substitute for contacts. Still she clung to it as a way of cushioning rejection. Fate was a useful weapon in the hands of an out-of-work actor. It proved less of a consolation, however, when it came to the loss of her lover.

Despite his defection Jay Bowden had not entirely loosed his grip on Alice. He returned her phone calls, channelled through a jaundiced researcher called Bob with whom he shared an office in Bayswater, made vague promises about 'always being there for her', and then, just when even Alice was reaching the point of admitting it was over, there he would be on her doorstep with a bottle of wine and tub of Haägen Daaz ice-cream, telling her he couldn't live without her another minute.

He obviously couldn't live with her for very long either because after a hectic bedroom tussle, three glasses of wine and most of the ice-cream he would be screeching at her to find his shoes and tearing off to the connubial home to await another very important phone call. 'Work, honey. Work, work, work. Still, that's what it's all about, I guess. We creative guys are never off the hook.'

Alice, who had been off the hook for several months, was always deeply hurt by the undisguised priority her lover gave to his profession, particularly as there was no evidence that his own opinion of his skills was widely shared.

She knew he made a living – his name often appeared in the

credits for series that had been running for some time – but, try as she might, she could not detect any genuine originality in anything he wrote.

She hated herself for this. Part of Jay's enduring hold on her, setting aside his corn-gold hair and velvet voice, was his status as an artist. He was a creative writer, Alice his muse. He had said so very early on in their relationship and it had struck her as unbearably romantic. For this one reason she had put up with all his heartless snubs – his selfishness, unreliability, periodic indifference and suspected infidelities – because in the end it was to her he returned. He needed her to inspire him. Without her he was nothing. With true strength of mind Alice rigidly refused to question where the newly reconciled wife stood in this scheme of things.

Sitting disconsolately in front of the television, she sometimes wondered if it was a fault in her that the sum of Jay's inspiration was a continuing dialogue between two pathologists about the best way to lay out a corpse. At times like these she would turn to her horoscope.

This particular Tuesday Alice had more need than usual of cosmic comfort. She had knocked a pint of milk over in the fridge, cracked her head on a cupboard while clearing it up and had a letter from her bank saying the manager would be grateful if she could ring for an appointment. She doubted it was to offer her an overdraft.

She debated telephoning her agent to see if there were any auditions in the pipeline, but calls to Surtees Management Inc. generally left her feeling more dejected than before. If they had anything they would let her know, Giles Surtees' headgirl assistant would assure her crisply. She hardly ever got to speak to the man himself. Alice sometimes wondered if he even knew who she was.

It was therefore doubly surprising when the phone rang and it was Giles Surtees on the other end. 'Good morning, Alice, my pet. I've got something here I think might interest you. We've had a call from Gareth Paynton's office.' He paused for her to take this in. Alice, while knowing of Paynton as both director and actor, thought mainly of him in his capacity of husband to Vanessa Stormont, a highly respected actress who had taught her at drama school. 'Well, you'll have read about him taking over the Millennium Players?' Surtees rattled on impatiently.

'Yes. Is he . . . ? Does he . . . ?' Alice's hopes began to soar.

'Yes. Audition. *Romeo and Juliet.* Thursday the ninth at the Welsh Centre. Up by Cambridge Circus. Well, you know where it is, don't you?'

'What am I auditioning for?' asked Alice, hardly daring to believe her luck.

'Juliet, you little ninny. It was hardly going to be Mercutio.' He gave a splutter of laughter. 'It's a tour. Not sure of the details. Tara took them down. Tara, my love, what did you do with those Millennium Players dates?' Tara's voice rose coolly in the background. 'Where? Oh, yes, here. Good God, what on earth are they going there for? Alice, are you still there, darling?'

'Yes,' she squeaked, heart pounding at the possibilities ahead of her. Juliet. A tour. Fame, romance, untold wealth . . . Suddenly it was all within her grasp.

'They're going to Estonia. Fancy that! I'm not even sure where it is. Sounds chilly to me. Then Scotland. That's definitely chilly. Twelve-week run, three-week rehearsal. Well, good luck, my darling. Give it your all. Half-past eleven, did I say? Let me know how you get on.'

There was a click as he hung up. Alice stayed where she was, gazing at the receiver, uncertain whether she was dreaming. An audition for the part of Juliet? She wondered why Gareth Paynton had asked for her. Presumably Vanessa Stormont had recommended her. That, too, boded well. A personal recommendation from your own wife was not something to be lightly ignored. Perhaps now, finally, with a change of scene and some real work, she would be able to shake off the last vestiges of her hopeless passion, to escape the downward spiral of her fortunes.

The phone made a buzzing noise, reminding her that she was blocking the Surtees empire's line to the world. She put it down and let out a screech of delirious excitement. Then she went to read her stars.

Jay Bowden gave a deprecating shrug as Bob the researcher handed him the phone. What can I do? it said. Is it my fault women are falling over themselves to get my attention? Bob pursed his lips. He had better things to do than act as go-between for a string of female callers, all apparently forbidden to ring his colleague at home. Why had he gone back to his wife if he intended to carry on exactly as before? That's what Bob would have liked to know.

'Jay here . . . Alice, honey, how are you? Good to hear from you . . . You what? . . . Well, that's great, really great . . . *Juliet*?' He gave a low whistle. 'A tour? Where're you going? . . . You don't say. That's marvellous . . . Of course you'll get it. You were born to play it. Didn't I always say so? . . . Tonight? Honey, I'd love to. I can't. I'm all tied up with this screenplay I'm working on . . . No, nothing like that. This one's for me. All I need's the dough and we'll be up and running.

'Tell you what, you give me a ring as soon as you hear. We'll squeeze in a little celebration. How would that be? . . . I know, honey. It's hard for me too, but I did tell you. I told you right from the start . . . I know. Oh, honey, don't get all miserable again. Think about the job. That's what counts. You're going to play Juliet. Six weeks from now you'll have forgotten you ever knew me . . .

'No, of course I didn't mean it, baby. Look, I've got to go. Got a meeting with the money men. V. important. I'll talk to you soon. Let me know how it goes.'

He replaced the phone. 'That was Alice.' His companion raised his eyebrows. 'Going to Estonia, wherever the hell that is. Touring. Shakespeare. She'll like that. She's a good kid. Deserves better than me.'

'You don't say?'

'I know. They all do.' Jay sighed and tipped a can of lager down his throat. 'Where's this Estonia place, anyway?'

'God, you Yanks are ignorant.'

Jay threatened him with the can. 'Call me a Yank again and you're dead.'

Bob grinned laconically. 'Tell you something, you want funding for your film – that's the sort of place you should be looking.'

Chapter Two

'My dear girl, it's a huge opportunity for you. Obviously it was a bit much to expect he'd offer you the lead on the strength of what you've done so far. They'll be going for a name. I really think you should accept. Four months' work. Good God, I've got actresses would give their eye teeth for that! Well-known ones,' Giles Surtees added unkindly then, regretting his callousness, 'Alice, my pet, it will do wonders for you. You'll be working with real pros, not that bunch of weirdos you were with in that thing I came to see. You need the chance to stretch yourself. Understudying four parts will do just that for you.

'And who knows? One of them may get ill. It does happen on tour, you know. Especially once you've crossed the Channel. You'd be amazed the things people go down with. I really do strongly advise you to accept. There's nothing else about at the moment. Theatre's dead and it's all repeats on the telly. Ask that friend of yours. The writer. He'll tell you the same thing.'

Alice bit back her tears and took a deep breath. 'I'll take it then, shall I?'

Relief flooded her agent's voice. 'Good girl. Yes, of course you must. Gareth Paynton was very impressed with you, by the way. He said to be sure and mention it. It was just that you lacked experience. Those were his very words. "Lacks experience". Well, here's your chance to get some. I'll tell

Tara to give you a call with the details as soon as they're through. Now I must rush. 'Bye, Alice, pet. Well done.'

Again she was left with an echoing line. This time she didn't hang on to it. She thumped it back so hard that a book fell off the table. She bent to pick it up then, seeing the title, left it where it was. *Romeo and Juliet – A Tragedy.*

By the time she got to the first day's rehearsal Alice was feeling more sanguine. Giles Surtees was right, she did lack experience. It was just that she had felt the audition had gone so well. She had pulled out all the stops, and there was no denying the electricity in the air as she sank distraught beside the outstretched reefer jacket which was standing in for Romeo.

Paynton had looked genuinely impressed. She had assumed his lowered eyes signalled concentration. They actually meant that the role of Juliet was already cast, but that the girl in front of him had a good voice and excellent legs and he would give serious thought to fitting her in somewhere. It would please Vanessa, who had not yet entirely given up the idea of playing the part herself. After all, she would not be fifty till October and Jean Forbes Hamilton had stuck to Peter Pan way beyond that.

Alice's stoicism was short-lived. By the end of the day she was a lot nearer to throwing herself under a train than the moment Jay had told her he was going back to his wife.

The cause of her despair was simple – the discovery that while she, an actress of some three years' experience, had been cast as lady-in-waiting, courtier and understudy for the Millennium Players' mould-breaking tour, the part of Juliet had gone to one Jasmine Ruddock, whose only claim to theatrical fame was to be the daughter of an ex-Tory MP who now had a chat show on Radio Penge, and to have been photographed drunk at the première of a Lloyd-Webber musical which had subsequently been withdrawn for drastic revision.

Jasmine had acquired her Equity card by playing herself in a drama documentary about the fate of women's hockey in a sport under threat from drug abuse. From the stills she had brought along to show them there was a general feeling amongst the cast that she was there to point up the dangers, not defend the spirit of amateurism as the film had set out to do.

To be fair Jasmine's prime ambition had never been to act, but to inveigle her way into the gossip columns, a 'Why Are They Famous?' slot and perhaps her own chat show. After all, if Daddy, who during his fifteen years in the Commons had never managed more than a follow-up question, could do it, why shouldn't she? All her reports had said 'chatterbox'.

Failing that she wanted to retain her place in the England B Ladies' hockey team for a couple more years, by which time she hoped to have worked her way through the rest of the England B Men's, and possibly moved on to the As.

In both these aims she had so far been disappointed, possibly due to their mutual incompatibility. Trials for the hockey team took place in the morning, and recovery from the social whirl kept Jasmine in bed till noon. Though not unduly bright, she had eventually come to realise that her stamina would be more usefully deployed in bed with the rich and powerful than labouring round a hockey pitch somewhere off the North Circular.

It was thus that she had fixed on Gareth Paynton, respected actor and now director of the Millennium Company. She had met him at the launch party for the new theatrical venture and, on hearing of the projected trip to Europe, had immediately offered herself for audition and anything else he might have in mind.

Paynton, for his part, was at an awkward stage in his career. No longer young (he was forty-five) and never handsome, he had become tired of seeing his name slip down the billing as newer and brighter actors came along.

He had therefore turned to directing. In a small way at first – a drama school production or two, a summer season here, a showcase there – but always with an eye to greater things. To this end he had allied himself to numerous worthy but uncontentious causes, defended the Arts Council, and concentrated single-mindedly on the classics, in the hope that this persistence might yet secure him a knighthood, the very summit of his ambition.

Then, just as the long years of toadying looked set to pay off, the Tories had been voted out of power. Not so much voted as booted, and Gareth Paynton's particular form of patriotism became dangerously unpopular overnight.

He had moved quickly to rectify this, startling even his own wife with the speed of the about face. Overnight he shed his Fat Cat contacts, dumped his plan to take *Lear* to Vienna, and turned instead to the British Council which was looking for someone to take a budget tour of Shakespeare to one of the less affluent parts of the continent, namely Estonia.

What no one else knew was that his motives were less than altruistic. Paynton had seen, and greatly regretted, that he had missed out on the opportunities which a few contacts in the developing countries could bring. For industrialists they brought contracts, for socialites privilege, and for middle-aged actors at the crossroads of their careers they brought dubbing, lucrative commercials and recognition. Who, outside Britain, would have heard of Laurence Olivier without the Kodak commercial? Thus Paynton reasoned. Estonia would be his Kodak.

The British Council for its part was immoderately grateful when Paynton's agent put him forward for the job. Already his reputation as a man who stayed within budget had reached them; also, he was in no sense *avant-garde*. His productions stuck rigorously to the text, his settings to the period. No Weimar Republic *Macbeth*s for him, or rap *As You Like It*s. No, Gareth Paynton was in every sense 'sound'. He was duly appointed.

The choice of play had been left to him beyond a stipulation that he avoid the Roman cycle (too reminiscent of recent events in that area), and anything too long. Electricity was still at a premium in many of the towns and the Council could not guarantee a lighting set beyond nine-thirty in the evening.

Gareth had settled at first on a comedy, then changed his mind and gone for a tragedy on the grounds that, while it was possible to miss the finer points of an Elizabethan pun, there was no way you could misinterpret a stage full of dead bodies.

Hamlet was out of the question because of its length, likewise *King Lear*. *Macbeth* looked promising till Gareth's wife declared her intention of playing Lady M. This frightened him considerably since one of the few perks of directing budget productions was the need to employ a quota of fledgling actresses. The last thing he wanted was Vanessa in tow as he arranged his private coaching sessions with the eager young acolytes.

Romeo and Juliet satisfied everyone. It was lyrical, thrilling, passionate, sad – and mercifully short as Shakespeare went.

Vanessa, though still toying with the thought that fifty was not too old if properly lit, accepted her husband's anguished assertions that he could not guarantee her that certainty, and settled instead for advising him on his cast.

Paynton's method was simple enough, based on the established theatrical tradition of ringing up his chums, eliminating any with political leanings or dyslexia, all those who gasped when he told them the subsistence levels, and anyone to whom he still owed money from his days in rep.

This left him with a ground base of secondary characters but as yet no hero or heroine. Here his wife stepped in again. If she could not play Juliet herself, she must insist that he consider her choice of substitute.

Paynton had hedged and humphed since, in his experience, his wife's protégés were generally of the 'dark and glowering' school of acting, the men gaunt and anguished, the women cropped and strident.

He was pleasantly surprised to find that Alice Hemingway was neither, being small, elfin and vivacious, but he was already sufficiently committed to Jasmine Ruddock to allow for no change of heart. He had therefore offered Alice the understudy position, on the grounds that she lacked sufficient experience to carry a major tour but would benefit mightily from seeing how it was done.

The rest of the cast were equally dismayed to find themselves the props of a girl whose chief talent seemed to be getting her tongue down the throat of their director before most of them had had time to take off their coats. There were rumblings of discontent and raised eyebrows but no one felt it as bitterly as Alice, huddled in a corner struggling with lines she would not be called upon to speak.

Nightmare scenarios began to take shape in her mind. The fantasies were mild at first: a slow puncture that kept Jasmine away from the first night; a heavy cold that robbed her of her voice. But as the days went by and it became increasingly clear that whatever the leading lady's failings, ill health was not one of them, Alice's imaginings began to take on a more bloodthirsty air. Jasmine would wake covered in boils; her bungee rope would break; her father would fart on the radio and the sponsors insist she be replaced.

It was while she was in the middle of one of these, stifling a hypocritical sob as Jasmine's cannibalised body was lowered into the ground, that Alice realised someone was speaking to her. She looked up. A tall young man was gazing down at her. He had speckly green eyes and a crop of unruly black hair which, had she not been so devoted to Jay, she might have found very attractive.

'Are you all right?'

Alice nodded. 'Yes, thank you. Why?'

The young man shrugged. 'Nothing. You looked a bit angry, that's all.'

She smiled unconvincingly. 'I was thinking about my landlord. That always makes me cross.'

The man held out his hand. 'I'm Philip Carter.'

Alice shook it. 'Alice Hemingway. Who do you play?'

Philip laughed a trifle humourlessly. 'No one.'

Alice frowned. 'Sorry. Are you the designer or something? Have I insulted you?'

He shook his head. 'I don't think anyone can insult me much any more.' He sat down next to her. 'I'm the understudy. "Chief" understudy, as I believe my contract says. Isn't that something?'

Alice eyed him warily. I hope he's not going to whine, she thought. I do hate moany men. 'Snap,' she said. 'I am, too. I don't think it says "chief" on my contract. That must mean you're vastly superior.'

Philip grinned. 'It probably just means you don't get stabbed. What are you doing at lunchtime?'

'Learning my lines,' she replied virtuously. 'You never know who's going to drop out.' Philip leant over and closed the book on Juliet's opening soliloquy.

'No, but you know who isn't,' he said authoritatively. 'Come and have some lunch.'

Chapter Three

By the end of the first week the company was beginning to gel. Several of the older members knew each other already, being stalwarts of the Gareth Paynton network.

Among these was Archie Frith who at fifty-five seemed dangerously miscast for Benvolio but turned out to have been Paynton's first director, way back in his days at Worthing Rep. His presence was partially explained when he confided to Alice one day that he was planning to write a 'warts 'n' all' account of the tour. He knew someone in publishing.

The Capulets were also played by friends of the director. Named, incongruously, Christine Pink and Marcus Lemmon, and known throughout the profession as the Pastels, they had been married to each other twice, twice divorced, and now maintained between them enough children and step-children to field a cricket team.

At present they were apart, Christine married to the brother of a former au pair, and Marcus still smarting from the rebuttal he had received when he'd suggested a similar arrangement to the girl herself. Though clearly experiencing considerable difficulties on the custody front, they had managed to set aside their differences for the sake of their work and, if anything, looked set for a third reunion as they bitched with touching unanimity about the appalling quality of Jasmine Ruddock's acting.

Their counterparts, Lord and Lady Montague, were a pallid affair by contrast. Axed recently from a failing soap opera and known only by their former characters' names as Jeannie and Ray, they were strangers to live theatre and seemed constantly embarrassed by the director's suggestion that they should try to make themselves heard beyond the second row.

Despite having been introduced on the first morning and given a copy of the cast list for back-up, Alice still found it a struggle remembering everyone's names. Twice she had offered Hilly Bates (Tybalt), a vegan and Born Again Christian, a sausage roll, thinking he was Clive Barry (Mercutio), a Born Again Carnivore. She decided to stop worrying after Paynton had called her Anita three times in one morning. If the director didn't know the names of his cast, how on earth could she be expected to?

Little by little faces began to slide into place. The part of Romeo had gone to an extremely handsome young actor called Craig Penforth. Straight out of drama school, he bore an uncanny resemblance to Leonardo di Caprio, although so far had failed to exhibit the same talent for acting. He was, however, a great deal better than Jasmine who made little secret of the fact that she was more than willing to rehearse with him privately, if necessary in the back of his car.

Craig had a long-standing girlfriend back in his home town of Preston and spent a fortune on phone calls to her from which he invariably returned looking depressed.

The one person who seriously bugged Alice, barring Jasmine Ruddock, was Marshall Vincent, a man of about fifty who had been cast as both Friar and Apothecary. He had recently recovered from an operation to cure his piles and, like the Ancient Mariner, plainly felt impelled to describe it in the minutest detail to anyone who sat still long enough. Since Alice was usually the only person who had nothing to do but sit around he had taken to making a bee-line for her as soon as he arrived, with the consequent effect that everyone else kept well away.

The only person genuinely interested in Marshall's condition, and everyone else's for that matter, was Bernice Wilde who was playing the Nurse.

She was married to Richmond Canning who, at seventy-two and playing the Prince of Verona, was firmly stuck in the Wolfit mould and had actually toured with the famous actor/manager on several occasions. Canning, despite certain health problems, was still a handsome man, tall and erect, with a mane of silver-white hair and brilliant blue eyes which twinkled roguishly when he saw a pretty girl.

Bernice was seven years his junior and by far the better known. This was mainly due to her role in a long-running prime-time series, *Sister Gillian*, in which she had played a district nurse travelling the countryside on a bicycle, and dispensing folklore and homespun platitudes till Birtism finally caught up with her and she was dispatched to an inner city housing estate, then quietly displaced by a gay black orderly as the focal point of the programme.

Since then she had contented herself with guest appearances, the odd Rattigan revival and the increasing needs of her husband on whom years of whisky and more whisky were finally taking their toll.

The couple saw themselves as the guardians of the company and rapidly became the focal point for the daily whingeing sessions which occurred around tea-time in the draughty corridor outside the rehearsal room.

If the actors seemed a little staid by theatrical standards, the same accusation could hardly be levelled at the stage staff. Led by the company manager, a stocky East Londoner called Sam Biggins, himself in the throes of a messy divorce, they consisted of Nobby Clarke, electrician, Simeon Balmforth, carpenter, two or three casuals, and Maeve and Jude, costume and wigs – a double act whom no one could remember working apart.

Nobby was an unprepossessing individual, shy of the bathroom and almost permanently inebriated. This in no way interfered with his conviction that he was God's gift to women, though it did interfere very heartily with his ability to light the set, a mammoth affair which Paynton had succeeded in hiring cheap from Opera North on the promise that he would put in a word for them with the Estonian Opera House.

Maeve and Jude were a colourful pair. At least Jude was colourful – a tiny fierce woman, much given to clapping her hands on which a knuckle-duster of rings flashed and sparkled. She was almost always in scarlet with occasional swirls of orange or gold, giving her the air of an escapee from a harem, although it would have been a bold sultan who chose to argue with Jude.

Maeve was tall and fair to the point of transparency. This she emphasised by the adoption of long flowing gowns, usually mauve or pale blue, and these, together with her invisible eyelashes and inaudible voice, always reminded Alice of a ghost story she had read about the soul of a woman trailing her reincarnation round the highlands of Scotland.

The thought of a reincarnated Maeve was not one that particularly appealed to her because she found the current version got on her nerves more than she would have thought possible. This had a lot to do with Maeve's air of condescension and the fact that she reserved it mainly for Alice. It was notably absent in her approach to the men of the company around whom she fluttered, tape measure in hand, with the persistence of a famished gnat.

'You must be Alice Jennings?' Maeve told her on their first meeting.

'Hemingway. Alice Hemingway.'

Maeve frowned suspiciously. 'Aren't you the understudy?'

'Yes.'

'It says Jennings here.'

'Well, my surname's Hemingway.'

'And you are the understudy?'

'Yes.'

'I suppose I'd better change it then.'

For all the difference it will make, Alice reflected, seeing that I haven't got any costumes. But she had. Three, in fact. Whatever her personal feelings, Maeve saw no reason why a lady-in-waiting should have fewer quick changes than the leading players. Indeed as the days progressed it became clear that this was to be less a play about love, passion, torment and death than about who could slip in and out of their farthingale the most times without hyperventilating or ending up dressed as a pall-bearer.

Jude was equally determined, having at her disposal more bundles of hair than a decent yak-shearing contest might yield, and she was damned if she was going to let any of it go to waste.

What she could not pile on the players' heads she looped around their ears, napes and shoulders, teasing enormous kiss curls on to their foreheads till poor Bernice was moved to protest that she looked more like Julian Clary than an Italian family retainer.

The men were buried behind a forest of whiskers and side-burns till Hilly Bates inhaled his moustache and immediately suffered an asthma attack, at which point Gareth Paynton stepped in to say he wanted all the young men clean-shaven. Jude acquiesced ungraciously, but from the expression on her face Alice suspected they had not seen the last of the hair mountain. She was right, as it happened, because a few days later Marshall Vincent sought her out to tell her that Jude had asked Gareth if the Apothecary could not be played as a hermit.

For the first time in her life Alice was genuinely unsettled to hear Jay's voice on the end of the phone. She had felt unable to ring him and say that, rather than playing the lead, she was about to set out on a three-month tour with nothing more exciting than a walk-on to illuminate her CV.

She knew how he would react, she had been through it so many times before. He would be kind, gentle, sympathetic – and she would feel even worse as a result, because for all his soft-spoken commiserations Jay never could resist patronising her. He was like it with everyone, even the surly Bob, but she alone seemed to mind. Maybe no one else noticed. After all, Jay's charm was legendary, a mixture of teasing, flirting and seriousness which melted the resistance of all but the most hardened. And even Alice didn't mind except where it came to her career. She liked how he joked about her taste in wine, clothes and music. It was only when he told her how to deliver a line that a tidal wave of resentment surged through her.

Now she would have to listen to it all again, just when she had hoped she was regaining control of her life. She should never have told him about the audition in the first place. What did he care if she was going away for three months? It was probably a blessed relief as far as he was concerned, and now she had met Philip – not that there was anything in it – she felt for the first time in ages that there was more to life than being Jay Bowden's cast-off.

Jay sounded uncharacteristically upbeat. 'Babe, I thought I'd've heard from you by now. How'd it go? Who's playing the guy? I always reckoned Juliet's a closet lesbian. You know, her and that Nurse. What's going on there, I wonder? Only kidding, honey,' as a furious hiss came down the line. 'So, when do you leave?'

Alice stared at the calendar. 'End of the month. The twenty-eighth.'

'Jeez, that's not long. Are you excited?'

'Not very.'

'Oh come on, Alice, honey. You must be. Big part, big bucks.'

She took a breath. 'I didn't get the part, Jay.'

'Didn't?' There was palpable disappointment in his voice. 'Oh, honey, I'm sorry. That's really rotten news. What did they do? Get someone from a soap opera?'

'It would have been better if they had.'

'So you're not going to this Estonia place?' For a moment Alice could have believed he really cared.

'Oh yes, I'm going. I'm *understudying* Juliet and all the rest of the women. And I play a courtier. It's just that . . .' She got no further.

'Well, honey babe, what are you moaning about then? I thought you meant you were off the tour. That's great! Look, I've got a few things to clear up here but how about I knock off early and buy us a bottle of something nice to celebrate? Do you want some ice-cream? What kind shall I buy? You get to choose.'

'Chocolate mint,' said Alice indifferently. It was Jay's favourite.

Waiting for him to arrive Alice's thoughts unconsciously reverted to her lunch with Philip Carter. How nice to have someone with whom she could share an innocent meal without the pressure of wondering where, if anywhere, it was leading. It was a new experience for her and one she felt sure she should cherish.

She had made herself a promise in the newfound maturity that losing both Jay and Juliet had brought, that if and when she ever did become involved with a man again, it would be for all the right reasons. Dependability, sobriety, a love of gardening featured high on her list. Looks would not count. Lust was no basis for permanence.

Sitting opposite Philip in the murky little pub next to the rehearsal rooms she had remembered this and struggled nobly to ignore his wicked sparkling eyes and the grin that sent buzzes up and down her spine. He was a fellow understudy, no more. They would be colleagues and, hopefully, friends. Try as she might she could not picture them exploring Ikea together. He was not a suitable candidate.

'Do you think,' he had asked as they sat down, 'that if the whole company went down with food poisoning when we get to Estonia, you and I could manage?'

Alice considered. Since so much of her free time was spent plotting the removal of Jasmine Ruddock it would be hypocritical to object. 'I'm sure we could. You might have to play the Nurse in one or two scenes.'

'I'd be happy with that.'

And they had spent the rest of the lunch plotting ways of finishing off the company.

As she sat on the tube that evening Alice had wondered casually if Philip would think it odd if she added Jay Bowden to the list of potential casualties. She also wondered if he himself had anyone who would qualify for disposal.

Jay arrived late and without the ice-cream. He was no longer so chirpy and chided Alice quite sharply for not having a proper corkscrew. She felt the customary sense of inadequacy flood over her. It was a tactic of Jay's to make her feel useless, one which he employed quite mercilessly if his own plans had suffered a setback.

After a couple of glasses of wine his good humour returned. He stroked her arm gently and assured her that anyone who turned her down for a part had no right to live, and that she had only to say the word and he would go straight round to Gareth Paynton's house and knock the bastard through the wall.

Looking at Jay's unblemished hands and the classic perfection of his features Alice knew he had never thrown a punch in his life, but she rejoiced in the thought that for her he was prepared to contemplate it.

Jay poured more wine and sighed deeply. He sat for some moments in silence then turned to her and said, almost conversationally, 'So you're really going away? Out of my life for good?'

Alice's heart gave a little jump. 'It's only for three months.'

Jay gave a brave little grunt. 'Sure it is. Three months. That's not so long.' He sighed again. 'Still, I guess by the time you come back you'll have forgotten all about me. And that'll be for the best. A new start.' He looked down into her eyes with wistful tenderness.

Alice felt a huge lump rising in her throat. 'I don't want a new start,' she mumbled. 'I never did. It was you. You're the one . . .'

'I know.' Jay squeezed her hand, the touch of his fingers sparking through her like a live current. 'I know I did. I had no choice.'

'You did,' said Alice tearfully. 'You didn't have to go back to your wife. Nobody forced you. You said it was what you wanted.'

Jay put his head in his hands. 'I don't know what I wanted. I just didn't think it was right for an old man like me to be playing around with a kid like you. You've got your whole life ahead of you. I just didn't want to mess it up.'

Alice turned away. 'So you dumped me?'

'I haven't dumped you.' Jay sounded quite indignant. 'How can you say that? I still see you. I ring you. I'm here now. Is that dumping you?'

'You went back to her.'

Jay groaned and slumped back in the chair. 'I guess you're too young to understand the reasons,' he muttered almost to himself.

'Too stupid, isn't that what you mean?' Alice retaliated bitterly. She hated it when he went on about the age difference. It hadn't mattered when she was twenty-one, why was it such a problem now?

Jay looked at her sorrowfully and stood up. 'I guess it's time I went. Goodbye, Alice. I hope everything works out for you. I hope it from the bottom of my heart.'

Shocked by the dramatic finality of his tone, Alice burst into tears. 'Don't just walk out on me like this. Please, Jay. I'm sorry. I know I'm stupid and awful and a nuisance to you, but I can't bear it if you just walk away and leave me.' She flung herself into his arms. Jay made soothing noises and smoothed her hair with his strong brown hand.

'There now, Alice, baby. Stop this crying. You said it yourself, three months is no time. I'll still be here when you get back. I'm not going anywhere. It's just Francesca needs me at the moment. She's had a bit of bad luck lately and – you know – we go back a long way. I couldn't just turn my back on her, could I?' Alice sniffed. Jay lifted her face and kissed her eyelids, then her cheeks then her mouth. 'It's not like you and me.'

Alice watched dreamily as Jay pulled on his trousers and searched around for his car keys. Lovingly she stooped to pick up the little white card that had fallen from his pocket. She glanced at it.

'Who's Bryony Douglas?'

Jay looked up sharply and almost snatched the card away from her. 'Oh, just someone I met at a script conference. She said she might be able to put some work my way. Jeez, is that the time? I'd better shoot. I've got a call coming from Geneva at eight o'clock. 'Bye, honey. Talk to you soon.' With a peremptory peck he was away down the stairs.

Alice went back and lay on the disordered bed, luxuriating in the memory of the past hour. She had been wrong to think it was over. Jay loved her, she felt sure – almost sure – of it now. He was only with Francesca for a while. Probably they didn't even sleep together, or if they did it was only for companionship.

Most exciting of all was his promise that he might manage to come out and see her in Tallinn. It wasn't all that far and he felt sure he could get a cheap flight on standby. He'd heard it was very beautiful – 'the poor man's Prague'. What more romantic setting for a lovers' tryst?

Chapter Four

Jay did not get in touch as promised. Alice had rung his office once or twice but Bob had put her off, saying Jay was out or in a meeting or busy. Could he give him a message? Alice had no desire to pass messages through Bob. The very thought of him rasping out her endearments left a nasty taste in her mouth.

'Could you just say Alice phoned?' she would murmur dejectedly.

'Alice who?'

'Just Alice.' She made a note not to invite him to the wedding.

She was brooding on this one day at rehearsal when Philip Carter caught up with her. They had seen very little of each other since the first day, mainly because Philip was only required for the men's rehearsals and she for the women's. The actual love scenes were being left to the third week in the hope that by then some sort of rapport might have been established between the two principals. No one was holding their breath.

'How's it going?' he asked, sinking down on to the disintegrating leather couch beside her.

Alice shrugged. 'Okay. I can't learn this "*Gallop apace*" bit.'

'Not that. The murder plot.'

She laughed. 'All right. How's this? You saw through the balcony, so that's Jasmine out of the way. I take the caps off the foils and the guys all run each other through. Christine and Marcus knock each other out. Marshall chokes on his own vomit.'

'What about Bernice and Rich?'

Alice hesitated. 'Well, they're so nice, couldn't they just sleep through the whole thing?'

Philip nodded. 'Suits me. Richmond does anyway, doesn't he? I thought perhaps Jaz could be strangled by her own hair when she goes through the floor?'

'Yes,' Alice enthused. 'And do you think she could land on top of Jude and Maeve? That would be really perfect.'

'What a bloodthirsty creature you are.'

'You started it.'

'Yes, and I'll look a damn' fool if it happens because I don't know a single line.'

'It's harder when you know you'll never get to play it,' Alice conceded forlornly. 'I just kid myself I'm going to, otherwise I couldn't learn a word.'

'We could always have a bet.'

'On what?'

'I'll bet you you can't learn Juliet by the end of the week, and you bet me Romeo. Whoever loses buys a drink.'

Alice grinned. 'You're on. What about the other parts?'

'Well, if this works we'll do them next week.'

'We could learn one a day. We'd be permanently legless.'

Philip laughed a trifle sourly. 'I don't see how else we're going to get through this tour.'

Not for the first time Alice wondered why he had accepted the job. He plainly detested understudying as much as she did. She knew why she was there, the alternative was filing, but it seemed unlikely to her that Philip could not have found other work. He was extremely good-looking in a dishevelled sort of way and had a lot more presence than the actors he had been employed to cover. Anyone could see that, including Christine Pink who had named him her Official Toy Boy for the tour, much to the amusement of Marcus Lemmon who suspected the au pair's brother must be on the way out.

Philip took it in good part, flexing his muscles outrageously whenever he passed her. He seemed less happy, however, with the attentions of Jasmine Ruddock who was beginning to tire of Gareth Paynton's niggling possessiveness and was clearly on the lookout for someone more robust to occupy her energies.

Alice noted how Philip tried to avoid her and warmed to him accordingly. She began to feel quite protective towards him, ruthlessly breaking in on tête-à-têtes which Jasmine had inveigled him into, and flashing threatening glares in the girl's direction if she chanced to look their way.

Philip was duly grateful. He was in an awkward position. If he rejected Jasmine's advances outright she would doubtless trash him to the director; if he encouraged them, the director would do his own trashing.

Neither Alice nor he referred to this unspoken agreement. It just seemed right that they should look out for each other. To which end Philip took to rescuing her from Marshall Vincent's anatomy lectures, whisking her away to practise the lines that neither of them knew.

She wondered if he had a girlfriend. He never mentioned anyone in the course of their conversations but, for reasons she wasn't quite sure of, she never mentioned Jay to him either. It was as though inside the walls of the rehearsal room they had entered a different world, a place unvisited by the trials of real life. It was a cocoon, a microcosm, complete with its own awesome array of problems – not least the quality of the production which showed very few signs of improving as the days went by.

'Better start saving,' Philip whispered to her during Richmond's opening address to the brawling citizens of Verona, of whom they formed the bulk.

'Why?' Alice whispered back, trying to look like a rumbling dissenter. Richmond frowned and lost his place. He hated any sort of interruption during his speeches, despite Gareth's assertion that a degree of heckling was essential to convey the turmoil into which his dukedom had been thrown.

'I know all of Act One,' Philip murmured, shaking his fist at Richmond who again lost his place.

'So do I. Nearly.'

Richmond stopped speaking and turned directly to the director. 'Look here, Gareth. I'm afraid I'm going to have to put my foot down about all this nattering. I know it's all the rage nowadays, but Sir Donald wouldn't have stood for it and I don't see why I should have to either.'

Gareth nodded appeasingly. 'No, I utterly agree with you, Rich. Or at least I would if it weren't for the fact that you're giving such a *brilliant* performance. What I particularly admire is the way you're channelling your frustration into the lines. I mean, you're absolutely bristling with rage and authority. It's quite electrifying. I'm sure everyone can sense it, can't they?'

Everyone said they could.

Richmond harrumphed and cast his eyes towards Bernice who was mixing his mid-morning powder. She beamed enthusiastically.

'Well, if you're positive that's how you want it?'

Gareth spread his arms wide. 'Rich, I'm in your hands. If you feel it would be better done in silence . . .'

'No, no, no. You're the director. Just wanted to be sure it was going okay, that's all.'

'It's going like a dream.'

'Good. Right. Better get on then.'

For the next few days Philip taunted Alice with little snippets of Romeo till she seriously thought she was going to have to pay for the whole evening. The pub plan had mushroomed into an Indian meal as well by now and she was really looking forward to it. It would be so nice to go out with someone who didn't spend half the evening on his mobile phone, or shuffling around in his seat because he was bored by the play.

She felt a pang of guilt at her disloyalty but consoled herself with the thought that if she and Jay were really going to make a go of things, she would have to accept that he was not entirely perfect, just as Jay had obviously accepted it in her. She imagined he would be pleased to know of her friendship with Philip. After all, Jay had a lot of women friends and insisted it was immature of her to object to them.

Just as she was leaving for rehearsal on Friday morning the phone rang. Alice was tempted to leave it. She was already running late and she wanted to buy some nail varnish on the way in, but a ringing phone has its own imperative. She flung down her coat and lifted the receiver.

It was Jay. 'Hi, honey. Glad I caught you. Listen, honey, I need to see you.' Alice's heart quickened.

'Yes, of course. I'm free from tomorrow lunchtime.'

'Hell, it can't wait till then. How about I pick you up after rehearsal today? We can go for a bite and I'll tell you all about it. What time do you finish?'

'Five o'clock,' Alice stammered, her head reeling.

'Fine. I'll pick you up. What's the address?'

Alice told him.

'That old barn? I thought it burned down. Okay, I'll be there. Hang around if I'm not. It'll be the traffic.'

'Jay, I can't . . . Not tonight.'

There was silence on the end of the line. 'What do you mean, you can't?'

'I've . . . er . . . I've arranged to go out this evening. With a friend. I'm free tomorrow afternoon. And all day Sunday.'

'Fuck all day Sunday!' snapped Jay aggressively. 'So who's this friend that's so important you can't spare your lover a few precious hours of your time?'

Alice baulked. She had never heard this tone in his voice before. 'Well, he's just someone . . .' She got no further.

'Oh, it's a he, is it?' said Jay in a quiet, cold voice.

Alice's heart froze. 'It's only someone I'm working with. The other understudy. We just thought we ought to run through the lines . . . in case anyone goes sick. I've got four parts to cover and Philip's got loads. All the men. No one ever rehearses us.'

'So you thought you'd have your own private little rehearsal after work?'

'Yes.'

'And where's this rehearsal taking place? Your place or his?'

Alice was overwhelmed by the injustice of his insinuation.

She took a breath. 'You have no right to talk to me like that, Jay. I'm not your property. I can see anyone I like, and go anywhere I like with them. You should know – you've never consulted me about who *you* go out with.' The receiver was shaking in her hand. I have to be strong, she told herself. He shouldn't have said that.

There was a palpable silence on the other end. Alice waited, trembling. Finally Jay spoke. 'Honey baby, I'm sorry. I'm just a jealous old lecher. Can't bear to think of you with any other guy, that's all. You can understand that, can't you? I should never have said that. I know you too well. You'd never cheat on me, would you?'

Alice felt her insides dissolving into a kind of puddle. 'You know I wouldn't,' she murmured huskily.

'You tell this guy,' Jay's voice was soft now, coaxing, 'tell him you're truly sorry but something urgent came up. Jeez, you see him every day, there must be another time you can do your lines?'

'I suppose so,' Alice wavered.

'Baby, I wouldn't ask you if it wasn't important. For both of us,' he added silkily. Alice closed her eyes. She hated letting people down – something which Jay had never cottoned on to. As far as he was concerned you arranged to do things and if it still suited you when the time arrived, you did them. If not, why bother?

'I'll pick you up at five. 'Bye, baby.'

She was late for rehearsal, not that anyone noticed. They were too busy studying the pile of brochures that Sam Biggins had distributed amongst them, following his return from the Estonian Consulate where he had taken everyone's passports for checking.

Thankfully no one had been pronounced *persona non grata*, although the official had looked very closely at Nobby Clarke's photograph since it bore an uncanny resemblance to almost every *mafioso* mugshot he had come across.

Philip came up to Alice. 'Have you seen this?' He showed her a leaflet featuring a brilliant sky over an inky blue lake dotted with tiny fishing boats. 'I'm actually beginning to look forward to this trip after all. Ready? "*Liberty, Freedom, Tyranny is dead*".'

Alice stared at him in horror. 'I don't remember that.'

'No, you wouldn't. It's from *Julius Caesar*. Just thought I'd throw it in for good measure.'

'Show off. Look, Philip, I've got a bit of a problem about tonight.'

He grinned. 'It's all right. I wasn't going to make you pay anyway. We'll go Dutch. Whoever wins. Okay?'

'Yes. No. It's not that . . . I can't come.'

Philip's face fell. 'I thought it was arranged?'

'It was. It is. Yes. The thing is the man I . . . Someone I know rang me first thing. Just as I was coming out, in fact, and said he had to see me after work today. On a matter of great importance.'

'Well, it won't take all evening, will it?'

Alice flailed around for the right words. 'It might. I can't be sure. You never know with him. I think it might. I asked if we couldn't put it off till tomorrow, but he said no, it was urgent. So I thought I'd better agree. I'm so sorry. I was really looking forward to tonight.'

Philip shrugged. 'Me too. Never mind. Can't be helped.' He turned away.

Alice touched his arm. 'We could go tomorrow,' she suggested tentatively. 'We finish at lunchtime.'

He smiled vaguely. 'No. Sorry, I can't do weekends. Not to worry.' He walked off. Alice watched him gloomily. So there is someone else, she thought.

'Come on, Orphan Annie. Come and have some lunch.'

Alice looked up. She had been miles away thinking if only she hadn't picked up the phone that morning. It was Sam Biggins who had spoken.

'My name's Alice,' she said firmly, suspecting he had made the same mistake as Maeve from costume.

'I know it is, but it don't go with "orphan", do it? Not so well. Are you coming or not?'

Alice sighed and nodded. She didn't particularly feel like lunch. She felt more like a double whisky. The morning's rehearsal had been unduly drawn-out due to a prolonged discussion between Maeve, Jasmine and Gareth as to whether Juliet could perform the balcony scene in the nude.

It was Jasmine's idea, based mainly on her theory that it was boiling hot in Italy and she jolly well knew she'd be starkers if she was out there in all that heat.

Maeve had pursed her pale lips and turned to the director for a decision. Paynton, whilst knowing full well that it was an impossibility, toyed lasciviously with the prospect of taking it as far as the dress rehearsal before succumbing to Maeve's entreaties for a chiffon shift.

All in all they had lost an hour of rehearsal time – time that could ill be afforded, judging by the trouble young Craig Penforth – who, it turned out, was dyslexic – was having with his lines, and the number of stops they had to make for Richmond to take his medicine or empty his bowels or simply sit down because he was feeling a bit 'you know'.

Sam led Alice through a spider's web of side streets to a sandwich bar called Uncle Fred's. It was curiously yuppified for the area, with wrought-iron furniture and a stark black and white tiled floor. The menu was written on a blackboard the length of the counter and the people making the sandwiches laboured to misunderstand every order with a determination bordering on the heroic.

'What'll you have?' asked Sam. Alice scanned the board.

'Chicken salad, please, and an orange juice.'

'With or without?'

'With or without what?'

'Stuff. It's all organic, you know. That's why I come here. Compassion in Farming. I'm into all that.'

'Oh,' said Alice. 'Yes.' Company gossip had it that Sam had not shown much compassion to his wife. Mind you, it also had it that she had brought her fancy man home and introduced him to the children as their 'new daddy', so the sympathy lay largely with Sam.

'Everything here's been grown organically.'

'Including the chickens?'

Sam chuckled. 'No. They're problem chickens. They insist on being shoved into a box eight by six and staying there for their natural. I'm going to have trouble with you, I can see that. I'll have a double bacon and egg, love, and a chicken salad for the lady. And a Grolsch and an orange juice. Ta.'

He guided her to a table. 'Gawd, I hate these chairs!' he complained, wriggling his broad frame.

'They're not all that comfortable,' Alice agreed.

'That's what I like about doing good,' said Sam cheerfully. 'It's always so bleeding miserable.'

Alice burst out laughing. 'Do you do a lot of good?'

Sam considered the question. 'Either that or I'm putting on weight. So, how are you enjoying yourself in the Millennium Players, young Alice?'

She shrugged. 'I am. On the whole. Yes, it's fine. I like it.'

'That's a mighty big "but".'

Alice stirred her drink with the straw. 'Well, I'm the understudy, aren't I? It would be different if I were playing something.'

Sam took a bite of his sandwich. 'I was talking to young Phil. He feels the same. Pig of a job, ain't it? Watching other people having all the fun. I couldn't do it. Still, if past form's anything to go by you'll be on before long, take my word for it. People drop like flies on these foreign tours.'

'Do they?' asked Alice, brightening.

'You bet. The last one I did half of them went down with dysentry. Mind you that was in Kuala Lumpur. But there's always something happens. You pack your medical kit, my girl, and don't go sleeping with the natives.'

Alice laughed. 'Anyone would think we were going to darkest Africa.'

'Africa's all right. Barring the mosquitoes. You know what

you're in for there. What do we know about these blooming Iron Curtain countries? Anything could happen. We might get nuked. Anything.'

'It looked very nice on those brochures you got us.'

Sam drained his glass. 'Well, it would, wouldn't it? You're hardly going to put Chernobyl on the front, are you?'

'That's the Ukraine.'

'Same thing.'

'I shouldn't say that to the locals. Anyway, why are you going if you think it will be so grim?'

'Because I need something to take me mind off things at home, that's why. What's your excuse?'

Alice sighed. 'It's work. And actually,' she hesitated, surprised at what she was about to say, 'I wouldn't mind getting away from things for a while, either.'

Sam glanced at her. 'Couple of lost souls, ain't we?' He looked at his watch. 'Come on, Orphan Annie. Don't wanna be late.'

She pulled on her jacket. 'For all the difference it will make.'

Sam helped her find the arm. 'Not for you, maybe. I'm company manager, remember. I'm indispensable.' He winked and Alice laughed.

'I'll remember.'

'You do. Mr Fixit, that's me. We hope. The way things're going, I'll need to be bleeding Mr Magic.'

As they were climbing the stairs up to the rehearsal room, Sam, who was ahead, suddenly stopped and turned to Alice. 'You don't want to let it get you down, you know.'

'What?' she asked in surprise.

Sam jerked his head towards the rehearsal room from where Jasmine could be heard murdering another soliloquy.

'Any of it.'

Chapter Five

The rehearsal was late finishing that afternoon so that Alice was beginning to panic by the time they were finally dismissed.

She needn't have worried. There was no sign of Jay in the tiny car park behind the building. She hung around by the exit for a bit then wandered round the corner to see if he was out the front. It had started to rain during the afternoon and the streets were wet and shiny in the lights of passing cars. One sped past splashing her. She retreated inside.

As she was hovering by the radiator Philip Carter came down the stairs, followed by Sam Biggins. 'What you hanging about for, ducks?' asked Sam. 'Boyfriend stood you up?'

Alice blushed. 'It's the Friday night traffic. He thought he might be a bit late.'

Sam nodded. 'Well, you can't stay here by yourself. All sorts of riff-raff about. Phil and I are just going for a drink. You come in the pub with us. The boyfriend's bound to guess, ain't he? There's nowhere else you'd be.'

'Oh, no, honestly,' Alice protested. 'He won't be long, I'm sure he won't. In fact, I think I can see his car now.' She craned ineffectually as a taxi cab zoomed past.

'Taxi driver, is he?' asked Sam approvingly.

'No. It's just the lights dazzled me.'

'Come on, Sam,' Philip broke in irritably. 'She doesn't want to come.'

'I'm not leaving her here on her own.' Sam's chin began

to protrude. 'There was a kid murdered round here a couple of months back. You go on. I'll wait with her till the geezer shows. Get one in for me, will you? Whisky chaser'll do fine.'

Philip, who had hardly looked at Alice, turned to go just as Jay came screeching into the car park. He slithered to a halt, effectively blocking the exit, tooted belligerently and flashed his lights. 'Oh, here he is now,' murmured Alice, feeling the blood sweeping up from her toes. 'He hates London traffic.'

'Well, there's a thing,' said Sam mildly. 'Come on, young Phil. See you Monday, ducks. Have a good weekend.' The two men left her. Alice noticed that as they passed the car Philip glanced briefly in Jay's direction.

Jay made no apology for his lateness. If anything he seemed to feel it was Alice's fault for rehearsing off the Euston Road.

'A drink. I need a drink,' he muttered, steering her across the road to a wine bar the cast had given the thumbs down. 'This will have to be quick,' he told her as the waitress brought an overpriced bottle to their table. 'I've written it all down, so there shouldn't be a problem.' He rummaged in his jacket and produced a buff envelope which he handed to Alice. 'Take a look at it and tell me if there's anything you don't understand.'

She opened the envelope, feeling there was very little she did understand. Jay was behaving as though she was his Cold War contact, not the woman he hoped would bear his children.

She stared at the contents in confusion.

'Huh?' Jay prompted. 'You're frowning. What's the hitch?' He poured some wine.

Alice looked up. 'Why have you given this to me? It's just a list of companies.'

Jay grinned and shook his head tolerantly. 'Not just any companies, though. All these guys have a business connection in this place you're going to – Estonia.'

'So?' said Alice, now totally confused. Jay leant forward.

'So, my little honey, I just thought it might be an idea for you to have a look round while you're over there and see if you can't put in a good word for me with one or two of them.'

Alice's frown deepened. 'Me? But what can I do? I mean, they're not even anything I know about. Look at this one. Mayfield Roofing and Guttering. You're surely not going to write a series set on a roof?'

'If you'd let me explain,' said Jay with restrained irritation. 'The products are irrelevant. They're just a way of soaking up some of the loot that's floating around out there. You go over, establish a branch, register your interest and sit back and wait.'

'Wait for what?' asked Alice, her head beginning to whirl.

'The grants, the subsidies. Eastern Europe's awash with money and nothing to spend it on. It's just what I need to get this project of mine off the ground. I've talked to Bob about it. He says it's a gift from God you going over there like this.'

'But I can't set up a company,' wailed Alice. 'I wouldn't know where to start.'

Jay patted her hand and waved to the waitress to bring some olives. 'Of course you can't. I'm not asking you to. All I'm asking is that you do a bit of detective work for me while you're out there. Ask around. You're bound to meet a few bigwigs at the first-night party and that. Just say you happen to know a guy, a very talented writer, who might be interested in setting up a production company out there. How would he go about it? That sort of thing.' He leant over and kissed her ear. 'Surely you can do that for me, baby?'

Alice wriggled pleasurably. 'And then, when you come over, you can finalise the details?'

Jay looked momentarily startled then rallied. 'Sure. Obviously that would be the ideal. It just depends how things hold up this end, whether I can get away.'

Alice stared at him. 'But you promised. That was half the reason I took the job.'

'Oh, come on, baby. You'd already accepted it before you told me.'

'Well, yes, I know, but . . .'

Jay reached across and clasped both her hands in his. 'Honey, you know there is nothing in this world I would rather do than come on this tour with you. And I'm going to do my damnedest to get myself over there, even if it's only for a day.' He kissed each of her fingers one by one.

The waitress, hovering with a bowl of olives, finally slammed them and the bill on the table and stalked away. Jay raised his eyebrows in mock dismay and Alice dissolved into giggles. He offered her the bowl. 'You might as well have some now she's gone to all that trouble.'

Alice shook her head. 'I hate them, you know I do.'

Jay looked surprised. 'I thought you loved them? When I took you to that Greek place . . .' He hesitated. 'Oh, Jeez, no, that was Bob and his wife. On their anniversary.' He grinned. 'That's what old age does for you. I'm losing all my faculties.' Alice stared at the olives and tried to smile.

From inside his jacket came the bleep of his phone. He whipped it out. 'Hullo . . . Oh, hi . . .' Though gifted with a voice that dripped honey in normal life, Jay turned into the obligatory stone-deaf power freak when talking into his mobile.

'Well, where are you? . . . Yes, I know I said seven. I got held up . . . Yes, traffic . . .' He looked at his watch. 'Half-past . . . No, that's fine. I'm through my business here. Just got to pay and I'm on my way.' He replaced the phone, extracted his wallet, scrutinised the bill, pulled a face and laid two clean notes on the table. Alice watched this with a sense of disbelief. Was he really about to go charging off to meet someone else? What about 'having' to see her? 'Too urgent to wait'? And here he was, about to shoot off somewhere else barely an hour after picking her up. What about her 'bite' to eat? She was starving.

Jay was already on his feet. 'Come on, honey. I'm in a bit of a rush. I'll give you a lift to the tube.'

Alice made no attempt to move. Jay shifted irritably. 'Baby, come on. I'm late as it is.'

'You go.'

'I'm giving you a lift.'

'I don't want a lift,' she responded, so forcefully that half the bar turned round. Jay stared at her angrily. He didn't like his plans messed about. 'It's raining out there.'

'I'm wet already,' said Alice, flaunting the leg of her jeans. 'Anyway, I haven't finished my wine.' Jay sensed that this was no time to argue.

'Fine,' he said in a clipped voice. 'Enjoy it. Christ knows, it cost enough,' he added for the benefit of the surly waitress who merely sniffed and carried on polishing glasses.

When he had gone Alice drained her glass. She didn't particularly want the wine. She had just felt she needed to make a point. She got up, added a tip to Jay's money and made swiftly for the door.

'Buy you a drink?' She looked down to see a sweaty-faced young man in a blue-striped shirt and braces beaming hazily up at her.

'No thank you.'

'Only I saw you had a bit of tiff. Never mind, darling. You come and have a drink with us. We won't upset you, will we, chaps?' He indicated his two companions, both equally drunk.

'No. Thanks, anyway,' said Alice and hurried out into the street. It was raining quite hard now and she almost wished she had taken Jay up on his offer. The underground was a good ten minutes' walk. She pulled her jacket tighter round her and was about to set off when the stripy shirt appeared again.

'My dear girl, you can't POSSIBL . . . EEY go out in this. Come back in and have another drinkie.'

He made to grab her arm. Alice pulled away violently but he had hold of her sleeve. 'I said NO,' she insisted, still trying to detach herself from his grasp.

'Naughty, naughty,' chortled the young man, hugely amused.

With a wrench Alice broke free and set off at a gallop down the street. To her horror, she found he was following her. She plunged across the road, the man in pursuit, hooting and guffawing like a paralytic huntsman.

Just down a side-street was the entrance to the pub where

the cast went at lunchtime. The landlord, though dour, would be more than capable of dealing with a sozzled Hoorah Henry. She fled towards it, hurling herself through the door of the saloon bar. It was empty save for one or two aged regulars crouched protectively over their pints. Alice rushed up to the bar. 'Is Geoff here, please? Only there's this horrible drunken man following me.'

'It's Geoff's night off,' said the young barmaid who plainly didn't relish having to deal with the situation herself. 'You can use the phone if you like, but we don't want no trouble.' The regulars grunted in agreement.

Alice had no time to phone anyone for at that moment the oaf came wheezing through the door and made a bee-line for her. 'Get away. Leave me ALONE,' Alice squealed as his great sweaty face loomed closer.

The next thing she knew he was flat on his back, still wheezing, with the bewildcred expression of beached sperm whale. A hand reached down and hauled him to his feet. 'I should go home if I were you,' said a voice. 'You're bothering the young lady.'

Alice opened her mouth to say something but nothing came out. The man made various conciliatory gestures, denoting that it was all a bit of harmless fun, that he was about to leave the country forever, and that he would prefer not to be booted in the kidneys again if that was all right with his attacker?

To all this Philip Carter smoothly acquiesced and, having seen him off the premises, returned to where Alice stood folded shakily over the bar and ordered them both a double brandy.

'But how did you manage to knock him down? I never even saw you coming.' Alice, now into her second brandy, was beginning to feel more cheerful. It made total sense of their understudies' bond that Philip should have been the one to rescue her, albeit in rather unusual circumstances.

'Total accident. I'd been practising my fights with Hilly all afternoon and that was the first time I got it right.'

'You could have damaged him for life.'

Philip regarded her impassively. 'Would you have cared?'

Alice was shocked. 'Well, of course I would have. He was only drunk. I don't think he meant any real harm.'

'That's what they all say,' said Philip coolly.

Alice was afraid she had sounded less than grateful. 'It was just so good you were still here. Otherwise I don't know what I would have done.'

Philip shrugged. 'Someone else would have stepped in.'

'I wouldn't like to count on it,' she said. They looked at the shrivelled-up regulars, hawking into the gas log fire, and both began to laugh uncontrollably. The girl behind the bar stared at them in alarm, making a mental note not to be free next Friday.

'Have you had anything to eat?' asked Philip when they had calmed down. Alice shook her head. 'I thought Jay was going to buy me dinner, but it . . . didn't work out.'

Philip nodded. 'Did you have a row?'

'No, nothing like that. He had another meeting. He's always very busy. That's why when he rang this morning, I thought I should go. I didn't mean to mess you around, honestly. If I'd known he was going on somewhere I would never have cancelled.'

'It's not too late.'

Alice made a face. 'I can't remember lines when I've been drinking.'

Philip grinned. 'I didn't mean the lines. I meant the meal.' He cast a telling glance around the dismal bar. 'I think we've done the pub bit.'

Settled in the warmth of the Indian restaurant, steam rising gently from her legs, Alice felt a lot happier than she had all day. It was nice being here with Philip – far more relaxed and peaceful than with Jay. An only child herself, she supposed this must be what it was like to have a brother. There was no implicit subtext between them. They just nattered and gossiped as though they had known each other forever, and yet they knew so little about each other.

'What shall we talk about now?' she asked, crunching on

the last of the poppadoms. They had completed their plans for the disposal of the company, throwing in Alice's landlord, the woman who had scorched a hole in Philip's favourite jacket, and Bob the researcher. Alice had fought shy of bringing Jay's wife into the net, for fear of revealing too much about her own position.

Philip drained the last of the wine into their glasses. 'I think now we're supposed to discuss our deprived childhoods, our terror of open spaces, that sort of thing.'

'Oh,' said Alice. 'You start.'

Philip laughed. 'Sad to say, I don't have all that much emotional baggage. Lovely mum, lovely stepfather. He's French. They live over there. By Lake Geneva. Lovely house.'

'Brothers and sisters?'

'A brother. He's my twin, actually. He's lovely too.'

'How old is he?' asked Alice.

'The same age as me.'

'Which is?'

'Twenty-five. Too old to be understudying.'

'Any age is too old to be understudying.'

Philip unwrapped a cube of sugar and ate it. 'You really hate it, don't you?'

Alice sighed. 'I do, yes. Particularly now I've seen who I'm understudying.'

'It's not just her, though, is it? Bernice might get ill, or Christine, or Jeannie. You've got a one in four chance of going on.'

'You must have a one in one, the number of people you're covering.'

Philip sat back. 'Yes, but what do you bet it'll be Marshall or Richmond who cracks first?'

'I suppose so. Oh, don't let's talk about the play. It depresses me.'

'Suits me. Tell me about you, then. Are you deprived?'

Alice smiled. 'Not really. Not in those terms, anyway. I'm an only child. Spoilt rotten. Dad's an engineer and my mother's a librarian. Couldn't be cosier.'

'What does he engineer?'

Alice shrugged. 'Not sure. Biscuits, I think. Something like that.'

Philip stared at his glass. 'My father's a solicitor. A senior partner. Carter and Venables.'

'That doesn't sound very French.' She stopped. 'Oh, sorry.'

'That's all right. They split up when we were tiny. I hardly saw him till I was fifteen. He was more interested in Paul. He's the brainy one. I was more . . .' He shrugged.

'Arty?' suggested Alice.

Philip laughed. 'Arty. Yes, I like that. "Vague" was how my mother described it. Dad just said I was thick.' His expression suddenly hardened. 'Right, that's brought us up to date, hasn't it? What next? Love life?'

Alice shuddered. 'No, thanks.'

Philip's face softened slightly. 'I was only joking. You are with that guy, though, aren't you?'

Alice stared at her glass, surprised to see that it was empty again. 'I don't know,' she said simply. 'I really don't know.'

'Married?' asked Philip. Oddly his questions didn't seem intrusive.

Alice sighed. 'Not to me.' Philip said nothing. She looked up. 'I expect you think I'm stupid?'

He frowned slightly. 'Why would I think that?'

Alice shrugged. 'Everyone else seems to. Even bloody Bob. D'you know, when I ring Jay and Bob answers, he always says, "Who is it?" He *knows* my voice. Who else is going to ring Jay there, for heaven's sake? Everyone else is allowed to ring him at home. They're certainly not going to bother going through that little freak, are they? It's only me that has to be kept a dirty dark little secret.' She stopped, aware that her voice had risen. 'I'm sorry. You don't want to hear all this.'

'How do you know?'

'Because it's not interesting, that's why.'

'Shouldn't I be the judge of that?'

Alice smiled half-heartedly. 'You sound like a psychiatrist. Tell me about you.'

Philip studied the menu. 'Do you want a pud?'

'No, thanks. Is that all I get?'

'You can have some coffee or a liqueur.' He squinted at the menu. 'I don't think I can afford both.'

'I meant, about you.'

Philip laid down the menu. 'I told you about me.'

Alice realised instinctively that the subject was closed. She smiled brightly. 'Anyway, you're not paying for me. We said Dutch treat, remember?'

'That was before.'

'Before what?'

'Before you got chased round the streets by a drunk.'

'Does that entitle me to a free meal then?'

Philip grinned. 'I think it might.'

'I must do it more often.'

'Not too often. An understudy's means are finite.'

Alice stretched out her arms. 'Wait till we've done them all in, then we'll be rich.'

'The richest lifers in Britain.'

'If you're going to be negative . . .'

Philip laughed and waved to the waiter to bring the bill. 'That's the end of our session for tonight, Miss Hemingway. Try not to fall over the mat on the way out.'

Outside the rain had slowed to a drizzle. Alice huddled her jacket around her. 'Thank you.'

Philip was buttoning his coat. 'What for?'

'Everything. A lovely meal. A lovely evening. Much lovelier than it started out.'

He grunted. 'Where did you say you lived?'

'Ealing.'

'That's a bit of luck. I'm in Acton.'

'Whereabouts?'

'Behind the post office. Down a dark alley.'

'Full of cats and dead prostitutes?'

'That's the one.'

They found a minicab office. 'Thank you very much for all this,' said Alice again as they sped along the Embankment, strains of Country and Western music crackling raucously from the radio. The warmth of the car had made her sleepy. She would have given anything to snuggle up to Philip, just for comfort, but even through the woolly fog that two brandies and a lot of wine had induced, she sensed that he was keeping his distance. For the first time it struck her that there might be a downside to platonic friendships. I'm sloshed, she told herself, otherwise I wouldn't think that. But looking up at Philip's profile as he stared dreamily ahead, she was hard pressed not to ask him if he ever shopped at Ikea.

Chapter Six

Alice woke with a hangover. She lay in bed trying to disentangle her recollections of the previous evening – mainly good – from the piercing throbbing over her left eye – extremely bad.

After several aspirins and a pint of coffee she set off for the rehearsal rooms, thanking whichever deity was on duty that they were due to finish at lunchtime.

If Alice was feeling frail, it was nothing compared with Jasmine Ruddock who looked as though she had hardly been to bed at all. This was apparently true, although Jasmine seemed to have very little idea of where she had spent the night, beyond something about a 'really whizz party'. Gareth Paynton looked suitably po-faced, having left her at her father's radio station on the understanding that she was going for a 'quiet dinner with Daddy'.

After several feeble attempts to run Juliet's scenes with the Nurse, Gareth abandoned his work plan and concentrated on the crowd scenes. This put a further nail in Jasmine's coffin as far as Alice was concerned, because she was in all of them and was certainly in no state to charge around the room waving staves at a bewildered Richmond Canning, himself under the impression that he had only been called in for a wig fitting.

Philip, looking horribly alert, steered her around as best he could, but by the time they broke for coffee even he was feeling the strain. Alice slumped in a chair. 'I'm sorry,' she groaned. 'I'm not usually this bad. I shouldn't have mixed them.'

Jasmine, who had been asleep on the couch, opened one eye. 'Get me a cup of that, will you, Philly my love?' She stretched languorously. 'And then you can come over here and rub my temples for me.'

'No, thanks,' said Philip calmly, but he did get her the coffee.

'I met a friend of yours last night,' Jasmine called across to Alice as she took the cup. 'Aren't there any biscuits or anything? I haven't eaten since yesterday.'

'Do you good,' Christine Pink told her. 'You could do with losing some weight.'

'Look who's talking,' said Jasmine crossly. 'You're no size eight yourself. An American guy,' she continued. 'Really dishy. A writer or something. He'd come to pick up Dad's PR girl.'

Alice felt a kind of cold slime in the back of her throat. 'Oh?' was all she could manage.

'Yup. Oh, bugger!' Jasmine had just poured coffee down her sweatshirt. 'Get me a cloth, someone, can you?'

Alice, despite herself, went and fetched one. 'How did you know he knew me?' she asked, her voice unnaturally high.

'Dad introduced us. When I said I was doing a tour of *Romeo and Juliet*, he said, "Oh, I know someone doing the same thing. She's going to Estonia." So obviously I knew it must be our lot he was talking about, so I asked who it was, and he said you. Where'd'you know him from?'

Alice swallowed. 'I've known Jay for years.'

Jasmine chucked the cloth at the sink and missed. 'Lucky you. He's scrummy! Bit old, but I don't mind that.' At this point a message arrived from Gareth Paynton to say that he was waiting for all those involved in the funeral scene and would they please get a move on? Jasmine sighed. 'He can't mean me, I'm dead. Tell you what, Ali, you do it. Ga won't mind. You don't have to say anything. Just lie there. Go on, it's your big chance.'

'Where is everyone?' came a bellow from the rehearsal room. There was a general scurry. 'Where's Jaz?' demanded Paynton as they stood around. 'I need her for this scene. I know she's under the weather but it's not much to ask, is it, at this late stage?' There was a horrible ring to that last phrase.

'She asked if I could stand in for her,' mumbled Alice unhappily. Gareth stared at her in surprise, then shrugged. 'I don't care who does it so long as we can get on. Richmond . . . Where's Richmond?'

'He's just popped to the gents,' said Bernice soothingly.

Gareth started to say something then changed his mind. 'Is there anyone involved in this scene who would like to have a go at it?' he demanded sarcastically.

As Alice was lowered to the ground on the wallpaper table standing in for a bier she heard Bernice whisper to Jeannie, 'Doesn't Alice make a pretty corpse?'

'Very realistic,' Jeannie agreed.

'By the way,' asked Jasmine as they were leaving, 'did you used to bonk that guy? The American one?'

Alice bit her lip. 'He's just a friend.'

Jasmine nodded. 'I didn't think you'd be his type. Mind you, I can't see what he sees in Bryony Douglas either.'

Philip caught up with her at the underground. Alice had heard him calling after her but had simply quickened her pace and hurried on.

'Alice . . .'

She said nothing, searching for her ticket. 'Alice, what's the matter? What's that bitch said to you now?'

Still she said nothing. Philip touched her arm. 'You mustn't let her upset you. She does it on purpose. Look how she rattles Christine. And everyone else for that matter.'

Alice nodded violently. She knew if she spoke the tears would start. Philip gazed at her sympathetically. 'Do you want to talk about it? We could have a coffee.'

She shook her head. 'No, thanks. Look, I'm sorry, I've got to rush. I'm . . . meeting someone.' She glanced up to see if he had bought the lie. It was impossible to tell. All she did know was that his eyes were strangely full of concern. He nodded briefly. 'Well, if you change your mind, you know where I live.'

Alice tried to smile. 'Down the dark alley.'

'That's the one.'

After he had gone, she deliberately waiting for the next train on the pretext that she was going into town, Alice reflected on the kindness of some people and the beastliness of others. Just her luck to be involved with a beastly one. Jasmine Ruddock was beastly, too; so was Gareth Paynton for not casting her, and Maeve Jenkins for not remembering her surname, and Marshall Vincent for being unhealthy . . .

She was disturbed in her reverie by the arrival of her train. Someone had left a newspaper on the seat. She seized it and turned to the horoscope page. *You are in danger of making a big mistake*, it said. *Avoid jumping to hasty conclusions. Watch out for hidden difficulties. Foreign travel promises new horizons.*

Alice folded the paper and put it in her bag.

Radio Penge was not something she would have listened to as a rule. She was not really listening to it now, beyond straining her ears every time the music stopped in an effort to catch the phone-in number.

She had a plan. Having spent half the afternoon in tears, tormented by images of a lissom Bryony Douglas rolling round Piers Ruddock's studio in the arms of the man Alice loved, she had decided to take action.

What the action was to be was not entirely clear in her mind, but the first step was to make contact, of this she was sure.

Call Piers Ruddock didn't start till six but they had been touting it all afternoon, beseeching listeners to call in with their favourite animal anecdotes or requests for 'really deserving' acquaintances. They still hadn't mentioned the phone number. Obviously Radio Penge's audience was very loyal and did not require reminding, or else – a more likely alternative in Alice's opinion – there was nobody out there listening to it. Well, now there was her and if they didn't say the number soon she would ring Directory Enquiries and force them to reveal it.

'Just time to tell you about what we've got lined up for

you this evening,' came the cheeky-chappy twang of the afternoon presenter. 'Later tonight we'll be bringing you our usual roundup of what's been happening in the area. News, views and comment on matters of interest to *you*. But first, just after the traffic, we have that champion of the consumer, Piers Ruddock, MP. Ooops! Ex-MP, I should have said. Sorry, Piers, if you're listening. He'll be here with the phone-in, giving you the chance to turn broadcaster with your favourite tales of . . . what is it this week?'

'Animals,' came a female voice in the background.

'Now is that any way to talk to the guys you work with? Right. Only joking. Sorry, Bry. Ooh, she's giving me the look now. She's a right women's libber, is Bry. True or false?'

'True,' came the woman's voice again. Good, thought Alice. Jay hates feminists.

'Now, here's that phone number you've all been waiting for . . . And don't forget, Piers would also like to receive any requests you've got for anyone who may be in special need of a bit of cheering up at the moment. So keep those phone calls rolling in. Till Monday it's cheerio from me, Denny Harman, and remember: keep your powder dry.' There was a whooping noise followed by a jingle and a female voice finally giving out the precious number. Alice scribbled it down, switched off the radio and made for the phone.

The line was busy. She waited a few moments then tried again with the same result. After ten minutes she was getting desperate. She dialled the number and, laying the receiver on its side, went and fetched a glass of wine. When she came back it was still beeping, but a recorded message occasionally intervened to thank her for her patience and tell her not to give up as Piers Ruddock was particularly anxious to hear from her. 'Huh!' said Alice, and took a deep swig. The message was repeated every minute till she was reduced to shouting abuse at it. She went to refill her glass and when she came back a glacial voice was asking whether she was a request or an animal story.

It took Alice a moment to register that the toneless female

on the other end was no longer a machine. 'Neither,' she said when the woman repeated the question.

'I'm sorry? I asked whether you had a request or an animal anecdote. Which is it?'

'Neither,' said Alice again, feeling quite belligerent in view of the time she had been kept waiting. There was a pause.

'This is *Call Piers Ruddock*. Are you sure you've got the right number?'

'Yes. I want to speak to Bryony Douglas. Are you Bryony Douglas?'

'No, I am not,' said the female crossly. Alice thought this boded well.

'Could you put me through to her then, please?'

'Look,' sang-froid was rapidly deserting the telephonist, 'this is a radio phone-in. It's not for private calls. It's for people who want to get on the air. Now do you have a request or a story? If not, I shall cut you off.'

'A request,' gabbled Alice, fearful of losing her slot.

'Right. I'm putting you through to Piers now. May I have your Christian name?'

Alice baulked.

'Are you still there?' Obviously there couldn't be many callers if the voice was prepared to put in this much effort.

'Yes.'

'What is your first name?'

Alice swallowed and crossed her fingers. 'It's Francesca.'

'Thank you.' The line went dead for a moment then crackled sharply. Alice froze as she recognised Piers Ruddock's unctuous tones. 'I believe we have Francesca on the line with a special request for someone she loves. Hello, are you there, Francesca?' Alice made a squeaky noise. 'Hello? Don't be nervous. There's nothing to be nervous about. Now, who would you like us to play some music for tonight?'

'My husband,' squeaked Alice.

'That's nice. And, silly question, I know, because you obviously think the world of him or you wouldn't have rung in, but is there any special reason you decided to give us a call tonight?'

Alice was silent.

'Francesca, are you still there?'

'Yes.'

'Thank goodness! I thought we'd lost you for a moment. Now, why do you want us to play something for your husband? What's his name, by the way?'

Alice took a breath. 'Jay.'

'Uh huh. That's odd. I met someone called Jay last night. He's not American, by any chance?'

'He's Canadian.'

'Ah. Not the same guy then. Is it a popular name out there?'

'Out where?'

'In Canada?'

'I wouldn't know.'

'No. So, has your husband had an accident or anything recently, Francesca? We usually like to keep our request spot for someone who's had a bit of bad luck. You know – redundancy, bankruptcy, that sort of thing.'

'I'm going to divorce him.'

'Yes, I see.' The line went dead. Alice tore across the room and switched on the radio. Mawkish music was issuing from it. When it finished Piers Ruddock, without a tremor in his voice, went on to say that they were just about to broadcast their first animal anecdote of the evening, so stand by all hamster fans.

Alice lay face down on her bed. I am mad, she told herself over and over again. I am completely and utterly mad. Supposing Jay heard it? He'll never speak to me again. Or Francesca, his bloody wife. He'll kill me. Or Jasmine. She'd've recognised my voice. She'll tell everyone and they'll all think I'm mad. Gareth will sack me. I'll never work again. Actors hate working with mad people more than children and animals. What will Philip say? He liked me up till today. If Gareth sacks me I'll never see him again . . . Oddly this was the thought which stayed with her longest.

She spent the rest of the evening trying to think of alibis

which would prove beyond all possible doubt that she had never phoned a radio station in her life, that the name Bryony Douglas meant nothing to her, and that for the past six months she had been praying nightly that Jay and his wife should still be together in forty years.

On Sunday she woke filled with fresh paranoia and rushed down to the newsagent's to see if any of the tabloids were vaunting such headlines as *We Reveal ID of Mad Radio Caller* or *Tragedy as Husband Kills Wife Who Wanted Divorce.* Even she had to admit the latter smacked of melodrama.

The absence of anything worse than a fresh Fergie scandal and details of a football manager's taste for choirboys calmed her somewhat. She bought supplies from the supermarket and spent a relatively peaceful day compiling lists of essentials to take to Estonia, a quick glance revealing that her flat could be relet as 'unfurnished' if she stuck to the items included.

It was now only eight days till departure and there was a decided frisson in the air at Monday morning's rehearsal, partly because the production was so far from ready and partly because they were all excited about going away.

Marshall had collared Sam Biggins and was interrogating him about the medical facilities in Estonia. Alice watched Sam nodding reassuringly as he ran through his list. Antibiotics, she overheard. Reciprocal provision. Enema.

Bernice, who had long ago ordered a double dose of everything Richmond needed, had no such worries. Her main anxiety was what she should take to wear. 'I don't want to be overdressed,' she appealed to the cast in general. 'Goodness knows, those poor people can't have much in the way of jewellery and so on. I don't believe I've ever seen an Estonian label at any of the Paris shows, though of course they must have their own fashion houses. What do you think, Christine? You always look so smart.'

'Darling, I'm taking my thermal undies, my bikini and a frock or two,' confirmed Christine Pink, who was more concerned about leaving her new young spouse in charge of the children.

Bernice frowned. She was too polite to say she thought Christine's choice inadequate, and too literal not to realise she was being teased. 'I think perhaps I'll have a word with Maeve and Jude,' she murmured, and hurried off in their direction.

Maeve and Jude protested that they hadn't given the matter a thought. They were far too busy trying to get the costumes ready to think about themselves.

'Just as well,' decreed Jasmine, who was being measured for her wedding dress. 'No one's going to look at you anyway, are they? Bugger!' as a pin went into her leg. 'Can you be a bit careful with those pins, Maeve?'

'Sorry,' said Maeve primly. 'You do move about a lot, don't you?'

'So would you if someone was sticking pins in you,' Jasmine retorted with some justification.

Craig Penforth had spent the weekend in Preston with his girlfriend, and seemed a lot more jolly as a result. 'She went through everything with me,' he told Richmond proudly. 'We were at it all weekend.' This drew lewd comments from the younger men. Craig blushed and went off into a corner to practise his sword fight.

Sam, who had managed to free himself from Marshall Vincent, was talking earnestly to Simeon Balmforth. It was the first time Alice had seen him look genuinely worried throughout two weeks of spiralling crises. He passed her on his way out and winked. 'You all right, Orphan Annie?'

'Yes, thanks. You?'

'Two steps from the madhouse. He's only gone and hired a set what won't fit half the theatres it's playing in. Poor old Sim's near in tears over there.'

'What will he do?' asked Alice. She admired the carpenter, mainly for his stoicism.

'Dunno. Pray for a bloody miracle, I should think. He'll think of something, will Sim, but I could do without it and that's not a lie.' He moved on then turned. 'By the way, you didn't half upset young Phil the other night.'

'Eh?' said Alice.

'Standing him up like that. I had a drink with him after the rehearsal. Well, two or three. He looked like he was settling in for the night when I left.'

'Oh,' Alice faltered. 'Actually, I did turn up. It was all a bit of a muddle. I got away earlier than I thought I would. We went out for a meal.'

Sam grunted. 'Nice, was it?'

'Very, yes,' she said evasively.

'Only from what he was saying in the pub, I reckon he's a bit keen, so don't mess him about if you don't wanna know, will you, ducks? Us blokes have got feelings, too, you know.'

Chapter Seven

Frisson had turned to crisis when Alice entered the rehearsal room next day. Clive Barry, who was playing Mercutio, had sprained his ankle falling over a paving stone on his way in. He had been to Casualty, escorted by a trembling Maeve who had been the only other person around apart from Gareth Paynton and Jasmine, neither of whom could sensibly be spared.

There had been further confusion when the receptionist assumed the patient was the distraught woman with pernicious anaemia rather than the bronzed young man reading a paperback, but once this had been sorted out and it proved that nothing was broken, Clive had been sent back to work in a taxi with instructions to rest his foot for a week and then use a stick.

'That is it,' snapped Paynton on hearing the news. 'That is bloody IT. How are we going to rehearse his death if he can't fight?' The matter was solved by installing Philip to do the moves while Clive emoted cheerfully from a makeshift chaise-longue, pushed around the set by two of the casuals who thought it a great laugh to project him at speed whenever they came to the end of the hall which sloped.

'For fuck's sake!' roared Paynton after Clive had narrowly missed going straight through the window. 'Are you trying to break his fucking neck, or what?'

Since their director had barely been known to raise his voice above a purr, the actors concluded he was not completely happy with the way things were going and took themselves off into corners to make sure they knew their cues a little better.

It was about this time that Jasmine Ruddock turned her attention to Craig Penforth. True to his intentions Paynton had kept the two of them apart till the third week but now, with the rest of the play chugging along, he began to concentrate on the main characters.

At first it was thought that Jasmine's need to fling her arms around Craig every time he came into sight was an attempt to create rapport, or at the very least to cheer him up. Craig had plenty to be depressed about. After his own mammoth weekend of line-learning he was at last free to concentrate on the performance of his co-star, and he didn't much like what he saw. Despite three years at drama school he was essentially a shy young man and seemed distinctly uncomfortable to find Jasmine's hands roaming so freely over his body.

Gareth, too, seemed a little uneasy about her interpretation. 'Darling . . . Jaz, look, try and remember you're a good Catholic girl. This is Juliet's first encounter with the opposite sex, apart from her dad and so forth. I think she might be a bit less – forthcoming.'

'Oh, rubbish, Ga! Girls today are much more forward than blokes. Aren't they, Craig? I bet Phyllis had your knickers off the first time she met you. Body like that.'

Craig blushed magenta. 'Her name's Felicity,' he murmured.

Gareth scowled and made a mental note to resume his press-ups. 'Anyway, pet, this is not now. This is sixteenth-century Verona, so I'd like a bit more decorum. Remember, you're wearing a heavy dress. You won't be able to charge around like that. Actually, Maeve . . . Maeve . . .'

Maeve leapt up from winding a stocking full of frozen peas round Clive Barry's ankle. 'Yes, Gareth?'

'I think it's time Jaz had a rehearsal skirt. So she can get the feel of the costume.'

'Oh . . . yes . . . right,' dithered Maeve, in the sure knowledge that she had made the remaining one into a beach bag.

'Now.'

'Yes, of course.' She scurried off. Clive picked up his stocking and swung it lassoo fashion over his head. The stocking burst, riddling the cast with ice cold peas. 'Oops! Sorry, everyone,' he managed, shortly before being bombarded from all sides by the rapidly thawing shrapnel.

By lunchtime order had been restored. Half the company had been sent home. Alice and Philip were required to stay so that they could mark the ever-changing moves Gareth was trying to instil in the young lovers.

'Jasmine, darling, let him make the first move. Remember this is your first sexual encounter. You are a virgin. Try and be a bit more . . .'

'A bit more what?'

'A bit more . . . reluctant.'

'RELUCTANT?'

'Not reluctant, no. That was a bad choice of words. Reticent – that's what I mean. Reticent. Don't you agree, Craig? Don't you feel Juliet would be a little more . . . erm . . . shy?' he translated, seeing that Craig had no idea what he was talking about.

'Definitely,' nodded Craig, tucking his shirt back in.

'Well, that's all very well,' pouted Jasmine, 'but the rate he's going I'll still be a virgin in the morning.'

'Let him go at his own pace,' begged Gareth. 'This is a rehearsal, remember. It's a time for experimentation and trial. This is when we find out what will work and what won't. No one expects a finished result first time.'

'Please yourself.' Jasmine folded her arms and slumped on to the sponge mattress Props had provided for the wedding bed.

'Let's move on,' Gareth sighed. 'To the vault.'

'And keep your bloody hands to yourself,' Craig snarled under his breath as he prepared to discover her lifeless body. Alice and Philip exchanged glances and went to get some coffee.

'I didn't,' came Jasmine's voice as they returned. 'I didn't touch the stupid thing. What are you, gay or what? Christ, I shouldn't think I could find it with a magnifying glass.'

'You bloody did,' came Craig's sullen response. 'I told you to watch it. I'm going to have you for bloody assault if you're not careful. You're a bloody nympho.' Alice noticed how his vowels reverted to northern in times of stress.

'I'm going to tell Gareth what you just said,' Jasmine retorted primly. 'I wouldn't be surprised if he threw you out.'

'Bit late for that, I'd've reckoned.'

'Don't you believe it. Romeos are ten a penny.'

'Well, Juliets must be pretty bloody scarce if you're the best he could come up with!'

They were interrupted in their exchange by the return of Gareth who had been called to the phone to be told that the company's flight to Tallinn was overbooked, and that in consequence they would have to fly to Frankfurt and change on to an Estonian Airways airbus, but that there should be absolutely no problem with this, apart from the four-hour wait at Frankfurt and the fact that the set was still going via Stockholm.

'Right,' he said, seeing their heated faces turned towards him questioningly. 'Let's take it once more from the top and then I think we'll call it a day.'

Philip leaned over and whispered in Alice's ear, 'I think it's time we had that line rehearsal.'

'I didn't mean you to cook a meal,' Alice apologised yet again as they carried the shopping up the narrow stairs to Philip's flat. 'We could have got a takeaway. I would have paid. It's my turn.'

'I told you, I like cooking.' Philip struggled to unlock the door without dropping everything. He switched on the light. 'Come in. Sit down while I open this wine, then we can get started.' He went off into the kitchen.

Alice took her coat off and sat down. She looked around the room. There was really nothing about the place to give her a clue to Philip's character. It was just a room: blue walls, blue and white curtains, shabby blue carpet, television in the corner, books in a pile under the window, National Theatre poster for *Electra* on the wall. She peered to see if his name was on it. It wasn't.

She felt strangely let down by the impersonality of the place. There was a photo on the window-sill. It was of a fair, gamine young woman holding a little boy. Otherwise the place was bare, no knick-knacks, not even any clothes strewn around. It was as though Philip was only passing through, not living there.

'Have you been here long?' she asked as he came back through with the wine.

Philip shrugged. 'About two years. I'm not here all that much.'

'Do you get a lot of work?' she asked innocently.

He gave a snort of laughter. 'Do you think I'd be doing this if I did?'

Alice blushed. 'I'm sorry. It's just you said you weren't here so I sort of assumed you must go away on tour or something.'

Philip grunted. 'I didn't mean to snap. It's just a bit of a sore point, me and work. Me and the lack of it, I should say.'

Alice sighed. 'Tell me about it! I've been filing envelopes for the last three months. I should be down on my bended knees to Gareth for just getting me out of that office.'

'But you're not?'

'No, I'm like you. A seething mass of discontent. I was quite pleased to start with. Well, I was, then I wasn't. If you see what I mean?'

'Not entirely.'

'Well, the thing was, my agent rang up and said I had an audition for Juliet. It came through Vanessa Stormont. She used to teach me, you see, and I felt I must have quite a good chance if she'd personally recommended me to her own husband.'

'Makes sense.'

'And to tell the truth, I thought the audition went okay. I really put my heart into it. I couldn't have done any better – at least, that's what I thought. And then Giles – that's my agent – rang up and said they'd offered me the understudy, so I thought, Oh, well, that's it. I'm useless. Then he said the only reason they hadn't given it to me was because I lacked experience, so I thought, that's fair enough. But then when I turned up that Monday . . .'

Philip handed her a glass. 'And saw our lovely leading lady. You must have felt like topping yourself.'

Alice hesitated. Self-destruction had never greatly appealed to her. 'I liked your idea better.'

'Which one?'

'Topping everyone else.'

Philip burst out laughing. 'You're right. You'll make a great Lady M.'

Alice felt suitably flattered by this. 'Should we start?' Philip fetched his copy of the play, turned on a lamp, lit the gas fire and dimmed the overhead light. 'Atmosphere,' he explained. Alice reached for her glass. Philip put his hand over the top. 'You only get to drink if you get it right. This is a serious rehearsal.'

Alice considered this. '*Romeo and Juliet*,' she said. 'A play by William Shakespeare.' They drained their glasses.

'We're brilliant,' Philip decreed when they had finished. Alice wasn't quite convinced, but she couldn't remember when she had laughed so much. Philip gave every part he played a different accent. This had gone quite well to begin with but by the time he came to his eighth he was running out of inspiration. They were on to their second bottle of wine.

'I can't understand a word you're saying,' Alice had objected. She was now down to dropping her aitches in an attempt to keep up. 'What is it? Afrikaans?'

Philip shook his head vigorously. 'I've bitten my tongue.'

This set Alice off again. 'I think perhaps we should leave it for tonight,' she whimpered, wiping her eyes and wondering whether stress incontinence could strike in your twenties.

'You're probably right. I'll make us some food.'

Alice followed him into the kitchen. It was a tiny galley-shaped room, smaller even than hers. 'Do you want me to do anything?'

'No. Talk to me if you want.'

Alice sat down. 'What shall we talk about?'

Philip was chopping mushrooms. 'Do you always say that?'

'What do you mean?'

'Well, you said it the other night in the restaurant. I thought it was a joke.'

'It is really. It's a habit. There are so many things I can't talk about to . . .' She stopped, feeling unaccountably disloyal to the man who was probably bonking Piers Ruddock's PR girl.

'You can say what you like to me. I shan't care,' Philip promised.

Alice laughed. 'People always say that, and then they do.'

He took a box of eggs and cracked them expertly into a basin.

'How do you do that?'

'What?'

'Crack eggs with one hand and not get them all over the floor?'

Philip narrowed his eyes mysteriously. 'It is an ancient art taught to me by Merlin when I was a boy at King Arthur's court.'

'I thought it might be.'

'Actually, you need big hands and nerves of steel.'

'That's me out then.'

'Hands or nerves?'

'Both.'

Philip opened some more wine. His hands were large, she noticed, but remarkably deft. She set the table, using odd cutlery and side plates that did not match. Silently Philip replaced them with those that did.

'You're a fantastic cook,' she observed when they had eaten.

Philip shrugged. 'Paul's better than me. He's had things in cookbooks. Mind you, Maxine publishes them.'

'Who's Maxine?'

Philip reached across for her plate and placed it on top of his. 'She's his wife. They've got a little boy, Danny. He's a smasher. I've got a picture of them somewhere.' He glanced vaguely around.

'Is it the one on the window-sill?' asked Alice.

'Oh, is that where it is? Yes, must be.' He made no effort to fetch it.

'Is Paul a chef then?'

Philip looked surprised. 'No. Why?'

'You said he'd had things in cookbooks.'

Philip shook his head. 'He's a photographer by trade. He's pretty good at that, too. Good at most things, is brother Paul.' He shuddered slightly. 'And here am I, unemployed, unemployable most of the time. What went wrong, do you think?'

'Acting's not like other professions,' Alice said stoutly. 'Being unemployed's part of it.'

Philip smiled very slightly. 'I must introduce you to my father. Perhaps you can persuade him of that fact.'

Alice detected an edge to his voice. She decided to change the subject. 'Did you have a nice weekend?'

'So, so,' said Philip. 'How about you?'

'Oh, yes, fine. Very nice.'

'What did you do?'

Alice sensed she was blushing. 'Well, I made lists of things to take on tour and I did some shopping. And I . . . listened to the radio quite a bit.'

Philip nodded. 'I like the radio. It's relaxing, isn't it?'

'Very,' said Alice, going even redder. 'What did you do?'

Philip reached behind him for a bar of chocolate. He broke a chunk off and offered it to her. 'Not much. Went to my brother's house on Sunday. It's become a bit of a ritual. Paul's away most weekends. Maxine gets upset if I don't show. She's a twin, too, you see. She gets lonely on her own. Twins tend to.'

Alice bit into her chocolate. 'That's an amazing coincidence. Both of you being twins, I mean. It's a wonder she didn't have twins as well. A twin and a twin getting married. What's her sister like? Are they identical?'

'She hasn't got one.'

'But I thought you said . . .'

'Her twin's a brother. They're very alike, though. Much more than Paul and me. Quite telepathic.'

'Is that when you can feel each other's pain?' asked Alice.

Philip was momentarily caught off guard. 'I imagine all families do that,' was all he said.

'I wish I was a twin,' said Alice suddenly.

'What on earth for?'

'Just to have someone to share things with.'

Philip solemnly broke the remaining chocolate in two and handed half to her. 'You can share things with me. I shall make you my honorary twin.'

Alice beamed. 'Thank you,' she said gravely. 'I shall endeavour to grow taller. By the way, I thought of a wonderful way of getting rid of Gareth Paynton the other night.'

'Oh yes?'

'Yes. I thought he could be mistaken for a descendant of Rasputin and stoned to death by the locals.'

'Rasputin was Russian.'

'Oh. Well, all the better. I thought we could wrap some of Jude's spare hair round him while he was asleep and stick a note on him.'

'"Please Stone Here"?'

'Something of the sort.'

The phone rang. Philip went into the bedroom to answer it. When he came out his face was very pale.

'Is everything all right?' she asked, since it plainly wasn't.

Philip stared at her for a moment as though trying to remember why she was there. 'That was my father,' he said flatly. 'Speaking of the devil. He certainly knows how to choose his moments.'

Alice nodded sympathetically. 'Parents can be a pest sometimes, can't they? My father's always telling people I have a degree in psychology.'

Philip frowned. 'Have you?'

'Of course not. He does it to annoy. I could kick him sometimes.'

'I don't follow.'

'Well,' Alice hesitated, 'I sometimes . . . once or twice in the past I've . . . er . . . made a bit of a fool of myself. Over men, that is. And Dad reckons it's because I don't sort of . . . erm . . . think things through.'

Philip was silent. 'And do you?' he asked at last.

Alice gazed at her fingernails. 'No, not really, I suppose.' She looked up. 'Not at all, actually.'

'He probably worries about you.'

'Oh, he does. I know he does.' She laughed awkwardly. 'He thinks I'm still his little girl, you see. I expect your father's the same.'

To her dismay Philip burst out laughing, but it was not the friendly, teasing laugh she had heard earlier. It was a horrid cold laugh, totally devoid of humour. 'My father! Worry about us? Yes, I suppose he does. We don't see him for fifteen years and suddenly he thinks he can turn up and run our lives for us. Just because he's got money. "Treatment"! If I hear that once more . . . There is no bloody treatment. Anyone would think you got it from drinking tap water. I think he probably does. If we can all cope with it, how come he can't? I thought that's what families were for.' He slammed his fist against the table. The crockery jumped and so did Alice. She stood up.

'I'd better go.'

Philip scowled at her. 'Yes, why not? There's nothing worse than other people's dirty linen, is there?'

Alice gripped the back of her chair. 'I didn't mean that. I just thought you'd prefer it. I seem to be getting on your nerves.'

Philip's face changed instantly. He looked chastened. 'You're not. Honestly. I'm sorry for sounding off at you like that. God knows, it's not your fault. He always has this effect on me, the bastard. I wish he'd never interfered. Why couldn't he just have let us be?'

'It's none of my business,' said Alice cautiously, 'but if he wasn't around when it mattered, why do you care what he thinks?'

Philip shrugged. 'Truth is, I don't. But it's not just Paul

and me, you see. It's Maxine. He's driving her to a nervous breakdown – all the things he's going to do for Danny if, if, if . . . It's blackmail, that's what it comes down to. He wants to run our lives. And I'm not having it. Let him rot. And his fucking trust funds.' He stopped. 'Still, it's easy for me to say that. I haven't got a kid.'

'But surely, if Paul's making a good living anyway . . . ? I mean, why do they need your father's money?'

Philip was silent for a long moment as though deciding whether to reply. Having done so he raised his eyes and, looking straight at Alice, said, 'because Paul may not always be there, and there's no way I can support them on what I earn.'

Alice sensed she was getting out of her depth. 'Is Paul ill?' she asked softly, her heart pumping.

Philip lowered his head. 'No, not ill. The marriage is in trouble.' He hesitated. 'Paul's involved with someone else. Maxine is trying to come to terms with it but she doesn't want to be left with nothing. She's right. I saw how my mother struggled till Jean-Claude came along. I wouldn't wish that on anyone. And if there's a way of making that bastard pay for what he did to her, I'll be first in line to make it happen. It's tough, though, listening to his ranting. Our best hope is for him to set up a trust for Danny, then at least we know he'll be okay.'

'But don't you think, if he's got in touch after all this time it must show that perhaps he wants to make amends to the two of you?'

Philip was silent for a while. 'I think he did till he found out what his years of neglect had produced.'

'How do you mean?'

Philip picked up a tray and piled the dinner things neatly on to it. 'If there's one thing on God's earth my father hates worse than tapioca, it's Labour supporters and homosexuals. And, unfortunately for him, it turns out he's spawned one of each.'

Alice sat for a moment, the chocolate in her mouth turning to gall. 'I think it's time I went home,' she said quietly.

'Thank you for putting up with my outpourings,' said

Philip, more cheerfully. 'Still, that's what you get for being an honorary twin.'

Alice tried to smile. 'It's certainly different.'

Back in her empty flat she put out the light and got into bed. It was suddenly so obvious. His aversion to Jasmine, the table-setting, the egg-cracking, his love of cookery, devotion to his mother, loathing of his father. I bet he likes garden centres, too, she thought. Her toes touched something crackly in the bed. It was the newspaper she had picked up on the train and fallen asleep re-reading the previous night. Angrily she forked it on to the floor. *You are in danger of making a big mistake* glared up at her from the floorboards. Alice crinkled up her face and began to sob. 'When did I ever do anything else?' she bellowed wretchedly.

Down below someone thumped on the ceiling.

Chapter Eight

The final dress rehearsal was on Saturday afternoon. It took place before an invited audience in Alice's old drama school, arranged by Vanessa Stormont in return for a free improvisation class.

Fortunately term had finished. Alice didn't think she could have borne seeing the students' confident young faces and remembering just how hopeful she had been before the realities of life on the boards struck home.

It was all a bit of a sham really, not only because the audience was made up of friends, but because most of the set was already on its way to Heathrow airport.

They struggled through, Clive Barry still limping noticeably and Richmond twice losing his place due to the noisy antics of Jasmine's friends from the hockey team, who had come straight from their victory over Cardigan Bay and were in no mood for sombre entertainment. They wolf-whistled and cheered every time a new actor appeared, beseeching him to show them his willy with a persistence bordering on the fanatical.

At the end Gareth Paynton gave a small speech, thanking the audience for their attention, enlarging on the value of taking Shakespeare to countries hitherto starved of such delights, and positively grovelling in his praise for the sponsor, a ball-bearing manufacturer from the Midlands whose motive for involvement was very similar to his own.

After the show they went backstage and drank copiously from wine boxes, while Gareth gave them notes. Sam Biggins stepped in to remind them to be at the airport by two o'clock on Tuesday afternoon and on no account to forget their passports. He then handed out comprehensive itineraries for the forthcoming tour, adding with breath-taking sang-froid that these might just conceivably be subject to minor changes as they went along.

Philip bumped into Alice as they were leaving. The past few days had been so hectic, what with technical rehearsals and last-minute costume fittings, that they had seen very little of each other. Alice, still reeling from Philip's revelation, was not sorry. Jay's infidelity had paled beside her discovery that the man she had unwittingly been earmarking for his replacement was not interested in women at all.

It was not until Philip had told her he was gay that she had realised quite how much stock she had been setting by their friendship. It had come as a cruel blow to have her prejudices confirmed, i.e. that there was no such animal as a kind, funny, sexy, compatible, available, heterosexual man. At least not for the likes of her.

'Not so hot, eh?' he observed laconically as they made their way out.

'Could have been worse, I suppose.'

Philip raised an eyebrow. 'Do you really think so?'

'I have to,' said Alice, 'otherwise I'd shoot myself.'

He smiled. 'Do you want a lift? Paul's got his car here.'

'You never invited him to watch, did you?' asked Alice, appalled.

Philip shrugged. 'We like to share our pain. Come on, I'll introduce you.' He led her to the stage door where several people were hanging about waiting for friends. The hockey team had moved on, though the distant bellow of their voices could still be heard as they headed for the pub.

Philip caught hold of a man's arm. He turned. 'Paul, this is Alice. My fellow understudy.'

She held out her hand. 'Hullo,' she said, trying not to stare. He didn't look at all like Philip. He was shorter and his hair was almost fair, compared with Philip's dark thatch. He wore glasses, too, which underlined the difference, but when he smiled, as he did now, Alice could see that they must be brothers. 'Delighted to meet you, Alice,' he said. 'Philip's told me all about you.'

'Has he?' she asked warily.

Paul laughed. 'Only the respectable bits.'

She smiled and crossed her fingers. 'Same here.'

'Go on. Say it,' Philip intervened.

'Say what?' asked Alice in terror.

'We don't look at all alike.'

'Well, you don't very,' she acknowledged in relief. 'Not to start with. You've got the same smile.' They both grinned.

'Thanks for telling me where you were.' They all turned to see a fair young woman stalking towards them. Alice immediately recognised her from the photo in Philip's flat. She was tall and willowy with a kind of boyish grace that reminded Alice of a model. Perhaps that was how Paul had met her if he was a professional photographer. 'I've been hanging around at the front with all those gruesome females screeching away,' continued the newcomer peevishly. 'I've got the most excruciating headache. I'm petrified I'm starting a migraine. Why didn't you say you were coming out the back way, Philip?'

'I thought you realised,' Paul intervened, embarrassed.

'Actors always come out the back way,' said Philip in a voice frozen with sarcasm. 'You should know.' Their eyes met.

'Please don't start,' said Paul's wife wearily. 'It's not my fault you're starving in a garret.'

'I won't starve,' retorted Philip viciously. 'And if I do, you'll be first in the pot.'

Alice was totally shocked by the way he spoke. It was so out of character. She glanced nervously over to see how his sister-in-law would react. It was then that the bombshell hit her. She stepped back, unable to take in for a moment what was now so patently clear. Philip saw and with almost sadistic pleasure drew her back into the circle.

'Let me introduce you two,' he said calmly. 'This is Alice.

We work together. Alice, this is Robert – Paul's brother-in-law.' Rarely had she seen such unhappiness in anyone's eyes as she saw that moment in Paul Carter's.

The journey home was virtually silent. Alice asked to be dropped in the Broadway. Philip offered to walk with her to her flat, but she refused outright. 'I've taken you enough out of your way already. Thank you very much,' she added to Paul, who was driving. He grunted and continued to stare straight ahead as he had throughout. Philip got back in the car. He looked curiously unmoved by the effect his behaviour had had on them all. He used me, Alice thought resentfully, as she turned to cross the road. He used me to get at them both. Poor Paul. It's not his fault if his brother's got a thing about his brother-in-law. For why else would Philip have taunted him so savagely? She shuddered involuntarily. Perhaps there was something to be said for being an only child after all.

As the car drove away Philip lowered the window. 'See you Tuesday,' he called. Alice frowned and nodded, trying to remember what she had arranged to do on Tuesday. Then she remembered. She was going to start a new life.

'Bobs, could you come over here, please? I'm having a little trouble reading this.'

Richmond Canning, glasses on the tip of his nose, was seated on a luggage trolley, studying his copy of the first week's itinerary.

'It says here Frankfurt. I didn't know we were playing there. I haven't got any German currency. I suppose they'll take travellers' cheques, will they? I do think Sam might have said. I hope we're not going to have to eat all that ghastly cabbage stuff. Is that our flight they're calling?'

'No, dear. It's someone wanting a wheelchair.'

'Ah. Well, it's all very unsettling. Have you got enough Rennies, precious? I don't want to run short.'

'I've got eleven packs, dear. Nothing to worry about. And we're not playing Frankfurt,' soothed Bernice who had been just about to treat herself to a Hermès scarf when Richmond summoned her.

'Well, perhaps I could have a couple now? Just for safety's sake. You never know with this airline food. How long did you say the flight was?'

'Two hours, thereabouts.'

'That doesn't seem very long.'

'Well, it's not that far away.'

'Isn't it? I always thought the Baltic was a hell of a way off. I suppose that's because no one ever goes there.'

'It's two hours to Frankfurt.'

'I thought you said we weren't going there?'

'It's just a stopover. Which do you prefer, blue or brown?'

'I've never had blue before. What flavour are they? Come to think of it, I don't think I've tried brown. Are they coffee or chocolate? I don't want nut.'

'Not the Rennies, Richmond. I've seen a pair of adorable headscarves in the boutique over there, but I can't make up my mind quite. The blue would go with my Chanel suit, but the brown would look lovely with my Aquascutum. I really can't choose.'

'You're not buying things already, are you, precious?' asked Richmond in a voice redolent with gloom.

'No, nothing. Just a little thing for the journey. You know how I like to get the odd souvenir.'

'Couldn't you make do with a postcard?' asked Richmond hopelessly.

'Well, of course I could if you're going to be sticky,' replied his wife.

Richmond protested that there was nothing he would less like to be. Bernice pressed a kiss on his forehead and was back in no time with her purchases.

Jasmine was being seen off by her friends from the hockey team who had become a lot fonder of her since she had forsaken the playing field for the stage and left them to work their own way through the Men's B, albeit at a more sedate pace. They had brought an inflatable penis which they had paraded through the airport as far as the check-in and were now intent on attaching to Jasmine's luggage trolley.

Gareth, accompanied by his wife, was watching with some dismay. While officially leaving the business of cast control to Sam Biggins as company manager, he was not entirely relaxed at the prospect of being accompanied to Tallinn, or even Frankfurt, by an inflatable penis labelled 'Romeo'. He would draw the line if Jaz wanted to take it as hand baggage.

Vanessa Stormont, witnessing her husband's discomfort, felt a stab of unworthy pleasure in view of his rejection of her own offer to play Juliet. Soothingly she squeezed his arm. 'Never mind, darling. It's only a bit of fun. These young things . . .' She left it there, knowing how any reference to age upset him.

Gareth humphed and looked at his watch. He was expecting a representative of the British Council, together with someone from the Estonian Consulate, to appear at any moment. They had expressed a desire to bid the tour *bon voyage* and to that end the management had laid on several press photographers and a man from the *Mail*, all of whom, he suspected, would find far more to interest them in the presence of a giant penis than speeches about culture and *entente cordiale*.

Alice sat with a magazine, staring unseeingly at articles about how to tell if your partner was being: unfaithful; disloyal; dishonest. Since, as far as she could tell, Jay had been all of these, she felt the article had very little to offer her.

Maeve and Jude came tottering by, both looking like walk-ons from *Murder on the Orient Express* with their hair piled high under pill-box hats and their legs encased in pencil-slim skirts and stilettos, scarves trailing down their backs like fish skins.

She looked around for Philip. Odd that now she had seen him with his lover – for it seemed fairly obvious that he would not have spoken to Robert like that unless some sort of intimacy existed between them – she wished even more that he could have transferred his affections to her. The admission was just about bearable, the evidence was pretty hard to take.

Still, even if he couldn't fancy her, he could at least take her mind off her problems. She had a knot in her stomach which no amount of measured breathing could disperse. It was like stage fright, only worse. At least with stage fright you knew why you had it, and also that it would eventually go away. With this she had no way of knowing whether it was a temporary inconvenience or whether it would travel with her the entire length of the tour and possibly beyond. The thought was weighing her down.

In one last tearful phone call to Jay she had virtually promised to secure him the names of suitable sponsors for the production of his much-vaunted screenplay. It was ridiculous, pathetic, that a woman of her years and emotional maturity should have fallen for his patter yet again.

She had rung to tell him that she would like formally to put an end to their relationship; that she had heard from Jasmine Ruddock that he was involved with one of her father's employees, and that, while wishing him all possible happiness for his future life, she felt she could no longer be a part of it.

She had rehearsed what she would say till the bathwater stagnated around her, coating her in chalky scum and sending chilly ripples up and down her body. Then, having perfected her speech, she had dried herself and gone to the phone.

It had started well enough. She had been firm with the odious Bob, requesting with quiet dignity to be put through to Jay directly and even adding that, as the call was of a personal nature, she would be grateful if he could leave the office for a few minutes.

She had waited patiently while he put her on hold, and even more patiently while he tried to connect her to a patently unwilling Jay.

It was only when Alice heard his voice – anxious, warm, caressing – that her resolution had crumbled into dust and less than dust. He knew why she was angry. She had every right to be. He had felt dreadful deserting her in the wine bar, and all for nothing as it had turned out. Bryony Douglas, who had absolutely promised to put him in touch with the major sponsor of Radio Penge, had done no more than introduce him to that pompous reptile Piers Ruddock and his sex-mad daughter. How he had kicked himself for turning down the chance of an evening with Alice for that. Still, at least they could look forward to their weekend in Tallinn. She needn't worry about finding contacts. He already had the names of a couple of guys who would be only too happy to get the ball rolling. He had faxed her details to them so that they could get in touch direct. Everything was going to be fine.

He would be over as soon as he heard from her. What a weekend that would be! Tax-free, too. All she had to do was be nice to them. A couple of drinks, perhaps some comps for the show? It hadn't seemed much to ask.

Nor would it now, if she had not accidentally come across an article in one of the Sundays, stating that Eastern Europe was currently a haven for criminal activity, a lot of it connected with the setting up of non-existent companies to launder drugs money. Of course that was just a rogue fringe. Most of the business deals being struck between the West and these emerging nations were wholly legitimate and, indeed, provided a valuable boost to the economies of the poorer nations, but *caveat emptor*. Alice had looked this up and discovered that basically it meant she would be to blame if anything went wrong. This did not greatly encourage her.

'Hullo, Sunshine. You all right?' Sam Biggins was doing his final checks. Having disposed of the luggage amidst panic-stricken cries from Bernice to make sure her hat boxes were the right way up, obscenities from Marcus Lemmon who had been surcharged for the transportation of his exercise bike, and general whimpering from the rest as they saw their possessions being shot into the void below Air Argentina, he was now doing a head count.

This was marginally more difficult than rounding up sheep on a motorway for as quickly as he bullied the men away from the bar, he lost Marshall to the lavatories, Bernice to Pastimes and Richmond to The Fudge Factory.

They were finally brought together by a screech of operatic intensity from Jasmine on discovering that, in attempting to scrawl a farewell message on the penis, the team's reserve goal keeper had pierced it with her Biro.

Being of tougher stuff than the average phallus, it had not yet given up the fight and was deflating gradually, a wistful hiss the only sign that it could no longer double as a life preserver.

'Do something, someone,' entreated Jasmine, pressing her finger over the hole.

'What?' snapped Hilly Bates, suspecting it contained gelatine.

'I don't know – mend it. Ask Marcus if he's got a puncture kit. He must have if he's got an exercise bike. Quick! If it goes down we'll never get it up again. Marshall, have you got any plasters with you?'

Marshall Vincent looked distinctly defensive. 'Of course I have.'

'Well, give me one, there's a love. I'll pay you back.'

'You can't. They're prescription only. They've got ointment on.'

'Oh, for God's sake!' stormed Jasmine. 'Some help you are.' Marshall went away to sulk, by which time Sam, having hauled Nobby Clarke out of the bar for the third time and threatened to 'slam him one' if he moved again, came into sight.

'Hullo, hullo. What you been doing to your flexible friend, young Jaz?'

She giggled. 'That twit Carly stuck her Biro through him. Oh, do help me, Sam. Look at him. He reminds me of G—' She stopped, remembering that the director's wife was present. 'Oooh, this is hopeless.' With a petulant shove, she knocked the penis to the ground and stalked off in the direction of a BA hostess who was trying to shepherd them into the VIP lounge where the First Secretary to the Estonian Embassy was waiting to address them.

Hilly Bates took the opportunity to cram a Duty Free bag, over the corpse, watched with mounting interest by the security guards now clustered round the monitor in a room on the second floor.

'Is that them actors?' asked one, his face taut with disapproval.

'Think so.'

'Whatever do they think they're at? He'd better not leave it there for someone to fall over.'

'Well, there's nowhere else, is there? Now there's no bins.'

'He can't leave it there.'

'Better call Establishments.'

'They won't touch that.'

'Well, it's not one of ours, is it?'

'No, definitely not one of ours.'

The penis lay for two hours before a sniffer dog was summoned after a lady passenger complained that someone had left a bag unattended in the main concourse.

The VIP lounge was occupied, as it turned out, by an American soap star on her way home for Rehab, so they were relocated to a soundproofed management suite from where they could watch the planes taking off and landing with all the insulated calm of a giant aquarium. Hilly, having been more than a little intrigued by the Halle-Bopp apostles, edged his way towards the window and gazed rapturously at the giant machines trundling silently past on the tarmac.

Gareth and Vanessa were chatting to a small man in a light-coloured raincoat. Beside him stood a distinguished-looking man in an expensive suit, smoking a cigar.

After a few moments during which the company hunted in vain for signs of refreshment, the small man nodded to Gareth who stepped forward and held up his hand for silence. 'Ladies and gentlemen of the Millennium Players, it is my great good fortune to introduce to you now Mr Gavin Furlong from the British Council, who has kindly found time to come along this afternoon and see us off. And, most particularly, to Mr Andrei Rikov, First Secretary to the Estonian Embassy in London, who has generously expressed a wish to say a few words to us all before we set forth, with excitement and a sense of profound privilege, to perform one of Shakespeare's immortal plays for the people of his country.'

There was a ripple of applause. Mr Rikov stepped forward.

'I am most honoured to take this opportunity to thank you all for your kind participation in this most historic enterprise. It is the wish of His Excellency and, of course, our government, that this may be the first of many such cultural endeavours.

'Estonia is home to all forms of artistic expression. We have many opera houses, concert halls, art galleries. Everywhere you go you will see signs of our artistic heritage. You will hear the beauty of our music; you will see the skill and passion of our dancers; you will gasp with wonder at the beauty of our architecture. And everywhere you will find the warmest of warm welcomes, because Estonian people are a fine and loving race. You will eat our food, you will drink our beer and fine wines, you will wander in our beautiful forests and stop to sigh by the crystal sweetness of our lakes . . .'

'What is that guy on?' whispered Clive Barry, whose ankle was giving him gip.

'In the evening, till late into the night when the first stars are hiding in the cobweb shawl of dawn, you will sit and listen as our poets enthrall you again and again with the mysteries of our origins.' Mr Rikov drew a large handkerchief from inside his jacket and pressed it poignantly to his nostrils.

'I must conclude simply to say how deeply I envy you this return to the land of my boyhood and the cradle of all my dreams. Naturally, I am enjoying my stay in Great Britain very much.'

He sat down so suddenly that he nearly squashed Gavin Furlong's briefcase. Furlong whipped it away just in time. He patted his hands together encouragingly and the company followed suit, led by Gareth who had the expression of a man who has just put a bet on a three-legged greyhound.

Gavin Furlong now spoke, briefly and almost brutally to the point in comparison with his predecessor. He told them they were lucky to have been given this opportunity to visit Eastern Europe, they would find some things there a little different from back home and they were to remember at all times that they were envoys for HM British Government and as such should conduct themselves in an appropriate manner.

The two men then departed through a side door whereupon a BA hostess appeared and shovelled them back into the Departure Lounge with all the ceremony of a Rentokil man on night duty.

Their flight was just being called, which elicited fresh panic from Richmond. Alice wondered that anyone, even an elderly actor given to theatrical outbursts, could react so violently to calls for missing children, cleaning staff, flights to Abu Dhabi and the latest score in the test match, but there he was again, grabbing at every passing arm and asking if that was what he thought it was. Since Richmond had not yet got as far as telling anyone what he did think it was, the general reaction was to nod and detach his hand before any permanent damage could be done to the person's jacket.

They filed off down the travelators, Marcus Lemmon and Jasmine racing each other and nearly flattening Marshall in their endeavours to get past.

Craig Penforth was in tears, having spent forty minutes on the phone to Felicity who had not felt up to making the massive journey from Preston to Heathrow to see him off. Bernice was with him, patting his arm and murmuring encouragement, much to Richmond's alarm because he had never been on a travelator before and wasn't at all sure how to get off the other end.

Maeve Prentice had come within an inch of being asphyxiated when her chiffon scarf got hooked on a passing umbrella just as she stepped on to the moving track, but quick thinking by the owner had prevented a major catastrophe and the incident had actually brought the tiniest hint of colour to Maeve's pallid cheeks, as any form of strangulation is wont to do.

Safely installed, seat-belts straining, ears popping, hearts pounding, the Millennium Players sat back and waited as the captain made his final checks and the plane soared away through the clouds on the first leg of the tour.

Chapter Nine

'All right, all right! Do you not see I am coming?' screeched the stewardess.

Nobby Clarke, who had spent the entire four-hour stopover in Frankfurt pouring beer down his throat, gazed at her fuzzily and waved his plastic beaker. He alone seemed oblivious to the variations wrought by the change of airline.

These were particularly acute for Gareth and Jasmine, the latter having succeeded in getting them upgraded to Business Class on the way out with the promise of a birthday request for the steward's mum on her father's radio programme.

Now they sat tetchily crammed between Jeannie and Ray who, despite their usual weediness, were putting up a brave struggle in the fight for elbow room.

Nobody liked their stew. Opinion was divided on what poor animal had perished to furnish a hundred and seventy people with the irradiated gristle now before them, but they remained united in their determination not to eat it.

The stewardess collected their trays, sighing aggrievedly at the sight of so much waste. She was a stunning girl, with almond-shaped eyes and thick golden hair worn in a plait. Even the restrictions of the uniform could not hide her contours. Only her temperament seemed better suited to a Class One detention centre than the glamorous world of the Jet Set.

To be fair, Estonian Airways' ex-Aeroflot airbus was possibly not the most exotic location for one who saw herself as a potential Bond girl, or if not that then at least the bride of a senior politician, but it was hardly the fault of those on board if they could not provide her with these alternatives. It seemed a little unfair that they should pay for her frustrated ambitions by being made to eat sludge and wait thirty minutes for someone to take away their sick bag.

It had been nearly midnight by the time they boarded the plane. Everyone was fractious, the excitement of the afternoon long gone and the effects of too much airport coffee making them jumpy. They shifted and twitched in their seats, grumbling and apologising in equal measure as the stewardess, who seemed to be virtually alone save for the occasional shadowy presence in the serving hatch, plunged up and down the aisle, flinging blankets and bottles of water indiscriminately in all directions.

'Excuse me . . .' came Marshall's familiar whine. 'Excuse me . . .'

'What?'

'There's someone smoking over there. I distinctly asked for a non-smoking seat.'

'You have a non-smoking seat.'

'Yes, but all his smoke is coming over here.'

'This I cannot help.'

'Can't you ask him to stop?'

'He is in a smoking seat.'

'But surely the smoking and non-smoking areas shouldn't be so close together?'

'This I cannot help. I do not make the plane.'

'But surely . . . I'm recovering from an operation.'

'You have permission to travel?'

Marshall sat back, alarmed at the intensity of her question. 'I don't need permission. I've been discharged. My consultant's very happy with my progress.'

'So, this is not then a reason to ask the gentleman to stop his smoking.'

'But . . .' But she was gone.

Alice twisted round in her seat. She was on the end of a row, next to Richmond who was the only person who had managed to fall asleep and was now snoring so violently that the chances of anyone else dropping off were effectively zilch. Looking up, she saw Philip watching her from his seat opposite. 'Glad you came?' he murmured, shuffling his legs in an attempt to get comfortable. The stewardess stomped past, kicking him on the ankle. Philip winced and withdrew his foot.

'I shall be glad when we get there,' Alice whispered back. For some reason the hush of a dentist's waiting room had descended on the plane, probably because it offered the same degree of comfort. 'I wonder what the hotel's like.'

'It looks pretty posh according to the brochure.' Philip pulled a wad of leaflets from his jacket. '"*Hotel Mirus is a fine example of modern Estonian architecture, its fine rooms rising above the city to give a breathtaking view of the harbour, the fine old town and the bus station. Each placement is provided of a washbasin and some have with bath. There are several fine restaurant and bars for your refreshment and also one may use the Sauna after a heavy day of seeing. English is available.*"'

Alice smiled. 'It sounds perfect.'

Philip grinned and closed his eyes. 'Perfect indeed.'

'I'm sorry, but I cannot stay in that room. I have a medical condition. I must insist that I have a bath at my disposal.' Marshall, who had not been in the hotel ten minutes, had already discovered that the single rooms were the placements with washbasins.

'But I am afraid only the double rooms are with bath,' apologised the receptionist, who was also ridiculously beautiful. Alice was beginning to wonder if the idea for *Baywatch* had come from Estonia. She looked around for a token Ugly but even the night porter looked like a young Jeremy Irons.

'What's the problem?' Sam, back from escorting Richmond and Bernice to the fifteenth floor, Richmond having developed a pronounced distrust for the lift which was glass-sided, came hurrying back to the desk.

'The gentleman is unhappy with his placement,' explained the girl, 'because it is with washbasin but not bath. Only the double rooms are with bath.'

'Right,' said Sam. 'Leave it with me. You give the others their keys while I think this one through.'

Although annoyed to think that Marshall's whining might result in an en suite room, the others were basically too tired to argue about it there and then. It was now nearly five in the morning and most of them would have settled for a night on a stone floor if it meant they could stretch their aching limbs and get some proper sleep.

Maeve and Jude who were, of course, sharing, collected their keys and went off looking smug. Likewise Christine and Marcus who had done too much touring to let divorce stand between them and a private bathroom. Alice joined them in the lift.

'If that old wanker gets his own bath I'm going to complain to Gareth about it,' Christine announced as soon as the lift doors shut. Alice and Marcus looked at her in surprise. Of them all, Christine was generally the most laid back. 'Don't you see?' she spluttered. 'If he gets away with this it'll be just the beginning. I know his sort. They're like water on a stone. Drip, drip, drip. He'll be travelling by private ambulance by the time he's through.'

Alice could see her point but was still surprised at her vehemence considering she had agreed to share a bed with the man she had twice divorced, for precisely the same reason that Marshall was now dangling his piles.

Dawn was breaking as Alice at last crawled into bed. The blind was broken so she could just see the paling sky through a gap in the curtains as she sunk exhausted on to the hospital-hard bed. What was it that man from the embassy had said? Something about a cobweb shawl? She liked that. What a fairy-tale place Estonia was, the women all fabulous, the men all poets. Perhaps here, in Estonia, her luck would change.

With these philosophical thoughts, Alice fell asleep.

She woke to the sound of thunderous rain, ping-ponging off the window ledge like sniper fire. Looking out at the asphalt-grey sky, her optimism began to slip.

The first person she encountered was Christine Pink. She was sitting in a corner of the coffee shop under a large spiky plant which seemed to have staked a claim in both the sugar bowl and the actress's hair. Christine beckoned her over.

'Guess what? Sam sorted Marshall.'

'Oh?' Alice tried to remember what the problem had been.

'Yes. He said he was perfectly happy for Marshall to have a double room with a bathroom if that's what he felt he needed, but that obviously the budget wouldn't run to paying for a single room they didn't require, so what he suggested was that he cancel two single rooms and Marshall could share with Nobby. That was the last he heard of that idea.'

Marshall's disaffection was underlined by his appearance some five minutes later, looking peevish and haggard. 'Come and join us, Marshall,' Christine called, her good humour entirely restored. 'Marcus will be down in a minute. He's just having a lovely loungy bath. I wouldn't be surprised if he's used the hotel's entire supply of hot water.'

Marshall Vincent's lips quivered. 'I think it's perfectly possible he has, Christine. I couldn't get anything but tepid from my taps. It really won't do. Everyone knows I've got a problem.'

'Yes, and everyone thinks it's something different,' growled Christine to Alice who choked on her coffee and had to be patted on the back by a passing waiter.

'Cheer up,' she continued. 'You'll feel better when you've had some coffee.'

'I'm not allowed coffee. Caffeine has a binding effect. I could probably manage some herbal tea.'

'Whatever,' said Christine. 'Ooh, look at those.' A waiter had arrived with a plate of assorted Danish pastries which he placed solemnly in front of her. 'They're not all for me, are they? Oh my god, I only ordered a couple of croissants. Come on, you two, you're going to have to help me out.'

Alice had no objection but Marshall, though plainly starving, refused to have anything, and instead set about describing his condition to the waiter who shifted from foot to foot as he tried to decide whether this was an official complaint about the Mirus' pastry cook, or the desperate attempt of a middle-aged homosexual to engage his sympathies.

He was rescued by the arrival of Jasmine and several of the male contingent, exchanging ribald jokes about things to do in a glass lift, and hurried away to attend to their orders.

At midday Sam came by to tell them that an official from the British Council had arrived and was waiting to talk to them in the lounge bar. They trundled down.

The official, one Brian Berrell, was if anything smaller than Gavin Furlong. He was balding and slightly overweight, and gave the impression that he too had better things to be doing than nursemaiding a troupe of actors. He spoke very quickly in a disapproving voice and generally put Alice more in mind of a tax inspector than an advocate for all that was finest in British culture.

Their afternoon was free, he informed them, as though this was the result of some canny negotiation, but a small soirée had been arranged at the headquarters of the British Council that evening to allow them to meet some of their hosts. 'Jeans must not be worn,' he had added fiercely, his eyes fastening directly on Bernice who was wearing a Jaeger two-piece with pearls.

When he had gone plans were laid for the afternoon. Nobby had long since departed in search of a beer cellar, Clive Barry had gone back to bed, Craig Penforth was trying to book a telephone call to Preston, and Hilly Bates was interrogating the receptionist on the whereabouts of the nearest Baptist church. Outside the rain continued unabated.

Maeve and Jude intended to go exploring, and to this end had bought a map which they now studied with the zest of Victorian missionaries. 'Oh, look,' trilled Maeve, 'that must be the cathedral. Or is it the castle?'

'It's the Indian restaurant we passed on the way in,' came Jude's emphatic response.

'Not that. Next to it. Honestly, Jude . . . I'm not a complete idiot.'

There was no response at all to this.

Alice watched them set off, Maeve swathed in a lilac mackintosh with matching sou'wester, and Jude jangling behind her in dazzling array of shawls and headscarves. The doorman eyed them curiously as they passed, which led them both to haul in their stomachs and toss their heads coquettishly – a mistake on Jude's part because one of her hooped ear-rings came loose and struck him rather forcibly on the lip, thereby wrecking all hope she might have had of returning later to seduce him.

Gareth Paynton wandered around amongst those remaining asking if anyone was planning to visit the State Art Gallery or the Toompea Castle, and if so could they possibly pick up a few postcards for him?

His wife, sensing that he would have more free time on his hands than he could usefully deploy, had given him a list of essential places to visit that would have tested the stamina of a Japanese tourist.

Gareth, whose own view of this trip was to spend as much time as possible in bed with Jasmine Ruddock, when not required for the practical purposes of socialising, making small speeches and occasionally patching up the production, had hit upon the idea of delegating his sight-seeing to the more enthusiastic members of the company.

In this he was sadly let down because, apart from Maeve and Jude, and Archie Frith in search of copy for his exposé, no one was particularly keen to tramp round the Old Town in the pouring rain for the purposes of buying postcards or anything else.

He eventually bullied Marshall Vincent into going as far as the Raekoja Plats by informing him there was an apothecary's shop there which had been used by Peter the Great, and that it was in the interest of Marshall's performance that he should hotfoot it up there immediately and, if possible, be photographed outside with Gareth's own camera which he was going to lend him as a special favour.

Marshall was duly seen trudging out into the wet, encased in a trenchcoat down to his ankles and 'one size fits all' Norfolk hat he had purchased through a mail order company, Gareth's camera strung round his neck like a Scarlet Letter.

More coffee was ordered while Hilly fetched his Scrabble. Heavy arguments were soon erupting between poor Craig, whose dyslexia did not make him ideally suited to the game, and Christine Pink who refused to let him have 'heebive' despite Bernice nearly losing an eyelash in her attempts to wink some pity out of the woman.

Alice had excused herself from the game and was half thinking of going back to bed herself. Idly she picked up the tourist guide that Gareth had been waving in his efforts to tempt them.

> *Estonia is the most beautiful country in the world,* she read. *Its magnificent forests interspiced with limpid lapping lakes render it a truly beneficial area for peaceful fortitude.*
>
> *Its cities boast of architecture from the eleven century through to current modernism with a magnificent blend of harmony.*
>
> *There are many fine art galleries, concert halls and opera palaces. The famous Estonian poet, Mihail Rikov, has said, 'Estonian people are born with music in their hearts, like flowers that open to the kiss of gentle raindrops'.*

Alice closed the book, wondering how less successful poets got by in Estonia.

She was prevented from further reflection by the sudden arrival of Philip Carter, looking slightly unnerved. He hurried over to her.

'Look, Alice, I don't want you to worry or anything . . .'

Her heart started to pound. Jasmine had fallen down the lift shaft, broken her leg. *Gallop apace, you fiery-footed steeds towards Phoebus*' . . . What? It had all gone from her. She had forgotten every word.

'Only there are two guys downstairs asking for you.'

Jolted back to reality, she stared at him. 'For me? Why? Who?'

Philip shrugged. 'They didn't tell me their names. They just kept saying "Alice Emingvay", so I thought I'd better come and warn you. I think they might be Immigration or something. Do you want me to get Sam to sort them out?'

An icy chill began to crawl up Alice's spine. 'They're not . . . ? They aren't . . . ?' Philip gazed at her in bewilderment.

'Aren't what? Were you expecting someone?'

'Yes. No. I don't know. They're not . . . um . . . are they?'

'Not what? They're just two guys. One's about forty, the other's a lot younger – twenties, I'd guess. It's definitely you they're after. Look, I'll get Sam. He'll sort it out, whatever it is.'

'NO.' Philip was stopped in his tracks. 'Umm, it's all right, I think. It's just someone Jay fixed up for me to meet. I was sort of hoping they wouldn't turn up on our first day.' She gave a weak laugh. 'I'd better go and see what they want.'

'Do you want me to come with you?'

'No. Please. I'm sure it will be all right. Downstairs, you said?'

'In Reception.'

'Right. See you in a bit.' With a noble effort she tried to walk casually to the lift. Philip followed her.

'Alice, stay in Reception. Don't go anywhere with them, will you?'

She gave another weedy laugh. 'In this rain? You must be joking.' Philip nodded slightly and bit his lip. The lift arrived.

'Remember what I said,' he told her as the doors opened. 'Stay in the hotel. Promise?'

'I promise. Stop fussing. They're just a couple of friends Jay wanted me to say hello to.'

'Well, make sure that's all you do do.' The doors started to close. Philip suddenly stuck his foot between them. They parted again.

'I don't want to frighten you or anything. It's probably perfectly normal round here . . .'

'What is?' asked Alice, imagining them both with beards to the ground and pigtails to match.

Philip withdrew his foot. He looked very worried indeed. 'I think they're both armed,' he said.

Chapter Ten

As the door closed on the lift Alice felt her life passing before her eyes. Before the eyes of everyone else in the hotel, too, as she was transported with silent ease down the goldfish bowl tube to her fate. She knew exactly how it must feel to ride on a tumbril, except that the lift in the Hotel Mirus had none of the charms of an early-morning jaunt in the fresh air.

How do I get out of this was all that she could think. What has Jay let me in for? Is this a plot to have me murdered so that he can run off with Bryony Douglas? Or Francesca? Or bloody Bob, for that matter? Not that Jay had ever indicated . . . But if you'd asked her a week ago about Philip Carter . . . Her honorary twin! And to think she'd always wanted a brother. She still did. She just didn't want it to be him. And yet perhaps sibling love was the best kind? She tried to picture Jay in similar circumstances. It was very hard to imagine him worrying about her safety.

No, only Philip really cared about her. Philip, who had offered to come with her. To fetch Sam. Why had she not let him? Why, oh why, not? Because he had failed to mention till it was too late the fact that the two men waiting for her were hired assassins. *Rogue Fringe* came into her mind and refused to be dislodged.

She scanned the wall feverishly. If she punched the button for the fifteenth floor surely it would take her up again? She thumped it hard. The lift registered the fact and continued imperviously on its way to the ground. Every spy film she had ever seen flashed through her mind. She saw the gleaming lift awash with blood. Her blood. She heard the crack of the shattering glass as the bullet smacked through it. She felt a pounding in her ears as she sank slowly, finally to the pseudo-marble floor . . .

There was a hiss as the door opened. A man stepped forward. Alice shrank back. 'Miss Alice Emingvay? Good afternoon. I am Alexei Morkov. This is my colleague, Janni Viszla. You are well?'

She stared at the two men. The one who had spoken, squat and bearded, the other . . . Alice continued to gaze, slack-jawed, at the cornflower blue eyes, the aquiline nose, the glistening bronze skin, the floppy ash blond hair. If she had not known he was a thousand miles away in London, she could have sworn she was looking at Jay, or better still his younger brother.

Small black dots were still zooming at her from various points in the room. Morkov eyed her with concern. 'You are a little heated from the lift? I myself hate these lifts because there is no clear air in them. They are a source for infection.'

He led her courteously to a sofa tucked away in the corner and surrounded by another plantation of house plants.

Alice, dazed, did not struggle. Plainly her execution was not to take place in full view of the hotel's other occupants after all. She was to be found slumped behind the aspidistras by the cleaner the following day. She wondered vaguely if she would be missed at the British Council soirée.

Settled on the couch she became aware that the two men were watching her with some anxiety. 'You will take tea?' suggested Morkov, plainly versed in the last wishes of about-to-be-liquidated Britons. Alice opened her eyes wide and nodded.

'You will like cake with this?' added the younger man. This was the first time he had spoken and Alice noted that he had a very sexy voice, low and caressing with just the hint of a sibilant 's'. This, combined with his looks, made the prospect of death a tiny bit more bearable. She hoped he would be the one to press the trigger. He went away to order the refreshments.

Alexei Morkov, clearly feeling the onus was on him to make her last moments memorable, leant forward. 'Here is a small gift for you, from Janni and myself.' He put his hand inside his coat and Alice screamed, though the only sound to emerge was a kind of violent hiccup. Morkov removed his hand and gazed at her compassionately. 'You are perhaps a little tired after your flight?' He smiled roguishly. 'I hope you have not eaten a meal on the aeroplane?' Alice forced the sides of her mouth upwards in a rictus grin.

'Not really,' she croaked.

'I am sorry to have to say it, but our airline meals are not absolutely A1. Don't you agree?'

Alice conceded that this was a fair appraisal.

'But our national cuisine is second to nought. It is A l. Ah, here is Janni with cake.'

Janni was approaching, followed by a small procession of waiters armed with teapots, crockery, and another selection of gâteaux that would not have disgraced a royal wedding.

Alice entertained a brief *Thousand and One Nights* fantasy that if she strung the tea out long enough her captors would come to love her and be unable to carry out the killing. She particularly hoped this in the case of Janni, beside whom the doorman paled into insignificance. And where was he, anyway, while she was here being murdered?

The waiters set down the trays and departed. Alice tried to catch their eyes but they were expecting a party of thirty-eight Finns at any moment and couldn't waste time on an unknown British actress.

Janni lifted the lid of the teapot and stirred the contents. 'I shall be mother?' he asked, and gave a deep fruity laugh. Alice chirruped sycophantically.

'You will take milk?'

'Yes please.'

'Sugar?'

'No thank you.'

'This is because you are sweet enough already?'

The two men guffawed at their grasp of Western humour. Alice wondered if she asked to go to the lavatory whether she could squeeze through a window and find the police station before either of them noticed.

She sipped daintily at her tea.

'Which cake will you like?' asked Alexei, indicating the spread.

'Oh, really I don't mind. They all look so scrumptious,' wittered Alice. 'You choose first.'

Alexei's face went a peculiar colour. 'But of course, you are a guest. You must choose.'

'Also a lady,' purred Janni, running his dreamy blue eyes over her.

So the cakes were poisoned, Alice discerned, trying to remember how V.I. Warshawski had got round the problem.

'I think I might have the apple,' she murmured, her eyes flicking between them.

'By every means,' beamed Alexei, turning the plate towards her.

Alice gave a pathetic giggle. 'Oooh, I've just spotted the almond custard. Would it be too wicked to change my mind?'

It was the men's turn to exchange glances. 'Please,' said Janni. He reached over and lifted the cake on to her plate. 'Be my visitor.'

Obviously they were all poisoned. Alice made a mental note that if she ever came across Jay again, even if it was fifty reincarnations down the line, she would stand on him.

Janni had the apple slice. Alexei said he could not have a cake at all or his wife would beat him. They all laughed heartily at this, especially Alice who, having moved a morsel of the almond custard round her mouth for ten minutes, trying to detect whether it was Amaretto or arsenic, was beginning to wonder just why these two men should want to kill her anyway. After all, she'd done nothing wrong, apart from her affair with Jay, so unless his wife had put them up to it . . . ?

'You do not like your cake?' Janni was watching her with the eyes of a wounded deer.

'It's very nice,' Alice faltered. 'I'm trying to make it last.' This delighted the two men who roared with laughter and signalled for the waiter to whom they spoke rapidly.

A plate of almond custards duly arrived.

These were followed shortly by the long-awaited Finns who appeared to be very drunk. Alexei and Janni tutted furiously. 'These people are a disgrace to their homeland,' Alexei decreed. 'They are here for only one thing.'

Alice hoped fervently it wasn't to see a performance of *Romeo and Juliet* as they tumbled over the furniture, pushing and shouting at each other indiscriminately.

A man stumbled backwards into her chair, nearly upending it. He staggered off without a backward glance. Janni rose silently. 'Excuse me,' he said politely and followed the man across the room. Alexei sighed. 'Janni is a very proper person,' he murmured. 'He will encourage the man to apologise.'

Alice shook her head vigorously. 'There's no need, really. It was just an accident.' Too late. A dull thud and a hiss of expelling air, followed by a brief lull in the rumpus as the rest of the party watched the culprit heaving himself back towards Alice.

'The young man would like to apologise for his behaviour.' Janni smiled encouragingly at the Finn like a teacher prompting the school play. The man curled his lip threateningly, then let out a yelp and sank to his knees as Janni cracked his foot into the back of his legs.

Alice blanched. 'There's really no need,' she stammered.

'There is every need,' said Janni tonelessly. The man mumbled something in Finnish. Janni snapped back at him. The man repeated the phrase more feelingly. Alexei stepped in. 'He has said it was discourteous of him. He hopes you will forgive the incident?'

'Oh yes,' quavered Alice, who was now more fearful of causing someone else's death than precipitating her own. 'Thank you.' She smiled feebly at the man who was regarding her with such unadulterated hatred that she made a mental note never even to fly over Finland unaccompanied.

Janni jerked his head and the man retreated. They resumed their seats. 'Now,' said Alexei as though nothing had happened, 'let me see how many cakes you can eat.' Alice ate them all.

'And now, to business,' he chuckled as she sat creaking under the weight of her almond custards. He opened his briefcase and withdrew a sheaf of papers. Janni mounted guard, though since the Finnish interlude no one had come near them except to offer fresh hot water and remove the surplus plates.

Alexei leant forward. 'You know what this is all about?' Alice twitched her face in several directions. If she knew too much she would definitely be eliminated; too little and they might conclude she was a spy. 'Jay did mention, briefly, most of the details to me,' she murmured, hoping this was sufficiently broad.

Alexei beamed. 'I have spoken to my contact, General Vassili Rikov – you know of him, perhaps?'

Alice frowned. The name was certainly familiar. Probably a hero of some sort. 'Oh, yes. Well, who hasn't?'

Alexei raised his eyebrows very slightly but let it pass. 'He is on the Committee for Industrial Enterprise and, as such, is responsible for doctoring all foreign investment in our country.'

'Doctoring it?' echoed Alice nervously.

Alexei looked up. 'But yes, of course. All business transactions must be doctored. It is the law.'

'Is it?' asked Alice in bewilderment. Janni, who had remained silent during this, reached into his pocket and pulled out a compact dictionary. The two consulted it.

'Alternatively I may say "vetted",' said Alexei a little huffily, and moved on to explain that he would need a specimen of Jay's signature and details of his bank account before proceeding further.

'You can convey this to your fiancé?' he asked, piling the papers back into his case.

'Oh, yes,' promised Alice, overwhelmed to be called Jay's fiancée. 'I can phone him tonight if you like.'

Alexei snorted violently. 'No communication by telephone. This is imperative. Do you not know about GCHQ?'

Alice blanched. 'But why would they be interested?'

Alexei and Janni exchanged glances. Janni came and sat down next to her.

'Alice, my dear friend,' he purred. She felt her heart doing peculiar little jumps. 'You are not experienced in these matters. You must trust Alexei and myself.'

'Oh, I do,' she promised. 'I absolutely do.' Janni smiled. The jumps moved lower. Concentrate, she ordered herself. Your life may depend on it.

'What we would like is for you to send to your fiancé some faxes with the details of our arrangements.'

'Faxes? But surely anyone can read those?'

Janni nodded forgivingly. 'Precisely, but they will not understand them.'

'Oh.' Alice smiled brightly. 'I see.'

'Ha!' interrupted Alexei, beaming from ear to ear. 'But no one else will.' This was too much for the two men who dissolved into laughter. Alice tittered unconvincingly. Alexei wiped his eyes, blew his nose and continued. 'We will tell you how to put the arrangements, but you must send them because no one will find it strange for you to communicate with your loved one like this.'

'By fax?' It sounded pretty strange to Alice.

A tiny cloud appeared on Alexei's brow. 'Trust me,' he said gruffly. 'I have had many dealings of this sort. I know what I am saying.'

'Oh yes,' Alice retreated. 'Whatever you think best. I'm in your hands completely.' The cloud disappeared. Alexei patted her arm. 'If I were a somewhat younger man that would be my best wish,' he chuckled amiably. Janni said nothing, fastening his attention on the rogue aspidistra.

Alexei finished putting his papers back in the case and locked it. He rose. 'This has been a most valuable meeting,' he informed her.

Alice rose uncertainly. 'Good. That is . . . erm, what exactly do you want me to do – about things?'

Alexei pressed his finger to his lips. 'Nothing for the moment. We will be in touch.'

'But the faxes? Do I send them from the hotel?' Craig Penforth had still not succeeded in booking his phone call.

'No, no, no,' Alexei tutted. 'From the British Council. We have a contact there. A very good man.'

'Oh. Right. Er, do I need to ask for him or anything?' A little whinny of despair came from Janni who was putting on his coat. Alexei shook his head. 'That will not be necessary. He will find you.'

'Oh, right,' said Alice again, not daring to ask how. Alexei held out his hand and she shook it energetically. She turned to Janni. He lifted her hand and pressed it gently to his lips. The jumps turned into cartwheels. 'It has been a pleasure to meet you,' he murmured, his eyes conveying a thousand other messages, each of which Alice would spend a sleepless night interpreting.

They turned to go. Just as they got to the door, Alexei spun round and came hurrying back. 'Nearly I have forgotten.' Once more his hand reached inside his jacket. Once more Alice froze. He pulled out a brightly coloured paperback. 'Here is a small gift from Janni and myself.' He pressed it into her hands.

'Thank you,' said Alice. 'Thank you very much.' Alexei nodded and hurried back across the hotel foyer and out into the pouring rain.

Alice looked at the book. *Estonia: Everything You Need To Know*. What I would really like to know, she thought, is, Is Janni Viszla married? True he didn't meet many of the criteria on her list for a perfect soulmate, but who did? Only Philip Carter so far, and he was definitely off limits.

Chapter Eleven

Alice's enjoyment of the British Council soirée was marred by paranoia that her alleged 'contact' was somewhere on the premises, poised to pounce and spirit her away to commit treasonable offences on the fax machine.

With Janni's departure and the subsequent slowing of her heartbeat, doubts and fears had begun to creep back in. Why on earth was it necessary for her to communicate with Jay by fax? And why her? Surely these things were better arranged man to man? She was an actress not a fixer. Her role was purely social. Wasn't it enough that she had eaten five almond slices in the cause of Jay's screenplay? Pelicans paled in comparison.

Haunted by Alexei's reference to GCHQ, with its connotations of laser pens and truth drugs, she scurried around the elegant salon, avoiding eye contact with all but the most mumsy of its occupants, and finally coming to rest in front of an enormous floral wall-hanging by the fireplace.

Here she was cornered by Marshall Vincent who had managed to develop a full-blown cold in the space of only two hours, following his sortie into the Old Town. 'I feel dreadful,' he told her, exploding into another sneezing fit.

'For God's sake, Marshall,' snapped Jasmine, who was near enough to feel the blast, 'would you please not sneeze all over my food.'

'It's not my fault,' Vincent sniffed. 'I didn't ask to go out in all that rain.'

'A bit of rain never hurt anyone,' Jasmine scoffed. 'I used to play hockey in my blouse and knickers in a lot worse than this. You're just unhealthy, that's the trouble with you.'

She moved away to talk to a burly bodyguard she had been eyeing up all evening.

Marshall raised his eyes to heaven. 'Some people . . .'

Alice was saved having to hear the rest by a hand on her shoulder. She started so violently she nearly knocked Marshall's glass out of his hand. 'Careful,' he said crossly. 'Found those wigs yet, Sam?'

Alice turned to see that it was indeed the company manager and felt a wave of relief. If she stuck close to him no one would dare abduct her.

Sam grunted. 'Gone to Helsinki. Some geezer thought they was for the prison. Gawd knows why, unless they were planning to slide down them and do a runner. Three in the morning I've got to pick 'em up. I dunno. Her ladyship's kicking up stink, by way of a change.' He jerked his head in Jude's direction.

Jude did, indeed, look strangely animated as she engaged in what appeared to be a boxing match with a very large Estonian woman in turquoise. The fight was being refereed by their host, Brian Berrell, his face mottled with sadistic delight. 'Madame Skikne is a renowned singing teacher,' they heard him say as Jude struggled to recover from a particularly stinging blow to the ribs. 'Her technique is much admired.'

'So was Mohammed Ali's,' muttered Sam. 'Rather her than me, mate.'

Madame Skikne now turned her attention to Gareth Paynton who had been lurking conscientiously nearby. Although in truth he would love to see Jude Jenkins laid low, it was too early on in the tour to dispense with her entirely. He was a little taken aback to find that Madame Skikne's methods also encompassed placing her ample hands rather low down his own vertebrae. In fact had he not been a professional himself, and therefore used to the unorthodox, he might have said she was groping his buttocks. He wheezed slightly as she expelled the air from his rib cage with a series of short sharp thumps. Out of the corner of his eye he could see Jasmine drinking out of the bodyguard's glass. Someone had said the man was in fact the Curator of Estonian Antiquities, but that didn't ease Paynton's suspicions.

Madame Skikne turned to Brian Berrell and murmured something. Berrell swallowed nervously and endeavoured to smile. 'Madame Skikne says she will be happy to train your voice while you are here,' he informed Gareth. 'She suggests you meet for lunch during the week to arrange a suitable time.'

Gareth smiled a winning smile. 'Nothing would give me greater pleasure, Brian. As I'm sure you know. However, sadly our timetable is so tight, I'm horribly afraid it just won't be possible. Maybe next time?'

Brian Berrell looked at him as though he were entirely mad before rattling off several lengthy sentences to Madame Skikne. To everyone's surprise she beamed and, seizing both Gareth's hands, compressed them into a small ball and went on her way, punching at will.

Gareth looked notably relieved. 'I was afraid she wouldn't take no for an answer,' he confided to Berrell. The British Council man threw him a forgiving glance.

Alice turned to Sam. 'Are you going to have to wait up till three o'clock to pick up the wigs, then?'

'Looks like it. It's no sweat. The worst is I've to take Jude with me to sign for them. She don't trust me to manage on my own. I ask you! How many crateloads of yaks' pubes are going to turn up at three in the morning? Even in a place like this?'

Alice tucked her arm under his. 'You sound fed up.'

Sam frowned. 'I am, but not about that.'

'What then?'

'If you must know, ducks, it's you.'

'Me?' Alice frowned. 'What have I done now?' She meant it jokily but Sam continued to look grave.

'You tell me.'

Alice gazed at him, bemused. 'I don't understand.'

Sam sighed. 'Phil was saying you met a couple of geezers in the hotel foyer?'

Alice let go of his arm. 'I didn't pick them up, if that's what you mean. They were . . . business acquaintances of someone I know.'

Sam nodded and sucked in his cheeks. 'That's what Phil said. Only you want to be a bit careful about doing business over here, my duck. There's a black market and it's a lot blacker than you might think.'

'I wasn't buying anything,' protested Alice, feeling horribly guilty. 'We just had tea together, that was all.'

'They didn't ask you to take nothing back to England for them or nothing?'

'No . . .' She hesitated, aware that Sam was watching her keenly. 'They did give me – well, you can look at it for yourself. They gave me a guide book to the place. It's the same one as Gareth had. All full of "pattering puddles" and things. Surely there's nothing wrong with that?'

Sam shook his head. ''Course there ain't. I just wouldn't want you being taken advantage of. You know – if these guys asked you to do a favour for them, for "old times' sake", that sort of thing. There was none of that?'

'No. Nothing.'

'And they didn't ask you to send any messages for them, or nothing? 'Coz that's another scam. Get some innocent tourist to telephone a message through. Seems harmless enough at the time and it turns out to be the buzz word for a drugs consignment on its way. I just wouldn't want you getting mixed up in anything, that's all. The police are very hot on it over here. They lock you up first and ask questions after.'

'Oh, stop it,' wailed Alice, feeling sick. 'There was nothing like that. They were just friends of a friend. I don't know what Philip's been telling you, but that's all there was to it.'

Sam nodded. 'Right. That's okay then. Here he is. Ask him yourself.' And he was gone.

Alice looked up to see Philip making his way towards her with two glasses of champagne. He held one out to her. She took it silently. Philip sat down. 'Are you all right?'

'Of course I am. Why shouldn't I be?'

'You look a bit . . .'

'A bit what?'

'Fractious,' said Philip.

'Well, you'd be fractious if you'd had my evening.'

'Why? What's happened?'

Alice sighed. 'Nothing, really, I suppose. Sam's just been giving me the third degree about Alexei and Janni, thanks to you.'

'Is that those two men you were having tea with this afternoon?'

'How did you know I was having tea with them? The last I heard from you was they were waiting to blow my brains out. It wasn't a very good joke, in my opinion.'

Philip looked grave. 'It wasn't meant to be a joke. If you'd seen the way the doorman got out of their way when they came in, you'd've been worried too.'

'I was worried. I nearly fainted in the lift, I was so worried. Why didn't you tell me before I got in?'

'I didn't want to worry you.' He ducked as Alice threw a nut at him. 'Anyway, I followed you down to make sure you were all right, and you were having such a good time I thought I might as well clear off.' He stared darkly into his glass.

Alice looked at him curiously. 'You actually checked to see if I was all right?'

'Well, of course I did. I couldn't very well just leave you, could I? They might have been anybody. We're not in England now, you know.'

'And we're not in a small town in Germany. You've been reading too many spy stories.'

'Yes, well, I worry.'

'Why?'

'Why? Because . . .'

'Because what?'

Philip looked at her. For some reason Alice couldn't interpret what she saw. 'Because you don't want to understudy the women too?' she suggested lightly.

He inclined his head. 'Got it in one.'

* * *

The company was taken back to the Hotel Mirus in a fleet of taxis. Richmond immediately suggested a nightcap but Jasmine was already organising a trip down town in search of 'a bit of life'. Gareth tried to dissuade her on the grounds that they had a gruelling day ahead of them, but Jasmine merely rubbed salt in the wound by saying if he was past it, she would find someone else to take her. Remembering the Curator of Antiquities, Gareth duly changed his shirt and was last seen heading out into the sticky night with Jasmine on one arm and Nobby Clarke, who was too drunk to distinguish gender, on the other. Maeve and Jude brought up the rear, both the worse for wear.

Nobody else seemed keen to prolong the evening. They sat around in the bar for a while and then drifted off to bed till only Sam, who had to stay up anyway, and Alice, who could not be bothered to move, were left. He came and sat beside her.

'You not tired, Orphan Annie?'

Alice yawned. 'Yes, a bit. I just don't feel like going to bed. I mean, we're only here for a fortnight. I sort of feel I should be out doing things.'

'What sort of things?'

She shrugged. 'I don't know. Things.'

'Why didn't you go with Jaz and the guv?'

Alice made a face. 'Not those sort of things. Besides Maeve and Jude can't stand me.'

'They wouldn't even see you, ducks, when they're on the pull. Where's young Phil? He'd've gone out with you, surely?'

Alice looked away. 'I don't know where he is,' she said, suddenly realising she had not seen him since they got back to the hotel. 'Anyway, it doesn't matter. I'll go to bed. The Midnight Sun will have to wait.'

Sam chuckled. 'Tell you what, you can come over to the airport with me if you fancy it. We could go the scenic route then at least you can say you've seen Tallinn by moonlight. How'd that be?'

Alice sat up. 'Oh yes, do you think we could? I mean, if you don't mind? But what about Jude? Won't she object?'

'If I know Jude Jenkins, she'll be way past objecting to anything by the time we pick her up.' He looked at his watch. 'It's one o'clock now. I've got some things to sort out. I'll be back here at two. If you still want to come, be here. If not, I'll go without you. How's that?'

'Oh brilliant. Excellent. Thank you, Sam. You are smashing.' Now wide awake Alice rushed upstairs, had a shower, changed and was back in the bar by twenty to. The barman looked at her curiously as he polished the glasses and stacked them in readiness for the return of the Finns.

Sam took her down the back way to where the hired van was parked. As they drove past the front the Finns were falling out of their coach and up the steps to the hotel, stopping to be copiously sick on the way. Glancing out Alice could not be sure but was almost certain she saw Philip making his way unsteadily between them. She glanced at Sam to see if he had noticed but his eyes were glued on the road ahead.

Jude did not want to come to the airport. She had, after several failed attempts, managed to secure the attentions of a redundant bouncer, who had been downgraded to 'cloaks' at the Hotspot Nightclub after having both legs broken in a disagreement over the cost of entry. She now perched precariously at the apex of his splints on what little lap remained to him, both arms locked vice-like round his neck.

Sam had left Alice in the van while he went looking for Jude and she was beginning to get nervous when, after ten minutes, he still had not returned. She wondered about going after him, but the pavement was lined with people being sick – plainly a popular activity in Tallinn – and the thought of threading her way through them and past the bouncers was not one she relished.

Sam duly returned, dragging Jude by one arm. She looked anything but pleased. He unfastened the back of the van and shoved her unceremoniously on to the floor. Jude swore, sang two verses of 'Ave Maria' and fell asleep.

'Do you want me to go in the back?' Alice asked as Jude rolled about between the tarpaulins.

'What for?'

'Well, she might bump her head or something. She'd be better off with a seatbelt.'

'A crack on the head might knock some sense into her,' said Sam harshly, and Alice was reminded of the stories about his wife.

He drove slowly along the cobbled streets, allowing her to peer at the quaint old buildings to either side. In the half light they looked like pantomime flats for *Dick Whittington* with their gables and ancient pulleys overhanging the pavements.

'That's what I call a church,' Sam observed as they came on the enormous onion-domed cathedral at the top of Toompea Hill. Alice nodded, fighting the impression that it looked more like something from Eurodisney than a genuine house of worship.

Leaving the town they drove along a deserted road, past the port and out into the open countryside. It was very quiet, the distant sounds of the sea blending with Jude's snores till they seemed part of each other. Alice snuggled back in her seat. She felt strangely peaceful, remote and detached from her surroundings. Fairyland, she thought again, closing her eyes to see if she could conjure up Janni's face.

As Sam turned into the airport car park she felt him crunch his foot down on the brake. The van screeched to a halt, stalling as it did so. Jude let out a furious growl from the back. Before she realised what was happening Alice felt a cold draught of air as both side doors were flung open. Two men stood on either side of the van. They wore expensive leather coats, their arms folded across their chests with military precision. Alice turned to Sam in panic. He was staring straight ahead, his face very pale in the moonlight. 'Shit,' was all he said.

The men were very nice. Their leader spoke good English and was able to reassure Sam that his consignment of wigs had arrived safely from Helsinki and was now awaiting collection in the Special Deliveries section of the airport. The only problem was that in order to ensure the continuing safety of the wigs they had had to pay a small sum to the security guards. This they would be grateful if Sam would now reimburse, preferably in American dollars.

He was led away to inspect the goods and verify that they had not been damaged. There appeared to be no need for Jude to sign for anything. Presumably they had requested her presence as a potential hostage if Sam proved awkward.

Though he would happily have handed Jude over and the money as well, if it guaranteed he would be free of her for the rest of the tour, the quartet seemed unwilling to take advantage of the fact so, with much smiling and waving of hands the van was duly loaded and the three of them returned to Tallinn, Sam two hundred pounds the poorer.

'I suppose,' said Alice when she had found her voice again, 'it was lucky you had the money on you.'

Sam grunted. 'I can't believe I fell for it. I cannot bleeding believe I fell for that one. The oldest trick in the book. How long have I been doing this? Twenty bleeding years, and I fall for that one. "Three o'clock in the morning". From Helsinki? Pull the other one.'

Alice said nothing. She felt guilty. Perhaps it wouldn't have happened if Sam had come on his own, although she couldn't really see why not. Unless she was bad luck? Hastily she crossed her fingers and tried to think of three poets beginning with S.

'He fancied me.' Jude's face, blotched with mascara, appeared between their seats. 'That tall one with the moustache. He was making eyes at me all the while you were gone. Wasn't he?' She jabbed Alice sharply. 'She saw. He had the real hots for me, didn't he, you . . . understudy person? What's your name again?'

'Alice,' said Alice fiercely. Jude might be drunk but that was no excuse for calling her 'understudy'.

'Yes. All right. The real hots.' Jude burped and sank back on to the tarpaulins.

Sam glanced across at Alice. 'They didn't give you no trouble, did they, ducks? Them geezers? 'Coz if they bleedin' did . . .'

'No,' said Alice quickly, visions of Janni and the Finn fading beside the prospect of Sam and the entire Russian Mafia. 'No, honestly. Nothing. They were very polite.'

Sam nodded. Alice thought she detected relief on his face. Clearly he hadn't fancied taking them on much himself.

Back at the hotel they loaded Jude into the lift and delivered her to a fretful Maeve who resented being woken at that hour and even more having to deal with her drunken friend.

That done Sam went to park the laden van in the hotel's lock-up garage. 'If they're gone again in the morning, that's it,' he said grimly as he punched the lift button.

Alice hovered. 'I'm awfully sorry about tonight, Sam,' she murmured.

'Not your fault.'

'I feel as though it was.'

The lift arrived. Sam shoved his foot in the door. 'What on earth for? How could you have known it was a set up? I'm the c— the one what should've, not you, ducks. Now you get some sleep and think no more about it. All part of life's rich whatsit.'

Alice nodded dejectedly. 'I just hope I didn't bring you bad luck, that's all.'

Sam screwed up his face in despair. 'Bad luck? You? I'll tell you something, ducks. There's no such thing as bad luck. Or good luck either, if it comes to that. You make your own luck and don't let anyone tell you different. You could lie down in a field of four-leafed clovers and still wake up under a tractor. Remember that.'

He leant forward and kissed her cheek. 'Now get to bed before I forget I'm old enough to be your dad.'

Chapter Twelve

'*"A plague a' both your houses"*. Oops! Aagh . . . FUUUUUCK!'

This last accompanied Clive Barry as he rolled, slowly at first, then with gathering momentum, down the glass-smooth surface of the stage.

The angle of the rake was acute by any standards, and not helped by the sheen of beeswax bedded into it by the enthusiastic daughter of a tallow merchant, now serving her apprenticeship as a set designer.

Clive's ankle, still weak from his sprain, gave way beneath him as he lunged at Tybalt then fell back mortally wounded. Hilly and the others watched helplessly as he spun past them, thinking at first this was yet another piece of improvisation (Clive was much given to milking his exits), so that by the time they realised that he was in real trouble it was too late and Mercutio was teetering over the orchestra pit, prior to a spectacularly noisy descent into the timpani section.

Fortunately no one was underneath or the charge might well have been one of manslaughter, but by the time Clive came to rest, his cloak impaled on a series of music stands, his codpiece lodged between two triangles, there was very little left of the kettle drum.

The actors edged forward like novice skiers, to peer in dreadful silence into the abyss.

'What's going on?' boomed Richmond from the wings,

horribly afraid he had missed his cue. 'Is it tea?' Bernice slithered off to humour him.

'Clive,' came Gareth Paynton's stilted voice, 'are you okay?' A groan issued from the depths. 'Oh, well, at least he's alive.' Gareth stumbled out from behind his makeshift desk in the stalls and hurried down the aisle.

Maeve was there before him. She had installed herself in the front row to see if you could tell Jasmine was wearing no knickers in the balcony scene, and almost fell on top of Clive in her desire to be the harbinger of doom. 'He's looking dreadfully pale,' she imparted tragically. 'Speak to me, Clive. Can you feel your toes?'

Clive strove to convey that if something wasn't done and quick, he would feel the throats of the first six people to come near him. 'I think he's delirious,' Maeve affirmed, getting in everyone's way.

The local stagehands, who had seen similar things many times in the past, chatted and shrugged their shoulders till ordered unambiguously by Sam to help free the poor man. This they did swiftly and with some ease since a grown man was nothing compared with the succession of Toscas they had had to resuscitate over the years.

Jude, hearing the rumpus over the Tannoy, forsook her wigs and raced to the scene.

'Call an ambulance, someone,' she bellowed into Clive's face as he was lowered to the ground in front of her. 'Has anyone called an ambulance?'

Clive, who felt he had more than fulfilled his role in the sideshow, hauled himself wincing on to one elbow, and asked her rather forcefully if she really thought he was the person to do it.

'Not you. Of course I didn't mean you,' snapped Jude sulkily. 'Here, you might as well let me take your wig while you're at it. I'll have to start again from scratch. I don't know where I'm going to find the time.'

With this she made a determined effort to wrench Mercutio's curls from the actor's head, but since they were glued to his temples the ensuing screams were a great deal worse than anything any of the Toscas had managed. The stage crew gathered round in silent admiration, each one planning to report this new torture to his Mafia boss in the hope of gaining kudos.

It was during this interlude that an ambulance did arrive, summoned by a quick-thinking usherette who had sneaked in to watch the rehearsal. Clive was borne away on a stretcher, his foot at an ugly angle and his face twisted with pain and dreams of revenge.

'Okay, everyone. I think we'd better get on. We've lost a lot of time,' came the director's voice from the mid stalls.

'Yes, but, Gareth dear, who's going to play Mercutio?' called Bernice from the wings where she was administering Richmond's evening laxative, collecting for flowers for the invalid, and trying to decide whether she should tell her husband about the charming little brooch she had bought in an antique shop while he was having his pre-prandial zizz.

'Bernice, my love, the man's dead.'

'WHAT?' There was a clatter as Bernice dropped the glass with Richmond's medicine and rushed on to the stage. 'Oh, Gareth, this is DREADFUL. When did it happen? But he was here just now. I know he was in pain, but oh, oh . . .' She stood centre stage, a tiny trembling figure, her hands clasped before her in anguish.

Gareth raised his eyes to the ceiling, once more fought his way out from behind his desk and came to the edge of the stage. 'Bernice, no. Not CLIVE. *Mercutio*, I meant. He's just been killed in a sword fight, remember. So we don't need anyone to play the part. We just need to get on with the play,' he added through gritted teeth. Bernice gave a weak little laugh.

'Oh, of course. What a fool I am. It's just you gave me such a fright, saying it like that, Gareth dear. So he's all right . . . Clive? Who's gone with him in the ambulance?'

'No one. He didn't want anyone,' added Paynton hastily. 'He didn't want any fuss.'

'Bless him. So brave. But I really don't think he should go

on his own. He doesn't speak the language or anything. Suppose he has to sign a form?'

'Well, who can I send?' demanded Paynton, growing flustered. It was true he should not have allowed one of his leading actors to be carted away in a foreign ambulance without anyone to keep tabs on where they were taking him. For all he knew Clive might be on his way to a transplant farm to have both his kidneys removed.

'Shall I go?' Maeve was on her feet and halfway up the aisle before Gareth stopped her.

'No, you damn' well won't. Who's going to sort out Jaz's wedding dress if you go haring off to hospital? She looked like Miss Haversham when she tried it on.'

'That was because of her hair. There was nothing wrong with the dress,' Maeve responded defiantly.

'Excuse *me*,' stormed Jude, 'it's not my fault if the actress won't let me dress her wig properly. If you ask me she looked more like Lady Macbeth.'

A gasp of horror ran through the theatre. Jude had to go down two flights of stairs, turn round three times and spit. 'See how Clive is while you're there,' shouted Marcus Lemmon belligerently.

Sam Biggins, who had gone to see Clive into the ambulance, came hurrying back. 'Sorry, guv, but they say someone's got to go with him. Preferably a translator.'

Paynton slammed shut his notebook. 'Oh, fine. Well, which of my twenty-three Estonian-speaking actors shall it be, Sam? Or do you want to go? Better still, why don't I?'

Sam, who was well used to directors' tantrums, shook his head. 'What about young Phil? He's spare, unless anyone else goes AWOL.'

'Yes, yes, Philip can do it. Where is he? See to it, will you, Sam, or we won't be through by curtain up tomorrow.'

Philip was located in the café, mumbling nervily into his coffee cup. Sam beckoned from the door. 'Come on, mate, you've got to go to hospital.' What little blood was left in Philip's face now drained away.

'What? Why? I'm fine, honestly. It's just nerves. I'll be okay, trust me.'

'Someone's got to go with Clive and you won the raffle.'

'Oh, God, no. Not a hospital?' Philip shuddered pathetically. 'Honestly, Sam, I hate them. They make me feel ill. I can't stand the smell. I come over all funny.'

'Would you like me to go?' suggested Alice who had offered to hear Philip's lines. She was still feeling guilty about the airport fiasco, and though she had no great affection for hospitals either, thought she could put up with one for the sake of peace.

Sam shook his head. 'They want a bloke in case the orderlies are on strike again, apparently. I could've sent Maeve, but you'd be no good for lifting, little Alice, would you?'

'I don't mind lifting him, so long as I don't have to hang around,' said Philip, ashamed of his own feebleness.

'Why don't we both go?' said Alice, standing up to show the decision had been made.

Sam led them down to where the ambulance men were sitting on a wall outside the stage door, smoking and throwing stones at pigeons. Clive had had a swig of the local fire-water and now lay snoring gently, strapped to the stretcher – a sensible precaution as the vehicle bounced and rattled over the cobbled streets and away to the south of the town.

Philip and Alice sat side by side, Philip looking profoundly unhappy. 'Would you like to run the lines again?' whispered Alice in the hope of diverting his attention from matters medical.

Philip's face brightened slightly then fell. 'We can't, can we? With Clive here.'

'Whyever not?'

'Because it's . . . well, how would you feel if you were lying there and someone started rehearsing your lines right in front of you? It'd be like hearing your will read on your death bed.'

'Don't be so melodramatic,' Alice snorted, crossing her fingers behind her back. 'Well, it's up to you, but don't go panicking if you have to go on tomorrow night and you don't know them.' She shifted up the seat and reached in her bag for

Estonia: Everything You Need To Know. It had become something of a talisman to her, partly because she knew nothing, but more because it had occurred to her that Janni might have hidden a message in it for her. Why else give it to her?

She thumbed the pages. '*Sup with me in the romantic cellar bars of Old Tallinn. Let the music of winsome fiddlers kiss our ears as we sit, side by side, in the softening twilight in Kadriorg Park.*'

It was practically an invitation. She wasn't sure about the 'winsome fiddlers'. If anyone was going to kiss her ears she would like it to be Janni, but you could hardly be that explicit in a guide book. She certainly wouldn't want Maeve and Jude having their ears kissed by him. Or Gareth Paynton, for that matter.

'If you're sure he's asleep . . .' Alice realised Philip was talking to her.

'Sorry, what?'

'If you're sure Clive's asleep, perhaps we could just run through the big speeches? If you're sure it's not too much trouble?'

Alice controlled a sigh. 'No trouble,' she said.

The hospital was old-fashioned, the nurses nuns, garbed in long grey dresses with triangular teatowels on their heads and cumbersome wooden crosses which swung from their necks like pendulums as they padded silently about, occasionally flattening themselves against the walls in deference to the doctors, who strutted around looking like extras from *Dr Kildare*.

The orderlies were not on strike, though they might as well have been for the speed with which they approached the ambulance. Clive was eventually off-loaded with much spitting and rubbing of backs under the watchful eye of a senior nun, and wheeled away to a side ward where he was placed in a cubicle while formalities were completed.

There was some speculation about his injuries and also his clothing (purple doublet with leather jerkin, ruff, matching tights – laddered, and black ballet pumps), but this was replaced by knowing grunts as Alice flipped to the Concert Hall diagram in her guide book. Such wounds, it appeared, were not uncommon from that quarter.

She was given a form on which she wrote Clive's name, his occupation and the address of the Hotel Mirus. The rest was beyond her. Philip hovered by an open window, gulping in air like a landed fish till a passing oblate offered to put his head between his knees. This frightened him considerably and he went and sat on a chair by the exit while Alice continued to struggle with the paperwork.

Clive having awoken, periodic demands for aspirin, hamburgers and the use of a mobile phone began to emerge from the cubicle. These were ignored with all the sang-froid of a National Health Service casualty department, inspiring Philip to suggest that perhaps he should go and look for a late-night chemist, a phone, or at the very least a hamburger bar.

Alice was blowed if she was going to be left on her own to sign away Clive's kidneys so refused to sanction anything of the kind, waving her guidebook as proof that they were miles from anywhere.

Clive was duly wheeled away to X-ray, and Alice and Philip were transferred to the reception area, amongst a throng of coughing, bleeding out-patients and enough small children to start a nursery. Philip stared fixedly at his feet.

So far no one had required them to interpret anything. A doctor had made a preliminary examination, prodding Clive at various points, each of which had elicited cries of 'Ouch!', 'Aaaagh!', and finally 'JESUS CHRIST!', which seemed to have been fairly well understood by those present.

The doctor emerged again to say, with the aid of hand movements, that Clive had a lot of bruises but no bones broken. They would keep him in overnight. Thus much Alice comprehended. Clive was trundled away to a ward, now very resentful at the lack of dope and hamburgers. Philip breathed a sigh of relief. 'Thank God that's done. How are we going to get back?' He was already on his feet.

Alice frowned. 'I'll look in my book.'

'What good's that going to do?' demanded Philip. 'It's hardly going to have a Good Hospital section, is it?'

Alice took exception to this. 'This doesn't happen to be an average guidebook,' she retorted primly, and began to study the section on taxis. It was not noticeably helpful, making much of the fact that a bus between Tallinn and Riga only took six hours and was very good value for money.

'Do you think we ought to have another look at Clive before we go?' she suggested to give herself time to think.

'Go where?' said Philip gloomily. 'Unless you fancy a five-mile walk back to town?'

'Well, you think of something,' she snapped. She, too, was fed up. At least Clive Barry had a bed for the night. And to think she was only here out of the kindness of her heart. There was clearly a downside to being an honorary twin.

'I could ask if I can phone Sam?' Philip suggested. 'He'll sort something out.'

'Yes, okay, do that. I'm going to say goodnight to Clive. Any messages?'

'Tell him I hope he's fine in the morning,' said Philip, thumbing through his pocket for some change.

'Liar,' said Alice.

She never got as far as Clive's ward. As she was retracing her steps past Casualty a figure stepped out of a cubicle, halted, and said with some surprise, 'But here you are, in the hospital. Where we have not expected you.'

Alice looked up and the fly-blown strip lighting exploded into fireworks. 'Hallo, Janni,' she said. 'Fancy seeing you here.'

Chapter Thirteen

'This man has only his self to blame,' Janni explained as they sped back towards Tallinn in the sleek black Mercedes driven by a man in dark glasses, a Rayban sticker stuck firmly across one lens.

He was referring not to Clive Barry, currently the envy of his ward as he sat with a plate of blood sausage and gherkins, trying to remember what he had done to deserve such indigestion, but to the man Janni himself had been visiting – apparently a local footballer of some prowess who had lately thought of deserting his team for a Portuguese club. 'Naturally his friends will not be happy to see him go.'

'What's happened to him?' asked Alice, still not over the excitement of meeting Janni again, albeit in slightly macabre circumstances.

'Nothing. He has a small trouble in his knee. It is nothing. He will soon recover.'

'Will he still be able to go to Portugal?'

Janni smiled and shrugged. 'Naturally. But I think maybe he is no longer so keen. Now, what has happened with your friend? He will be ready to act tomorrow night?'

'We don't know,' said Alice. 'He fell off the front of the stage, right into the orchestra pit. The doctor says it's just bruises. They're keeping him in overnight. The thing is, he's playing Mercutio. He has to fight and leap about like crazy.'

Janni frowned. 'And if he is not better, what will happen? The play will be cancelled?'

'Oh, no, certainly not. The show must go on. No, Philip will play the part. He's his understudy, you see.'

Janni looked at Philip with interest. 'But who will play Philip's part?'

'No one. I haven't got one,' said Philip sullenly. Alice felt embarrassed. Here was the divine Janni, saving their necks by giving them a ride in his beautiful car, ordering food for Clive, being as charming as it was possible to be, and here was Philip, acting as though the man were Public Enemy Number One.

'Philip and I understudy all the parts between us,' she said brightly. 'That way if anyone's ill there's always someone to go on in their place.'

'What if two people are ill at the same time? Or three? Or ten? What will happen then?'

Alice laughed. 'Well, I think if it was ten they'd have to cancel, but honestly you don't know actors if you think they'll willingly miss a performance.'

'Why is that? In the army the men are always wanting to be ill.'

'Acting's different though. If you let someone go on in your place the audience might decide they were better than you. Think of that.'

Janni smiled. 'And who will you go instead of, Miss Alice Understudy?'

Alice crossed her fingers. 'Oh, all the women, but I hope I never have to. I wouldn't want anything to happen to any of them.' There was a snort from Philip.

Janni looked down at her, his brilliant blue eyes alight with mischief. 'Not even to play the star part?'

Alice demurred daintily. 'It would be nice,' she conceded. 'Just to give it a go.'

The car swept up to the Concert Hall. The chauffeur got out and opened the doors. Philip shot out and away up the stairs calling 'Thanks for the lift' over his shoulder.

Janni raised his hand. 'It is my pleasure.'

'I'm sorry about him,' said Alice desperately. 'I don't know what's got into him. I know he doesn't like hospitals but he's not usually so rude.'

Janni shrugged. 'He is a very fine young man. I hope he may play this part tomorrow. Perhaps I shall come and watch.'

Alice swallowed nervously. 'I wouldn't if I were you.'

'Why not?'

'Things tend to go wrong on first nights.' She sighed. 'Not that much more can go wrong with this production, if you ask me.'

Janni put his hands on her shoulders. 'You are unhappy. Have you spoken with your fiancé yet?'

Alice shook her head. Jay was a million miles from her thoughts. 'I thought I was supposed to wait till someone contacted me? From the British Council? Was that wrong?'

Janni burst out laughing. 'No, it is not wrong. I just thought you would want to speak to this man you are going to marry before now. You will make a very good wife to him if you are always so obedient.' He took her hand and once more raised it to his lips. 'Goodnight, Miss Alice. I hope you will get your wish.'

'Which wish?' she asked, her heart in her mouth. Janni was already halfway to the car.

'To play the star part, of course. Do you have another?'

Alice smiled forlornly. 'No,' she murmured. 'No others.'

Philip was talking to Sam in the foyer. Sam waved to her. 'Thanks for that, my love. Phil was just telling me what happened.'

'I'm surprised he knew,' said Alice aggrievedly.

'What's that supposed to mean?' asked Philip, equally truculent.

'You had your head out of the window the whole time. For all you know Clive could have had his legs amputated. And for all you care.'

'Now, now,' said Sam. 'Don't you two start. I've had Maeve in tears, Craig threatening to fly home, Nobby falling out of the flies, near as, and then some bloke from the British Council comes prowling round saying does anyone want to use his fax machine? I ask you. Ten o'clock at night.'

'Did anyone?' asked Alice jerkily.

'How should I know? Archie said something about it. Anyway the bloke's gone now. Come on, you'd better go and hear the boss's words of wisdom. The way things are going, you'll be the only ones left tomorrow night.'

They crept in. Bernice fell upon them immediately. 'How is poor Clive? Is he going to be all right? I've organised some flowers. That nice little usherette's going to see to it. What did the doctor say? I really thought I ought to pop over and see him, but Richmond says it's too late. He'll be asleep. What do you think? Is it too late? I could go first thing in the morning, after I've had my hair done.'

'As far as I know he's fine,' Alice told her. 'He hasn't broken anything. Just bruises. He looked okay when we left.'

'Thank goodness for that. Oh, there's poor Philip. He looks exhausted. Poor love, having to sort all that out and worry about whether he's going to be on or not. How's he been coping?'

'I think he's dealing with it in his own way,' said Alice stiffly.

'Yes, still, the lad could probably do with a drink,' declared Richmond, who could certainly do with one himself. 'Let's get back to the hotel and have a snifter or two.'

In the bar the company gathered round, demanding to know how Clive was and when, if ever, he would be returning to them.

'He was in quite a lot of pain when we left,' Alice heard Philip telling Marcus Lemmon. 'I can't see the doctors letting him out in time for tomorrow night.'

You wish, she thought malevolently. She had still not forgiven him for being so off with Janni.

'So how did you explain what had happened?' Archie Frith chimed in, pen poised.

'Oh, well, I . . .' Philip caught Alice's eye. 'It wasn't too bad, really. Apparently they get a lot of patients from the Concert Hall.' Nobody was surprised by this.

'Well, Philly, my baby, if you want to run over Mercutio's lines, just tap on my door.' Jasmine Ruddock gave a long, lingering stretch and wandered off towards the lift. Craig Penforth put a brotherly hand on Philip's arm. 'I wouldn't, if I were you,' he warned him. 'You'll not come out alive.'

'Oh shut up, you eunuch,' yelled Jasmine from across the room.

'Shut it yourself, Big Ears,' retorted Craig, blushing at his own audacity. Archie scribbled wildly.

Sam Biggins put his arm round Alice's shoulder. 'Come on, Florence Nightingale, what can I get you?'

'I'm a bit tired.'

'Just one.'

'All right. Just one.' She trailed him to the bar. Sam ordered double whiskies. Maeve and Jude were perched either side of Philip, now looking nearly as haunted as he had at the hospital.

'You'd better come to me first thing in the morning so that I can measure your head,' Jude was announcing.

'No, Jude. I'll have him first in case the costume needs altering.'

'What costume? It's still at the hospital, isn't it? Unless you brought it back with you?' Philip was obliged to confess that he had not.

Maeve looked suitably agonised. 'Well, that's it. I shall have to go over there first thing in the morning and fetch it back. Honestly, I do think *you* might have remembered, Alice. You had nothing else to do.'

'I'm awfully sorry,' replied Alice levelly. 'It quite slipped my mind.'

'I think we were both worried about Clive,' put in Philip quickly. 'It was all a bit of a strain.'

'Yes, well, I can see it would be for you,' Maeve conceded, 'but Alice only went along for the ride, didn't you, Alice?'

'That's right,' said Alice, adjusting Maeve's position on the death list.

'And what with us all being so busy . . . it would have helped if you'd thought to bring Clive's costume back.'

'Since it's Philip who's planning to wear it, shouldn't he be the one who thought to bring it back?' Alice retaliated. 'Besides, what's Clive supposed to wear when he's discharged?'

'He can hardly get on a bus in a doublet and hose, can he?' tittered Jude.

'There aren't any buses on that route,' Alice informed her. 'The nearest one passes the corner a quarter of a mile down the road and only runs on Tuesdays.' She tipped the remainder of her whisky down her throat. 'Thanks, Sam. I'm off.'

Philip caught up with her at the lift. 'I'm sorry.'

'What about?'

'Everything. Tonight. I know I was rude to that guy.'

'I thought so.'

'But, Alice, surely you can see? He's trouble. You ought to keep away from him, honestly. Even if he is a friend of . . . what's-his-name?'

'I assume you mean Jay?'

'Yes, Jay. I knew it began with a J.'

'Well remembered,' said Alice frostily.

Philip looked downcast. 'I just don't want you to get involved in something you can't handle, that's all. I worry about you. After all we are . . .'

Alice raised an enquiring eyebrow. 'What are we, Philip?'

Philip became interested in a broken tile by his toe. 'Mates, I suppose.'

Alice gave an exhausted laugh. 'Oh yes. Mates. Of course we are.' She thumped savagely at the lift button. It arrived, full of Finns who fell strangely silent when they saw her. She got in. 'Are you coming?' Philip shook his head. 'I promised Sam I'd buy him a drink. I'll see you tomorrow.'

'Room for us?' called Bernice, dragging Richmond by his elbow. Alice held the lift. 'I thought we might have stayed for another,' grumbled Richmond. Bernice shushed him. 'You know you always get nightmares if you mix your drinks.'

'I wasn't mixing them. I was sticking to whisky.'

'Whisky and Milk of Magnesia. Last time, he did that he thought he was back in Malaya,' she confided to Alice.

Alice smiled. 'At least it doesn't rain all the time in Malaya.'

'Does in the rainy season,' said Richmond huffily. 'And the insects! Ants an inch long. Get everywhere: in your bed, in your hair . . .'

'Stop it, Richmond,' said Bernice firmly. 'Or we'll all be having nightmares.'

'That's a lovely brooch you're wearing,' said Alice to change the subject. Bernice's face contorted very slightly.

'Oh, do you like it, dear? I've had it for ages. I bought it when we were in Hungary that time. Do you remember, darling?'

Richmond frowned. 'I don't remember the brooch,' he said suspiciously. The lift stopped. Bernice glided out. 'Here we are. Well, goodnight, Alice dear. Sleep well.'

'Goodnight,' said Alice. She was just putting the key in her lock when she felt a tap on her arm. It was Bernice. 'Alice, my pet, I know it's a pest, but could you try not to mention anything I'm wearing when Richmond's there? He's a dear generous man, but he sometimes gets a bit sticky about things like that. He doesn't understand how important it is to look one's best in this business. Well, it's easy for men, isn't it? Especially if they're as handsome as Richmond. Did I ever show you that photograph of him in his captain's uniform? My dear, Cary Grant paled by comparison.'

'Bernice . . . what are you up to? I can't find the liver salts,' echoed down the corridor.

'Coming, my love. I must dash. Thank you so much for that, Alice, dear. I wonder if Clive will be all right for tomorrow. Of course we all hope he is, but it would be nice for Philip to have a go, wouldn't it? Such a nice-looking young man. You're a lucky girl.' Bernice whirled away.

Alice stood for a moment in the corridor, trying to take in what she had said. I can't believe, she thought, I am the only one who knows about Philip.

Chapter Fourteen

The dining-room was nearly empty when Alice came down next morning. The Pastels were still in bed, the professed purity of their arrangement rekindling passions they had imagined long buried under a welter of decrees nisi, maintenance and teenage children.

Jeannie and Ray were out trawling the streets in search of a decent fry-up and most of the men were sleeping off the effects of an impromptu poker session in Sam's room the night before.

Marshall was there, clamped to a radiator, the reek of eucalyptus oil floating like a mushroom cloud above his head. 'Don't come any nearer,' he ordered as Alice approached. 'Looks like it's turning into flu.'

'Oh, poor you.' She retreated to the other end of the table.

'There's no need to treat me like a leper.'

Hilly Bates was dissecting a grapefruit with the precision of a brain surgeon. Archie Frith was crouched over his notebook in a corner. He was beginning to remind Alice of a Stasi agent. What on earth can he have to write about? she wondered. *Tuesday: rain. Wednesday: rain. Thursday: Clive fell off stage. Showers.* The tabloids would be falling over each other for that. Still, if whoever wrote her guidebook could make a flat wet country sound like Arcadia, why shouldn't Archie pipe some frenzy into his scribblings?

'Alice, dear, how are you this morning?' Bernice came breezing in, looking like a visiting dignitary in a ruby toque with matching coat.

'I'm fine, thank you, Bernice. You look . . .' She stopped for fear of inciting Richmond.

'Do you like it? It's my hospital visiting outfit. I always used to wear it when I was asked to open a ward or anything during my *Sister Gillian* days. Richmond always says it makes me look like a blood clot. Horrid man!' She beamed affectionately at her husband. Hilly Bates shuddered and pushed his grapefruit away.

Bernice advanced on him. 'Hilly, dear, I'm organising a little party to go and see Clive. Sam's going to sort out some transport. Would you like to come?'

Hilly straightened his back. 'I wouldn't awfully, Bernice, to tell the truth. But I'm going to say a few prayers for him this morning, if you could give him that message?'

'Oh how lovely. Certainly I will.'

'Remember me in them, will you, Hills?' Jasmine came tottering in. She was suffering from a hangover, having persuaded Gareth to order a bottle of champagne, the bulk of which she had drunk herself. 'Anyone got any paracetamol?'

Alice had, but she had no intention of fetching them. Besides if Jasmine felt ill enough there was always the chance she might have to step into the breach at the last moment. Some hope! Jasmine had pounced on Marshall's jacket and was rifling through his pockets like a truffle hound. 'What's this?' she gurgled, pulling out a pack of postcards.

'Give those back,' yelped Marshall, moving very fast for someone who was ill.

'Aha!' Jasmine had found some Alka Seltzer among the collection of pills and purgatives. 'These will do.'

'Do you want to come and see Clive with us, Jasmine, dear?' asked Bernice.

'Yuk, no thanks. I hate ill people.' Jasmine emptied the Alka Seltzer into a glass of orange juice and swigged it down.

'People can't help being ill,' sniffed Marshall peevishly,

thinking it was all very fine for people to take his medicine and then blame him for needing it.

'Yes they can.' Jasmine wiped the froth from her mouth. 'I'm never ill. It's a waste of time. Anyway, give Clive my love. Say he needn't hurry back 'cos Philip's ten times better than him. That'll get him on his feet.'

Bernice laughed indulgently. 'You're a naughty girl, Jasmine. Ah, here are the others.'

The 'others' turned out to be Maeve and Jude, looking very clinical in navy dresses with white button-down collars. Nobody asked which play they'd pinched them from.

'Has anyone heard anything?' enquired Archie Frith, licking the tip of his pencil. 'About if Phil's on, or what?'

'Ga's told him to come in at twelve if Clive's not back,' Jasmine informed them. 'Could be his big night. God, I feel dreadful.' She slumped into a chair and helped herself from Hilly's coffee pot. He frowned very slightly then, unable to contain himself any longer, set down his own cup and folded his hands on the table. 'Jasmine, I really do wish you wouldn't do that.'

'What? Have a drop of your coffee? Oh, don't be so mean, Hilly babe. I thought you Christians were meant to share things. Chuck me the sugar, would you, Marshall, there's a pet. On second thoughts, don't. I don't want your disgusting germs.'

'I thought you never got ill,' said Marshall disagreeably.

'That's because I keep away from people like you. Ali, be a pet and pass me that sugar behind you, would you?'

'It's not that,' said Hilly heavily. 'It's just I would prefer it if you could stop taking the Lord's name in vain. I know you don't mean anything by it but it's blasphemy nonetheless.'

Jasmine stopped with the cup halfway to her mouth. 'Blasphemy? Does that mean I'll go to hell?'

Hilly was taken aback. His doctrine decreed he should strike while the iron was hot, but natural diffidence stood in his way. 'Well, no – not if you're sorry,' he temporised.

'I am,' Jasmine assured him. 'Jolly. Oh, nuts, is that the time? I'm meant to be meeting Ga on stage at ten. Has anyone seen that ratfink Penforth? We've got to spend all morning on the balcony, just 'cos he dried in the dress. Jeez, when I think of all the men who could have played that part. And here comes one of them.' This as Philip came wandering in. He looked pretty washed out, too. Alice wondered idly if there was to be a photo call for the first night, in which case *Ill People from England* might make an appropriate caption.

'Cheer up, sexy,' Jasmine admonished him as she scooted past. 'I'll get round to you in time.'

'Philip,' Bernice was upon him, 'I'm just sorting out who wants to come and see poor Clive at the hospital. Would you like to? I know Gareth wants you later on, but we should be back . . . No?' as Philip's face contorted. 'Well, perhaps another time. Now come along, everyone who's going. Sam's meeting us in Reception at ten to. It's nearly that now. Come on, Alice. Where's your coat?'

'I wasn't actually planning . . .'

'Well, if you're sure. It's a lot warmer than yesterday, I grant you, but I still think you should have a jacket of some kind. Never mind. I know these hospitals. They're always overheated.' Taking Alice's arm, she shepherded her towards the lift with the others. Alice gave in. At least there was safety in numbers.

Sam was waiting for them. He had managed to hire a very old minibus from the uncle of one of the stagehands and it now sat outside the hotel, black smoke belching from its exhaust and an equal quantity from the driver's pipe.

Bernice was ecstatic. 'Oh goodness, is that for us? Well done, Sam. Now, who's going to sit next to the driver? I think it had better be Alice because she knows the way.'

Several people protested at this: Alice because she didn't know the way, Jude because she thought *she* did, and Richmond because he had the longest legs and didn't like travelling sideways.

It was finally arranged that Richmond would go in the front with Jude directly behind him to give directions, should they be needed. Alice sat next to Bernice who was as excited as if they were off to the seaside, and Maeve sat stonily opposite, plainly feeling that her importance in the matter of retrieving Clive's costume was not being given due attention.

Sam drew Alice aside as she was about to get in. 'Listen, ducks, I wouldn't go worrying that lot about what happened at the airport, okay?'

Alice nodded.

'I don't want the old lady flapping, or nothing,' he continued. 'Any trouble, get straight on the blower, right? I'm at the theatre. The driver geezer'll know the number.' He waved them off and the minibus lurched wretchedly over the cobbles and then back on to the main road out of town.

They travelled mainly in silence, the driver periodically swivelling his pipe in order to launch a phlegm attack on the unsuspecting verge. Alice noticed that the grass nearest the curb was a lot greener than that further back and had to chew hard on her gums to stop herself being sick.

Their arrival at the hospital caused some confusion, partly because, on hearing of five people arriving from the theatre, the Casualty staff immediately assumed that a catastrophe had taken place, and took all their doctors off the wards, placing their own theatres on Red Alert to await the admission of five sets of mangled limbs. Since Maeve's was the first face they saw a runner was sent hotfoot to the hospital's blood bank to tell them to defrost the lot.

Once it had been established that the group was merely visiting the organisation clicked back into slack mode with awesome promptness, and the five of them were left to twiddle their thumbs for twenty-five minutes while a junior nurse was dispatched to ascertain the condition of Clive, now touchingly rechristened 'the English Patient'. The charm of this almost took his mind off his indigestion.

A doctor eventually appeared and endeavoured to convey to them that Clive was perfectly healthy, barring the severe bruising to his ankle, his ribs and his manhood, and that they were happy to discharge him, provided he rested all three until the swelling had disappeared.

Clive was then lent a dressing-gown and made to sign a form in Estonian which none of them understood although Maeve insisted she had seen the word 'transplant' amid the gobbledegook. No one took the slightest notice of her until they went outside to find the minibus gone and in its place a brand new Mercedes People Carrier.

A young man in jeans was sitting in the driver's seat. He leapt out when he saw them and came hurrying across. 'Hi,' he said cheerfully. 'All is well? I am glad. Let me help you.' He began to manhandle a protesting Clive into the vehicle.

Richmond stepped forward. 'Young man, there appears to be some mistake. Where is our driver? Where is our minibus?'

The young man's English immediately forsook him. He grinned inanely, shrugged his shoulders and continued to prod Clive into the car. Richmond, who had fought in both Spain and the Malay swamps, was not going to be brushed off so lightly. 'Young man,' he boomed in a voice that would have carried in Wembley Stadium, 'I demand to know what is going on.'

For those who have ever scoffed that shouting loudly in English is no substitute for learning the language this would have proved a cruel rebuttal. The youth let go of Clive's foot, which thudded with accompanying groans to the floor, and turned to face his inquisitor.

'Unhappily your driver has had a small incident to his finger. He must not drive. I, nonetheless, am in lieu of him.'

They were all too flabbergasted by his grasp of idiom to argue and were duly herded into the vehicle, gaping at its luxurious upholstery, seat belts and individual air conditioners.

The young man turned on the ignition. A roar, a rasp and a rattle issued from the engine as it first jerked, stalled, then jumped its way past the grinning ambulance men, who waved and whistled at the car as if it had been a local beauty queen.

'Well, isn't this nice?' beamed Bernice, having got over her initial anxiety. 'And so much better for poor Clive. How are you feeling, dear? You must go straight to bed when we get back and rest that poor leg.'

Clive was sorely afraid that he would have to. Loath though he was to miss a performance, he could hardly play Mercutio bandaged like the Invisible Man. It was a shame, but he doubted if Philip knew any of the words. Understudies never did. He would have to go on with the book and everyone would make allowances and be very sweet to him afterwards. Clive could handle that.

'Now you mustn't worry about a thing,' Bernice reassured him. 'Gareth's going to run through everything with Philip this afternoon, and Maeve here says the costume's no problem. I'm sure everything will be fine.' She winked fiercely at Maeve to stop her contradicting.

Maeve sighed. 'No, I'm sure I shall be able to manage. Philip's a bit broader in the chest than you, isn't he, Clive? And taller, of course, but actually I think he'll make a very handsome Mercutio.' Clive shuffled slightly and tried to see if he could move his toes.

'Dark men always look good in purple,' said Jude authoritatively. Clive frowned, thinking that red-headed men did too.

'And at least he knows all the lines,' added Bernice. 'Thanks to Alice. Philip was telling me what a slave-driver she is. Is that true, dear? I do think men need that.' Richmond harrumphed. 'Goodness, isn't this road bumpy? I don't remember that on the way and this is a much newer car.'

The young man, either from pique or determination to prove her wrong, thrust the accelerator into the floor. The People Carrier leapt forward, roaring like an angry lion, rocketed to eighty miles an hour, then with a sickening clang, followed by crackling and the stink of burning rubber, ground to a halt.

The young man got out and opened the bonnet from which smoke was now pouring. He stared grimly into the depths then slammed it down and erupted into a diatribe, kicking viciously at the vehicle as he stomped round it, alternately thumping the sides and making throat-slitting gestures as he went.

'I wonder if it's petrol?' said Bernice blandly. 'I don't remember passing a garage on the way and these big things must use an awful lot.'

'It's a trap,' said Jude suddenly.

'Oooooh,' whimpered Maeve, unsure whether to be thrilled or afraid. The young man was very good-looking even if he did have gold fillings.

'What sort of trap?' asked Richmond, trying to remember which leg a commando crawl started on. Not that his darling wife would be willing to crawl through the undergrowth, of which there was precious little, in her hospital visiting kit. And poor young Clive was in no state for a long trek. He supposed they'd have to leave him and hoped the Estonians knew how to treat their POWs.

He was brought back to reality by Alice's voice. 'He's got a mobile phone. I expect he's calling the AA or whatever they have here.' From the look on the young man's face he was not getting very good service from whoever was on the other end. His voice rose, then sank. His gestures degenerated from violent to desperate to helpless as he threatened, pouted and whinged into the receiver. Finally he slammed the aerial down, stood for a moment staring at his feet then, without a word to his passengers, flagged down a passing lorry, hauled himself into the driver's cab, exchanged a few quick words with him, and was driven away towards Tallinn without so much as a backward glance.

'I say,' said Richmond, thoroughly annoyed and beginning to want his lunch.

'Has anyone got any painkillers?' asked Clive who had the beginnings of cramp.

'I expect he's gone for help,' Bernice soothed them.

'Don't you believe it,' Jude insisted. 'Or if he has, it's to finish us off.' Maeve wailed and had to fan herself to keep from fainting. Alice sat silently, horribly afraid there might be more truth in what Jude said than she realised.

They never found out. Fifteen minutes later the sound of crunching gears and a puff of distant black smoke heralded the arrival of the original minibus. The driver drew to a halt, surveyed the scene, spat expressively into the middle of the road and loaded them back in. Alice noticed that his index finger was in plaster.

He dropped them at the theatre before careering off into the Old Town. Sam came out to meet them. 'Where you lot been? I thought we was down to five-a-side.'

'Oh, the strangest thing . . .' Bernice regaled him with the details. Sam chewed silently at a piece of string. 'Oh well, all's well that ends well,' he said stoically when she had finished. 'How's young Clive?'

'Oh, not at all well,' said Bernice. 'Straight to bed for him, I should say.'

Clive, however, had other ideas. Bravely he hauled himself out on to the pavement. 'I'm fine,' he assured Sam, wincing as he spoke. 'Just a few bruises. Nothing to worry about.' Sam surveyed him dubiously.

'Up to you, mate. The boss's in there. You'd better sort it out with him. You don't want to worry about Phil letting the side down, though. I've been listening to him rehearsing. He's bloody good.'

Clive straightened up and with all the courage of Charles I ascending the scaffold, went to reclaim his part.

Sam shrugged and came over to Alice. 'I hope I didn't do that.'

'Do what?'

'Lose the kiddo his big chance. Me and my big mouth.'

Alice smiled dejectedly. 'I think he'd already made up his mind when Maeve said Philip looked good in purple.'

Sam nodded. 'You'd better go and try and cheer him up.'

Alice retreated. 'Me? I'm the last person. Everything I do seems to annoy him these days.'

Sam gave her an odd look. 'Yeah, well . . . So what's all this on the road back, then? Was the old lady telling the truth?'

'Of course she was.'

Sam shook his head. 'I didn't mean it like that. I just thought she might have been exaggerating.'

'I don't think she was, actually. But why would a brand new car break down like that?'

'Fuel. There's none about. Probably running it on pigeon shit. This whole place is a bleeding farce, if you ask me. I've had half the bleeding set pinched while I was on the phone. Two back flats for the ballroom – gone to make someone's garden shed, I wouldn't be surprised. It's not the local lads. They're fine. Bloody good workers. It's all these bleeding racketeers. That was nothing the other night, you know, at the airport. Half the blooming budget's gonna go in back-handers at this rate. I'd rather be in Nigeria and that's not a lie.

'Oh, by the way, the girl on Reception asked me to tell you there's a fax arrived for you. Right little cracker she is an' all. Have you noticed how pretty the girls are out here? No wonder the terrible twins are having problems. Anyway I can't hang about here nattering. See you later, love. Don't get lost. And *don't,*' he added, suddenly looking serious, 'do anything I wouldn't do.'

Chapter Fifteen

Alice saw Philip before he saw her. He was sitting at a curbside table outside one of the chichi little cafés in the Raekoja Plats, the main square of the Old Town, a half-empty glass of beer in front of him. He was staring grimly at an inoffensive statue of some local dignitary on the pavement opposite, but his thoughts were clearly elsewhere.

Alice approached with caution. She found almost everything she did nowadays had a hint of espionage about it. Even collecting her fax from the receptionist at the hotel had felt like a scene from an early Hitchcock. The girl had been patently nervous as she handed it over and when Alice had asked who had delivered it, had positively begun to shake.

'I am very sorry, madam. I did not see the man at all. I could not describe him.'

Alice had decided not to pursue the matter. Instead she had tucked the paper conspiratorially inside her jacket and not opened it until she was safe inside her room. The prosaicness of its contents was sadly out of keeping with her effort.

Hi, honey. How's it going? Did the guys get in touch? Let me know soonest. Jay

'I miss you, too,' she muttered resentfully. 'And, yes, it was a lousy flight.' Then, fearing that the room might be bugged, 'But it wasn't the fault of the airline.' She caught sight of her reflection in the mirror and decided to go for a walk before whoever was listening arrived with a straitjacket.

Collecting her guidebook and a plastic rainhat Jeannie had pressed upon her and she would die before she wore, she set off.

Tallinn by night had been eerie but Tallinn by day was magical, at least away from the hideous concrete blocks surrounding the hotel – itself no beauty spot, with its jagged towers stabbing the sky like an angry Toblerone.

She went first towards the port and took several photos of a forbidding-looking building which her book informed her was: *Fat Margaret, a sixteen century bastion of much importance*. It didn't say why. She passed several churches and tried to drum up the enthusiasm to go inside, but she was, and always had been, a hopeless tourist and after a couple of tentative sorties, mainly past elderly women queuing to light candles, she gave up and headed for the square.

Wandering along, it occurred to her that the cobbled streets, medieval buildings, pastel-washed houses with their intricate iron twirls and precipitous red roofs would make an ideal setting for *Romeo and Juliet*. If Jay had any sense he would forsake his screenplay and concentrate on finding funds to film the Millennium Players on tour.

Idly she wondered just when the British Council contact would catch up with her. What would he be like? Surely not smaller than Brian Berrell, who had been smaller than Gareth Furlong? Perhaps they were employed on a descending scale. Small, smaller, smallest. Maybe he had been at the soirée after all, but she had missed him because he only came up to her knees. Realising that madness was getting the upper hand, she returned to *Estonia: Everything You Need To Know*. A very short acquaintance with it suggested that the Estonian world view owed more to Kafka than hard fact.

Toompea Castle on top of Toompea Hill was now the seat of the Estonian Parliament, but this didn't stop the author explaining in some detail that it was also the grave mound of the folk hero Kalev, whose mother had taken the unprecedented step of weeping a whole lake for him just beyond its boundaries.

Alice pondered what on earth the son could have done to encourage such a deluge. Probably married an unsuitable girl. Maybe a Russian. She had noticed on her wanderings how little reference there was to the people who formed so large a proportion of the population, and that those there were were hostile. Underneath all the picturesque charm and friendliness of the locals there must be a political cauldron bubbling. She only hoped they kept the lid on till the Millennium Players had gone home.

It was as she crossed the square in front of the magnificent town hall, the fifteenth-century Raekoda, that she spotted Philip. Newly armed with information that *Here was dauntless Vana Toomas ruthlessly slain*, although not who he was or even who had felt moved to dispose of him, she made her way towards him.

'Hullo.'

Philip looked up in surprise. 'Hullo.'

'Can I join you? My feet are killing me.'

Philip shrugged and pulled out a chair. A waiter came over. Alice ordered a beer. 'Do you want another?' Philip shook his head, then changed his mind.

They sat in silence while the waiter fetched the drinks.

'I've been for a walk round the town,' said Alice.

'What's it like?' asked Philip listlessly.

'Nice,' said Alice. 'This guidebook of mine has come in really useful. It's got all sorts of snippets about the history and things.'

'What sort of things?'

'Well, did you know, for instance, that just over there Vana Toomas was ruthlessly slain?'

'Where?'

'Over there. Outside the town hall, I suppose. Although presumably it wasn't built at the time.'

'Presumably not. It's double-glazed.'

'It's been there since fourteen hundred and four,' Alice informed him. 'I expect the double-glazing is an addition.'

'Do you know, I hadn't thought of that.'

'And just the other side of the castle is a lake composed entirely of Kalev's mother's tears.'

Philip finished his first beer and took a long drink of the second. 'You don't say.'

'It's all here in my book.'

'Should make the bestseller list.'

Alice set the book down. 'Philip, I'm really sorry about Clive.'

'What about him?'

'Being better and that.'

'Yup. Thanks.'

'But it isn't my fault.'

Philip frowned. 'Whoever said it was?'

'So there's no real need to be beastly to me, is there?'

Philip scowled. 'I'm sorry. I was rather hoping not to run into anyone up here.'

Alice stood up, slapped some money on the table and picked up her book. 'I beg your pardon. I only came over because I felt sorry for you.'

The scowl deepened. 'I think I can do without that, thanks all the same.'

'You'll bloody well have to,' snapped Alice, and stalked off back to the hotel.

'I thought he did remarkably well, considering. It brought a whole new dimension to the role. Don't you agree, Richmond?'

Only an optimist of Bernice's ranking could have thought Clive's first night Mercutio improved by the addition of a limp and the restaging of his fight along the lines of a pavane.

Richmond was too much of a professional to lend his support to the claim, so merely grunted and enquired whether anyone knew where he could get a copy of the *Daily Telegraph*.

The general feeling amongst the cast was that they were damn' lucky to have got through the performance at all, given that Clive could not move, Marshall could not speak and Jasmine could not act.

The theatre had been nearly full and the audience warm

and responsive. There had been cheers at the end, and flowers thrown on the stage. Alice was surprised that so many people should turn out to watch a play in a foreign language. Maybe wooden acting went down better if you couldn't understand a word.

They'd certainly had their money's worth. Partway through the second act one of the struts supporting the balcony had come loose. Jasmine had retained her balance by clinging to the artificial ivy Craig Penforth was attempting to climb. Since she was no weakling this had the effect of a ship weighing anchor, and Craig had been unceremoniously winched skywards, his feet scrabbling feverishly to maintain a hold on the trellis.

Alice was watching from the wings as Sam shot past, hammer in hand. 'Bleeding Batman!' drifted back to her.

Marshall had a coughing fit in the marriage scene which further delayed the action, and Jeannie and Ray, who were watching themselves in a dubbed episode of their erstwhile soap, nearly missed their final cue.

All in all it was both gratifying and amazing to Alice as she stood in the back row to hear the sound of genuine applause from the darkened auditorium.

One down, she thought, fifty-nine to go.

There were drinks laid on in the bar for the cast. Several of the notables from the previous evening were in place, including the redoubtable Madame Skikne.

Alice hid behind Sam when she came past. She had never enjoyed singing lessons and was not at all sure that Madame Skikne's methods would bring out the best in her. In doing so she felt the unmistakable squelch of toes beneath her heel. She turned to apologise and found herself face to face with a dark-eyed ferrety man, squinting morosely down at her through rimless glasses.

'I'm so sorry,' she babbled. 'I didn't know you were there.'

The man made a clicking noise with his tongue. 'You are Alice Ermingway?'

'Erm, yes. Hemingway, but it doesn't matter,' Alice reassured him, her heart beating faster.

'If I can speak with you?'

'Oh, certainly. Yes. Of course. Here? Now?'

The man clicked again. 'Perhaps we shall make for a more tranquil place?'

Not for the first time Alice wondered who taught the Estonians their English. They seemed to have a profound grasp of the least-used phrases in the language and an equal determination to resurrect them.

He jerked his head towards the far corner and strode purposefully in that direction, followed more slowly by Alice.

Once there the man turned and surveyed her irritably. 'Yesterday I have been at the theatre and spoken to your company about the fax machine.' He paused.

'Yes, I heard about it. I had to go with Clive to the hospital. I'm sorry I missed you.'

'I think also you have missed the reason for my visit. I have today had placed a fax at the hotel for you from England.'

'Oh, that was you, was it? The receptionist was a bit vague. Thank you. Erm . . . do you want me to send Jay any message?'

The man looked taken aback. 'I?'

Alice nodded. 'Yes. From Janni and Alexei. They said I had to send everything by fax to Jay, in case it got intercepted by GCHQ.' Her voice trailed away. The man was staring at her very hard.

'I am afraid I am not following you. I wish merely to convey that the British Council fax machine is available to all members of your company for the sendage, and I stress *only* for the sendage, of vital and urgent messages. We have made this available only because it is sometimes difficult to obtain contact through the telephone system. This is not the fault of the Estonians,' he added sharply.

Alice swallowed. 'I'm sure it's not.' The man clicked his tongue once more and left her. Alice sank down on to a chair. Oh, my God, she thought. What have I done? Given *everything* away. Alexei and Janni will kill me, I know they will. Look at that poor man who only wanted to play football in Portugal. She put her head in her hands.

'Cheer up, Ali.' Sam was standing over her with a glass of wine. 'It wasn't that bad. Look on the bright side.'

'What bright side?' she groaned. 'There is no bright side.'

''Course there is. You didn't forget none of your lines. Here, try this.' He handed her the glass. 'I don't like it much but I'm a beer man. See what you think.'

Alice took a deep gulp and shuddered.

'That bad, eh? Or is it something else? Saw you talking to the new boyfriend just now. You sure get through them, don't you? What's wrong with us Brits, that's what I'd like to know?' He sat down opposite and patted her knee. 'Come on. Tell Uncle Sam. That's what I'm here for.'

Alice braced herself. 'Sam, do you think I could go home?'

''Course you can, ducks. You feeling a bit rough? It's been a long day.'

'Not the hotel, Sam. Home. England. I want to go home.'

He sat back and gave a low whistle. 'What is this? I spent half yesterday talking Craig out of it, and now you're at it. We've only been here a couple of days. I have it straight from the Almighty it's not going to rain all summer, if that's what's pissing you off. What is it? Missing the boyfriend?'

Alice shook her head violently. 'Sam, I'm serious. I think I may be in trouble. Awful trouble. I can't tell you why. Just believe me, I wouldn't ask otherwise.'

Sam was silent for a moment. 'Who's going to do the understudying?'

Alice flung up her hands in despair. 'For God's sake, Sam. No one's ever going to be off, are they? Look at Clive tonight. They'd rather die than let Philip or me on. I'm surplus to requirements. We all know that. I can't stay. I just can't.'

Sam patted her hand reassuringly. 'Sure I can get you home if that's what you want, but you gotta promise me two things.'

'What? Anything.'

'One, you sleep on it. Things may look a lot different in the morning. And two, if they don't, you tell me the real reason you want to go. No messing about. Agreed?'

Alice nodded in relief. 'Oh, thank you, Sam. Thank you so much.'

He grunted. 'Right. Well, I think the best thing might be for me to get you back to the hotel. I've got a taxi coming at half-past. You can hitch a ride in that. Should be here by now. Come on, I'll take you down. Quick, before Chris Ewbank over there gets her mitts on us.' He led her away.

The taxi was just pulling off but Sam flagged it down. 'There you go, ducks. You get a bit of sleep and we'll talk about it in the morning. Straight home, mind. No clubbing.' Alice smiled and kissed his cheek in gratitude.

'You are wonderful, Sam.'

Sam grunted, 'So they tell me.' He opened the door for her. Alice clambered in, expecting to find Richmond and Bernice installed, or at worst Maeve and Jude.

'Oh,' she said uncertainly. 'Couldn't you stand it, either?'

'I wasn't in a party mood,' said Philip tersely and turned his attention to the window.

They rode for a while in silence. Despite the atmosphere Alice was glad he was there. Away from the bar her panic seemed a bit overblown. After all, the man had not understood what she'd said to him, so it was perfectly possible that no one else need ever know about their conversation. It wasn't her fault if she'd mistaken him for her contact. Alexei should have been more explicit. She couldn't bring herself to think that Janni was in any way to blame for the mix-up. Perhaps she had over-reacted. It would be awfully stupid to give up the whole tour after two days, just because she'd annoyed some minion at the British Council.

One thing was for sure. The moment she stepped on that plane home Jasmine Ruddock would be sure to fall down a mine shaft and break every bone in her body.

Philip paid the driver when they got to the Mirus. Alice offered her share but he shrugged it off. 'I was coming back anyway.'

'Yes, but still.'

Philip walked towards the lift. Alice trotted after him. 'I really am sorry about tonight, Philip. Clive and everything.'

He grimaced. 'I didn't believe you when you said actors would die before they missed a perf.'

Alice shrugged. 'I daresay we'd be the same. Particularly if the understudy was any good.'

Philip laughed shortly. 'That's some sort of consolation, is it? Word got back to Clive that I actually knew the lines so he hotfooted it from his deathbed at the eleventh hour.'

'It certainly looked as though he had,' said Alice, 'but I am sorry you didn't get to go on. Truly I am.'

Philip smiled. 'Me, too. Especially as I was up all night rehearsing it. Probably just as well. I might have done a Richmond and fallen asleep halfway through.'

Alice laughed. 'And it is early days, isn't it? I mean, tonight was the first night. We've got ages yet. Come on, let me buy you a drink.'

'That would be nice. We can plot who we're going to dispose of next.'

Alice began to giggle.

'What's so funny?'

'I was just thinking about when the balcony gave way and poor Craig was bobbing about on the end of that ivy.'

'He looked like Catch of the Day.'

'And then when Marshall started coughing. He really is disgusting. I never thought I'd agree with anything Jasmine said, but in his case she's right.'

'Poor old Clive looked like death, didn't he?'

'So did Gareth. Do you think he arranged for those flowers the audience were throwing at the end?'

Philip considered. 'Must have done, I suppose. If it had been left to me they'd've been hand grenades.'

The lift opened and they headed for the bar. It was surprisingly quiet, but the Finns were out getting drunk somewhere cheaper and there didn't seem to be many other guests apart from the Millennium Players in the hotel. *Tourism is in its infants,* Alice recalled from her book's introduction.

'What would you like?' she asked as they settled themselves.

'Beer would be fine.'

'Beer's boring.'

'Can you run to a vodka?'

'Dozens if necessary.'

'They may be. Do you know, I had such a good feeling about this tour,' said Philip suddenly, 'and it all seems to be draining away.'

Alice swallowed. 'You're just fed up because the Mercutio thing fell through. It's understandable.' She ordered the drinks.

Philip smiled slightly and shook his head. 'Maybe you're right. But it feels deeper than that somehow. I can't help wondering if it's worth it.'

'What?'

'Any of it. Acting. I mean, it's a pretty daft job really, isn't it? Am I really going to spend my life pretending to be someone else?'

'I don't see why not. It's better than just being yourself, wouldn't you say?'

Philip laughed. 'I see we're going straight to the "What's it all about?" stage.'

Alice sipped her vodka. 'You started it. God, these are strong.'

'Good. No, it's just being twenty-five, and nearly getting to play a good part, and then having to stand back and grin when some middle-aged twat of a director says, "Oh, by the way, we don't want you after all. Just get to the back of the line again." I mean, why do I put up with it? I should have stood my ground.'

'How? Refused to give Clive his tights back?'

'I should have said, "Look, Gareth, I've been up all night learning this. I'm as good as he is. Clive's in no condition to go on, he can hardly move. You owe it to the company and the audience not to foist them off with a sub-standard performance." Something like that.'

'And what would Gareth have replied?'

Philip swigged his vodka. '"P45 in the post", I expect. But at least I'd've made a stand. Are we going to have another?'

'Might as well.' Alice was feeling better all of a sudden. 'Look, Clive's had two accidents already. He could easily have another. And if not him, someone else. That's the beauty of understudying. You never know who you might have to play. Much better than just having one lousy part.'

The barman brought more drinks. 'Why don't we ask him to leave the bottle?' suggested Philip.

'Good idea. Put it on my bill.'

'Mine.'

'Mine. I have invited you. That is the end of it.' The barman stood patiently by. 'Please may you leave the bottle and put it on my bill?' requested Alice. 'And could we have some more ice? Please. Thank you.'

'And some crisps,' suggested Philip. The man looked confused. 'Please?'

'Bits. Snacky things. Nuts,' said Alice in a moment of inspiration.

The man took her room number, returning with a tray of assorted gherkins and the bottle.

'Thank you very much,' said Alice, refilling their glasses. 'These look . . . like gherkins.' The man retreated.

Philip sat back, savouring his drink. 'You're right,' he confirmed eventually. 'You're talking utter rubbish, but you're right.'

This made total sense to Alice. She drank deep. The vodka wasn't actually all that strong. Not once you'd got the taste for it. 'And I'll tell you another thing,' she began, trying to remember what it was.

'Tell me.'

'I will.'

'Go on then.'

'Can you just top up my drink?'

'I can do that small thing.'

'Do yours too.'

'I am.'

'And I'll tell you something else . . .'

Chapter Sixteen

Maeve and Jude, who had had a singularly unsuccessful night, having failed to attract even the attention of the drunken Finns when the party moved on to a cellar bar from the theatre, now stood outside Gareth Paynton's room.

It was eight o'clock in the morning but this was not a matter they felt should be left till a more civilised hour. This was an emergency and should be dealt with as such.

'I think I heard something,' whispered Jude, her head bent low to the keyhole.

'Knock again,' urged Maeve.

Jude rapped sharply. There was a pause, then the sound of someone's voice, or to be correct two people's voices, for Jasmine had decided to stay the night, despite her lover's rather nervous suggestion that it would be safer if she crept back to her own room in case there was a fire alarm.

The sound of someone knocking at his door at eight o'clock in the morning when he had only been in bed since three was rather less attractive than a full-scale assault by water cannon, as far as Paynton was concerned. He had discovered a slightly unendearing habit of Jasmine's to hog the blankets. Vanessa did it too. It was one of the reasons they had agreed to sleep in separate beds, and now here was the divine Jasmine exhibiting similar trends of selfishness. All in all he had passed a restless night, and what sleep he had managed had been haunted by dreams of wheelchair Mercutios ranged in battle order before him and all demanding to be allowed to sing in the Estonian Song Festival. Madame Skikne had not actually appeared, but the spirit of her being had hovered in his subconscious like Banquo's ghost, knocking endlessly on a door which Gareth knew he would eventually have to open.

When he finally surfaced to discover that the knocking was real and, on staggering to the door, found himself confronted by Maeve, ashen with migraine, and Jude, scarlet with PMT, his first thought was to rush back to bed and abandon himself to whatever frenzied fantasy the Estonian southpaw had in mind for him.

It was not to be.

'I hope we haven't woken you up, Gareth,' said Jude, casting a keen eye at the humped bedclothes under which Jasmine slumbered like a great she-elephant, regal in repose, 'only it is a matter of some urgency.'

'No, no. I was just getting up,' mumbled Paynton, fumbling with his pyjama cord and wishing Maeve would look at something else.

'Only we thought you'd want to know,' Maeve twittered, her eyes still fixed on his crotch.

'Yes, yes, obviously, if it's urgent. Could you just hang on a minute while I finish getting dressed? I could meet you in the restaurant in five minutes?'

The women nodded gravely and made their way downstairs.

'Now, what's all this about?' Gareth, dripping blood from his rush to shave, sat down heavily and looked around. 'Have you ordered coffee? I'm afraid I can't function without it.'

'We haven't,' said Maeve piously, 'because we had too much on our minds.'

Gareth refrained from saying what was on his. He signalled a waiter. 'Could you bring us some coffee, please? A large pot.' The man hurried away. 'Now, what precisely is the problem? I know Richmond's wig was a bit lopsided last night, but I'm sure no one noticed. He carried it off very well.'

Jude bristled. 'It looked all right to me.'

'There you are, then. It was probably just me. Maybe I had my head on one side.' He laughed chokily. Jude pursed her lips.

'I know it's probably none of our business . . .'

Gareth froze. They're going to lecture me on sleeping with Jaz, he thought in horror. What on earth shall I say? I can't sack them. I'll never find replacements out here. Good God, if a man can't sleep with his own actresses on tour, what are things coming to?

The waiter arrived with the coffee. There was a pause while he poured three cups.

'The point is,' Jude continued, her dark eyes piercing into Gareth's very soul, 'it reflects badly on the company.'

'Er – does it?' he flailed. 'I wonder if you could pass me the sugar, Maeve?' Maeve passed it.

'I should have thought that was obvious,' Jude continued ominously. 'In private's one thing, but in the bar of the hotel! Anyone could have come along.'

Paynton frowned slightly, trying to remember just what he and Jasmine had done to excite this outbreak of righteousness in Jude Jenkins, whom he knew for a fact spent her life trying to get laid.

'It's just as well it was only us,' broke in Maeve supportively.

Jude frowned. 'I don't know what you mean by "only", Maeve. As if our opinion didn't count.'

'No, well, no I didn't mean that . . .' Maeve studied her fingernails.

'Perhaps you two ladies could come to the point,' said Gareth aggressively. If they had anything to say let them get on and say it then perhaps he could snatch another half hour in bed before the day's trials began in full.

'Very well.' Jude pulled herself up in her chair. Gareth straightened his back so that he could still look down on her. 'Last night, when we returned to the hotel, we saw Philip Carter and Alice Hemingway in the bar.'

'And?' said Gareth, unable to believe he had been dragged out of bed for this.

'And they were drunk. Very drunk.'

'So?' As far as he could remember every single member of the cast had been drunk last night, and with good cause. And Richmond Canning's wig *had* been lopsided, so Jude had just better watch her step.

'It was worse than that,' droned Maeve remorselessly.

'How? Were they sick?' Gareth was already planning to blame the Finns.

'No.' Maeve shook her head. 'Nothing like that. They were saying things.'

This was too much for Gareth. 'I see,' he said evenly. 'So you have actually got me out of bed, after the worst night's sleep I've had in my entire life, dragged me down here, forced me practically to sever an artery in the process – to tell me what? That the entire cast has been killed in an earthquake? That Estonia has declared war on the United Kingdom and we are all to be interned? No. You have got me out of bed to tell me that last night when you got back to the hotel you spotted two members of the company sitting in the bar *saying things*.'

The other occupants of the restaurant looked up nervously and the waiter came flying over with fresh coffee.

Maeve wilted under Paynton's gaze, her cheeks flapping in and out like moths' wings. Jude was not so easily routed.

'It's what they were saying that we thought you might be interested in, Gareth,' she said accusingly. 'But, of course, if you feel we're wasting your time, perhaps we'd better forget all about it.'

'Well, come on, then. What were they saying?' he demanded, feeling on firmer ground now the emphasis had shifted from his private life.

'It was horrible,' whispered Maeve. 'Quite horrible.'

'In what way?'

The two women glanced at one other, heads dipping forward conspiratorially. Gareth followed suit. 'They were talking about ways,' murmured Jude through a slit in her lips, 'of getting rid of people.'

'Of what?' Gareth sat up sharply and nearly knocked the tray out of the waiter's hand.

'Getting rid of people,' she repeated, eyes darting in search of potential eavesdroppers.

'Who?' asked Gareth, mystified. 'You mean, like Jehovah's Witnesses?'

'No,' moaned Maeve and Jude in chorus. 'You know, Gareth, people – actors – the company. They were talking about how to get rid of everyone, so they could take over their roles.'

Gareth rubbed a weary hand over his brow. I'm too old for this, he thought. Either I must get eight hours' sleep a night or I must not employ psychotics on my stage management team. He squeezed his eyes tightly together then opened them, hoping to find this was a part of his nightmare. If it was, it was still going on. Jude and Maeve sat opposite him like a pair of premenstrual lurchers.

'I see,' he said, striving to keep his voice level. 'And how, precisely, were they planning to do this?'

'All sorts of ways,' said Maeve enthusiastically. 'They were going to flood the stage with melted candle wax so everyone slid into the orchestra pit.'

'Philip said he would rebandage Clive's legs so his circulation stopped,' added Jude, fighting to control her excitement.

'They were going to do awful things to poor Jasmine,' Maeve quavered.

'What sort of things?' demanded Gareth, who so recently had been planning a few of his own.

'Oh, you wouldn't want to even hear,' Jude insisted.

'I would. That is . . . Look, girls, you said yourselves you thought they might have had a bit too much to drink.'

'They were paralytic,' Jude corrected.

'Well, there you are. I'm sure they meant no harm by it. They're a couple of nice kids – probably not used to the alcohol over here. Let's face it, it's a bit stronger than your average pint. I don't suppose they'll remember a thing about it this morning. I really don't think it's grounds for having them taken into custody.' He laughed to show that this was a joke. Maeve and Jude watched him stony-faced.

'Am I to take it that you intend to do nothing about this?' asked Jude at last. Paynton gave a deprecating shrug.

'Be sensible, Jude. What can I do? A couple of my actors get drunk and fire off a few unfortunate remarks. Does that mean I sack them both? Have them clapped in irons for the rest of the tour? I haven't got the staff to guard them, even if I wanted to. Anyway, suppose someone gets ill, or Clive breaks what's left of him? Who's going to go on? The company needs its understudies.' More than it does a couple of old hens like you, he thought, gazing at their resentful faces.

Jude gave a deep sigh. 'Well, we've done our best. Nobody can blame us if anything happens.'

'I'm sure nobody will.'

Jude harrumphed. 'Come on, Maeve. We've got jobs to do even if other people aren't interested in doing theirs.' They rose indignantly and thudded away.

'Perhaps you should have told him what they were going to do to *him*,' came Maeve's spindly voice as they trotted towards the lift.

Gareth Paynton had been right about one thing: Alice could not have, under torture, revealed what she had been planning with Philip the night before when she woke up.

At first she thought she must have hit her head on something – an iron bar at least – then, gradually, as she felt her stomach rising up to meet her tonsils, it occurred to her that she was in the throes of the worst hangover of her life. 'Oooh,' she whimpered, stumbling towards the wash-basin. 'Oooooh!'

Further down the corridor Philip was not doing much better. He hung, grey-faced, by the open window breathing in great gulps of air and trying to swallow the wodge of codeine tablets now clinging like wet cement to the sides of his mouth.

Back in his room, Gareth ran himself a bath and thought. Although he had dismissed Maeve and Jude's testimony as the fiction of two frustrated old bags, he was not entirely happy with the idea that his understudies were planning to dispatch the entire company before the tour was over. Obviously it was just a bit of harmless fun, but from acorns mighty oaks might grow. He didn't actually believe that they would go so far as to hospitalise the complete cast but he had known in the past of actors getting other actors drunk just so they could step into their shoes, and Alice and Philip were plainly no strangers to alcohol. Also rumour had it that Alice had been seen consorting with known Mafiosi – although that was probably just another of Jude's fantasies. She had got much worse since coming off the Prozac.

Nevertheless he had better do something about it before things started to mushroom out of control. But what? He had enough on his plate without worrying about the two least important members of the company. An idea struck him. Mightn't it be their very insignificance that was getting them down? Of course. Why hadn't he thought of it before? He sent for Sam Biggins.

'Gawd, Ali, what you been on? Heroin?' asked Sam when she came to the door. Alice clamped her hands over her ears.

'Please, could you not shout?' she croaked. 'I've got a bit of a . . .'

'Only a bit? Well, you're going to like my news then. Gareth's called an understudy rehearsal. Just you, Phil and him. Eleven o'clock at the theatre.'

'Eleven o'clock?' wailed Alice. It was ten past ten already.

'That's it. Skates on. I've ordered a cab for a quarter to. See you downstairs.'

The understudies swayed miserably around in the cab. Sam had to shovel them out on to the pavement outside the theatre and steer them towards the rehearsal room where their director was waiting.

Christ, they look like death, crossed Paynton's mind as the two of them entered the room. He twitched his face into a smile. 'Now, please don't think I'm looking for perfection. It's just, what with Clive's little mishap, I felt it would be a wise precaution to make sure you're on top of the moves as well as the lines. We'll take it very slowly. In fact, we may not get through the whole play this morning. I've got a luncheon appointment with . . . erm . . . Madame Skikne, Sam informs me.' His face drooped more pathetically than theirs. 'But let's make a start and see how we get on.'

They began. It was hopeless. That it was always going to be hopeless was clear to all of them. Only the National Theatre of Brent could have recreated the full tragedy of *Romeo and Juliet* with two actors, both of whom felt a lot nearer death than any of the characters in the play.

'I think you should be over by the window there, Alice. You're looking out for the Nurse, remember. You're very wound up and agitated.'

'Oh yes.' She sloped towards the imaginary window and cast a cursory glance out for her tormentor. '"*The clock struck nine when I did send the nurse . . .*"'

Gareth looked up. She can't have dried already, he thought. But she had. '"*In half an hour she promised to return*".'

'Oh yes, thank you. "*In half an hour she promised to return*".'

There was a pause. 'I'm awfully sorry, Gareth. I seem to have lost it again.'

'"*Perchance she cannot meet him*".'

They ground on. Philip was no better. Gone were his assorted dialects and quirky characterisations. Husky and dehydrated, he staggered through the text till the director could bear it no more.

'I think that's probably enough for one day,' he burst out with more feeling than he had known himself capable of. 'Not bad. Not bad at all. Just brush up on some of those long speeches, will you, Alice? And, Phil, try not to turn your back in the fight scene. You'll get yourself killed.' His laughter rang hollow round the room.

Alice hung her head in despair. So much for her big chance. Jasmine must be in line for an Oscar by comparison. They watched him go. 'Jesus!' said Philip, rubbing his eyes. 'He must be praying no one goes sick again.'

Alice was nearly in tears. 'I can't believe I didn't even know my first speech.' Philip put his arm round her.

'Cheer up. It could have been worse.'

'How?'

Philip was silent for a moment. 'You're right. It couldn't have been worse.'

'Ooooh!' Alice leant her head against his shoulder. 'I feel so terrible. I wish I was dead.'

Philip stirred slightly. 'No you don't. Today was different. An aberration. Mitigating circumstances and all that. Come on. Live to fight another day.'

'What's the point if you're never going to win?'

Philip looked down at her. Although he smiled his eyes were dark with discontent. 'I keep hoping that's not true,' he said.

As Gareth Paynton stood at the door of the restaurant, *Vana Kungla*, he felt his life ebbing away. A python had somehow got loose and was intent on compressing his body into a flat-pack. Its grip relaxed slightly and he was able to gasp in a small supply of oxygen.

He turned and saw that the python was in fact a leopard, or rather Madame Lareshka Skikne, swathed in the skin of one endangered species and now hotly in pursuit of another – the middle-aged Englishman without a wife in tow. 'But, hullo, Mr Paynton,' she purred seductively. 'Now we may have a very good time.'

Later that afternoon it was reported that a deeply drunk Gareth Paynton had been seen throwing up in a fountain in the Raekoja Plats. He had only escaped arrest due to the prompt intervention of two local businessmen who had sworn that he was related to the Minister for Public Transport and had returned him to the hotel before verification of the claim could take place.

By the time Alice heard it the story had grown to full-scale fisticuffs with an armed militia man and the confiscation of the

Millennium Players' subsistence budget for the rest of the tour. This had come via Archie Frith, whose copy she now concluded must be headed for the *Sunday Sport*.

Sam caught up with her at the stage door. 'Feeling a bit better?' he enquired.

'Yes, thank you. Lots. I've been asleep all afternoon. What's this about Gareth beating up a general?'

Sam whistled and raised his eyes to heaven. 'Bloody actors. Don't know why you don't write your own plays. No, poor old Gareth's just got a touch of what you had last night, from what I can gather. Can't say I blame him. He was having lunch with the man-eater.'

'Jasmine?' asked Alice in some surprise.

Sam grinned. 'Not her. The other one. Madame Skitterbug. The one that sings.'

'Serves him right. Making us rehearse like that when we were so ill.' Her face contorted. 'Now I'll never get another part in anything he does.'

Sam patted her shoulder. ''Course you will. He's not going to remember any more about today than you do about last night. Speaking of which, do you still want to fly home?'

'Do I what?'

'See what I mean.' Sam shook his head and went off to check the balcony had been repaired.

Chapter Seventeen

'Alice, dear, I've got a message for you.' Bernice, sporting an exquisite pair of amber ear-rings with matching pendant, came bustling into the dressing-room. 'I should have told you yesterday but it quite slipped my mind what with poor Gareth and everything.'

Apparently Bernice had been in the foyer when their director had been delivered to the hotel the previous afternoon. She had wasted no time in taking over, escorting him to his room, sending Richmond to order lemon tea and generally making sure that the incident attracted as little public attention as possible.

A lifetime of dealing with her husband had taught her the best way to minimise potential scandal was to behave as if it were the most normal thing in the world for a well-known figure to be found collapsed in the gutter outside his lodgings. This effectively deflated any accusation of concealment and more often than not led to a paragraph citing Bernice's own involvement with charity and a smiling picture of her, Richmond hovering in the background like a curious passer-by.

'It was actually from the young man who kindly brought Gareth home after he was taken poorly in the market place. He said he was a friend of yours. A very handsome young man. Called Janni? Was that right?'

'Yes.' Alice stopped, her heart beginning its customary lurches. 'What did he say? Was it urgent?'

'No, no, no. It was something to do with hoping to see you after the performance this evening. I'm afraid I wasn't really concentrating. I was more worried about getting poor Gareth up to his room.'

Alice smiled, cursing 'poor Gareth' from the depths of her heart. 'But you thought he said tonight, after the performance?' she prompted.

'Yes, I'm almost sure that was it. Or it might have been last night. No, it can't have been, can it? Or you would have bumped into him.'

'I suppose so,' murmured Alice wretchedly. She had gone straight home after the show without going near front-of-house. Suppose he had been there, and she had missed him?

'No. Now I remember, it was tonight.' Bernice unclipped her ear-rings and placed them lovingly on top of her make-up tray. 'Because he told me he knew where I could get really cheap amber. That was after he'd admired these, you see, and I told him I thought they were a tremendous bargain, but when I said how much I'd paid he made a face, and that was when he told me he could show me somewhere cheaper. Yes, a very nice young man. Speaks beautiful English, too. I hope you're not going to go making Philip jealous.'

'Philip?' said Alice blankly, her thoughts still fixed on Janni. 'Why should he be jealous?'

Bernice smiled. 'I know, but men are funny creatures. Just be a bit careful, dear. You're a sensible girl so I don't need to say any more.'

They were interrupted by the arrival of Jasmine, late as always, her arms full of carrier bags. 'Ga took me shopping to make up for being such a slug yesterday. We found this marvellous indoor market and I've got loads of things. Look at this,' she flung a tasselled tablecloth round her shoulders and pranced excitedly round the room. 'Who am I? Go on. Guess.'

'Jude?' suggested Bernice tentatively, moving her make-up tray.

'Carmen,' Jasmine snorted indignantly. 'It's perfectly obvious.'

'Only to a bull, my sweet,' drawled Christine Pink, showering everyone with air freshener. She had found an excellent source of cannabis through a roadie friend of her current husband's, and had hardly been seen for the past two days. Marcus Lemmon, though initially reluctant, had eventually succumbed and was at that very moment trying to negotiate his doublet and hose, which had suddenly become mysteriously fluid.

Jasmine made a face and slumped herself down in front of her mirror. 'By the way, Alice, Ga said he'd never seen anything as awful as you and Philip in the understudy rehearsal the other day,' she remarked petulantly, slapping foundation all over her freckles.

Alice sat silent, humiliation engulfing her.

'You are a little cow, aren't you?' observed Christine, shocked from her inertia.

'That is a very unkind thing to say, even though you obviously don't mean it,' Bernice rebuked her.

Jasmine looked genuinely aggrieved. 'Why are you having a go at me? *I* didn't say it. I just thought Alice might like to know, that's all.'

'I bet you bloody did,' said Christine, aggression taking hold. 'The same way you'd like to be told what we all think of your acting?'

'Let's all calm down,' said Bernice in her best *Sister Gillian* voice. 'Remember, we've got a show to put on.'

'I bet,' continued Christine, ignoring Bernice's advice, 'Alice would make a better Juliet, blindfold, gagged and tied to a tree than you do, Jazzy baby.'

'Oh thanks,' said Jasmine sarcastically. 'Well, if you don't mind me saying, Smackhead, with a mother like you it's a wonder I'm not in therapy.'

'It's bloody well where you belong,' shrieked Christine, picking up the nearest thing which, fortunately, was a powder puff, and flinging it at Jasmine's head.

'Everyone . . . please . . .' begged Bernice, cramming her ear-rings into her handbag for safe-keeping.

Jeannie, who had been cowering in the corner with a box of

Pontefract Cakes, made a whimpering sound and fled in search of Ray.

She found Sam first and, quivering, dragged him towards the ladies' dressing-room.

'Oi, oi. What's all this, then?'

Jeannie had opened the door just as Christine was aiming the last of Jasmine's plums which had already travelled the length of the dressing-room twice. Sadly, though Sam saw her and ducked, Jeannie did not and was nearly floored by the impact of the soggy missile. She sat down very sharply on the edge of the fire extinguisher and let out a squeal that amazed them all with its resonance.

'There,' said Bernice without thinking, 'I knew there was a voice in there somewhere, Jeannie dear. All it needed was a prod.'

Jeannie, who was not terribly bright, was quite bright enough to suggest there were other forms of prodding which might have worked just as well, and that a rotten plum in your eye and an inert pressure pump up your rectum were not her preferred methods.

Sam was more alarmed by the fact that the fire extinguisher had failed to go off and made a mental note to check the whole of backstage at the earliest opportunity. Meanwhile he had to restore calm.

'Come on, girls. You've had the half. We've got a full house out there tonight, near as. And the telly.'

This had the desired effect. The women stopped squabbling and swung their attention to the company manager.

'Telly?' asked Christine, automatically tightening her stomach muscles.

'That's right. The local station. Something to do with Gareth's girlfriend.'

'His what?' demanded Jasmine, more surprised than angry.

'You know, Madame Acne – the singing one who keeps trying to get inside his trousers.'

'That shouldn't be too hard,' muttered Christine. 'We all know he's not choosy.'

'That's *enough,*' roared Sam, seizing a cup of water that Jasmine had been about to pour over Christine's head. 'If there's one more word out of any of you I'm going out there and saying the show's off. Got it? Then where will your telly stardom be? Now, get your frocks on and let's get this thing over with. Okay?'

The women, grumbling, resumed their preparations. Bernice caught Alice's eye in the mirror and winked. She fought off an urge to giggle. The other three all looked so pious as they dabbed silently at their faces, for all the world like novice nuns preparing to take their vows.

The show ran more smoothly than the night before, which was not saying a lot. Marshall had OD'd on his cold-cure potions and spent the entire evening with an inane grin on his face, which wasn't terribly suitable for someone responsible for sending two young people to their death.

Clive was lamer than before, having spent the day in bed resting his bruised limbs which had consequently set like rigor mortis. Gareth had seriously contemplated giving him the night off, but his experience of the understudy rehearsal made him unwilling to put Philip on in his place. Better a cripple who spoke with passion than an able-bodied zombie, was his reasoning.

Alice had never been sprightlier in her courtier's role. She danced, dimpled, 'ooohed' and 'aaahed' as though her life depended on it.

'You're in good form tonight, Alice,' Marcus Lemmon remarked after she had flirted outrageously with him during the ball scene. Now safely installed in his costume he was once more relishing the pleasures of an afternoon spent smoking dope. 'Why don't we go on somewhere for a drink after the show?' Obviously the exercise bike was paying off. And Alice was a pretty little thing. Reminded him of Christine the year they met.

Alice smiled enigmatically. 'I'll have to see, my lord,' she whispered, making wild promises with her eyes.

None of this was for the television crew which, true to

Sam's promise, had set up a couple of cameras either side of the auditorium. It was for Janni Viszla whom she now felt convinced was out there somewhere watching her. I'll show him who the real actress in this production is, she swore to herself, deliberately upstaging Jasmine in the gavotte. I'll show Gareth Paynton too. How dare he comment on her efforts to that tart? He'd said himself he wasn't expecting miracles. To be fair, he probably hadn't been expecting the unmitigated disaster Philip and she had chalked up for him, either, but what had fairness to do with acting?

The dressing-room fracas seemed to have been forgotten by the time the curtain came down, the actresses more concerned with rushing front-of-house before the television crew decamped.

Alice was the last to leave. She didn't really want to get caught up in the palaver of not being interviewed, not being photographed, not being required. On the other hand she did want to see Janni, and if she hung around too long he might give up on her and go.

There was a tap on the door.

'Come in.'

The door opened. It was Philip. 'I saw the light was still on. I thought it might be you.'

Alice smiled. 'I didn't want to get trampled in the rush.'

'Me neither. Listen, do you fancy giving the bun fight a miss? We could get a drink somewhere else. Probably be cheaper than the bar here anyway.'

Alice hesitated. Philip misread the signs. 'I promise – no vodka.'

She laughed. 'No, it's not that. It's just I'm supposed to meet Janni out front. He gave Bernice a message yesterday. I think I'd better go and find out what he wants.'

Philip's face stiffened. 'I can't think it'll be to your advantage,' he said coldly.

Alice blushed. 'I wish you wouldn't be so nasty about him all the time. He's been very kind to us, and to Gareth. Did you know it was him and Alexei who brought him back yesterday after he was sick in the fountain? He'd probably be languishing inside Fat Margaret or somewhere.'

'I hope he checked his pockets,' said Philip.

Alice stood up. 'I've had enough of this. Janni is a friend of mine. Probably the best friend I've got in this bloody country. You're entitled to your own opinions but perhaps you'd be good enough to keep them to yourself as far as I'm concerned in future.' She stalked past him into the corridor. 'Could you turn the light off, please, when you go?'

Philip snapped off the light, slammed the door and came after her. 'I didn't mean to upset you . . .' he began.

'Well you have.'

'Alice,' he put his hand on her arm. 'I just don't want to see you get hurt or anything, and I just know this bloke is after something, and I don't think it's what you think it is.'

She turned on him, crimson with mortification. 'What do you know about what I want?' she said, her voice tight with the effort to control herself. 'How could someone like you ever know?' She whipped her arm away from him and almost ran down the corridor and through the pass door to the bar.

'Here she is.' Bernice, glowing like a forest fire in her amber jewellery and gold cocktail dress, reached out and drew Alice into the circle. 'We were beginning to wonder what had happened to you. Janni you know, of course.' Alice made a small squeaky sound at the back of her throat as Janni took her hand and squeezed her fingers conspiratorially. 'And Richmond.' They all laughed. Bernice turned to the fourth member of the party, a young man, stocky, with eyebrows that met in the middle and a ragged moustache. 'And this is Igor, Janni's brother.'

'Brother?' exclaimed Alice, then checked herself. She held out her hand. 'I'm so pleased to meet you. Janni didn't tell me he had a brother. You're not twins, are you?' Everyone stared. 'Sorry. Bad joke. It's just I know a set of twins and they don't look at all alike.'

'I bet you mean Philip and his brother,' chortled Bernice. 'She's absolutely right. Chalk and cheese.'

'And your Philip is not here?' said Janni, glancing around.

'No, he . . . He's gone somewhere else,' said Alice hurriedly.

Janni shrugged. 'This is a pity. What a fine actor that young man is.'

'Philip?'

Janni looked at her. 'But of course. Why do you seem surprised?'

She shook her head. 'No, he is. Of course he is. I just wondered how you could tell. I mean, he didn't have much to do tonight.'

Janni smiled and Alice felt her nervous system go into overdrive. 'Ah, you are talking about the play. No, I am afraid we were too late to see it this evening. I was thinking of how he hides what he is thinking.' Before Alice could respond he carried on, 'Has Madame Bernice told you of our plan?'

'No,' said Alice.

'Well, of course I haven't. We've only just made it, silly boy,' gurgled Bernice. 'Janni has had the most marvellous idea. Tomorrow morning he is going to drive us into the country to look at some amber and other things a friend of his is hoping to sell. He's primarily an art dealer but Janni thinks he might have something to tempt our fancy. All very cheap,' she added hastily as Richmond began to rumble. 'And then we're all going for a picnic by a huge lake that Janni's been telling us about. You can even swim in it. Isn't it exciting?'

'Yes,' said Alice, at something of a loss.

'And, of course, you must come with us,' said Janni quietly, his eyes caressing her face till Alice thought she would fall through the floor.

'Thank you,' she murmured. 'I'm not sure I can afford to buy any jewellery.'

Bernice, Richmond and Janni all found this very funny, Richmond suggesting that she might like to change places with Bernice because he'd always longed for a thrifty wife. Only Igor remained sullenly unamused. Alice concluded he was probably a lot younger than he looked and going through a teenage crisis.

The bar was closing. Alice caught a quick glimpse of Jasmine looped round one of the cameramen and trailed by a decidedly peeved-looking Gareth as they headed off for whatever dive had been earmarked for the night's continuing revelries. They were followed by Hilly Bates earnestly trying to convert the female reporter, Marshall Vincent, still wearing his silly smile and, a long way behind, Clive Barry who had managed to borrow a walking stick from Props and went crashing across the room like the Grim Reaper in pursuit of his last bus.

'Hey-ho,' said Bernice, suppressing a yawn. 'Time for bed, I think. Come along, my precious.' She took Richmond's arm and began to steer him towards the door.

'How about a nightcap back at the hotel?' came her husband's ever-hopeful voice.

'I don't think so, dear. We've got a long day tomorrow.'

Alice picked up her jacket. Janni helped her into it. 'So, you will come with us tomorrow, Miss Alice?'

'Yes please. If you're sure you don't mind me not buying anything?'

Janni smiled. 'Perhaps if you are a very good girl I will buy something for you. But first Igor has something to say to you.'

'Has he?' asked Alice doubtfully. He'd been looking at her all evening as though he would like to run her through.

Janni gave Igor rather a sharp rap between the shoulder-blades and the young man leapt forward. 'Yes,' he said rapidly. 'When Janni will give you information to send to England you must come to the British Council building and ask for me, Igor Rikov, by name.'

'Rikov?' repeated Alice.

'That is correct.'

'But I thought you were Janni's brother?' She looked from one to the other. Igor had gone very red. Janni merely smiled.

'Igor is what you call my half-brother, I think? One mother, two fathers. That is why we laugh when you ask if we are twins.' He gave Igor another rap, though slightly less violent, and Igor crumpled his face into a grin.

'Oh. Right. Thank you. When do you think that will be?'

Janni looked thoughtful. 'I think perhaps very soon. There are one or two small problems. I think I can solve them, then I will come to you.' He gazed at her for a moment then abruptly turned to Igor and spoke rapidly in Estonian. Igor's face resumed its surly expression. Janni returned to Alice. 'Now we will drive you to your hotel.'

'If you're sure it's no trouble?'

'Of course it is not. Alexei sends his regards to you, by the way. He would have come tonight but he has one or two tasks to perform in connection with his business affairs.'

Alice nodded understandingly.

In the car she closed her eyes and tried to imagine Janni whisking her away to his secret hideout in the mountains. Not that there were any in Estonia, but the guidebook certainly knew how to build up its mole-hills. At the entrance to the hotel Janni helped her out. 'We will see you in the morning. At nine o'clock. This is not too early for you?'

'Oh no. I'm always up early,' Alice lied, wondering if she'd have time to try her face pack before they went.

'I wish you goodnight, then.'

'Goodnight, Janni.'

He looked down at her. 'That is the first time you have use my name.'

Alice blushed. 'I think it's a lovely name.'

Janni smiled. 'I think also Alice is lovely.' He bent down and kissed her cheek and was away into the car before she had caught her breath.

Inside in the foyer Craig Penforth was sitting like a condemned man waiting to see if his pre-booked phone call to Preston was going to be cancelled yet again.

Chapter Eighteen

Please don't let it rain. Alice stood at her window gazing out at the threatening sky. If it rains he's bound to cancel, she thought. Gone in a flash all her dreams of lying by the *limpid lapping lake* in a gauzy shirt and cutaway denim shorts. She'd have to slog round some cellar full of artefacts in the jersey she'd been wearing for two days and second-best pair of jeans. *And* Janni would take no notice of her because the trip to the friend's house was purely for Bernice's benefit so he would spend all his time with her.

She opened the window and leant out. Was there moisture in the breeze? She wiggled her nose. Hard to tell. Her alarm clock shrilled. Whatever the weather, if she wasn't ready at nine o'clock they'd be sure to go without her. Bernice was a stickler for punctuality and Alice suspected Janni was not the kind of man who liked to be kept waiting.

She had a shower and washed her hair, tried on her shorts, changed into her jeans, swopped the gauzy shirt for a check cotton, went back to the gauze, discarded it for a smudgy pink tee-shirt, changed back into the shorts and concealed the entire outfit under a cable knit Aran she had pinched from Jay in happier times.

Satisfied that she had covered most climatic contingencies outside the Pacific rim, she re-did her eye make-up, unplaited her hair, twisted it into a French roll, ran out of clips, brushed it loose and finally scooped it up into a pony tail.

There was a buzz on the hotel intercom. Alice rushed to

it. 'Please, there is two gentlemen waiting for you in the hotel lobby, Miss Ermingway.'

'Oh, thank you. I'll be right down. I'm on my way. Thank you.' Alice zoomed frantically around, grabbing her bag, her key, her camera, discarding it as being too touristy, then recovering it in case Janni thought she wasn't interested in the sights of his beautiful country.

Bernice and Richmond were already down, Bernice in a huge straw hat and floral silk sundress with matching parasol, Richmond dapper in an alpaca suit and panama. 'Ah, there you are, Alice, my pet. Goodness, what long legs you've got! I never noticed. Right up to your armpits. How lovely. Richmond, come and look at Alice's legs.'

Richmond made the most of the invitation, as did fifteen Finns who were waiting for their coach to the ferry. Alice blushed mightily.

'Actually I think I might go and change, if you don't mind just waiting two minutes for me?' she began. But it was too late.

Igor, looking crosser even than yesterday and nursing rather a large bump on his forehead, came bounding into the hotel. 'So now everyone is here?' he barked. 'We must depart before the tourist buses or it will be a very slow journey.'

They followed him out. The Mercedes was parked right in front of the entrance, much to the annoyance of the Finns' coach driver who had been forced to stop in the main street and was being hooted at by the entire population of Tallinn, it appeared.

Janni was sitting in the front passenger seat, a pair of designer sunglasses masking his eyes. He got out when he saw them coming and stood smiling in welcome while the coach driver bounced up and down furiously at a safe distance.

Janni held out his hand to Bernice, then Richmond. When he saw Alice his smile deepened. 'I see you do not believe we will have a sunny day like our friends?' He gestured to Bernice and Richmond.

'I do,' stammered Alice. 'I just wasn't sure. It looked a bit overcast. I can easily go and change if you wouldn't mind hanging on for a few minutes?'

'But why shall you change? You are quite perfect in your big fisherman's sweater. If you are too hot we will buy you a dress in the market and you may pretend you are a gypsy princess. Who knows? Maybe you will meet a prince.' He opened the door and ushered them into the wide back seat. Alice sat in the middle because apparently Igor, who was driving, couldn't see past Bernice and Richmond's hats.

They sped through the streets at a frightening pace. At least it would have been, had not the other traffic mysteriously chosen to pull into the side as the Mercedes shot past. Road Rage was clearly not something that had taken off in Estonia.

Once out of the city Igor relaxed his speed a little to allow them to take in the sights of a drive through the countryside. Alice had taken care to bring her book and was sycophantically regaling them all with snippets of information. '"*Sometimes the orchards are blessed with blossom late into the spring.*" Oh, how lovely! Imagine cherry blossom in June. Wouldn't that be a marvellous sight? Just like *The Cherry Orchard*.'

There was a snarling sound from Igor. Janni, who had removed his glasses in deference to the slate-grey cloud cover, looked back at Alice. 'I am afraid Igor is not so fond of the Russian writers,' he murmured confidentially.

'Not even Chekhov?' asked Alice in surprise. She had never seen anyone who looked so much like a character from one of his plays.

'Most especially Chekhov,' spat Igor, spraying the windscreen with saliva.

'I played Madame Ranayevska once,' said Bernice dreamily. She nudged Richmond who was dozing off. 'Do you remember, darling?'

He leapt to life. 'Yes. Is it? Ancient, you say? Well, of course, some of them came over with the Vikings.' This had the effect of quashing further discussion.

Surprisingly the sky did seem to be clearing. Little streaks of blue began to prise their way between the clouds and a hazy yellow glow to soften the gloom.

By the time they got to the village where Janni's friend housed his collection the sun was fairly scorching down on them. Janni had resumed his sunglasses, Igor, in Adidas tracksuit, was letting off a powerful stench, and Alice had removed her Aran jumper and now sat self-consciously between Bernice and Richmond who remained as cool as the Mountbattens on a progress through the Hill District.

They arrived just as the locals were coming out of church. For some reason Alice had assumed the Estonians would be Catholic but the ornate design of the building was more reminiscent of a mosque. 'Orthodox,' Bernice whispered as they slowed to let several elderly matrons cross the road. They were dressed poorly but with enormous style, their headscarves wound jauntily round their once handsome faces. Black was definitely the new navy blue as far as they were concerned, although the men, particularly the younger ones, had clearly fallen victim to M & S button down striped cotton leisure shirts in a variety of pastel shades. These they wore with braces and black trousers, and generally looked more like extras from a yoghurt commercial than stalwarts of a striving European economy.

Igor swung the car into a small courtyard off the main street. It was surrounded on three sides by rough stone houses from which a variety of children began to stream. They ranged in age from about fourteen to babes-in-arms, these being carried by the older ones. With one accord they advanced upon the car, shyly at first then with increasing excitement as they circled its gleaming chassis. Igor leapt out and shooed them back, but it was an impossible task for no sooner had he dispersed one group than another closed in from the rear. It reminded Alice of Grandmother's Footsteps.

Janni got out and opened the door for Bernice, before motioning to Igor to do the same for Richmond. Alice climbed out his side as she had become unaccountably twitchy about her legs. The emergence of the three of them did unnerve the children slightly. They shuffled back, whispering and giggling amongst themselves and pointing at Bernice's parasol as though it were a witch's broomstick.

There was a bellow from the house on the right and an enormous man with a bright red beard and braces to match came charging out of a side entrance, waving his arms in greeting. He hugged Janni and Igor, and chatting the whole time in Estonian, advanced upon the visitors.

Janni introduced them. 'Bernice, Richmond, Alice, this is my dear friend, Nicolai.' Nicolai beamed and crushed their knuckles between his hands. The children began to move in again. Alice wondered if they were all his. He looked more than capable of fathering a tribe. She revised her opinion in the next moment, however, for out of the same entrance came a small thin woman with a beaked nose, very grey hair and her arms clamped across her bosom as though she were trying to push it out through her shoulder-blades. This, it appeared, was Nicolai's wife. The trio dutifully held out their mangled hands but she merely screwed her face into a scowl and kicked disconcertingly at the gravel at her feet. Alice wondered if she was perhaps Igor's mother as there was a definite resemblance in the way their eyes narrowed when confronted with guests, but then she remembered that it was on the maternal side that the brothers were related and nothing would make her believe that this hag had brought forth Janni.

They were ushered inside the house, Igor still mounting guard over the car and beginning to get shirty with the more persistent of the children.

Inside the house it was hot and dark. Although it was June a fire blazed in the grate and several large saucepans were chuntering on a stove in the tiny kitchen which led off the main living area.

The walls were covered in mock beechwood wallpaper, giving the impression of being inside a box. Alice controlled her claustrophobia by concentrating on the fact that Janni was only six inches away from her and she would probably never have an excuse to get so near to him again.

Painted plates hung on wire frames on the wall over the fireplace. They were crude and amateurish and again Alice wondered if they were the work of some of the children milling around outside. She could not relinquish the thought that they were more to Nicolai than mere neighbours.

She felt a hand on her shoulder and looked up, alarmed, to see her host towering over her, his eyes alight. As far as she could tell he had not drawn breath from the moment they'd arrived, and seemed in no mood to do so now. A torrent of words poured down on her. She wondered if she were being subjected to immersion therapy and would leave the village speaking perfect Estonian.

Janni, plainly, was not a disciple of this theory because he angled his way round Bernice's hat and came and stood between them. 'Nicolai is pleased you like his paintings,' he said cheerfully. 'If you wish he will let you buy one for a very economical price.'

Alice gazed at him in dismay. 'But I told you I hadn't got any money. I couldn't possibly buy an original work of art, Janni.' She felt rather proud of this piece of diplomacy and watched to see its effect.

Janni said something to Nicolai who burst out laughing and charged into the kitchen to stir whatever was in the pots.

'If nobody minds,' gasped Richmond, who had gone very red and was fanning himself with his panama, 'I think I might just step outside for a moment. Little bit warm, if you know what I mean.'

'But of course, let me escort you.' Janni was at his elbow, Bernice fussing along behind him. Suddenly the room was empty but for Alice and Nicolai's wife. Alice smiled nervously and began a detailed study of the pictures on the adjacent walls. They were uniformly horrible, featuring either large-eyed children in rags with mongrels tearing bread from their hands, or gunmetal blobs of water on which solitary cranes pecked posily at bullrushes.

'You like this pictures?' Alice fairly leapt. It was Nicolai's wife. For reasons she could not justify she had not expected the woman to speak English.

'Erm, yes. They're very nice,' she responded, casting a quick glance through the window to see if the others were coming back.

'They are shit,' said the woman.

Alice opened her mouth once or twice, but could not think of a reply.

'If Nicolai sees you watching them he will try to sell them to you,' said the woman casually and, picking up the poker, prodded the fire.

'Oh. Thank you,' said Alice. 'I haven't actually got very much money.'

The woman looked at her quizzically. 'Then why have you come?'

Alice blushed. 'I was invited,' she said weakly. 'We're meant to be going for a picnic afterwards. It's Bernice and Richmond who are interested in art,' she added treacherously, seeing the woman still had the poker in her hand.

She nodded. 'I see. So they are rich?'

'Oh, I don't think so,' protested Alice. 'They just like nice things.' Their eyes met. Alice looked away embarrassed.

'You are in love with Janni?' asked the woman, as if she were talking about the weather.

Alice baulked. 'No, of course not. I hardly know him. As a matter of fact, I only met him because of my . . . fiancé. He's back in England. It's all a bit complicated. Jay's hoping to make a film.'

'Hah!' The response was so sharp that Alice jumped.

'Is there something wrong with that?'

The woman stared at her for a moment then stiffened her jaw in stoic contempt. 'So Janni will help your man with this film?'

'Well, not the film itself. But Jay was thinking he might be able to get some financial investment from over here. That's where Janni comes in, I think.' She fell silent, sensing that the woman found the idea as preposterous as she did. She only hoped she was not going to go 'Hah!' again.

She did not. Instead she went into the kitchen, returning with a thin earthenware mug. 'Here is some coffee for you.'

Alice thanked her. The coffee was black and sickly sweet but it did not occur to her to ask for milk. Hospitality was finite, it seemed, among the residents of Estonia.

'Has Janni worked in investment for a long time?' asked Alice when she could bear the sound of her own swallowing no longer.

'Janni?' The woman heaved a deep sigh. She leant over, opened a small wooden box and extracted a thin cigar which she tapped rapidly on her wrist before lighting it. Alice waited, thinking perhaps she had forgotten her enquiry.

'Janni,' said the woman suddenly, 'has worked in many things. He is a rich man. Powerful also. How he makes his money, I don't know. Your man is rich?'

'Goodness, no,' said Alice, caught off guard. 'He's always complaining he hasn't got two pins to rub together.' The woman frowned, though possibly because she couldn't see the point of rubbing pins.

'Well,' she said at last, 'I hope he knows what he is doing. Janni will want a lot of pay for helping your man. If not, he may not be so kind with you.' She swung her legs round and went outside to where Richmond, who was feeling much better, was now seated on the stone wall performing conjuring tricks, much to the delight of the children who squealed and shrieked delightedly every time he got it wrong.

'Your husband is well now?' the woman asked Bernice.

'Yes, thank you. He just got a bit overheated. Look at him. I don't know how I'm going to drag him away.'

There was a peal of joyful laughter as Richmond chose the wrong hand again and another child pocketed a coin. Bernice chuckled. 'It's costing him a fortune. We won't have any money left if he keeps it up much longer.'

The woman's face changed instantly from indifference to alarm and she charged over to where Nicolai and Janni stood talking. With much shrugging and finger-snapping she managed to persuade them that it was time to show the visitors around Nicolai's workshop.

Alice had watched this from the window. She felt strangely unsettled by the woman's words. Although she did not like her particularly she sensed that she was telling the truth. Janni, for all his effortless charm, was capable of great ruthlessness, as witness their first meeting at the hotel. But surely he wouldn't blame her if Jay's plans came to nothing? After all, he must know that business projects often fell through. It was no one's fault, least of all hers. She was merely the messenger.

Nicolai was ushering Bernice and Richmond towards a short flight of steps leading down to his workshop. Janni was talking to Igor who had refused to move away from the car. Suddenly he looked up and caught sight of Alice watching him from inside the house. He came bounding over.

'But, Alice, you must come and see Nicolai's beautiful art works. You do not have to buy anything. You may simply look, otherwise Nicolai will be insulted.' He smiled and Alice felt her doubts slipping away. There was absolutely no question of Janni ever harming her in any way. She just knew. Women did.

He escorted her across the courtyard and down the steps. The workshop was larger than she had expected and was laid out almost like a gallery, with glass-topped cases full of delicate amber necklaces and bracelets, over which Bernice cooed while Richmond marched quickly around, saying 'very nice, very nice' in a negative sort of way.

Alice liked the jewellery too. She noticed there were no price tickets attached to anything, but possibly you were supposed to bargain. It seemed to be pretty much *de rigueur* in foreign countries. Only the British stood rigid with embarrassment when asked to alter the price of something.

'Come and look at this, Richmond,' Bernice summoned him.

'What is it, precious?'

'It's a set – ear-rings, necklace and bracelet. Oh, do look.

Did you ever see anything so exquisite? Come and look, Alice. Isn't it pretty?'

It was indeed very attractive but, even to Alice's unpractised eye, it was clear that the amber was of a far higher quality than the other pieces Bernice had treated herself to in Tallinn market. 'It's lovely,' she murmured hesitantly.

'There. Alice loves it. She insists you buy it for me, my darling. It can be our anniversary present.'

Richmond looked anxious. 'I'm just wondering if there mightn't be something a bit smaller? I mean, three pieces, you see, Bobs, is bound to be a bit of a price, and I don't suppose Nicolai takes Visa.'

Janni translated this for Nicolai, convulsing him with laughter. He slapped Richmond on the back. Richmond wheezed and tried to look as though he thought it hilarious too.

Nicolai and Janni now began a very rapid discussion at the end of which Janni turned to Bernice with a deprecating smile. 'Because you are a friend Nicolai has said to me he can make you a special price.' Bernice's face lit up. 'But,' Janni raised his hand in caution, 'because it is his finest piece he must ask for two hundred *kroon*. I have said to him this is too much, but he tells me he must live. He has a family to feed.'

Alice did a rough head count as to how many of the children had red hair.

Bernice and Richmond were both staring at Janni as though they'd been struck by lightning. 'How much did you say?' asked Richmond stiltedly. Janni shrugged. 'Two hundred *kroon*. He will not take less.'

Bernice turned to her husband. 'But that's . . .'

'About ten pounds,' said Richmond in the same bewildered tone.

'It is about ten English pounds,' Janni agreed. 'But look around. There are other things, much cheaper. Not so pretty, I confess, but pleasant.' His voice was drowned by the sound of Bernice counting out the money.

They stayed half an hour. Richmond bought a carved birch walking stick which he swished around jubilantly while

Bernice toyed with pewter mugs and cuff-links for Richmond's approaching birthday. Even Alice treated herself to an amber pendant for five pounds. Janni offered to buy it for her, but she refused resolutely, citing Jay's jealousy in the hope of spurring some sort of reaction from him. Janni merely smiled and suggested they adjourn to the house where Amelia (at last she had a name) had prepared coffee and refreshments for them.

These consisted of some rather dry ratafias which did not look as though they were the fruit of Amelia's home-baking, or perhaps they were, which was even more depressing.

Conversation turned to the Millennium Players' tour, Amelia wanting to know why English actors were so bad at Shakespeare. This produced great huffing sounds from Richmond and the danger that he would have to go outside again to cool down.

Bernice tactfully said that perhaps Amelia had been unfortunate in the performances she had seen because Shakespeare was always being produced in Britain, and not necessarily by those best qualified. This seemed to satisfy her although, unspoken in the air, hung the fear that she was proposing to honour their own production with a visit. They were put out of their misery by her forthright admission that she thought *Romeo and Juliet* the poorest of the lot and would not go and see it for all the tea in Russia.

Igor, who had refused refreshment, now pressed his face against the steamed up window to indicate that they should be making tracks, whereupon Nicolai leapt to his feet and insisted on taking them on a tour of the village. Alice was happy to go. Her head ached from the coffee and heat and she was beginning to think that they would be there for the rest of the day and forced to picnic off stew and dumplings by a roaring fire, rather than peaches and pale cheeses beside a limpid lake.

Richmond led the way, swishing his new cane. Janni caught up with Alice. 'How do you like my friend Nicolai?' he asked.

'He's very nice. I can't imagine how he makes a living if he sells everything so cheaply,' she added somewhat guiltily, aware that she had leapt on her pendant.

Janni shrugged. 'He is okay. You can see he is not a starving man.' They both laughed. Alice found that her headache had completely disappeared.

'Are any of those children his?' she asked.

Janni shook his head. 'Sadly Amelia can have no children.'

Alice said no more, thinking that was hardly the answer to her question.

It was only when they reached the church and were about to circle back that they noticed Bernice was missing. They waited a few moments to see if she had stopped off to look in the shop windows, but when she failed to appear it was decided that Nicolai should take Richmond and Alice on past the school and Janni would retrace their steps.

When they got back Bernice and Janni were sitting on the wall talking to Amelia. They all looked up as the others approached. Bernice got to her feet. 'I'm so sorry, I didn't mean to worry you. It's just I had to use the bathroom and by the time I came down you were out of sight, so I asked Amelia if it would be all right for me to stay here and wait for you. We've had a lovely chat. I am so much enjoying my day.'

With renewed thanks they all piled back into the car. The children came out again to wave them off, plainly hoping for another deluge of loose coins from Richmond. As they drove away and he fell into his customary snooze, Bernice nudged Alice conspiratorially. 'I'm afraid I've been a little bit naughty,' she whispered. 'It's a secret, mind. You mustn't tell a soul.' Alice looked at her enquiringly. 'Janni knows. It's a surprise for Richmond's birthday. It was a little bit dear, but I know he'll forgive me when he sees it. And, after all, we hardly spent a thing on my amber, did we?'

After this preamble Alice half-expected to see a sacred white stallion being led up the road to meet them, but Bernice fumbled silently in her bag and produced a tiny package wrapped in rough brown paper. Carefully she unfolded the paper to expose an exquisite miniature icon, its colours glowing like the Book of Kells, the Virgin's head picked out in pure gold, her ivory skin merging with the cobalt blue of her gown. 'Isn't it the most beautiful thing you ever saw in your life?' breathed Bernice rapturously. Alice nodded, speechless. Her eyes moved to Janni who was watching them both with amusement.

'Whatever did it cost?' she breathed, in view of Nicolai's cash only policy.

Bernice gave a tiny smile. 'Too much. Four hundred and seventy pounds, but I don't regret it. Of course I didn't have that much on me, but Janni has been an absolute saint. When he saw how much I loved it he arranged to pay Nicolai for me till I get the chance to get to a bank. I signed an IOU and this sweet little man from the baker's shop agreed to witness it for me. He didn't have to, but he'd brought the bread round and didn't seem to mind at all.'

'But when did all this happen?' was all Alice could think of to say.

'While you were on your walk. Janni whispered to me that Amelia had something she thought I might like to see so I pretended to have lost you all. I know it was a bit of a fib, but it was for a good cause so I don't think it really matters, does it? Oh, look at that lovely church. Now that must definitely be from the Hanseatic period. Look at the way the windows arch. You don't get that with the Russian architecture. What does your guidebook say about it, dear?'

Alice just handed it over.

Chapter Nineteen

'Are you not pleased now you came with us, Miss Alice?' Janni was lying in the shade of a clump of birch trees. They had laid the picnic out on the grass just above the waters of the lake. Alice had never seen anything more picture-postcard perfect. It was straight out of Sam's brochure.

The sky was now blue with only the slightest traces of filmy white cloud brushed along by a soft southerly breeze. Strange dark ducks with teal-coloured tail feathers floated by in formation and only the sound of birdsong and the occasional rustle of reeds broke the tranquillity. That and the rhythmic snoring of Richmond as he lay with his hat over his face a few feet away from his empty glass.

The picnic had exceeded all their expectations. According to Janni, Igor was responsible for it, and their groans of pleasure as the immense cold meat platter appeared, garnished with pickles and varieties of cress, brought the first glimmer of genuine pleasure to his eyes that any of them had seen.

This was followed by bread, cheeses, smoked fish, an enormous cherry flan and 'for our friend Alice, almond slices'.

She felt a flicker of panic but it seemed they were for everyone this time, so she breathed again and returned to the business of handing round plates.

They drank Russian champagne and a rich fruity red wine from unlabelled bottles. Richmond had pronounced the spread worthy of *The Wind in the Willows* and, seeing the confusion on their hosts' faces, gone on to give details. 'The rat's the one responsible for it all,' he explained, managing by that one sentence to restore Igor's ill humour. 'He takes Moley and Badger for a picnic by the riverside. I don't think Toad's along on that one, is he, Bobs?' Bernice wasn't sure. She thought not.

'Excuse me.' Janni leant forward intently. 'People take vermin for picnics in England? This I had not heard.'

'There are no people in *The Wind in the Willows*,' Alice broke in. 'Only animals. It's a story about animals. Very famous. At least it is in England,' she finished shyly for fear of questioning Janni's literary knowledge.

'Ah, of course.' His face cleared. 'We know of the famous British love for animals. This book is like *Animal Farm*, no doubt?'

'A bit,' said Alice, glancing at the others. They accepted the comparison without comment. Janni poured more champagne and Bernice told him he was a naughty boy and she hoped he wasn't trying to get her tipsy. This he protested against, saying that no lady of her quality could ever become drunk on champagne, which pleased her mightily.

Richmond clearly applied the same principle to the red wine *vis-à-vis* himself which was why he had fallen asleep by the time Janni produced a fine slim bottle of colourless liqueur which, with finger on lips, he informed them was distilled by a silent order of monks in a monastery on the outskirts of Tartu.

One sip persuaded Alice that she, too, would probably be rendered silent if she drank much of that. Bernice, whose stomach was clearly lined with lead, sipped cheerfully away, regaling them all with past theatrical triumphs and anecdotes about herself and Richmond in careers that spanned the better part of forty years.

'When are you and Igor coming to see our play?' she asked suddenly, wiping away the last of her tears at the passing of Sir Michael Redgrave.

Igor started visibly at the mention of his name. He had been making noticeable inroads into the firewater and his normally mottled skin was taking on a purplish hue. Alice hoped fervently that they would have time for a walk before driving home.

Janni shrugged. 'Of course we will like to come any time. I have heard it is magnificent.'

'Who from?' asked Bernice and Alice in unison.

Janni smiled. 'Ah, so many people. My friend Raina from the television station, Mr Berrell naturally, Madame Skikne . . . Many, many people. Perhaps I shall come tomorrow night if my business affairs will allow me.'

'Don't come on a Monday,' said Alice instinctively.

'Why not?'

'Mondays are always awful, aren't they, Bernice? Come at the end of the week, if you're going to come at all.'

'Really, Alice, anyone would think you were trying to put them off,' said Bernice a little reprovingly. Alice blushed.

'That is because she will like me to see her playing Juliet perhaps?' said Janni lightly, fixing her with his heavenly eyes. The blush deepened.

Bernice sighed. 'Well, yes, that would be nice, certainly, but Jasmine's not likely to be off, is she? She's such a . . . robust sort of girl.'

Richmond stirred. His hat had fallen off his face. Unwillingly he raised one eyelid. 'Hanseatic, you say? Well, that would explain it,' he muttered before turning on his side and starting to snore again.

'Would you like to take a walk, ladies?' Janni suggested.

'Yes, please,' said Alice, leaping up. Bernice shook her head.

'I think I'll stay here if you don't mind. I don't really like to leave Richmond on his own.'

'Igor will stay.' It was clear he had no say in the matter.

'It's very sweet of you, but to tell the truth I think perhaps the wine has gone to my head a little. I think I'll just sit here in the shade, if you don't mind?'

'Not one bit,' said Janni. 'Alice and I will tell you everything we have done when we return.'

'That will be nice,' said Bernice contentedly. Alice wasn't so sure.

They set off. The trees, which actually formed part of quite a large forest, thinned out towards the water's edge, allowing the sun to filter through on to a mossy path. The ground was soft and spongey, slippery in places so that more than once Alice nearly lost her footing. Janni was always there to catch her arm, dropping it again as he strolled ahead of her, knocking the overhanging branches out of the way and swiping at the clouds of mosquitoes with a stick he had found in the undergrowth.

Strange fungal growths sprouted from the trunks of some of the trees. Grey and flat – quite unlike any toadstools Alice had come across. 'Janni, what are these mushroom things?' she asked. He glanced down at them, taking a vicious swipe at one with his stick. It plopped on to the ground with a noise like a rubber sucker. Alice stepped back quickly in distaste. There it lay, flat and grey, its corrugated frills fanning out like a discarded petticoat.

'That,' said Janni, 'is the most deadly thing in this forest. More than the bears, more than the snakes.' He poked it again, swivelling the stick around until he had skewered a small piece of the flesh on the end, then he raised it towards her. 'Just one touch of this on your lips and you are dead.' Suddenly he lunged towards her like a swordsman. Alice screamed and turned away, covering her face with her hands. The stick flew past her and landed in the lake. She felt Janni's hands on her trembling shoulders. 'There. It is only a joke. I have not meant to frighten you.'

Gingerly Alice uncovered her face. 'Suppose you had touched me? I could have been dead.' Janni laughed.

'Oh, but it is just a common mushroom. We have eaten them in the pâté today for our picnic.'

Alice stared at her feet. 'I think I'd like to go back now,' she said.

Janni frowned very slightly. 'I have told you, it is a joke. I will not make any more. I thought British people had a very good sense of humour. I am sorry I have upset you. It is unfortunate.' He gazed into her eyes.

Alice melted. 'I'm sorry. I overreacted. You just frightened me, that's all. You fence very well. Where did you learn?'

'In the army. I was a champion for three years till I left.'

'Perhaps you should have a part in our play. Poor old Clive can hardly move since he fell off the stage.'

'Must he fence?'

'Oh, yes. He's Mercutio. He's always spoiling for a fight. That's how he gets killed.'

'So,' said Janni teasingly. 'You will like me to be killed because I have frightened you?'

Alice was aghast. 'No, of course not. Not for the world. I mean . . . It's just in the play. It's not for real.'

'Not for real,' repeated Janni, smiling slightly. 'No, nothing is for real. It is all acting. Come, I must talk to you about your fiancé's film. We will walk to that boat, do you see it by the clearing? There we may swim and then I will row you back to your friends. How will that be?'

Alice no longer bothered to enquire if Janni should take someone else's boat.

'There has been one small problem,' he told her as they walked along. 'It is very small. Of no importance, but it has delayed matters a little. That is why we have not asked you to make contact with your fiancé. But now I think it is time. I would like you to fax to him a message.'

'Yes, certainly,' said Alice, eager to find out what was happening.

'I would like you to tell him that in order to make his company registration he must send a Banker's Draft for ninety thousand *kroon*, also the details I have asked for. It is not so much,' he added, seeing the shock on Alice's face. 'Perhaps five thousand sterling? This is nothing.'

'Who should he send it to?'

Janni considered. 'To Alexei I think will be best. Yes, this will be the best thing.'

'What else shall I tell him?' asked Alice, wondering how Jay would react to the request.

Janni shrugged. 'Whatever a young girl tells to the man she loves,' he said enigmatically. 'You must know that more than I will. Now, here is the boat. The water here is very clear. You would like to swim?' He peeled off his shirt. Alice felt slightly faint. 'Come on. I will race you.' He unzipped his designer jeans and stood before her, a god in burgundy boxer shorts.

'I can't,' she stammered. 'I haven't got a costume.'

'You can swim as you are.'

'Or a towel.'

'The sun is hot. Soon you will dry. If not I will wrap you in my shirt and that will dry you. Come, Alice, do not disappoint me.' He dived with the grace of a swallow under the boat and out the other side, laughing and golden and unputdownable. Alice closed her eyes and jumped. Bloody hell, passed through her mind as the water, newly thawed from the Finnish ice floes which fed the lake, turned her throbbing young blood to Slush Puppy. I cannot believe I have fallen for this.

Janni, having completed a bold two-hundred-yard sprint to a rock and back again, arrived glistening and panting by her side. 'Is it not wonderful?'

'Yeees,' shivered Alice. 'I'm a little bit chilly actually.' Janni laughed, executed two or three egotistical manoeuvres round the boat and finally hauled himself, beaming like a cover for *Healthy Life*, on to the shore. 'Give me your hand.'

She required no second bidding.

Janni rowed boldly towards the distant shore. It was possible, even from that distance, to pick out the sleek black lines of the Mercedes.

Alice, shaking like a victim of delirium tremens, sat wrapped in Janni's shirt which was providing about as much warmth as a paper bag. Her skin, etched like an Ordnance Survey map with goose pimples, refused to glow no matter how she rubbed. Once or twice she sneezed. Bugger Ursula Andress! was running through her mind, as she recognised Bernice's elegant outline waving frantically to them from the shore.

'Oh, goodness, you two, how romantic,' she squealed as they came nearer, then turned and pounced upon her sleeping husband. 'Richmond, darling, wake up. Look, Janni's taken Alice for a row. *And* they've been swimming. Isn't that fun?'

Janni helped a frozen Alice ashore. 'Perhaps you will like a ride in the boat, too?'

Bernice was clearly tempted, but Richmond was adamant. 'Last time we tried that sort of thing we both ended up in the water.'

'Did we? Oh yes, so we did. But it was such fun! It was when we were doing *Cavalcade*, wasn't it? And it was someone's twenty-first. I know we'd been to Spindles and we were all frightfully tipsy. Oh, do let's, darling. We did so enjoy it last time.'

'Darling Bobs, it was over forty years ago. Do you want me to go to my grave in this foreign field?'

Bernice was finally dissuaded by her husband's reminder that the hotel laundry service was not up to scratch and that she would be mightily disappointed if her floral sundress fell victim to its 'boil in the bag' policy.

Igor had packed up the picnic and was sitting rather pointedly in the driver's seat, his feet hanging out of the door. He didn't seem to have taken advantage of Alice's and Janni's absence to sober himself up at all. In fact his colour, if anything, was deeper than before.

'So, you will not come with me in my little boat?' said Janni, affecting a pout.

Bernice shook her head apologetically. 'Perhaps another time? When we're dressed for it?'

Janni's face broke into a smile. 'But of course. We shall have a swimming party. Even Igor will enjoy that, won't you, my little angry brother?' He reached over and pinched Igor's cheek quite savagely. Alice wouldn't have been surprised if the youth had kicked out at him but instead a sickly grin spread across Igor's blotchy face. 'Swimming is good,' he grunted before turning away to study the speedometer.

Janni produced towels from the boot of the car. She might

have known he would come prepared. The upholstery was too precious to allow for wet bodies. Igor again drove at breakneck speed, and at one point nearly hit a cow which had made its way on to the road from a nearby field. It was difficult to decide who got the worst fright, but Igor won by a nose, presumably because if he had dented Janni's car brotherly love would have received its cruellest test.

It was nearly nine o'clock when they drove back into Tallinn but there was no sign of dusk. 'Whatever time does it get dark?' Alice asked. Janni shrugged.

'Sometimes midnight, sometimes later, sometimes not at all. Not really dark like you are used to in England.'

'But it was dark yesterday when we came out of the theatre,' said Alice, confused.

'That is because it was raining. When it rains it is dark all the time.'

She sat back. 'Imagine being light all night. How beautiful.'

Janni gave her a long look then turned away. 'Me, I prefer the dark.'

Neither Janni nor Igor wanted to come in 'just for a nightcap, old lad', as Richmond put it. He was allowed one if they had guests and not if he and Bernice were on their own. Assuming rightly that Alice would not count in this context, he tried desperately to change their minds, but Janni was adamant.

'We have to start very early in the morning. Igor must drive me to Narva. It is nearly three hundred miles all round. We have some business there that I must attend to.'

They said goodnight. As Janni raised Alice's hand to his lips in the now customary style he whispered, 'Go to the British Council building by ten o'clock in the morning. Igor will meet you.' She nodded nervously and watched as the two men hurried down the steps and got into the car.

Bernice clapped a hand on her shoulder. 'Wasn't that a lovely day? I can't remember when I've enjoyed myself more.'

'Are you coming, Bobs? I can't find my Rennies.' Richmond, thwarted of his nightcap, was now feeling tired and fretful.

'Coming, darling. I'm just saying goodnight to Alice.' She lowered her voice conspiratorially. 'You won't forget our little secret, will you?'

'No,' Alice replied, trying to remember what it was.

'Only I'd hate Richmond to find out before his birthday. I always let him have a whisky for breakfast on the day so he never minds what I've spent on his presents. That reminds me, I must get to a bank first thing tomorrow. Dear Janni. What a gentleman. One of the old school. Not many of those about nowadays, sad to say.'

She pattered off after her husband. Alice wandered over to Reception to pick up her key. Sad to say, she reflected as she waited for the lift, Janni has just told you a lie.

Chapter Twenty

Alice was right in assuming that Janni had been less than truthful with Bernice. Igor was no more driving to Narva the next morning than he was pleased to see her.

The British Council delegation was housed in a splendid Gothic building dating from the sixteen hundreds. In true British style its occupants had made every effort to preserve it in its original form, whilst on either side similar constructions had been converted into cafés and arty souvenir shops by the locals, with scant regard for the heritage they sought to peddle.

Alice was shown into a little side room while Igor was located. No one seemed particularly sure which department he belonged to. The receptionist, a serious girl on a sandwich year from Cardiff University, thought he was probably in Translation, and when this brought forth no response, perhaps Press. This proved more hopeful, because someone on the magazine section had definitely heard of him, although he couldn't remember him actually filing any copy.

They finally tracked him down in the Public Relations department, which was the very last place Alice would have thought of, and his expression when he arrived confirmed her initial instinct.

'You have it?' he demanded when they were alone.

'Yes.' Alice handed him a folded piece of paper.

'You should not bend the paper. It makes difficulties.'

She apologised, thinking that Igor would make difficulties no matter what.

He scanned the fax, disapproval oozing from each premature wrinkle. 'But this is no good,' he said finally, handing it back to her.

Alice swallowed. 'Why not? I put Janni's message in.'

Igor snorted in derision. 'But it is not hidden. How will it pass? You have written here,' he flicked the paper contemptuously, '"Dear Jay, Thanks for your fax. Please will you send a specimen signature, the number of your bank account and a banker's draft for ninety thousand Estonian *kroon* made out to Alexei Morkov. It has rained a lot, but yesterday it was sunny and we went for a picnic which was nice. Love, Alice".'

Alice felt herself reddening. She didn't much like being lectured on how to write in her own language by a surly spotty foreigner. 'What's wrong with it?' she asked haughtily.

Igor raised his mono-eyebrow so high it blended with his hair. 'Is this how English girls make love?' he sneered. '"Dear Jay, it has rained a lot"? So it is true what they say about the British?'

'That depends what they say,' retorted Alice. 'We tend not to wear our hearts on our sleeves, if that's what you mean.'

Igor looked confused. This was clearly not an expression he had come across. 'Here in Estonia if a man will send a love letter it will be full of deep passion and beautiful words.'

'Perhaps you'd better write it then,' Alice suggested curtly. 'You're obviously far more experienced in these things than I am.'

'I think this is certainly true,' Igor conceded.

'Do you get many replies?'

He made a rattling sound in his throat. 'Here.' He flung the paper back at her. 'You may write on the other side. I will assist.'

Alice snatched up the paper, pulled out a pen and sat staring at him coldly, liking a pupil awaiting dictation.

Igor closed his eyes and threaded his fingers through his hair. Silently he paced about the room.

'"My Darling Beloved . . ."'

'WHAT?' said Alice. 'You can't start a fax like that. Anyone could read it.'

'This is WHY,' explained Igor, tried beyond belief. 'They will be so interested in all this love that they will not notice anything else. Believe me, I know about this.'

'I've never called Jay that in my life,' protested Alice. 'And to be honest, I don't really want to start now.' She hesitated, afraid of admitting the truth even to herself. 'We're not as close as we once were.'

Igor rattled again, and it suddenly occurred to Alice that he had asked for a room where they could be alone. She decided to put protest on hold till she was back in the living world. 'Go on, then. What do you want me to write?'

Igor began again. It was intriguing to see how such a taciturn young man could be transformed when committing his thoughts to paper. '"My Darling Beloved, How I aitch . . ."'

'How I what?' asked Alice, genuinely confused.

'"I aitch to feel your arms around me."'

'Ah.' She corrected her spelling.

'"I see your lips everywhere."'

'Oh, please . . .'

'"I would like to have more and more of them, maybe ninety thousand *kroons* of them. Very soon."'

'Ah,' said Alice again. 'I think I understand.'

'"Please send me immediately some news and an answer to my fervent prayer. Oh, my knightly suitor, I am yours forever, your adoring Anna."'

'Alice,' she corrected, thinking it might as well be 'Igor'.

He looked decidedly pleased by his efforts. 'So now you will understand how to do these things?'

'Oh certainly,' said Alice. 'Though I doubt I'd ever come up to your standards. You have such a way with words.'

'My uncle is a poet,' confided Igor with silent pride.

When Alice got back to the Hotel Mirus another crisis was brewing. Hilly Bates, who had spent all of Sunday performing an extended yogic meditation, sustained by bottled water and the occasional banana, had ricked his neck doing a headstand. There was no way he would be able to get into a ruff that night.

Philip had once more been called to the theatre, this time to rehearse the part of Tybalt, thankfully a less taxing role than that of Mercutio – for him, if not for Maeve and Jude, who had immediately forsaken their plans to go to a dating agency, and rushed after him in a cab with a view to measuring his head and inside leg anew.

When Gareth Paynton, who was taking Philip through the scenes and had an important meeting with Brian Berrell at half-past eleven, pointed out that it was unlikely that either Philip's head or leg had grown much since Friday, they set up a wailing that would not have disgraced a Shi'ite funeral.

Tybalt's hat was a completely different shape from Mercutio's, as was his wig, his codpiece and his garter. Gareth bore this as long as he could before reminding them that he had twenty-five minutes to make sure that Philip was word perfect, cruelly adding that if his performance today was anything like that at the understudy rehearsal, each one of those minutes was more precious than gold to a director who ever hoped to work again.

The two women retired huffily, debating whether to hang around or make a quick dash before the agency closed for lunch.

In the event they were disappointed because, not only had it closed, but when it re-opened they were greeted with the unhelpful news that its main purpose was to supply brides to ageing GIs and fat cats from British industry who regarded Eastern European women as the next best thing to their mothers' apple pies.

Jude fought hard and long for the right to register along with the lissom beauties whose photographs the manageress had patiently showed her. 'What's so special about her?' she demanded, jabbing a scarlet nail at a white-blonde creature in a leotard.

'This is Lilla,' said the woman longingly.

'So?' persisted Jude.

'She is a very . . . special sort of person.'

'Well, everyone's special. I'm special. Maeve's . . . Everyone's special in their own way.'

'Of course, of course,' the woman agreed. 'But the men who use our agency are looking for a certain kind of specialness, if you understand me.'

Jude scowled. 'Looking at these photographs it strikes me they're very limited. Not all men like blonde women, you know. Anyway, Maeve's blonde.'

The manageress cast a weary eye at Maeve's cobweb tresses. 'Yes, but even so . . .'

'And we can speak English,' said Maeve, edging a little nearer.

The woman closed her folder. 'I am sorry. I cannot help you. Here I can deal only with Estonian females. It is the law. I wish you luck in your search for happiness.'

Jude and Maeve trailed out into the street again. They were getting sick of having to do all the searching. Why couldn't happiness take a few steps in their direction?

'You know Hilly?' sighed Maeve as they waited to buy ice-creams from a man with a barrow outside the History Museum.

'What about him?' asked Jude grumpily. 'No syrup. I don't want syrup. I said, NO SYRUP.' The man beamed and gave her an extra spoonful.

'Nothing. Only I mean – well, he's not married, is he?'

Jude counted her change. 'He's a Christian. They quite often don't.'

'Don't what?'

'Get married, of course. And he's a vegan. And he's hurt his neck.'

'But do you think he's . . . you know . . .'

Jude stopped counting. 'You mean gay? How should I know? Why? Do you fancy him?'

Maeve blushed. She didn't really, but they'd been working on this show nearly a month now and she was getting a bit desperate. There had been none of this trouble when she'd been at the National. Always a trail of broken marriages to be mulled over in the intimacy of the Wardrobe Room, frequently leading to a night of prolonged drinking, weeping and a perfunctory bonk, with the actor leaving at first light to return to the arms of his wife, and Maeve lying, misty with love, between the covers of her Easy Plan sofa bed.

'I don't know,' she murmured. 'He's very nice, isn't he? Kind and everything?'

Jude grunted. Although she had no very strong feelings about Hilly Bates either way, she didn't want Maeve fixing herself up before she had. She supposed she could take him over herself, but the trouble with men like Hilly was, although they were reasonably easy to persuade into bed, they were generally a lot harder to get out. They wanted mothering, and they whined a lot and wanted to be cuddled, whereas Jude's idea of a decent relationship was to have her clothes ripped off her with the minimum of preliminaries and to be flung on to the bed and ravaged sweatily for ten or fifteen minutes, after which time she expected the lover to depart and not be seen again for at least a month. That was why she preferred foreigners. She had to admit that Estonia, despite its generous quota of highly desirable specimens, had so far proved a disappointment.

They returned to the theatre, Maeve still brooding on the possibilities of Hilly Bates and fantasising about life as a vicar's wife, Jude wondering if she hung about outside the dating agency for a couple of hours whether she might manage to waylay a customer or two by offering to act as translator.

Gareth had left his meeting with Brian Berrell a little irritated. What did the man take him for, for Christ's sake? He was a director not a male escort. Berrell had suggested, nay, practically insisted, that he accompany Madame Skikne to the opening night of the Estonian Song Festival on Thursday with a view to persuading her to mention *Romeo and Juliet* over the loudspeakers to the fifty thousand odd visitors who were expected to throng Kadriorg Park for the event.

Obviously it made sense, as the pompous little squirt kept

reminding him, but why couldn't Berrell perform this vital service for the Millennium Players himself? He was supposed to be the British Council representative. On him should fall the responsibility of publicising the play.

Berrell had been quite evasive when Gareth had hinted as much to him, citing other duties, advance press releases, annual auditing – a dozen excuses which all led back to one point, Gareth Paynton must be the man at Madame Skikne's side on Thursday night.

'That bloody woman,' he muttered to himself as he went into the green room to pin a notice about Hilly's accident on the board. Jude, who was steaming Richmond's wig over the kettle in an attempt to right the tilt, heard this and assumed, as she always did, that he was talking about her.

'I'm sorry if you find working with me difficult, Gareth,' she said without turning round. 'I can only say that no other director has ever had cause to question my professionalism.'

'I'm sorry?' said Paynton, trying to remember whether he had sworn at her during Philip's rehearsal. Thankfully that had gone better than he'd anticipated after the fiasco of Friday morning. It must be the girl who'd put him off. She really was a disaster. He couldn't imagine how Vanessa had ever thought her talented.

'If you've got anything to say, I think you should say it to me direct,' continued Jude. 'Not swear about me when you think I'm out of earshot.'

Paynton clapped his hand to his head. 'My dear girl – Jude – how could you think I was referring to you? No, good God, without you this production would be lost. Absolutely lost.'

'It's nice to know someone appreciates me,' said Jude, wondering what Gareth was like in bed. He was a bit stocky for her taste, but he had good teeth and a reasonable amount of body hair from what she could gauge through his polo shirt.

'Everyone does,' he continued unctuously. 'It's just we've all been under a lot of strain over the last few days, what with Clive's accident and now Hilly. I must say I really am surprised at him. He struck me as very much the reliable type.'

Jude humphed knowingly. 'They're always the ones. I've done what I can with the wig. Philip's head is a lot bigger.'

'That's probably because he's got the chance to do a bit of acting.' Gareth chuckled uncomfortably, aware that the joke was a poor one. Jude humphed again, thinking that her director talked too much for her purposes. She became aware that Gareth was watching her. Or less watching than boring through her with his eyes. She decided to tackle him. 'Why are you looking at me like that, Gareth?'

He jumped. 'Was I? I do apologise. I was thinking. Miles away. I say, Jude . . .'

'What?'

'You like music, don't you?'

'What sort of music?'

'Well,' he shrugged desperately, 'any. Modern, classical, folk?'

Jude considered the question, stroking absently at Richmond's wig. 'I like some,' she said cautiously. She was not going to spend her free time scouring Tallinn for some wretched tape for the man to send home as a souvenir.

'It's just I've been asked to represent the company on Thursday evening at the opening night of the song festival and I'm practically tone deaf, as I expect you know.' He gurgled boyishly. 'I'm terrified they'll play something and I won't recognise it or something. I just don't want to let everyone down. That's why it would be so much better if someone really musical could take my place. Oh, I know it's a lot to ask, but it's quite an occasion, I believe. Real VIP treatment. And of course you'd be introduced to all the stars – lucky woman! Jaz was saying she'd give her eye teeth to get to meet some of those rock 'n' roll chappies.'

This was good enough for Jude. She sucked in her cheeks dejectedly. 'I'd love to help you out, Gareth . . .'

'But?' His face crumpled pathetically.

'Who'd see to the wigs?'

'Oh, is *that* all?' he burst out, then corrected himself. 'What

I mean is, I'm sure something could be sorted out. Couldn't Maeve . . . ?'

'Maeve knows nothing about hair.'

He could not dispute the truth of this. 'Well, perhaps . . .'

'I suppose I could come in early and see to them in the afternoon.'

'Could you? Would you? Not if it would be an imposition, obviously,' he added craftily in case she wanted overtime.

'I think I could probably manage that. What time does this thing start?'

'Seven o'clock. You really would be doing me the most tremendous favour, Jude. I shan't forget it.'

Jude shrugged. 'If it's for the good of the company . . .'

Chapter Twenty-One

Alice was still upset with Philip over his remarks about Janni, the more so because at the back of her mind was the creeping suspicion that he might conceivably be right. Try as she might she could not erase the memory of Janni's eyes when he had lunged at her with the disgusting mushroom thing. It had been a look of pure sadistic delight. Differences in national humour were not enough to account for that. What is it about me, she wondered wretchedly, that I can only ever fall for the wrong kind of men?

She bought a postcard depicting a very thin man bending over a fish pond with a bull charging up behind him. Scrawling 'Good Luck' across it she went in search of Philip.

She found him sitting in the green room, muttering Tybalt's lines and scratching wretchedly at the glue attaching his wig. 'I bought you this.'

Philip took the card. 'Thanks.'

'How's Hilly?'

He shrugged. 'Don't know. I haven't seen him. Maeve says he's taken to his bed. Marshall was moaning because Sam made him hand over all his aspirins.'

'I thought Hilly relied on faith healers?'

'Only when he's well. He was happy enough to take them, according to Sam.'

Alice sat down. 'Are you nervous?'

'A bit. To tell the truth it's a bit of an anti-climax after the Mercutio thing.'

'Still. It's a part.'

Philip nodded. 'I know. I shouldn't complain. Poor you. The women are holding up much better than the blokes, aren't they?'

Alice nodded glumly.

'Still,' continued Philip, looking straight ahead, 'you've got other ways of occupying yourself, haven't you?'

Alice stiffened slightly. 'What other ways?'

'Bernice was telling me you all went on a picnic yesterday, with the marvellous Janni. He seems to have got her under his spell as well.'

'Perhaps it's because he's a very nice person,' Alice responded, stung yet again. 'It's odd that everyone he meets seems to like him except you.'

'What's odd about that?'

'It doesn't occur to you that maybe you're the one with the problem?'

Philip snorted contemptuously. 'Oh, I've got my share of problems, Alice. Don't you worry about that. Falling for some . . .'

'Some WHAT?' she demanded, determined to bring things to a head.

'Some . . . oh, what the hell does it matter anyway? It just isn't one of my problems.'

'No. And it isn't any of your business, either,' she snapped. 'What did you do yesterday that was so much better than going on a picnic?'

Philip was silent. 'I wrote a couple of postcards, walked around for a bit, had a meal.'

'What an exciting day.'

He grinned half-heartedly. 'I'd bought a couple of tickets for a trip to Pirita beaches, barbecue thrown in.'

'Why didn't you do that then?'

'Because I wanted someone to go with me.'

'And no one would?'

'I'm sure a lot of people would have.' The Tannoy crackled the quarter. Philip got up, stretched and ambled towards the door, still fiddling with his wig. 'It was you I wanted to take.'

Alice was still reeling from this when Jasmine came bouncing in in search of a cloth. 'Stupid cow Christine. Leaves the lid off her foundation and then yells at me just because I knocked the stupid stuff over. It was over my side anyway. If I had her skin I'd be using Polyfilla not stupid Christian Dior or whatever it is. Here, do me a favour, Ali. Take this cloth back and have a mop round, there's a sweetie. I'm gasping for a coffee.'

Christine Pink was still fuming when Alice entered the dressing-room. 'Twenty-seven pounds fifty. *And* that was in Duty Free. I've a damned good mind to make her pay for it. I'll get Gareth to deduct it from her wages. That'll teach her to throw her bloody clothes all over my make-up.' She picked up Jasmine's tasselled shawl and flung it the length of the room. It struck Jeannie on the back of the head, causing her to smudge her eyeliner. 'Sorry, Jeannie. Accident.'

Jeannie pursed her lips, found a tissue and began again.

'Jasmine asked me to bring this cloth,' said Alice, handing it to Christine.

'Oh, that's right. Not only does she cost me twenty-seven pounds fifty but I'm supposed to clear it up myself, am I?' Christine seized the cloth and began to scrub furiously at the bronze puddle spreading along the shelf.

'Have you had an enjoyable day, Alice, dear?' asked Bernice blithely. She herself had had an excellent one. She had found a newsagent who had promised to obtain copies of the *Daily Telegraph* for Richmond. They would be three days in arrears but as he only wanted them for the crossword and the cricket she didn't think that would matter.

She had also been interviewed by a very nice young man for an article for the local paper. Apparently *Sister Gillian* was into its second series over there and had gathered quite a following. She rather longed to see herself speaking fluent Estonian, as the reporter had assured her she did, having been dubbed by one of the country's foremost actresses. To this end she had enquired at Reception into the possibility of someone videoing it for her.

This had been greeted with a bewildered stare and a request that she convey the hotel's apologies to Mr Penforth yet again, as his call to England had been unavoidably postponed.

Alice said that she had had a very nice day.

'I can't help feeling sorry for poor young Igor,' Bernice chattered. 'Having to drive all the way to Narva and back in one day. It's an awfully long way, you know, and he looked positively exhausted when we got back last night.'

'Did Janni mention to you why they were going?' asked Alice, ashamed of her subterfuge.

Bernice frowned. 'I think he said something about a bank account. It was while we were having lunch. I wasn't listening properly. He's got business connections there, that I do know he told me. Such an enterprising young man. I'm sure he'll rise to enormous heights. Oh, here's Jasmine back.' She lowered her voice. 'I do hope those two aren't going to quarrel all night. I do so hate an atmosphere in the dressing-room, don't you?'

They had no time to quarrel. Jasmine, as always, had left herself far too little time to get ready and Christine had gone off to phone her supplier.

'Give me a hand, will you, Ali?' pleaded Jasmine as she struggled into her costume. 'Jude's going to go bats if I'm not in Wigs in ten secs. She always sticks the clips in me when she's in a mood, which is every bloody night as far as I can see.'

Alice reluctantly began the marathon task of lacing her into her costume just as the spectre of Jude Jenkins appeared at the door, demanding in glacial tones whether Jasmine was planning to wear her wig at all that night.

Jasmine unwisely said not if she could bloody help it, which presumably set her up for a dozen extra jabs.

At the door she clapped her hand to her head. 'I knew I had something to tell you, Ali. There was a fax for you from England. It was delivered to the hotel and they asked if I could give it to you. I forgot all about it, what with Smackhead moaning about her make-up.'

'Where is it?' asked Alice urgently. The last thing she wanted was Jasmine Ruddock getting hold of her coded messages.

'Not sure. In my coat, I think. Or my bag. You can have a look. Don't eat my toffees, though. They cost a fortune over here.'

Alice found the fax in Jasmine's coat. Whatever the rarity value of British toffees, she rather wished they had been stored in a different pocket. Plainly the hotel receptionist had not felt bound by Igor's strictures. The fax was as creased as a concertina.

Hell, Alice. What are you playing at, for God's sake? You'd better stall the bastards and NO MORE MONEY TALK. *Okay? Jay.*

Alice stared at the sheet of paper. 'I am a dead woman' floated through her mind like a refrain. What is Igor going to say when he sees this? Apart from all else, it was an insult to his poetic temperament.

She leant forward, wondering if it might be possible to insert a few flowery adjectives to soften the impact of what was unquestionably a negative response.

Reaching for Christine's eyebrow pencil, she tentatively added an '*o*' to '*Hell*'. Her imagination failed her. How did you convert '*Stall the bastards*' into a lyrical declaration of enduring love?

She read it again. If Jay's last message had been terse, this one was positively aggressive. It was a new side to his character and one she did not particularly welcome. Perhaps the most sensible thing would be for her to bow out of the negotiations altogether? Janni would understand – probably he would prefer to deal with Jay directly anyway, and then she could concentrate on winning his affection on her own account, not as a go-between for some dubious business deal.

She suddenly became conscious of a strange voice over the Tannoy. At least, it wasn't strange, it was familiar. It was Philip being Tybalt. With a yelp of excitement she bounded out of the dressing-room and rushed to watch from the wings.

He *is* good, she thought, standing silently by the great

ballroom flats that they now knew would not fit the theatre in Tartu. He is a good actor. And a great wave of pride swept through her.

'What was all that about then, Ali?' asked Jasmine as they were changing after the show.

'All what?'

'You know. Your fax thing. "Kill the buggers", or whatever?'

It was unfortunate that Maeve Prentice chose this moment to come and collect the women's tights and sweatpads for washing.

'You shouldn't have read that fax,' grumbled Alice when Maeve had gone, her face an interesting combination of ash and fuchsia.

'Why not? It wasn't sealed or anything. That's the point about faxes. Anyone can read them.'

'Well, anyway . . .'

'Oh, don't be such a wimp. Who are you planning to kill?'

'You, with any luck,' issued from Christine's corner. 'And you can pay me for my foundation before she does.'

'I'll name you in my will,' said Jasmine carelessly. 'Here, have this. It's just as good.' She tossed a tube of Number Seven Spot Eraser in Christine's direction. Christine took one look and chucked it in the bin.

'Oi!' said Jasmine, genuinely annoyed. 'There's no need to do that. It's good stuff.'

'Only if you've got spots,' hissed Christine.

'Well, give it to your husband, then,' retorted Jasmine. 'Tell him it gets better once you're twenty.'

Jeannie slipped silently away in search of Sam.

When he arrived Bernice was dressing a minor wound to Christine's temple from a mis-hit by Jasmine's souvenir programme and Alice was mopping up the remains of Jeannie's glass of Ribena which had made a permanent stain on her wimple.

'I don't know what I'm going to do with you girls,' he said stoically. 'Five of you and ten blokes, and they're not half the trouble you are.'

He was called away at this point to separate Archie Frith and Craig Penforth, after the former had suggested that perhaps the reason Craig's girlfriend never got through to him on the phone was because she was having it off with the window cleaner.

'Alice, have you ever thought of the reason you were put upon this earth?'

She was sitting in a corner of the bar, nursing a very expensive orange juice and trying to decide whether she should renew her request to Sam to get her home on the next available flight. Hilly Bates, his head curiously angled, placed his glass of tonic water next to her orange and sat down opposite, knees crossed and hands folded purposefully around them.

He had received that day a long letter from his personal guru, stating that he was one hundred and seventy pounds behind with his Glory Donation Direct Debit, and that he was the only graduate from the Spring '98 recruitment class to have failed to enrol the standard ten sinners to the 'Hi there, Heaven' campaign.

That all seventeen of the other candidates had received the same standard letter was as yet unknown to him, and Hilly had spent a wretched day nursing his neck and drawing up five bar gates in an effort to single out the ten most likely sinners to fill his quota. Alice Hemingway had come top.

Alice gazed at him unseeing. 'Sorry?' she murmured.

'I said, have you ever wondered why you were put upon this earth?'

She twiddled her glass. 'Once or twice.'

Hilly's eyes glowed. 'And I bet that's what you're asking yourself this very minute.'

Alice shifted in her seat. She was actually asking herself what she had done to deserve the chance of being converted by Hilly on top of all her other problems.

Hilly took her silence as a sign that she was indeed keen to be led to greener pastures. He fumbled in his trouser pocket and produced a wad of single-sentence tracts which he proceeded to read to her before slapping them down on the table like the banker in pontoon.

'Consider the lilies of the field, how they grow.'

'No man, when he hath lighted a candle, covereth it with a vessel.'

'Swear not by thy head, for thou canst not make one hair of it white or black.' Tell that to Jude, Alice reflected.

'Many are called but few are chosen.'

This was a little too near the mark as far as Alice's career was concerned. 'Just why are you showing me all these, Hilly?' she interrupted.

He raised his eyes in concern. 'I haven't quite finished yet,' he stammered. His training had emphasised the necessity of getting to the end of the twenty or so tracts, in order to confuse ('open' in Guruspeak) the mind of the recipient to the point where they were sufficiently fuddled to go on to the next stage of salvation.

In the true course of events this should involve a Revivalist meeting where they would be engulfed in the love and support of their fellow sinners. They would also have the opportunity of applying for stage three, a Halo Card, not so far accepted in many retail outlets, for which they would need to give details of their bank account and agree to pay a fixed monthly sum for the privilege of becoming one of Christ's official warriors.

Just what Jesus would have made of all this was not something the followers were encouraged to dwell on at any length, their time being fully occupied in the pursuit of more lost souls to swell the organisation's coffers.

Hilly had been relieved to find a Special Dispensation appended to his reminder stating that his being abroad allowed him to omit stage two and go straight for the Halo Card option.

Alice yawned. 'I'm sorry, Hilly. I'm a bit tired. Do you think we could talk about this some other time?'

Hilly's face fell. 'There's no time like the present,' he muttered disconsolately.

Alice smiled apologetically, struggled to her feet and was making for the door when Archie Frith leapt out on her. 'Don't go, Alice. I want your version of what went on in the ladies' dressing-room tonight. I gather it was mayhem?'

Having heard about his own little fracas, Alice thought this a bit rich. 'Ask Hilly,' she said quickly. 'I've just been boring him to death with it.' Archie's eyes lit up as he loped off in Hilly's direction.

Alice's last impression was of the two of them beaming at each other in mutual anticipation.

Chapter Twenty-Two

By Thursday Hilly's crusade was beginning to wind down. He had had high hopes of Alice and the failure to get her 'on board' had considerably dented his confidence.

Archie had been a complete waste of time and cost him half a day's subsistence in Vana Tallinn, a devil's brew that Archie, despite swearing that he was now dry, drank in half-pint tankards, extolling its medicinal qualities as he sank slowly beneath the table.

He had had more luck with Maeve Prentice who had even offered to go to church with him. The two of them had knelt quietly at the back of the enormous Lutheran church in the Old Town, but on regaining his seat Hilly had been disturbed to find Maeve's scrawny white hand installed beneath his buttock. After that he had suggested she seek her Maker through other channels.

Marshall Vincent had come very close to espousing veganism but was far too concerned with his mortality to trust it to someone already officially dead.

Dejected and disillusioned Hilly sent a cheque to the 'Hi there, Heaven' campaign and in the loneliness of his room, ceremoniously cut his Halo Card in two.

It was doubly surprising to him, therefore, to find someone actively seeking his help, rather than scurrying away whenever he came into sight.

The person in question was Bernice Wilde.

Hilly was sitting alone with his slab of soya bean loaf when she came hurrying towards him, her normally rosy face quite white beneath its make-up. 'Oh, Hilly, here you are. I've been looking for you everywhere.' She sank down opposite him then seemed to have forgotten why she was there.

He set aside his breakfast. 'Er . . . why did you want to see me, Bernice?' he enquired politely. Bernice looked up, gazed at him in confusion then clasped her hands together and took a deep breath. 'Do you know anything about churches?' she asked.

Hilly sat up. A lesser man might have felt insulted, considering the energy he had put into talking about them all week. 'What did you have in mind?' he asked cautiously. His faith, though discovered at a fringe meeting, was orthodox in the main. He was not *au fait* with the legion cults that had sprung up around Europe in recent years.

'Icons,' said Bernice.

'They're sacred paintings,' explained Hilly in relief. 'Usually quite small, I believe. You know, of the Blessed Virgin, the saints and so on.'

'Yes, I know what they are,' Bernice informed him heavily. 'I just wondered if you knew much about them?'

'I think they're usually quite valuable,' ventured Hilly, wishing she could have quizzed him on the New Testament instead.

Bernice shuddered. 'Yes, yes. I thought so. Thank you, Hilly, dear. You've been a great help.' She let out a sigh so deep and despairing that, had it not been Bernice, Hilly might have thought she was being sarcastic.

Bernice gathered up her bag which, oddly for her, didn't go with her outfit, and hurried away towards the lift. Alice was coming out of it. 'Morning, Bernice,' she said cheerfully. She had heard no more from Igor since Jay's fax had arrived and was beginning to think she might not have to show it to him at all. She could plead ignorance of having received a reply or, better still, blame the receptionist for handing it over to Jasmine Ruddock.

'Alice, I must speak to you.' Bernice was hovering halfway in and out of the lift. 'Have you got a moment, dear?'

'Of course I have,' said Alice. 'Gosh, Bernice, are you all right? You're not ill, are you?'

Bernice shook her head distractedly. 'No, not ill. It's worse than that.'

'Richmond? Is he all right?' asked Alice, her anxiety growing.

'He's fine. He's upstairs doing . . . doing . . .' She got no further. 'Oh, Alice, do you think we could go somewhere quiet, just for a moment? The most dreadful thing has happened.'

Alice guided her back into the lift. 'Come up to my room. We won't be disturbed. If there's anything I can do . . . ?'

Bernice shook her head pitifully. 'There's nothing anyone can do. It's all my own fault. I shouldn't have been so greedy. Richmond's always telling me I'll come a cropper one day with my bargain hunting.' Her head drooped. The lift stopped and Alice led her silently to her room.

'Sit down. Would you like me to order some tea or something?'

Bernice shook her head vehemently. 'No, nothing. No one must know.' She got up nervously and peered out of the window. 'You don't suppose anyone saw us, do you? Coming up here?'

Alice felt a chill of anxiety. Was this how nervous breakdowns began? But why Bernice of all people? She always seemed so clear-headed and practical, if a little extravagant in her tastes.

'I don't think so,' she said lamely. 'Why? Would it matter?' Bernice shot her a look that said very clearly it would. She sank down on the bed, hugging her handbag to her, and for a moment reminded Alice of a bag lady who lived round the corner from her in Ealing, sitting on the damp stone steps of a mighty office building, gripping her plastic carrier bag as though her life depended on it. That was how Bernice looked now.

She sat down beside her. 'Tell me all about it. If I can help, I will. You know that.'

Bernice nodded agitatedly, staring at some fixed point on the floor. 'Yes, of course I do, dear. It's just so difficult to know where to begin.' She heaved another enormous sigh, braced herself and said, 'You know that birthday present I got for Richmond the other day? From Janni's friend Nicolai?'

Alice nodded.

'Well, I thought at the time it was a tremendous bargain. I said so to you, didn't I?' She gazed wretchedly at Alice as though her agreement might provide a panacea.

Alice nodded. 'You did.'

'I know why now,' said Bernice softly. Silently she opened her bag, pulled out a folded newspaper and handed it to Alice. Alice looked. It was a copy of Monday's *Daily Telegraph*, a large square missing, presumably where Richmond had cut out the crossword. 'Thank God, he only reads the cricket reports,' murmured Bernice. 'Look at that.' She jabbed her finger towards a quarter-page article headed *Church Relics Black Market Honey Pot*. 'Read it,' urged Bernice.

Alice read:

> Experts from Christie's Fine Arts department have called in Scotland Yard after the discovery that a number of religious artefacts, including a unique series of Eastern European icons, painted in the fifteenth century and till recently housed in the mighty Alexander Nevsky Cathedral in the capital of Estonia, Tallinn, have been offered to them with a view to sale.
>
> A spokesperson for Christie's pointed out that so far they had only seen photographs of the icons and so had no way of knowing whether they were genuine. They had become alarmed when the person purporting to be the owner, one Count Nicolai Rikovski, failed to produce the necessary export documents.
>
> It is feared that in the bureaucratic turmoil resulting from Estonia's recent independence, black marketeers may have bribed officials to turn a blind eye to what amounts to the full-scale pillage of church possessions by those able to trade in hard currency.
>
> The whereabouts of these precious artefacts at present

> remains a mystery, but experts fear that the series may be broken up to make it easier to sell to unscrupulous private collectors.
>
> The Estonian judiciary is famously Draconian in its treatment of speculators found to have breached the export regulations, handing out sentences of up to fifteen years for a first offence. Interpol has been called in.

The paper flopped on to Alice's lap.

'What am I going to do?' moaned Bernice. 'Whatever am I going to do? They'll put me in prison, I know they will. I'll never survive it. I'm too old. And who's going to look after Richmond? He's seventy-two. He'll be . . . he'll be . . . dead before I come out.' Her shoulders began to shudder and deep throaty sobs came choking their way out. Alice put her arm round her.

'Nothing like that's going to happen, Bernice. We've just got to think about this logically.'

Bernice fumbled for a handkerchief. 'How?'

This was precisely what Alice did not know. 'Where is it now?' she asked, staring apprehensively at Bernice's poppy-coloured bag.

'It's in here. It's been here since Sunday. I didn't dare get it out in case Richmond saw. And now I daren't get it out in case anyone else sees. Oh, Alice, what shall I do? Do you think if I flung the whole bag in the river they'd be able to trace it back?'

'You can't do that, Bernice,' Alice exclaimed. 'It's a work of art. Fifteenth-century. You can't just destroy it. That would be criminal.'

'Yes, but it would be criminal without going to prison for fifteen years,' Bernice pointed out.

'There must be another way.'

The two women sat side by side on the bed in silence. At length Bernice blew her nose. 'I must say I think it was a little unfair of Amelia to trick me like that. I know they need money – well, obviously with all those children around . . .'

'They're not hers,' interrupted Alice.

Bernice looked surprised. 'Oh, aren't they? She told me they were. Not all of them, but the rest are her brother's. They go in for extended families over here.'

'Indeed they do,' muttered Alice, her thoughts focusing on Igor and Janni.

'And then, poor Janni – lending me the money like that. Thank goodness I paid him back. I wonder if he knows about it by now. He'll be horrified. I feel so guilty. I hope he doesn't think I knew it was stolen.'

'I'm sure not,' said Alice quickly.

'But I have to get rid of it. I really must. That paper's three days old. Interpol are probably over here searching by now.' The hysterical note was returning to Bernice's voice. Alice sought to calm her down.

'Would it be an idea to tell Sam?' she suggested. Bernice's eyes widened in alarm.

'Oh no, dear. Please don't tell anyone. That would be fatal. There are no secrets in the theatre, remember. It would be round the company like a shot and then . . .'

'Sam's very discreet. He's been very helpful to me over one or two little problems I've had.'

Bernice stood up. 'NO ONE! No one must know. Promise me, Alice, please. Otherwise I don't know what I shall do.'

Alice caved in. 'Of course I won't tell anyone without your permission, I promise.' Bernice looked relieved. 'But,' she added firmly, 'you must promise me not to do anything without telling me. No throwing your bag in the river or down the rubbish chute. Promise?'

Bernice sighed. 'You have my word. Oh goodness, is that the time? I promised Richmond we could go to the pasta place for lunch. He's getting awfully sick of raw fish, poor love, although I think it's probably very good for him.' She flustered around, picking up the bag then putting it down again till Alice, who could see her leaving it behind on the restaurant counter, unwillingly offered to look after it until they had decided on the next move.

Ten years fell from Bernice. 'Oh, *would* you, Alice, my

dear? I should be so eternally grateful. Just for a little while, while I take Richmond for lunch? I wouldn't dream of asking you to risk getting involved, but no one's going to know, are they? And I'll only be gone an hour or two. You could hide it under your bed. The maid's finished our corridor for today, though between you and me I don't think she ever gets beyond the waste paper basket.' She permitted herself a little trill of amusement.

Alice walked with her to the lift, Bernice still extolling her virtues and bemoaning yet again the fact that she would probably never set foot on the stage. Alice fought off a wicked conceit that if Bernice were sentenced to fifteen years in jail, she would at least get to play the Nurse.

Returning to her room the situation became less surreal. Richmond's copy of the *Telegraph* was three days old. That meant that whoever was investigating the matter was three days farther forward. If the matter were serious enough to merit a quarter-page in an English broadsheet, how much more important must it be here, in the very city from which the icons had disappeared?

Alice closed her eyes and tried to imagine what she would do, were she an Estonian detective. Look for likely buyers for a start. And who more likely than western tourists?

Since the Millennium Players appeared to be more or less the only people in town who fitted that description, that further narrowed things down. All avenues pointed to them. Suppose the police decided to search their rooms? That very afternoon? It would be she and not Bernice who would be spending the next fifteen years in jail. Panic engulfed her. She must find somewhere safe to hide the dreaded item.

Bernice had left the newspaper cutting behind so Alice read it again, wondering if it supplied any hints about smuggling artefacts out of an hotel, let alone a country.

It occurred to her that the best place to 'lose' the icon must be the place from which it had originally come, the cathedral. Surely there must be some pillar or pew behind which it could be safely dumped, though not in a poppy red handbag? Stealthily she reached for Bernice's bag and undid the clasp. Her nerve failed her. She crossed to the window and drew the blinds, though how many people could be watching her on the fifteenth floor was not entirely clear.

She took the phone off the hook, locked the door, and as an extra precaution put the plug in her washbasin and turned the tap on. She had seen that in *The Hunt for Red October*. Now, assured that she had done all she could to maintain secrecy, she steeled herself for the task and opened the bag again.

Like someone picking a Lucky Dip she plunged her hand into the soft cluttered interior and felt around. The crisp edge of paper caught her fingers. She lifted the package out and laid it quickly on the pillow.

It frightened her.

Here, just a few inches away, was something that had been created five hundred years before, and created for the purpose of worship and redemption. The Virgin Mary, symbol of purity, the mediator between sinners and God. Stolen! And in her room.

A very creepy feeling swept over her. This went beyond a bit of fare dodging and the Poll Tax. A lifelong agnostic, she was now faced with the distinct possibility that He was watching her every move. She heard a plopping sound, gradual at first then more rapid. It gushed in her ears. I'm passing out, she thought. From down below came a sinister thudding. The ghost of Hamlet's father flashed before her eyes. The knocking became louder and more furious, as did the gushing.

With a cry of panic Alice flew across the room and turned off the taps.

Chapter Twenty-Three

Philip Carter was the last person Alice had expected to find in the Alexander Nevsky cathedral.

She was on a recce to try and pinpoint the best place to deposit the icon, and was so far torn between tucking it under a hassock, safe for her, dangerous for it, or dropping it in the collecting plate and running like hell.

It was while she was investigating the protective qualities of the hassocks that a muffled figure slipped hurriedly into the church, slid into her pew and slumped to his knees, covering his eyes with his hand.

Alice immediately reverted to praying stance, casting a cautious eye along the pew at the newcomer. She hoped he was not planning a long session. It was then she realised it was Philip.

'Philip? What are you doing here?' she hissed indignantly.

His head shot up. 'Oh, hello,' he muttered guiltily. 'Just thought I'd drop in. We've only got a couple more days here, haven't we, and I've hardly seen a thing. What brings you here?'

Alice crossed her fingers. 'The same, I suppose. I mean, it's such a beautiful building. I felt I had to see it.'

'From flat on your stomach?'

'I thought you might get a better view of the altar from lower down.'

'Can you?'

'No.' She clambered up. 'Well, I mustn't keep you from your prayers. I didn't realise you were religious.'

Philip glanced over his shoulder. 'I'm not. I was afraid Hilly was following me. I told him I was RC to get him off my back.'

Alice nodded. 'He tried it with me on Monday. I think he's working his way through the whole company.'

Philip sighed. 'Can't be having much luck if he's reduced to saving my soul.'

'Mine, neither.' She shivered violently. Philip glanced at her. 'Are you all right?'

Alice nodded. 'Why shouldn't I be? Just a bit chilly, that's all.'

'Someone walking over your grave.'

'Stop it,' she burst out. Several worshippers swivelled round.

'Sorry,' said Philip mildly. 'It's just a saying.'

'I know. I know. I'm sorry.'

'Alice . . .'

'What?'

'Is there anything you want to talk about?'

Alice held her breath. It was now or never. And if she told him, here in the church, perhaps it would be all right. Perhaps breaking a promise didn't count if you were on holy ground. Perhaps if you told the truth, even if it was an unpalatable truth, perhaps someone somewhere would take pity on you and make it all right. Especially if you told the only person you really trusted. She let the breath slide slowly out again. 'No,' she said. 'Nothing. Thanks all the same.'

Philip smiled rather sadly. 'Well, if ever you change your mind . . .'

Alice got up. 'I think I'll just have a wander round before I go.'

'Can I come with you?'

'If you like.'

'You can tell me all about it.'

'How?' she asked quickly. 'I've only just arrived.'

'Oh yes,' said Philip. 'I forgot.'

They clopped respectfully around the magnificent building. People came and went, mostly women, their heads discreetly covered, lighting candles and crossing themselves before the altar. Apart from that they seemed noticeably unawed by their surroundings, stopping to greet each other with the same noisy enthusiasm they showed in the street. Alice wondered if it was only people who didn't believe who felt the need to tiptoe.

'Had enough?' whispered Philip as they came full circle. She nodded. They dropped some coins into the collecting box and made their way towards the exit. Sunshine was trickling through a slit in the heavy wooden door and, without realising it, they both automatically quickened their pace.

'How are you anyway?' asked Philip when they were back in the open.

'All right.' Alice shrugged. 'Anyone would think you hadn't seen me for months.'

'It feels like that. I seem to spend all my time being groped by Maeve and Jude. They've got it into their heads that Marshall's about to conk out so they hauled me in for another fitting. I'm beginning to feel like a freak. None of these costumes fit me.'

'They don't fit anyone else either,' Alice reminded him.

Philip laughed. 'I'll tell you something wonderful.'

'What's that?'

'Jude was telling me – well, not telling me, complaining to Maeve, the way she always does – that apparently Gareth's got her to go to the opening ceremony of some song festival tonight instead of him.'

'What on earth for?'

'Because it's as the guest of that big woman who was punching everyone in the stomach the other night. Gareth's terrified of her. That's why he's sending Jude. I'm surprised she agreed, considering what she did to her.'

Alice made a face. 'I shouldn't think Madame Whatsit will be all that pleased if she's expecting Gareth and Jude shows up. She'll probably floor her.'

Philip grinned. 'I wouldn't mind being around for that one.

If Marshall survives the second act I'm going to have a look. Want to come?'

'What about the last scene?'

'Who's going to miss a couple of courtiers?'

Alice thought about it. What had she got to lose? She'd rather be fired with Philip than employed on her own. 'You're on.' To her surprise his face lit up.

'Good,' he said quietly. 'I've missed you.' Then, before she could reply, 'Now, what's next on this great cultural tour of the ancient and historic city of Tallinn, flower of Estonia and centre of economic excellence?'

'Coffee,' said Alice.

'Aliiiiii!' Jasmine rose from behind what was left of the lobby's aspidistra, having lost patience with it when it knocked the froth off her cappuccino. 'Come over here. Friend of yours wants a word.'

Alice's heart jumped. She had only one friend outside the company as far as she was concerned, and that was Janni Viszla. She had been disappointed not to see him during the week, although at the same time vaguely relieved. Till the business of Bernice's icon was sorted out she would rather not have to think about Banker's Drafts and setting up companies.

Will I never learn? she asked herself, watching Igor's furious face rise up between the dying leaves of the plant. Jasmine Ruddock would rather be dragged over red hot coals than hand a man like Janni over to me and fade quietly into the background.

She had left Philip at the theatre, checking up on whether Marshall was still alive. Just as well, she reflected. If he thinks Janni's bad news, wait till he sees Igor.

'I have expected a responding,' snarled Igor, ignoring Jasmine completely.

'I'll leave you two to it, shall I?' she volunteered. 'I'm afraid I've eaten all the cakes but they'll bring you some more if you ask. Iggy's treat, isn't it, Igs?' She gave his cheek a perky little pat. Igor recoiled.

For probably the only time in her life Alice blessed Jasmine. Arsenic slices were one thing, a *bombe surprise* from Igor would probably mean just that.

He remained standing, glaring at her with renewed ferocity.

'How are you?' stammered Alice.

'Now is four days,' responded Igor, holding up four fingers.

'Yes. Is it? Four?' Alice replied, trying to look as though this was a new and interesting discovery.

'You have had an answer from your lover?'

Alice flinched slightly. 'Lover' in Igor's mouth sounded distinctly obscene.

'Erm . . .'

'The loud girl has told me.'

'Jasmine? Yes, she is a bit . . . She's playing Juliet, you know. Have you managed to see the play yet?'

'What has he arranged?'

Alice experienced the well-known cotton wool swab phenomenon. Her mouth became completely dry. 'Nothing. As yet.'

To her amazement Igor's face broke into a beam of boyish delight.

'Nothing, you say?'

'Not as yet. I'm expecting to hear from him any day.'

'You must come with me.'

Alice shrank back behind the aspidistra. 'I really don't think . . . I have to be at the theatre by six.'

'There is time.' Igor seized her arm and frogmarched her across the lobby. The receptionist developed a sudden interest in polishing the keys on the board behind her, the doorman in his shoes.

'I have one or two things to sort out . . .' Alice whimpered as he steered her across town towards the British Council residence. Memories of Nigerian diplomats in attaché cases flooded her mind.

'Now,' he said, when they were safely installed in the

same side room, away from prying eyes, 'we will send another fax.'

'Are you bonking that arse-hole?' demanded Jasmine with her customary tact, as Alice rushed to get ready.

Bernice tutted and applied more powder. Jeannie spirit-levelled her lips.

'Don't hold back, sweetie, say what you really mean,' murmured Christine Pink. 'What arse-hole?' She turned to Alice. 'Reveal or die.'

'I don't know,' protested Alice. 'Anyway I'm not.'

'The spotty one with one eyebrow,' continued Jasmine remorselessly. 'He's not very chirpy, is he? He kicked up blue murder when I ordered another cake.'

'They're not as well off as us over here, you know,' Bernice murmured contritely, trying to avoid Alice's eye. Her lunch with Richmond had extended well past the couple of hours she had asked her to guard the unmentionable, and when she had finally got back to the hotel there was no sign of the understudy, just vague rumours that she had been seen crossing Raekoja Plats with a very angry young man. She only hoped it presaged well for Estonian literature.

Anyway, here she was, back safe and sound. Bernice was almost ashamed now that she had confided her fears to Philip Carter, but he was such a nice young man and it was perfectly plain that he adored Alice. What was she supposed to do? He had discovered her just after she had left Alice's room, shedding a few unseemly tears in the corridor, and it had made perfect sense for her to step into his room for a few minutes to compose herself. She certainly couldn't have let Richmond see her in that state. And Philip had been so kind and understanding. She hadn't meant to pin the cause of her distress on Alice, it had just seemed simpler at the time. And she could never have confessed to him about the icon.

Of course she hadn't mentioned Janni Viszla or the picnic, but it was clear Philip knew what she was talking about. Alice was a good girl – just a little romantic. It was easy to see how her head might be turned. These foreign tours always threw up a few broken hearts. She had seen it so often before. She just didn't want Alice to make a huge mistake . . . She hoped Philip didn't think she was interfering?

He had been remarkably calm about the whole thing. And had promised not to say a word, just to keep an eye on Alice.

Bernice sought her out in the interval. 'Alice, I'm so sorry we were late back from lunch. I looked for you, but someone said you'd gone out again – in a bit of a hurry?'

Alice nodded. 'It was something Igor wanted my help with. Nothing to do with . . . you know.'

'Oh, thank goodness,' breathed Bernice. 'I was just so worried in case anyone had come asking questions or anything.' She sat down heavily. 'I wish I knew what I was going to do. I really do.'

Alice hesitated. 'I've had a sort of idea.'

'What? Oh, anything!' Bernice's eyes shone with hope. Alice wished it was a better idea.

'I went to the cathedral this afternoon. You know, the one it disappeared from in the first place? I think it should be possible to smuggle the icon back in and just leave it in one of the pews when no one's looking. It's the most enormous place. It shouldn't be hard to find somewhere deserted. Especially late at night or very early in the morning.'

'No, no not early,' insisted Bernice, requisitioning the plan immediately. 'That's when the cleaners go in. They'd be bound to spot anything unusual.'

'Last thing at night, then? After the show?'

Bernice pressed her hands together. 'That would be perfect. And then the cleaners would find it next day. Now you're sure you absolutely don't mind, Alice? I know it's a lot to ask.'

'Me?' exclaimed Alice in alarm.

Bernice looked crestfallen. 'Well, of course, I know I should do it myself . . . Yes, you're absolutely right. I had no right to ask you. You've done more than enough already. Yes, of course it must be me. I'll just have to wait till Richmond's asleep. He's usually off by about two these days. And then I can creep out.'

Alice was shocked. 'Bernice, of course you can't go creeping around the city at two o'clock in the morning on your own. Suppose you got mugged?'

Bernice shuddered. 'That's a risk I shall have to take.'

'You'll do no such thing. I'll take it back. I'll do it straight after the performance while there are still people about.'

'Oh, Alice, I don't know. Supposing you were stopped and searched?'

'Why on earth would I be?'

Bernice gave a trembly little laugh. 'I don't know. I suppose I'm exaggerating. It's just I seem to be seeing secret police on every street corner at the moment. Oh, if I get out of this I shall never buy another bargain in my life. Truly, I shan't.'

The interval ended and Bernice trooped off to the stage. When she came back she found Christine and Jeannie in a state of some confusion. Christine turned to her. 'I don't suppose you know where Alice is, do you? She seems to have disappeared. Bernice . . .'

'You're not enjoying this, are you?' Philip asked as they stood jammed together in what could best be described as a cattle pen. On stage a group of musicians from Lithuania were performing a complex arrangement of Amen, or so it seemed from the number of notes they had allowed themselves. It had been going on for ten minutes now, and showed no sign of reaching a conclusion.

They had been preceded by a long-haired girl in harem pants and a Save the Whale T-shirt who had sung with agonising wistfulness while accompanying herself on the banjo, an instrument Alice had detested from birth.

She was hot, thirsty and in danger of being crushed. The back row of the Capulet court was looking better by the minute. 'You don't think we'll be sacked, do you?' she asked. 'I mean, we could probably make the curtain call if we ran.'

Philip shook his head. 'No point. They won't sack us for missing that.' Alice sighed. He was right. The damage had been done. And she'd forgotten how nice it was being with him, even if only as a co-opted twin.

Of Jude and the other VIPs there was no sign. She imagined they must be ensconced in the vast marquee they had passed near the entrance, from which sounds of merriment quite unconnected with the tenor of the festival were emerging. 'Shall we see if we can get a drink?' she suggested.

'Yes, okay.' They struggled back towards the tent, only to be stopped by a hefty man in a striped suit who clearly regarded them as gatecrashers. Philip produced their official invitations, doled out at the soirée the previous week. The man scrutinised them briefly before indicating with a stingingly graphic mime that they were forged. Philip then produced two hundred *kroon* notes which the man found no problem with and they were soon inside the sweltering marquee, edging their way through the sweating guests towards where half a dozen barmen were dispensing champagne in generous measures.

'There she is,' squeaked Alice as Philip handed her a glass. It was indeed Jude, dressed as for a fandango, and glaring ominously into the face of Brian Berrell who had made the mistake of saying that it was a 'poor show' that Gareth Paynton had sent her in his lieu. 'She doesn't look all that pleased to be here.'

'Jude wouldn't look pleased to be in heaven,' Philip reasoned.

'Do you think we should say hello?'

'Are you mad? Besides, she'll know we're skiving. Come over here behind this palm.' They slid guiltily away, Philip sweeping up a bottle as they went. 'There. She won't find us here. Now we can get drunk in peace.' He sat down on an empty crate and took a swig out of the bottle.

'Move up,' said Alice, cringeing as Brian Berrell passed them.

'I can't. You'll have to sit on my knee.'

'Oh, but . . .'

'Oh, but what?' Philip looked up angrily. 'It's all right, Alice. I've got no plans to tamper with your legendary virtue, if that's what you're worried about. I leave all that to your fancy man.' He took another gulp from the bottle. 'If he ever gets round to it.'

Alice blushed crimson. 'Don't be ridiculous. I didn't mean . . . And don't talk about Janni like that.'

'Why the hell not?'

'Because . . . he's not my fancy man.'

'No?'

'No. He's not like that. He's . . .'

Philip was staring hard at her. 'He's what, Alice? A pimp? A thug? A thief?'

'Stop it! How can you say that? How can you? You don't know anything about him. He's . . .'

'He's what?'

'He's twice the man you are.' She stopped. Philip lowered the bottle and gave her a long cool look. 'I expect you're right,' he said quietly. 'But that's not saying a lot, is it?'

'Philip, I didn't mean . . .'

'No, I'm sure you didn't.' He stood up and pushed past her and away through the crowd till he was out of sight, still clasping his bottle of champagne.

Alice stood quite still. He made me do it, she told herself. He made me say that. I wish I was dead.

Wretchedly she turned to find her way out. She had had about as much as she could handle for one day, what with Bernice's icon and that awful Igor who had stood over her while she wrote another ridiculous message to Jay. She had been tempted to sign it 'Mills and Boon', but Igor had made his rumbling noise when she suggested it, so she had left it as it was, 'your adoring Alice'.

How Jay would react she could only guess. She personally doubted that her 'burning entreaty' would produce any better result than her original plea for ninety thousand lips.

Hard though it was to admit, she knew she would actually be glad to leave Tallinn behind and make for the relative obscurity of Tartu. A girl could only take so much excitement.

'Miss Alice, but what are you doing in this place?' Alice

looked up. Alexei Morkov, on the arm of Madame Skikne and trailed by a very angry Jude, was walking purposefully towards her. With a cry of panic, she turned and fled.

'Where were you in the second half?' Christine Pink came marching across the hotel lobby. 'Bernice got in a right state when you disappeared. Richmond's had to put her to bed. God knows what's got into her. Overtired, I suppose. She was blathering about the secret police and holy relics or something. She seems to think someone's following her. Do you know anything about it?'

Jasmine came bouncing up, hotly followed by Archie Frith. 'What have you done with Philip? Marshall's got tonsillitis. Maeve's been having kittens. She wants to measure Phil's tongue or something.'

'He's . . . I don't know where he is.'

She stood there guiltily, surrounded by enquiring eyes.

'Well, you both went missing at the same time,' probed Frith, relishing the prospect of his first scoop.

'Did we? I didn't know that,' blustered Alice. 'I didn't feel very well. I went for some fresh air. I didn't think anyone would mind if I missed the curtain call just for once.'

'Hmmm,' said Archie, disappointed.

'Well, next time let one of us know,' said Christine, bored with the subject. 'I've had Jeannie wittering on at me all night about bodies under patios, white slave traffic, the lot.'

'Sorry.'

The group dispersed. Or Alice thought it had. Jasmine came hurtling back as the others got into the lift. 'You're not bonking him, are you?'

'Who this time?' she snapped, wondering if Jasmine ever thought about anything else.

'Philip, of course.'

For some reason Alice knew she would like to grab Jasmine by the hair and swing her round her head. She turned away. 'No,' she said wearily. 'I'm not bonking Philip.'

'Just thought I'd check. Oh, there's Ga. We've got to go

and have drinks with Ape Woman. Apparently she threw a wobbly when Ga didn't turn up at the song thingy, and that little chap from the BC says if he doesn't make it up to her we'll end up paying our own fares home. I've got to go, too. God knows why. I hate singing. Yoo hoo, Ga. Hang on. I've just been chatting to Alice.'

Alice waited till they had gone then sank down exhausted in the deserted bar. She wished now she had stood her ground in the marquee. What good did it do, running away like that? Alexei had probably only wanted to pass the time of day, but there had been something about the way he had made a bee-line for her that had panicked her.

She put her head in her hands. I don't know what's going on, she thought. It's all too much for me. Why have I got myself involved with all these people? Why can't everyone just leave me alone? The one person I do want doesn't want me.

The finality of it came like a sick cold pain into her head, pushing everything else into the background. She knew suddenly and without any room for doubt that she had fallen in love with Philip Carter – Philip who took care of her, and made her laugh, and understood what it was like to be an understudy, and who, if she had only had the courage to tell him, would have helped her get rid of Bernice's icon and not let anyone put her in jail. Philip, whom from sheer unadulterated frustration she had insulted and wounded beyond redress. And she also knew that, of all the stupid ill-conceived attachments she had made in her life, this was the most totally hopeless.

She closed her eyes and leant her head against the back of the seat. When she opened them again Janni Viszla was sitting opposite.

'I am not disturbing you, I hope?' he said as she shrank back. Janni leant forward. 'It is just that Alexei has told me you ran away from him tonight. I wondered why?'

'I didn't run away,' Alice blurted out shakily. 'It's just it was so hot in that tent. I thought I was going to faint. I just wanted some fresh air. I'm sorry if he thought that . . .' Her voice died away.

Janni smiled. 'I am glad he was mistaken. I felt sure it must be so. You are recovered now, from your faintness?'

Alice swallowed. She felt a lot fainter now than in the marquee. 'Yes, thank you.'

'Today I have also spoken with Igor.'

'Oh. Yes?'

Janni's eyes glinted very slightly. 'You must not mind his ways. Sometimes he is a little . . . careless in his approach.'

'No, no. He couldn't have been nicer. Very helpful.'

'He tells me you have received no answer from your fiancé regarding our request?'

'I . . .'

Janni reached across and took her hand in his. Very gently he began to massage her fingers one by one. Alice watched, mesmerised. 'I think perhaps you have received a reply, and that you did not want to tell Igor all about it? Is that so?'

'I . . .'

Janni exerted a tiny bit of pressure on her middle finger. Alice yelped. 'I'm sorry. I have hurt you. This is because tension has been allowed to gather in the joints and I must disperse it.' He pressed again. Alice winced but said nothing. Janni dropped her hand abruptly. He stood up.

'So, I am happy to have seen you again. On Saturday you leave for Tartu. I hope we will have received a satisfactory response from your loved one by then. Everything has been accomplished for our part. That is what Alexei wished to inform you. Now it is up to you.' For once he did not kiss her hand, but turned on his heel and strode quickly from the room.

Alice sat on, sick with fear. Something awful is going to happen, raced through her mind. And I'm going to be in the middle of it. She glanced out of the window. Oh my God, she thought. Bernice was right. A small squat man in a yellow waistcoat and black trousers was standing on the street corner opposite. He was eating a hot dog and staring right up at the hotel in the direction of the Cannings' bedroom.

Alice leapt up and rushed for the lift and the safety of her own room. Once there, she locked the door and, without putting on the light, crept over to the window. The man had gone. She breathed a sigh of relief. Somewhere a clock chimed midnight. Like an icy blast her promise came back to her. It's too late now, she told herself. I can't possibly go up to the cathedral this late. I'll have to get up early and go at first light. If I'm careful surely the cleaners won't see me?

She got undressed, set her alarm for five o'clock and slumped on her bed. For nearly an hour she tossed from side to side. It was no good. There was no way she was going to fall asleep till the icon was safely restored, or at least out of her keeping.

She wondered about leaving it in the hotel lobby, but that was too close to home if the police decided to investigate. No, she must do what she had said she would do. She got out of bed again, pulled on her clothes and went over to the wardrobe. Fumbling inside her boot she removed the tiny parcel and gazed down at it, so innocuous-looking in her hand.

If it had frightened her by day, it terrified her by night. It's watching me, I know it is, she thought and shivered, automatically pressing the paper tighter around it. This was ridiculous. The Virgin was a symbol of forgiveness, expiation not vengeance. Alice was doing a good thing in returning it. She had nothing to fear. Angels would guard her every step. She buried the package deep inside her coat pocket and crept over to her door. For some reason she had achieved all this in darkness. Dark deeds deserved dark nights.

She tiptoed along the dimly lit corridor to the lift and pushed the button for the ground floor. What the doorman would think she could only guess. Presumably she was not the only young woman to have ventured out alone at night from a hotel the size of the Mirus? She heard the hiss of the lift on its way up.

A hand fell on her shoulder, another closed around her mouth.

Chapter Twenty-Four

Alice sat on the edge of Philip's bed, a glass of local brandy in her trembling hands. 'How could you do that to me? Look at me. I'm still shaking.' Her initial relief at finding it was Philip who had waylaid her was turning to panic as she contemplated how to get away.

He sat down opposite her. Unlike Alice he seemed to have completely forgotten their row. 'I suppose you'd rather I'd let you wander round Tallinn all night on your own?'

'I wasn't wandering. I was going somewhere.'

'Where?'

'Somewhere. Out. It's none of your business.'

'You were going to meet that shyster, weren't you?'

'Who?'

'You know who.'

'What if I was?' asked Alice defiantly, thinking attack might be her best form of defence. 'You've had it in for him from the minute you saw him, haven't you?' She took a swig of the brandy and was seized with a coughing fit.

'I should sip that. It's fairly strong.'

'It's not strong. It's paraffin.'

'Where were you going?'

'It's none of your business.'

'I know that. Except that if you end up dead in a ditch I'll probably have to understudy your mob as well.'

'Thanks for your concern.'

'I just want you to appreciate my situation.'

'The way you have mine? Do you know, Philip, I actually find it a bit rotten that you've said what you just said.' She took another cautious sip at the fire-water.

He patted her shoulder. 'Don't worry. I promise I won't be as good.'

Alice shifted away from him angrily. 'I meant about ending up dead in a ditch.'

Philip's face became serious. 'What the hell did you think you were doing, creeping out of the hotel in the middle of the night, if it's not to meet that . . . ?' he stopped.

Alice considered. The truth was occasionally a good idea. 'I was going to church.'

Philip snorted disbelievingly. 'Oh, I see. He Man's finally popped the question, has he? Or were you going to practise the marriage scene? God knows, you could do with some rehearsal.'

This was too much for Alice. 'It's very hard to act you're in love with someone when you know the very thought of you makes them want to puke.'

Philip looked genuinely confused. 'Why do you say that?'

Alice shook her head. 'Nothing. No reason. Leave me alone. I've got to go to the cathedral. I promised . . . I just want to see it by moonlight, that's all. I've got nothing out of this trip, you know. I might as well be touring Surrey.'

Philip hesitated then went to fetch his jacket. 'You're right. I'll come with you.'

'No,' moaned Alice. 'That's the point. I have to go by myself. I . . . I don't want to be influenced. I don't want to see it through your eyes. I want to let it wash over me. That's why I've left it till now.'

Philip dropped his jacket on the bed and shrugged. 'Okay, Garbo. You win. As usual. Just don't go wandering off the beaten track, promise?'

'I promise.' At the door she turned. 'Philip, I'm so sorry about tonight. In the marquee. I didn't mean . . . I never meant . . . You do understand, don't you?'

He shook his head. 'Not really.'

'And I would like you to come with me normally. It's just . . .'

'You don't have to explain.'

Alice smiled forlornly. 'I wish I could.'

Philip walked across and kissed her lightly on the forehead. 'Get away with you, then. I've got four new parts to learn by the morning.'

Alice crept along the streets, eyes fixed on the distant onion domes of the cathedral, please let it be all right, her guiding prayer. Please don't let me be caught. Please don't let me meet anyone. Please don't let anyone see me. Please let it be all right.

By the time she reached the cathedral her heart was pounding like a marathon runner's. Shakily she slipped inside the mighty door. Candles burned, lighting up the unfriendly faces of the carved saints as they peered down on her with undisguised suspicion. She halted. The collection plate – so close, it had seemed, in the daytime – now lay acres away from her across an open expanse of mosaic. She took a step towards it. The sound echoed in the silence. The candles flickered suddenly and somewhere a door slammed. She shrank back, trembling and wishing with all her heart that she had paid more attention to Hilly Bates.

At the far end near the altar someone was moving about. Transfixed, Alice flattened herself against the wall as the footsteps came nearer, hesitated, then moved away again. After a while they ceased and another sudden flickering of the candles signalled the opening and closing of a distant door.

Alice waited, her heart thudding louder than the church bells, till she was sure the person had gone. Swiftly and without a thought for the icon's safety, she pulled it ruthlessly from inside her coat and rammed it into a crevice in the ancient wall behind her, then tore out of the building and didn't stop running till she was inside the hotel lobby.

The doorman gazed at her stoically. He hoped she had had

more luck than the gypsy woman and her anaemic friend whose advances as they returned unescorted from their night-time sorties were becoming ever more desperate. He was not averse to the odd tumble with visiting female tourists but he suspected these two came as a double act, and he was not sure he could cope with them both after a long night's work.

Alice almost fell out of the lift when it reached her floor. Fumbling for her key, she heard the sound of Philip's latch. His door opened. 'Good trip?'

'Yes, yes, perfect,' she gabbled, almost euphoric to be back in one piece. 'I wish I'd thought of going before. The cathedral's magic by night.'

'Really?'

'Yes, yes. Quieter, you know, and more . . . quiet. Peaceful. It gives you a lovely peaceful feeling.'

'Really?' said Philip again, ignoring her breathlessness and burning cheeks.

'Yes.'

'Do you fancy another brandy?'

'Why not?' Nothing could hurt her now. She had got rid of the icon. Bernice was safe. She was safe. Tomorrow they would leave for a quiet provincial town and in two days' time she would wonder what she had ever been worried about.

Philip poured the brandy. He watched her as she gulped it down. 'That was brave.'

'What?'

'The way you drank that. It's pretty powerful stuff.'

'I expect I'm getting a taste for it. Can I have another?'

'Not unless you want to feel as bad as you did the last time.'

'Oh, that was different. Look at me. I'm not remotely drunk.'

Philip shrugged. 'If you say so.'

'Oi, oi,' said Sam Biggins. He was up early to supervise the dismantling of the set. The cause of his observation was Alice Hemingway, tousled, dishevelled and looking decidedly furtive, staggering out of Philip Carter's room at six o'clock in the morning.

'Oh, morning, Sam,' she mumbled huskily.

'Morning, Ali. You're looking perky.'

Alice tried to laugh but it was too painful.

'So you two got it together in the end?'

She frowned. 'What are you talking about?'

'You and Phil. He's a nice bloke. Don't worry, I won't breathe a word.'

Alice shook her head. 'You've got it wrong, Sam. There's nothing between us. I just sort of fell asleep on his bed. I've just woken up, that's all.'

Sam shrugged. 'If you say so, ducks.'

'I do,' said Alice firmly. 'We're friends, that's all. Like brother and sister. Nothing else.'

'Right,' he said. 'See you in Tartu.'

'I only wish I could think of a way to thank you, you dear girl.' Bernice, radiant in cornflower blue – she had sworn never to wear red again – squeezed Alice's hands in gratitude.

'No, it's all right. It was nothing.'

'If there's ever anything I can do . . . You must let me buy you a present. A little souvenir.'

'NO!' begged Alice in terror. Bernice gave a guilty little smile.

'No, well, perhaps that's not such a good idea, but I shall definitely think of something.'

The way Alice was feeling, a promise from Bernice to wear only beige would have suited her. The violence of her outfit was doing nothing for Alice's hangover. Philip, grinning like a Cheshire cat, came over to her. 'Better now?'

'No.'

'I did warn you.'

'I knew you'd say that.'

'I'm a predictable sort of guy.'

Alice buried her head in her arms. 'I wouldn't say that.'

* * *

The coach journey to Tartu was long and largely uneventful. Alice slept much of the way, occasionally coming to as Maeve screechily identified some site of historical interest. She had purchased her own copy of *Estonia etc.*, and was intent on sharing its impressions with the entire company.

'We're just coming into Kehra. Let me see . . . "*Kehra village is memorable for its magnificent church of St Lennart. Here it is believed a miracle happened in the fourteenth century when the young shepherd boy, Lennart, while out tending his father's flock, found a silver stone, perfectly round and unblemmed.*" I think that should be "unblemished".

'"*He decided to throw the stone as far as he could and wherever it should land he would build a shrine. Sadly, when he threw the stone, it hit a passing peasant woman and robbed her instantly of her life, so Lennart immediately forsook his father's sheep and devoted his life to helping the poor.*" What a lovely story!'

'Young thug,' growled Archie Frith who did not like children.

'Goodness, this is where we came on our picnic,' Bernice suddenly exclaimed. 'I'm sure it is. Yes, that's the baker's shop where . . . where . . . Oh goodness, isn't that the man? He's looking straight at us. Oh, heavens, I hope we're not going to stop.'

The coach trundled on. It didn't seem unreasonable that the villagers should leave their homes to gaze at the colourful bus passing along its narrow streets. They probably didn't get many tourists on that route. The only odd thing was that the little man whom Bernice had spotted scurrying out of his baker's shop, looked remarkably like the man Alice had seen from the window of the hotel bar on the night of the song festival. She decided not to mention this to Bernice.

The scenery was bland. Birch forests divided by marshy plains and a scattering of lakes, not particularly 'limpid' in Alice's opinion. More like mud baths. Villages and the occasional town owing more to Communist architecture than historical antecedents flashed by, television aerials dotting the skyline like twisted coat hangers, then more flat colourless scrub and, more lakes, more trees. It reminded her of East Anglia.

Sometimes a house rose up, solitary, at the edge of the road, or a garage sporting garish advertising posters that might have come from the nineteen fifties. Tea seemed to be a big thing with the Estonians. Tea and cigarettes.

Alice closed her eyes. Her headache had more or less gone, but the lack of sleep was catching up with her. Vaguely she heard the sound of Jasmine complaining about the size of Craig Penforth's feet as she thundered up the bus on her way to annoy somebody.

She must have drifted off again because when she awoke Maeve Prentice was towering over her and the coach had come to a halt. 'Are we there?' Alice asked drowsily. Maeve nodded. She was staring down at Alice, eyes burning with grim despair.

'I just wondered if you'd like any help with your luggage?'

Alice blinked. 'That's very kind of you, Maeve. Won't it go on the trolley with everyone else's?'

'Oh yes, that,' said Maeve dismissively. 'I meant your hand luggage. Jude and I could see you were tired.'

To Alice's double dismay Jude, looking equally solicitous, poked her head round Maeve's shoulder. 'It's all right,' she stated authoritatively. 'I've seen to it. They're sending a boy.'

Sure enough a youth of about sixteen appeared at the door of the rapidly emptying coach and was immediately ordered to carry Alice's shoulder bag and two slim paperbacks up to her room in the Hotel Parva.

Alice followed, mystified, flanked by Jude and Maeve. What on earth were they up to? She looked around but Philip and Bernice had gone ahead and everyone else was more concerned with sorting out their own cases. Maeve waited while the receptionist gave Alice her key, then insisted on escorting her up the stairs, there were no lifts in the Hotel Parva, to the fourth floor.

'If I were you I'd lie down for a bit,' she intoned solemnly. 'Shall I ask Sam if you can be moved lower down? I'm sure he could sort something out.'

'No, thank you,' said Alice firmly, remembering the saga of Marshall and his bath.

'Well, if there's anything you need . . .' Maeve hovered for so long that Alice began to wonder if she should tip her. Seeing that there was not, Maeve finally retreated. 'Jude and I are in number forty-eight,' she told her. 'Just the other side of Philip, if you need us.'

'Thank you,' said Alice. Maeve turned to go, then with a hiccupping sound swung back and rummaged in her skirt pocket. 'By the way,' she mumbled, 'you were asleep, but Jasmine asked me to pass you this on the coach.' She handed Alice a crumpled sheet of paper. Alice unfolded it.

I'm afraid it's curtains, honey. I'll have to find someone else. Tell the guys it's all up with you. Your time is running out. Wish it could have been me. Jay.

Well, at least I'm away from Tallinn, was all Alice could think as she read Jay's fax. He really is a rat. Igor would have my fingernails out for this, and loath though she was to believe it, she fancied that Janni would not have been too pleased with the message either.

I'm safe here, she told herself. They'll have to sort it out with Jay direct. I was only ever supposed to have tea with them. How come I'm suddenly responsible for everything that goes wrong?

It occurred to her then that she had always been held to account for Jay Bowden's misfortunes. His unhappiness in his marriage and out of it. His failure to achieve artistic renown. And now this dubious business transaction. Always she had been there to pick up the tab. But no more.

Where once she had sought to excuse his cruelties via unfavourable astral shenanigans, now she could see this was no more than a pathetic attempt to avoid the truth about their relationship, which was that she was Jay's hobby, not his career.

He was not coming to Estonia. He had never planned to come. And now, when things had got so hopelessly out of hand, he was backing off in no uncertain way and leaving her to sort out the wreckage.

A fortnight away from her horoscope had done a lot for Alice. It had allowed her to start growing up.

She sat down on her bed and looked out of the window. A wide glistening river flowed gently past in the distance, unscathed as yet by the effluents pouring into it further downstream. Willows wavered serenely on the banks, the sun picked its way through yellow clouds. It was all very peaceful. Alice lay back and let the view wash over her. This is all very nice, she thought.

Bernice searched again in her purse for a larger handkerchief, lamenting the loss of her poppy handbag which had contained a special section for tissues. 'But are you absolutely sure?' she whimpered, dabbing at her eyes and clutching Richmond's arm till he winced.

'There can be no doubt.'

This was not definitive proof, since Jude Jenkins never approached any issue but from a conviction of certainty, but it certainly sounded pretty final.

Bernice turned to Maeve. 'What exactly did it say?'

Maeve studied her notes. Though grieved beyond imagining, she had made it her duty to copy Jay's latest fax to Alice word for word. '"I'm afraid it's curtains, honey,"' she quavered. '"Your time is running out. I wish it could have been me."' Here her control failed her. 'Oh, no wonder she wanted to kill everyone. It's perfectly normal. "Anger, then grief, then hopelessness, ultimately leading to resignation." My cousin did an Open University course in psychology. I remember him telling me about it.'

Bernice gave Maeve a quick glance, trying to decide if she was absolutely mad or merely upset. 'There must be something we can do,' she stated resolutely. 'Alice is just a young girl. It's not even as though she looks ill.'

'She did this morning,' Jude shot at her. 'She looked dreadful. And she slept nearly all the way here. That was four hours.'

'When I offered to help with her luggage she just gazed at

me dazed – as though she could hardly believe what she was hearing,' Maeve remembered. 'Oh, it's so dreadful! I could almost feel her slipping away from me.' She too searched for a handkerchief.

Richmond, who had so far remained silent, cleared his throat. 'What precisely is wrong with the dear girl?' he asked.

There was a brief silence. Everyone looked at Maeve.

'Well, it didn't exactly say,' she admitted. 'She must have had tests before we left. It definitely said her time was running out. What else could that possibly mean? "Wish it could have been me." Oh, that poor man. He must love her so dreadfully.' Here she permitted herself a fleeting vision of the distraught young fiancé at the funeral. Perhaps she would be able to comfort him in some way, just as she had so many afflicted husbands in the past.

It was too much for Bernice whose shoulders began to shake so violently that Richmond roused himself and ordered Maeve and Jude from their bedroom where this conversation was taking place. 'And if I were you,' he told them sternly, 'I wouldn't go spreading this about. Not till we know what steps to take. I'll have a word with Sam Biggins. He'll decide what's best.'

Jude and Maeve pottered off, each avowing that the secret was safe enough with them. 'Enough' being the operative word, for Maeve could no more keep a confidence than fly to the moon. By the end of the dress rehearsal the following afternoon everyone bar Jasmine and Gareth, who were too busy exploring the delights of their hotel bedrooms, and Philip Carter whose heart Bernice avowed it would break, knew that Alice Hemingway was not long for this world.

There was a feeling of shock and distress amongst the whole cast. Little though Alice had impinged on their lives so far, she suddenly became the focus of remembered kindnesses. 'She went all the way to the hospital with me that night,' Clive brooded into his tankard of beer. 'She didn't have to. Then she got that guy to get me some food. She was like an angel that night. An angel of mercy.'

'She was very sympathetic about my operation,' Marshall Vincent added.

The others sighed in agreement. They had reacted in the only way they knew to the news: by getting drunk. Even Hilly Bates, having spent a full hour sifting through his tracts for uplifting messages, had finally binned the lot and joined the rest of them in the bar.

The locals regarded them cautiously. They liked a drink themselves and were by no means averse to the odd binge, but this was more like a state funeral than a night out with the lads.

'She had so much to look forward to,' muttered Craig Penforth, who wasn't even sure of her surname. 'I mean, now she'll never get married, have kids, a mortgage of her own. Nothing.' Further silence ensued.

'I suppose I could speak to my consultant,' suggested Marshall.

'Oh for God's sake, Marshall. She's not dying of piles,' snapped Christine, who had been feverishly trying to contact her supplier to see if he could get her some *ganja* for Alice.

'I'm sorry I spoke. I just thought my surgeon might know someone,' said Marshall, puffing up like a pouter pigeon.

'It's a very kind thought,' soothed Bernice, gazing distractedly into her ginger cordial. Even Richmond had been permitted a second whisky in this orgy of despair.

Marcus Lemmon, who had said very little so far, suddenly leapt out of his seat, charged across to where Archie Frith was sitting, and ripped his notebook out of his hands. 'Sod you, Frith!' he roared, flinging it into the fire.

The locals exchanged glances and moved their chairs a little closer.

'I only thought it might help,' pleaded Frith as the party turned its vengeful eyes on him. 'The *Sun* and the *Mirror* are always getting up appeals for operations and things. Why not for Alice, a brilliant young actress trapped in a foreign country, dying of . . . Well, what is it she's got? Does anyone know?'

There was a rumbling as everyone speculated on what they

thought Alice's ailment might be. Maeve was still in favour of a wasting disease. She had noticed that Alice's waistband was a lot easier to do up than when they had first arrived in Estonia, overlooking the fact that there was nowhere to buy Terry's Chocolate Oranges.

Jude said rather prudishly that she suspected liver damage. Since she was on her fourth rum and lime juice no one took this very seriously.

It was Richmond Canning, perhaps because he sensed that his own days on earth were numbered, who came up with the most sensible suggestion. 'I think we must accept that there is no way, ladies and gentlemen, that we can effect a cure for an illness of which we know nothing. We are actors, not physicians. Should we not therefore be looking for a way to help that reflects our abilities, rather than our weaknesses?'

'You mean, like put on a show for her?' suggested Bernice, eyes aglow at the prospect. 'We raised an awful lot for Children in Need when we did that Noël Coward evening. Something like that?'

'I could do my Alan Bennett sermon,' Marcus Lemmon volunteered. It had been a great success at the Rotary Club dinner.

'I could sing,' enthused Hilly Bates, who was nearly a counter tenor.

'I learnt some magic tricks when I were busking,' Craig admitted sheepishly.

Richmond raised his hands. 'Ladies and gentlemen, please. This is not *The Hardy Boys*. Listen to me. What is Alice?'

They gazed at him in confusion. 'A girl?' suggested Clive Barry. Richmond shook his head.

'A dying girl?' offered Archie Frith, hoping to regain some kudos. There was a ripple of disapproval.

'I'll tell you what, Archie Frith,' said Craig Penforth aggressively. 'You'd be bloody better off on the *Sun*.' Frith subsided.

'She's a very talented little actress,' said Bernice firmly. 'That I do know. Vanessa swears by her, and if Vanessa says she's good, she's good.'

'EXACTLY!' Richmond clapped his hands together. 'She is an actress. We are actors. What do we want to do? We want to act. So does she. That poor child has had to haul herself halfway across Europe in her tragic condition, and for what? For NOTHING. Does she get to play a part? Does she get to feel the audience reaching out to her? To hear their applause and know it's for her? No. Who throws flowers to Alice Hemingway? No one. Does the poor child have to wait until she's dead before anyone casts a rose in her direction?'

There was a stunned silence, broken only by the sound of muffled sobs. These were coming mainly from the local clientele who had not understood a word, but knew a good performance when they saw one. They wiped their eyes and signalled to the barmen to supply more drink to the visitors. Embraces were exchanged. Everyone clapped each other. Flyers for the opening night were handed out.

It was Sam Biggins who brought them back to earth. 'So what do you suggest, Rich? I mean she can't play four women at once. Do we ask for volunteers among the ladies? Does she do one a night? What?'

'Well, she may certainly have a go at the Nurse,' Bernice affirmed stoutly. 'Whenever she likes.'

'And Lady C,' Christine Pink declared. 'Though acting with that milk cow's more of a punishment than a pleasure.'

'She's welcome to try Lady Montague,' echoed Jeannie. 'It's not large, but it's very meaningful.' No one had detected this in Jeannie's interpretation but it would have been churlish to say so at such a time.

Richmond bowed his head. 'I think perhaps further thought should be given to this matter. You ladies have been very generous. I think maybe if she were to start off with Lady Montague?' Jeannie inclined her head graciously. 'Then perhaps Lady C?'

Maeve raised a hand. The costume alterations for such an enterprise had not been thought through. It would entail hours of stitching. Instinctively she knew she could not raise this point. 'I'm just wondering, in her state of health, whether playing several different parts might prove too much for Alice? After all, we don't want . . . we don't want to hasten . . .' She drooped her head. Everyone followed suit.

Finally Sam spoke. 'We all know what would make Alice Hemingway the happiest creature on God's earth. To play Juliet. I know it's a big part and all that and it'll probably take it out of her. But, believe me, it's what she wants – more than anything else in this world.' He lowered his head. 'Except, perhaps, her life. And that we can't give her. This we can.'

This time everyone cried.

Chapter Twenty-Five

What had seemed such an obvious solution in the fug of the hotel bar became a logistical nightmare for Sam Biggins in the cold light of day.

First he had to oversee the opening night of the production. It had been agreed that nothing more could be done until the show was safely up and running. Following their experiences with the skating rink of the Tallinn Concert Hall no one wanted to expose Alice, let alone themself, to the uncharted dangers of the Tartu University theatre.

The theatre turned out to be surprisingly well equipped, due mainly to a gift from a visiting philanthropist who had envisaged Tartu as a future Bayreuth and only lost interest when confronted with the quality of Estonian composition.

The audience was mainly young, students by far outnumbering the local population, although Alice did notice one middle-aged man in a yellow waistcoat sitting on a side seat in the stalls. Yellow was obviously a popular colour among middle-aged men in Estonia. She tried to concentrate on looking grief-stricken. Romeo was dead and Juliet on her way out.

The audience was appreciative, if more circumspect in their applause than in Tallinn, presumably because their grasp of English was stronger, although their restraint in the auditorium was amply redressed as they congregated in the students' bar to offer congratulations and solicit autographs. Noise and laughter abounded.

'Are you all right, Alice?' Alice was shocked to find Maeve hovering over her with a beaker of iced water. 'It isn't too hot for you in here, is it?'

'No,' said Alice. 'It's fine.'

'I brought you this.'

She was obliged to sip the freezing water when all she really wanted was a mug of the fiery punch that everyone else was being offered. 'I shouldn't stay too long, if I were you,' Maeve advised. 'Jude and I will walk you back to the hotel. Just say the word.'

'There's really no need,' Alice muttered, wondering if she was under house arrest and someone had forgotten to tell her.

'You need your rest.'

She was rescued by Sam. 'Those two bothering you?' he asked when he had shooed them away.

'Not really. They are being most peculiar, though. More than usual.'

'How?'

'Well . . .' She hesitated. 'They're being sort of nice to me. I don't quite know how to handle it.'

'Just tell them to get stuffed if they get on your nerves. They understand that. What are you drinking?'

'Iced water. Not from choice. Maeve gave it to me.'

'For Christ's sake! Here, try some of this stuff. It ain't half got a kick.' Sam grabbed a tankard off a passing tray and handed it to her. 'Where's young Phil? He should be looking after you.'

'No he shouldn't,' said Alice sharply.

Sam's face creased with anxiety. 'You two haven't had another tiff, have you?'

'No, but I wish you wouldn't act as though we were a couple or something. It was true, you know, what I told you the other morning. Nothing happened. I do hate it when people jump to conclusions.'

She expected Sam to retaliate, but instead his worried look deepened. 'Calm down, Ali love. I didn't mean to upset you. Shall I get you some more water?'

Alice turned away. 'I don't want water,' she said desolately.

Sam took her arm. 'Come and sit somewhere quiet for a minute, my love. You look bloomin' . . .'

'Blooming what?'

He shook his head. 'I dunno. Bloomin' fed up.' He looked at her so sorrowfully that for absolutely no reason Alice found that she was on the verge of tears. Sam saw this. Quickly he led her out of the bar to his makeshift office.

'Sit down a minute, ducks,' he said. Then, 'Would it help to talk about it?'

'No.' Alice searched for a handkerchief. Sam said nothing. 'I can't help it,' she snuffled, dabbing furiously at her eyes.

'What can't you help?'

Alice gave a kind of heaving sigh. 'Philip.'

Sam waited a minute then said, 'You in love with him?'

Alice blew her nose. 'It's awful. I've tried everything.'

'Like what?'

'Oh, I don't know. Ignoring him, being with him, Janni . . . It's just so pointless. I just think about him all the time and how good it would have been if only . . . Oh, what's the use? You can't interfere with nature, can you?'

Sam stared grimly at his stubby nails. 'Have you told him?'

Alice shook her head. 'How can I? What would be the point? It would only make two people unhappy instead of one.'

Sam flinched. 'Even so, ducks, I think he'd like to know. I really do.'

'Why, for pity's sake?' Alice asked helplessly. 'Do you think it would make any difference? What do you think would happen? He'd suddenly declare his undying love for me? Pigs might fly!'

'Alice, ducks, don't talk like that.'

'Why not? It's the truth and I've got to face it. I've fooled myself a few times too often in the past. But that's over. There is no future for me and Philip. End of story. Sam . . . are you all right?'

'Yeah. Fine. I need a drink. You?'

'No thanks. I don't think I could face it. I'll just go back to the hotel.'

He nodded. 'Anything you need, Ali, you've only got to say the word. You know that.' She tried to smile.

'Thanks, Sam. You must be sick to death of hearing about my problems. I'm a terrible whinger, aren't I?'

Sam seemed suddenly very interested in finding his own handkerchief. 'I've known worse,' he mumbled. 'See you, Ali. God bless.'

She sat for a moment, wondering why she had opened her big mouth. She also wondered why Sam had taken it so much to heart.

Coming out into the corridor she collided head first with Jasmine Ruddock, fresh from a quiet grope with Gareth in the scenery store.

'Watch out, clumsy,' Jasmine grumbled, still feeling tender.

'Sorry, Jasmine.' Alice hurried on.

'By the way,' Jasmine yelled after her, 'did Maeve give you that fax?'

Alice turned. 'Yes, she did, thanks.'

'He's not a barrel of laughs, is he, your guy? Mind you, not many of them are, it seems to me.' Jasmine was momentarily touched by her own perception, so much so that by the time she remembered the other thing she had to tell Alice, she was gone.

Jasmine shrugged and went on her way. Alice would find out soon enough.

A gravel path led from the students' bar back to the main road in one direction, and between an avenue of silver birch trees in the other. The Hotel Parva lay halfway between the two some ten minutes' walk away. Since the road was noisy and the trees were quiet, Alice chose the avenue.

Moonlight trickled through the branches as she walked along. Despite the tranquillity she felt uneasy. Something strange was going on amongst the members of the Millennium Company and she was horribly afraid it had something to do with her.

It was as she came to the end of the avenue and was about to cross the car park that she saw someone come out of the hotel. He stood for a moment, hands deep in the pockets of his overcoat, staring at the ground in concentration then, as if on cue, the man looked up and saw her. His face broke into a smile of recognition as he came striding across the tarmac to meet her.

'Alice! I have been waiting for you. How could you leave Tallinn without saying goodbye?' Janni Viszla grasped her hand and raised it to his lips with almost savage delight.

Alice waited for the ground to swallow her up. It did not oblige. 'Janni . . . I . . . I didn't expect . . . I . . .'

He nodded. 'No, I had thought this was possible. But if you remember there are still matters to be settled. Come.' He took hold of her arm and wheeled her forcefully round to face the way she had come. 'We will take a little walk by the river. Do you know this river? It is the Emajogi. It is most beautiful by moonlight, don't you agree? Come, we will walk.'

'I'm a bit cold, actually,' croaked Alice, her teeth chattering with commendable authenticity.

'But it is not cold. It is never cold in Tartu in the summer. In the winter, that is a different matter. Then it will freeze you till your eyes explode.'

This was not a description that appealed to Alice who said no more. When they came to the bank of the river Janni stopped. The two of them stood silently gazing across the broad expanse of spangled water, both seemingly lost in thought. Alice was thinking how she had dreamt of standing alone with Janni Viszla in just such a setting, and how she would give everything she owned not to be there now. What Janni was thinking remains a mystery.

He turned to her suddenly. 'I think maybe you have misunderstood me when I told you the other night that it was up to you to arrange for your lover's deposit to be paid?'

Alice gaped at him. 'But . . . I mean, I had nothing to do with it. I tried. I did try, Janni. Honestly I did. He takes no notice of me. He never has.' She gazed at him desperately, praying for some flicker of compassion to graze his soul. Her prayer went unanswered.

Janni's face became stern. 'You have not been truthful with me, Miss Alice Hemingway. Have you?'

'I? What? How do you mean?' she stammered, backing away from him. Janni remained where he was. His eyes seemed to glow in the dark. Oh my God, he's a werewolf, suddenly occurred to her.

'You told to me that you had had no reply from your Jay Bowden.' Alice stood silent, like a rabbit transfixed by a snake. 'But your friend has told me a different story.'

'What friend?' she gabbled, wondering if she still had any.

'The friend whose part you would like to have in the play. Jasmine. I came to the hotel yesterday to speak with you, but you had already left. Your friend was just leaving too, so I asked her if she knew where you were. She said no, because she had been looking for you too, to deliver a fax message that had just arrived. Igor was not at work that morning, so they had sent it round to the hotel and the girl had asked Jasmine to give it to you. I asked if I might look at it. She is a simple girl, I think. She showed it to me.' Janni spread his hands in a deprecating little shrug. 'And so I have come here to talk to you about it.'

Alice's shivering was now assuming blancmange status. 'But surely you can see that it's not my fault?' she pleaded. 'I know nothing about Jay's project, except that he promised to come over for a weekend to sort things out and be with me. I was never meant to be involved in the negotiations and money and things, honestly. I swear to you I wasn't. I swear.'

Janni gazed at her silently, absorbing what she had said, then suddenly his face broke into its glorious smile. 'Well, then, I must say to you that you have been very unlucky, Alice, in this business. You are an innocent rook in your fiancé's dangerous game.'

'Pawn,' she said automatically.

'I am sorry?'

'It's an innocent pawn. Rooks can move as many squares as they like provided it's in a straight line. Pawns can only move one.'

Janni's smile faded. 'Thank you,' he said. Alice's heart

dropped like a stone. He turned away and stared across the river. 'Do you remember our swim in the lake?' he asked quietly. Alice nodded. 'Would you like to swim in this river? The Emajogi?'

'No,' Alice whimpered, tears of fright welling up in her eyes.

Janni looked at her unemotionally. 'Oh, but surely you will enjoy that?'

'No, please. I really don't want to. I'm so cold.' Even Janni could not deny she was shivering. He placed his hands on her shoulders and squeezed them till she felt she was being held in a clamp. The shivering stopped. 'Now you are not so cold. Besides, the exercise will warm you up. Because you see, Alice, because your fiancé has not been honourable with us he must be punished. Naturally you will agree that this is right?'

'Yes – yes, I do,' she whimpered.

Janni smiled. 'Normally of course this matter will be between him and us. But, as you know, he is not here at this time.'

'I could get him to come over. I'm sure I could,' pleaded Alice. Janni continued to smile.

'Unfortunately we do not have the time to wait for that. Our contact is very keen to have his payment. So Alexei and myself have decided to send him a little warning, so that he will send very quickly what we have asked for.'

'Do you want me to fax him the warning?' asked Alice breathlessly.

Janni shook his head. 'That will not be necessary. You see, he will hear about it soon enough.' He put his hand in his pocket and whipped out a piece of cord. Alice opened her mouth to scream but no sound came out. She turned to run but Janni had hold of her before she had taken two steps. Swiftly he bound her hands with the cord and dragged her towards the river's edge.

'Now we must see how good you are at swimming, Alice, my lovely Alice,' he murmured caressingly in her ear, and for a moment held her against him so that she could have felt the beat of his heart if he had had one. Then just as suddenly he twirled her round till she was hanging over the grassy bank, inches from the black glittering water. Somewhere inside her head there was an explosion. A body flew through the air. It could even have been hers. Alice felt the ground rushing up to meet her.

She woke up in an ambulance. 'What happened?' she mumbled. 'Where am I?'

The figure sitting opposite raised a sickly face to hers. 'On the way to hospital.'

Memory came flooding back. 'Have I been shot?' she panicked.

'No.' His teeth were chattering. 'You fainted. They thought they'd better take a look at you.'

Alice raised herself on one elbow. 'Oh, Philip,' she said, an urge to laugh nearly choking her, 'why on earth are you going with me?'

'I'm not going with you.' Philip shivered aggrievedly. 'I'm in shock. I'm being taken in.'

'*You're* in shock?' Alice tried to sit up. The ambulance man cast a nervous glance at her. He didn't like being called out to Mafia 'accidents'.

Gradually she recalled the evening's events. She too started to shake. The elderly ambulance ricocheted in sympathy along the pot-holed lanes.

'What happened? Did you . . . ? Where's . . . ? I thought I heard a . . .'

Philip rested a quivering hand on her arm. 'Calm down. It's all right. He's under arrest. Apparently the police had been watching him for months. That's probably why he was so desperate to get hold of some money.'

'Why?'

'Well, either to buy them off or pay for protection, I suppose. We'll find out soon enough.'

'But you still haven't said what happened. Oh, Philip.' Alice buried her head in the blanket. 'It was terrible . . . awful. He was so horrible. He dragged me right to the edge of the river with him and then he said he was going to give Jay a warning, and I'd deceived him. It's all Jasmine Ruddock's fault. She showed him Jay's fax and so Janni came after me and blamed me. He said he was going to punish Jay and I said I thought he should – only so that he'd let me go. I would have warned Jay, honestly I would, but I was so frightened, and he was speaking all quietly and it was horrible.

'Then when he said he was going to punish Jay and I said, yes, I thought he should, he suddenly said would I like to go for a swim in the river? And I said, no, I was cold, and he said I'd soon warm up. And then he pulled out a piece of string and I tried to run away and he caught up with me and tied my hands and . . . oh, it was awful! He was going to push me in the river with my hands tied and I would have drowned. Oh, what a terrible way to die! Drowning. That's the worst thing on earth, apart from your parachute not opening . . .'

The ambulance man, who spoke no English, indicated that an injection might calm the lady down. Philip shook his head, mainly because he knew he would pass out if the man produced a syringe. Instead, he gathered the quivering bundle that was Alice into his arms and rocked it gently to and fro in rhythm with the ambulance.

After a minute or two the bundle began to struggle as she fought to find an opening in the blankets through which to breathe.

When the ambulance arrived at the local hospital the nurses were confronted with the prospect of disentangling the two mummified foreigners before they could decide who was most in need of treatment.

Back at the hotel Bernice raised her hand for silence. The regulars, too, fell quiet as they waited to see what new emotions were about to sweep the Millennium Players.

'I'm afraid I have some very sad news.'

There was an intake of breath all round.

'Sam has asked me to tell you that Alice has tonight been taken into the local hospital.'

'I knew it,' burst out Maeve, clasping her rib cage for

want of a bosom. 'I spoke to her in the students' bar. She was flushed. I knew I should have insisted on bringing her back to the hotel.' She turned furiously on Jude who, up till then, had been nodding sagely. 'This is your fault, Jude. You said we couldn't force her.'

'Now hang on one minute,' rallied Jude.

'Please,' begged Bernice. 'Don't let's argue amongst ourselves. The point is, much as I hate to say it, Alice was not taken to hospital because her condition had worsened.'

'Surely that's good news?' interrupted Marcus Lemmon.

'Well, yes, it is. And it isn't,' Bernice continued. 'You see, the thing is . . .' She bowed her head then raised it again. Richmond patted her shoulder in encouragement. 'The reason Alice has been taken to hospital is because she tried to commit suicide.'

Chapter Twenty-Six

'What is this? A funeral?' Jasmine Ruddock, who had spent rather a good evening being shown round Tartu by the theatre's resident board operator, was surprised to find everyone still up when she crawled back into the hotel at three o'clock the following morning.

Gareth Paynton was not there, but that came as no surprise since she had definitely left him in an exhausted state after their little encounter in the scenery store.

Gareth had indeed been in need of a good night's sleep, not least because a letter had been handed to him on his return to the hotel stating that his wife had managed to squeeze a week's leave out of the production team of her TV show and was planning to arrive in Tartu in time for the last night's performance, adding somewhat unfairly that she had heard from a mutual friend that Jasmine Ruddock's acting abilities wouldn't fool a pig into thinking it was pink.

Since her beloved husband had got Jasmine past her solely on the grounds that the girl had all but conquered anorexia and was on the verge of entering a closed order of lesbians, Vanessa Stormont was naturally interested to see what sort of actress had actually been chosen to displace her own choice of Alice Hemingway.

Gareth had duly retired to bed with a large brandy and an even larger headache.

All eyes now turned to Jasmine. She gazed back, swaying slightly. 'What's up? Why are you staring at me like that?'

Bernice rose and took her by the arm. 'Come and sit down, Jasmine dear. There's something you ought to know.'

As she lay between the coarse starched sheets of the St Agnes' Female Ward in Tartu Infirmary, Alice wondered if she were awake or dreaming. She had been given a sedative, having been pronounced physically fit by a fierce little female doctor who spoke excellent English and seemed more concerned with discussing the moral dilemma of an under-age marriage (Romeo and Juliet's), and the possible harm pregnancy might cause to a pubescent female who had not finished growing.

This would probably have been enough to send Alice to sleep without the aid of a pill, but the combination had transported her to a kind of limbo, from which she was now re-running the events of the past few days like someone watching a video they had not known they were in.

So Philip had been right about Janni all the time? He had been using her. And not just her. It was impossible now to fool herself that he had not known about Bernice's stolen icon. The whole thing had been a set up. No money would have exchanged hands between Janni and Nicolai, only that which Bernice handed over the next day when she had been to the bank. It had all been a huge con.

Alice turned on her side. At least I'm safe now, she thought. He's under arrest. I was saved in the nick of time.

She sat bolt upright. 'How? How did they know? Who followed us? Why did they leave it so late? I might have drowned. I never want to see Jay Bowden again as long as I live.'

A nurse came scurrying over making shushing noises. Alice had been shouting at the top of her voice.

Philip, lying between equally stiff sheets in the Archbishop Rikov Ward for Male Geriatrics (they were short of beds in the men's section), closed his eyes even tighter to try and block out the smell of disinfectant and retching coughs and wheezing all around him.

He, too, had been severely frightened by the lengths that

bastard Viszla had been prepared to go to to get his money. Had he not bumped into Jasmine in the students' bar and heard how she had just seen Alice leaving, and if she had not added that 'that sexy guy' Alice hung around with in Tallinn had just driven past in his flashy car, he probably would stayed where he was, drowning his sorrows. He didn't understand women. What was it about the decent ones that drove them to get mixed up with the least suitable types?

The squeal of the night-time drugs trolley broke into his thoughts. He took a leaf from Alice's book and hid under the blankets.

'But why would Alice want to kill herself?' enquired Jasmine blearily. She had never heard anything so daft. 'Is it bloke trouble?'

'No, no, nothing like that.' Bernice cast around to see whether the others thought they should let Jasmine into their gruesome secret.

Marcus Lemmon shrugged. 'She's bound to find out sooner or later.' There were grunts of agreement.

Bernice sighed and took a deep breath. 'Alice is dying,' she said softly. Jasmine blinked rapidly once or twice.

'What?'

'She's dying. She's very ill. She hasn't got long to live.'

'What's the point of killing herself then?' demanded Jasmine with dreadful logic. There was a choral gasp from all those present.

'She's lost hope, you berk,' snarled Christine Pink. 'She's at her lowest ebb.' Jasmine struggled to take this in. She sat silently for several moments staring into the wobbling embers of the fire. Finally she roused herself. 'Does Ga know about this?' she asked.

Richmond shook his head. 'Not yet. We've only just found out ourselves.'

Jasmine nodded. 'I suppose I'd better tell him then.' The company expressed gratitude, daring to hope that she might yet make the ultimate sacrifice of her own volition. These hopes were short-lived.

'She can't share a dressing-room with us, that's for sure. Do you think it's catching, what she's got?' Jasmine clutched her throat, 'Oh my god, I gave her one of my toffees the other night. I let her get it out of my bag. I'll have to throw the whole lot away now. To think we've been sharing with her all this time . . . She might have said. It'll have to be fumigated, that's what they must do. They did it once when one of the girls got head lice in the second eleven. It stinks the place out but at least it kills the little buggers.'

The company sat silent, unable to deal with so pragmatic an approach.

'I think I'm going to bed,' said Clive Barry at last. By Jasmine's chair he stopped. 'I hope it is catching,' he said bitterly. 'I hope whatever it is, you've caught it.' Jasmine gazed after him as he stalked off up the stairs.

'I wonder what's got into him?' she murmured. 'Poor old Ali. It's not as though I don't feel sorry for her.'

'Who'd've guessed?' spat Christine Pink, preparing to follow Clive.

'No, but come on. The good of the play and all that. We can't go all falling ill and . . . well, whatever, can we?' Jasmine stretched and got up. 'I'm shattered. Where is Ali, by the way?'

'In hospital,' said Marcus Lemmon stonily.

'Oh, well, there you are. Probably the best place for her. I'll get her a card tomorrow, shall I? Then we can all sign it.' She ambled off.

'That girl is brain dead,' muttered Ray, who had hardly said a word all evening.

'So insensitive,' agreed Jeannie.

'Comes of riding to hounds,' Richmond opined. 'See death as a young 'un, it loses all meaning for you. I saw it in the war. You get hardened. Not her fault.'

'It bloody is,' muttered Christine. 'If she's not bloody careful there'll be strychnine in that vial tomorrow night.'

'I think we're all a bit tired,' said Bernice sadly. 'Perhaps things will look brighter in the morning. We can only hope so.' She took Richmond's arm and the two of them made their way slowly to the stairs.

Marshall Vincent prised himself gingerly out of his seat. 'Mind you,' he murmured, 'she does have a point. You can't be too careful these days.'

Hilly, who had been experiencing the pangs of withdrawal from the Hi there, Heaven club, picked up a cushion and flung it with all his might at Marshall's head.

It was very late when Sam Biggins got back. Having ascertained that neither Alice nor Philip was seriously harmed he had returned to the theatre to make sure no lights had been left on and then gone straight down to the police station to make his statement.

There wasn't all that much to say really. He had been walking back to the hotel and had seen two members of his cast, one in the company of Janni Viszla, making their way towards the river bank.

Curious as to why Philip Carter appeared to be stalking the couple and aware of his emotional attachment to Alice Hemingway, Sam had felt it his responsibility to make sure that no confrontation took place.

He had arrived just in time to see Alice Hemingway struggling with Viszla, and a small middle-aged man in a yellow waistcoat launching himself with commendable dexterity at the attacker from behind.

He himself had helped to overcome the accused, aided by Philip Carter who had also rescued Alice from where she had been in danger of rolling into the river. The two of them had then carried her to a place of safety while the man in the waistcoat summoned reinforcements and an ambulance. Of the three hefty kicks Carter had applied to Janni Viszla as he lay helpless on the ground, Sam made no mention.

Gareth Paynton had at last dropped into a fitful sleep full of dreams of Vanessa. She was playing Lady Capulet to his Prince of Verona and kept interrupting his final speech with screams of: 'She's young enough to be your daughter.' This had caused Gareth to lose his place and he was now trying to get rid of her by asking her if she had remembered to cancel the milk.

Into this mayhem now stepped Jasmine herself, reeking of alcohol and demanding to be told if he had known all along that Alice Hemingway was dying. It was some moments before he realised that the apparition now shaking him as though she were trying to turn a mattress was not going to be dispelled by his opening his eyes.

'Got back all right then?' was the best he could manage as Jasmine continued to pummel him.

'Did you hear me, you great ape? They're all down there in the bar saying she tried to kill herself and now she's dying as well.'

'What?' Paynton sat up, head pounding. 'What did you say?'

'Did you know about it? That's what I want to know. Because if you did, I think it's very selfish of you. We've all been sharing a dressing-room with her. I've been using her shampoo.'

'She tried to kill herself?' repeated Gareth, some sentences behind in the outflow.

'So Bernice said. Tried to throw herself in the river. Don't see how she could miss, do you? It's half a mile across. I think Phil or someone hauled her out. They've all gone to hospital. Have you got any aspirin? My head's killing me.' She giggled uncertainly. 'At least it isn't, but it is, if you see what I mean.'

'Go to bed, Jaz,' said Gareth in an exhausted voice. 'We'll talk about this in the morning. Just go to bed.'

He knew before he opened the door who it would be. Maeve and Jude stood outside, once more in their nurses' regalia. 'We thought we should speak to you first,' said Jude, adjusting the cuffs of her dress.

Gareth nodded. 'You did right,' he said solemnly. He had been rehearsing this reaction most of the night, having failed to get back to sleep after Jasmine left. He had never had to deal with a suicide on tour before, even a failed one. What on earth could have got into the girl? True, she couldn't act, but she must have known that all along. Anyway, everyone knew that understudies weren't supposed to be any good, otherwise they turned surly when you took the part away again.

He tried to think if there had been any tell-tale signs that he should have picked up on. Truth was, he had hardly noticed the girl. He'd had enough on his plate with half the men falling ill or over. Not to mention keeping his eye on young Jaz who, for all her charms, could be a bit of a handful. Now, here he was with Vanessa due to arrive in twenty-four hours and the girl that she had forced him into including on the tour, lying dying in the local infirmary, if Jasmine was to be believed.

'Would you like to come in for a moment?' he suggested. Jude and Maeve said they would, keeping a firm eye on the bedclothes for signs of unauthorised wriggling.

'We're on our way to visit them,' Jude informed him self-righteously. 'We thought you might like to come too.'

'Erm . . .' Gareth passed a weary hand over his forehead. 'Naturally, I would like . . . the thing is, I think I should . . . Have either of you seen Sam Biggins? I really think I should have a word with him first.'

'He wasn't around last night,' said Maeve. 'We were downstairs till very late and he wasn't back then.'

'So he won't know what's happened,' put in Jude. 'Well, if you don't want to come, Gareth, I'm sure that's perfectly understandable, but someone's got to be with that poor girl at a time like this.'

'I thought Philip was there?' responded Gareth, irritated by her tone. 'I'm sure he'll sort matters out. She won't want a huge crowd hanging round her if she's . . . not feeling quite the thing.'

Jude pursed her lips and led Maeve away. Gareth watched them go, thinking even by British standards 'not quite the thing' hardly covered suicide and terminal illness. He must find Sam. Despite Jude's avowal to the contrary, Sam would know what was going on.

Chapter Twenty-Seven

'So it definitely wasn't attempted suicide?' Gareth sat opposite Sam in the tiny study that had been set aside as the technical office.

'No, nothing of the kind. Ali's not that sort of girl.'

'I thought not,' beamed Gareth, relief coursing like brandy through his veins.

'It was attempted murder.'

'WHAT?' Gareth stood up so quickly that he knocked the table flying, bruising his knee as he did so. 'What are you talking about? ATTEMPTED MURDER? Has everyone gone mad? Who would want to murder Alice Hemingway? She's the understudy, for God's sake. As if it isn't enough I have Maeve Prentice and Jude Jenkins trying to tell me she and Philip Carter are planning to kill the entire cast, now I have you telling me someone's trying to kill *them*. This is a provincial tour of *Romeo and Juliet*, for God's sake, not a real life *Titus Andronicus*. When we finish here we go to Aberdeen. It's a "B" tour. Ask the bloody Arts Council. They haven't budgeted for twenty-four deaths.'

'I don't think it's quite the way it sounds, guv,' said Sam, setting the table straight.

'I should bloody well hope not. And I've got Nessie arriving tomorrow afternoon. I'm beginning to wish I was on this death list of theirs.'

'You are. You're top of it,' said Sam without irony. Gareth harrumphed and rubbed his wounded knee.

'Just tell me what you know, Sam. You're a sensible bloke. Give it to me straight.'

Sam shrugged. 'Ali got herself mixed up with some Mafia guys. I don't think she realised it. In fact, I'm sure she didn't. I think she had a thing about one of them and then it all turned sour. I don't know the ins and outs. Anyway he's the one who was trying to push her in the river. Luckily the police were on to him. He'd got his fingers in one pie too many and they set up a sting. Something about a stolen icon. He fell for it. He's off the scene now as far as we know.'

'But what's all this about an illness then? She always looked perfectly healthy to me, although . . .' He recalled Alice's pallor at the understudy rehearsal.

Sam sighed. 'I don't know. Apparently she had a message from some bloke in England. Grim, it sounded. "Time running out" and that. I don't know. You'd have to ask Maeve.'

'I'd rather not. Have you talked to Alice since all this? I mean, why's she in hospital now? And Philip with her? What's wrong with *him*, for God's sake? I can't have them both off at once.' The illogicality of this was lost on them both. Gareth looked at Sam nervously. 'You don't suppose it is catching, do you? Whatever she's got?'

Sam gave a short laugh. 'Only for some, I would imagine. I'm going over there to pick them up. Why don't you come?'

Gareth shuddered. 'That's an excellent idea. Yes, certainly. Good thinking. Only problem is . . .'

Sam saved him the trouble of trying to think of one. 'I'll let you know when they're back.'

Alice had got off very lightly as far as Maeve and Jude were concerned. She was sitting on her bed fully dressed when they arrived. She watched them trotting officiously down the ward, followed by a nurse. They stopped a few feet away and regarded her with theatrical dismay.

'You're dressed,' said Maeve dolefully.

'Yes.'

'What did the doctor say?' demanded Jude, prepared to

do battle on Alice's behalf. 'Surely they ought to be keeping you in?'

'There's nothing wrong with me,' said Alice blithely. Their mouths opened and closed again.

'Are you sure you feel okay?' asked Maeve.

'Yes, thank you. Wonderful. Never better. But poor Philip's not so good,' she added treacherously. The two women glanced at one other.

'Are they keeping him in?' asked Jude hopefully.

'I don't know,' Alice confessed, 'but I'm sure he'd like to see you both.'

'Well, if you're sure you're all right?'

'Oh yes, fine, thank you.'

'Don't move from that bed,' ordered Jude. 'We'll be back just as soon as we've seen him.' They marched away.

Though she hadn't known it, Alice had described Philip's state pretty accurately. A night spent listening to the baying of his geriatric colleagues, coupled with the clanging of bedpans, bells and trollies, had left Philip a nervous wreck. He now sat, dressed but unshaven (all sharp objects being in the gift of the staff nurse), on the edge of his bed, trying not to notice that the man in the next one was straining violently into a bedpan while trying with one hand to put his teeth in.

'There you are,' Jude announced, wondering why she had ever thought him sexy. 'You look dreadful. Have you seen a doctor yet?'

Philip nodded grimly.

'What did he say?' coaxed Maeve.

'I could go home.'

'Oh, that's good news,' said Jude, biting back her disappointment.

'We came by taxi,' Maeve volunteered. 'Perhaps we can all go back together. They're letting Alice out, too – for the time being.' She gave a brave little smile.

Philip stared at her oddly but said nothing. They were saved from the need for further conversation by the arrival of Sam. 'Come on, mate,' he said gruffly. He had a new respect for Phil after last night. 'Ali's in Reception. I've got a cab waiting.'

'Oh good,' chirruped Maeve. 'Room for two little 'uns?'

'Yeah, probably, but that counts you out,' Sam responded unkindly. 'I'll get him to phone for another. See you back there.' He led Philip away.

'I don't know what's got into him,' said Jude crossly. 'And where was he last night when we needed him? Out on the town, no doubt. Typical.' Maeve nodded dejectedly.

What had got into Sam Biggins was that he was deeply upset.

He liked Alice, possibly more than he did anyone else in the company, and it seemed to him the height of injustice that a nice kid like her should be cut down in her prime. More, he knew that when the time came, it would fall to him to tell Philip about it, and he was dreading it.

He knew also that the time could not be long coming. How else was he to avoid Maeve or Jude or even that idiot Jaz letting the cat out of the bag, and what could be more cruel than that Philip should find out from one of them?

He was also faced with the fact that Alice had failed to tell Philip herself, just as she had kept her dark secret from the rest of them. What a brave, gutsy little creature she was, to keep such bitter ill fortune to herself. She must love Philip very much to want to spare him the truth. Whatever she said about 'brother and sister' and all that, Sam knew better.

The other thing that was preoccupying him was how to dispose of Jasmine Ruddock before the final performance. Normally it should not have presented too many problems. Jasmine was clumsy, unreliable, and susceptible to alcohol. These combined should have been enough to guarantee her absence for at least one night of the run. The snag was Gareth Paynton. The man had already allowed her to hack her way through a fortnight's worth of dud performances. Why should he think mere drunkenness a reason to suspend her?

It was Gareth himself who paved the way for Sam's eventual triumph. The Millennium Players' director was angry with

Jasmine for frightening him like that. She had caught him at a very low ebb. Brian Berrell had been on to him from Tallinn saying that Madame Skikne had taken gross offence at his failure to squire her on the opening night of the song festival. She had apparently expressed her displeasure to the Minister for the Performing Arts who had promptly cancelled all plans to invite Vera Lynn to the Tartu Rock Festival. This was a disaster for cultural relations between the two countries.

Gareth had come within an inch of telling Berrell just what he thought of an organisation whose success depended on the sexual harassment of happily married men, but this raised the awkward question of why one such had felt the need to bring a mistress on tour with him.

It was all an awful pain. How he longed for his days as an 'also ran' in the interminable history cycles at Stratford.

It was while he was reminiscing that an idea came to him. He sat for a few moments savouring the delicious simplicity of his plan, then went in search of Jasmine.

Alice and Philip said nothing in the taxi back. She knew that she owed him an enormous debt, if not her actual life, and yet she could not bring herself to mention it. All she could think of was that he had been right and she had been wrong. Janni had used her. Worse than that, he had deliberately led her to think he cared about her and then dumped her, quite literally, when her usefulness ended. Jay, too, she realised, cared no more for her than for any of the other women cooing round him. Only Philip had stuck by her through thick and thin. And she had nothing to offer in return.

Philip seemed no more inclined to discuss their adventures than she was. He sat silently, staring out of the window. Sam was in the front with the driver, his head buzzing with all the difficulties ahead.

Jasmine slammed her glass down on the table. 'Certainly not. Of course I'm not going all the way back there. He's a ghastly little man, anyway. Why should I want to go and see him?'

'It's ambassadorial,' pleaded Paynton. 'It would make such a marvellous impression if you were to say you'd come 'specially, and missed a performance just to let him know how important his help has been and everything. Please, Jaz, otherwise they'll cut off all our funding, I know they will.'

'You go, then. If you're so worried.'

'Jaz, how can I make you understand? It will be a grand gesture. The star of the production gives up her final performance to plead personally with Brian Berrell for the life of the Millennium Players. You'd be famous. I could ask Sam to get in touch with the telly people. How would that be?'

Jasmine wavered. 'It's a hell of a long way, back to Tallinn. I'd have to go by train, I'm not going by bus.'

'No, of course not. I wouldn't dream of it. And you'd have to stay the night. I couldn't possibly ask you to come back the same day. Sam will sort it all out. I could even write you a little speech if you like. Something about how grateful we are for the warmth and hospitality we've received and how desperate we are to come back again. You could learn it on the train.'

'Yes, all right, if you like,' murmured Jasmine, who had no intention of going anywhere near Brian Berrell, but of making a flying visit to the Museum of Estonian Antiquities in search of her friend, the curator.

'So that's settled then?' asked Gareth, years falling from him like dandruff.

'Yup. Okay. I'll need some money for spends.'

'Yes, yes, all right. How much would see you through?'

Jasmine named an extravagant sum. He winced and handed it over.

Sam was delighted with the news. 'Does Ali know?'

Gareth shook his head. 'I suppose I'd better call a words rehearsal. I don't suppose we'll get much more out of her. Serves Vanessa right. Perhaps it'll stop her foisting all these misfits off on me every time I do a play.'

Sam started to say something then bit his lip. No point arguing with the prat now. 'Do you want me to tell the others? We'll need to walk her through it.'

'Yes, okay, would you, Sam? But keep it low key, can you? I don't want Jaz changing her mind.'

Bernice clasped Sam's hand, her huge eyes moist with gratitude. 'Oh, Sam, how can we thank you enough? You are so clever. So diplomatic. What did the dear girl say? I suppose once you told her why we wanted Alice to have a go, she couldn't help being moved?' She turned to Richmond. 'Isn't this just the most marvellous news, darling? Jasmine has agreed to let Alice play Juliet for our final performance. I really do think we should club together and get her a little present. Just to say "thank you". What do you think? Perhaps a brooch?'

'Certainly not a brooch,' thundered Richmond, who had been more than a little disturbed to find that Bernice's 'friendly baker' was in fact a member of the Estonian Flying Squad, and that it was only his devotion to the re-run of *Sister Gillian* that had stopped her amber jewellery from being confiscated on the spot.

'No, all right, dear. But some flowers, maybe?' pleaded Bernice contritely.

Richmond grunted. He had been shocked by Jasmine Ruddock's reaction to the dreadful news about Alice the other night, albeit the girl had been blotto. Perhaps this was her effort to atone. He must not be ungracious. 'We'll see.' Bernice beamed and turned to Sam.

'What does Alice say? Is she excited? Of course she is.'

'I haven't told her yet.'

'Not told her?' exclaimed Bernice. 'But you must. Immediately. So that she can get ready.'

'Gareth's calling a rehearsal for after lunch.'

'Not that.' Bernice flapped her hands around. 'She'll need to get her hair done. Have a manicure. So many things. She must certainly be told as soon as possible. Would you like me to do it?'

Sam shook his head. 'That's all right. I thought I'd get Phil to. Fellow understudies and all that.'

Bernice nodded gravely. 'Very wise. Poor man. Oh, the poor man.' She was overcome by tears and led away by Richmond who recommended a stiff brandy for them both.

To Sam's surprise Philip Carter was neither pleased nor grateful for the opportunity to break the news to Alice. 'You tell her. You fixed it,' he responded morosely. Sam was about to chin him for the callous bastard he was when he remembered that Philip did not know Alice was dying, and that that was why he wanted him to tell her. What better chance for her to come clean with him than when he told her her greatest dream was about to come true. (Second greatest, he corrected himself.)

'Look, mate, I'm up to my eyes in it, all right? Nobby's been on a blinder and it looks like I'm going to have to get one of the students to do the board. Do us a favour, eh? Just pop your head round the door and tell her she's on tomorrow night. She'd do it for you.'

Philip scowled. 'I think you're wrong about that,' he muttered, 'but if it's got to be done, it's got to be done.'

'Thanks, Phil. I won't forget.'

'No. Neither will I.'

He found Alice in the makeshift green room. She was sitting with her back pressed against the wall and her eyes tight shut. Philip kicked the door noisily and cleared his throat. Alice hardly moved. 'Am I disturbing you?' he asked aggressively. She opened her eyes. He was alarmed to see that she had been crying. Quickly he looked away. 'I've got some good news for you.'

Alice struggled to compose herself. 'Oh?'

'Yes. Sam says you're on tomorrow night.'

Alice stared at him. 'I am? Who as? Is Bernice . . . ?'

'Bernice is fine.'

'Jeannie?'

'They're all fine. You're playing Juliet. Jasmine's off somewhere for Gareth. Can't remember the details. Good luck. I'm sure you'll be great.' He turned to go.

'Philip,' Alice was on her feet. 'What is this?' He halted. She came over to him. 'Why are you being so horrid? I mean, suddenly? After all you've done. You . . . well, you saved my life, didn't you? And last night you were so kind . . . Now today, well, it's as though you can't bear to be in the same room with me. Why? At least give me a reason.'

Philip crushed a piece of dirt under his foot and spread it

around with his toe. 'I'm sorry. I've been thinking. Quite a bit. All last night, as a matter of fact. In that bloody hospital. No offence, but I've come to the conclusion I really don't want to be around you any more.'

Alice stared at him. 'I see,' she said quietly.

'Do you? I doubt it.'

'Of course I do. I'm not completely stupid, you know. And there's no need to try and spare my feelings. As a fellow understudy you should know by now they don't count.'

Philip gave a hoarse laugh. '"*Scratch me with a pin, do I not bleed?*" Your feelings count all right, Alice. They count so much they cancel out everyone else's, it seems to me.'

Alice frowned. 'What do you mean?'

'Nothing. Good news about Juliet, isn't it?'

'Bugger Juliet,' screeched Alice, suddenly sick of it all. 'Juliet's in a play. I'm here. I'm real. In case you hadn't noticed.'

'Yes, well, so'm I,' Philip roared back. 'And I don't plan to spend the rest of my life watching you hurling yourself at no-hopers like the pair you've come up with so far. How do you do it? Do you advertise in the Lonely Hearts? *Dim actress in search of bastard*. That sounds about right, doesn't it?'

'I didn't know he'd turn out like that,' Alice wailed.

'Which one?' asked Philip savagely. 'The one who's been cheating on you from the day you met or the homo with the glittery eyes?'

There was a ghastly silence.

'What do you mean?' she asked at last.

'What about?'

'You know.'

'Oh, didn't you realise? I thought once Igor showed up you'd get the message.'

'Igor is Janni's brother,' said Alice, feeling strangely sick.

Philip shook his head in despair. 'Is he just? Alice, only you would believe that a Neanderthal like that came out of the same womb as your fancy man. Think about it. Surely you've met enough gays to recognise the signs? Janni was no more interested in you than he was in sewing mailbags. He took you for a ride. Nearly a very expensive one. Funerals come dear these days.'

Alice stared at her feet. 'I'm leaving my body to science.'

There was a collective gasp from the dressing rooms where the entire encounter was being relayed, due to a fault in the Tannoy system that meant everything from the green room was broadcast all over backstage.

Philip shrugged. 'I doubt they'd have wanted it after you'd been in the Emajogi. The pollution is appalling.'

'We shall never know.'

'No, that's right. By the way, it's only eighteen inches deep where he was planning to turf you in. You'd have had to work at it to drown.'

'I daresay I would have managed.'

Philip heaved a deep sigh. 'I daresay you would.'

Tears were rolling down Alice's face. 'Is Jay queer as well?'

Philip shrugged indifferently. 'How would I know? He certainly sounds narcissistic, from what you've told me. That's often a sign.'

Alice nodded. 'Perhaps that's the best I can hope for.'

'What?'

'Men who aren't sure.'

Philip closed his eyes. A video camera would have revealed that he too was close to tears. 'Perhaps.'

Chapter Twenty-Eight

Vanessa Stormont arrived in Tallinn after a journey similar in all ways but one to the company's, at eight-thirty in the morning.

She, too, had been insulted by the stewardess, nauseated by the food, and irritated by the smokers. The difference was that she had travelled in the company of Felicity Wells, fiancée of Craig Penforth, who had brought with her an armful of magazines regarding the care of the body during pregnancy and the importance of early bonding between father and foetus.

To this end, on discovering the results of Craig's weekend visit home, the young woman had set aside her lifelong distrust of anywhere outside Preston, rushed round to Craig's mother and demanded to be put on the next train to Estonia.

Mrs Penforth, a sensible woman, had insisted first that Felicity check with her doctor that this journey was indeed advisable, and having received an assurance that it would be an excellent idea, if only to give the girl a taste of life beyond Preston, had contacted Equity and thence the director's wife who, with her usual efficiency, had immediately arranged a bucket shop ticket and undertaken to meet Felicity at Euston station and transport her to Tartu.

That she had begun to regret her undertaking within fifteen minutes of meeting the girl, Vanessa kept stoically to herself.

Felicity Wells, twenty years old and never before in London, nevertheless felt competent to lecture her companion with all the confidence of a resident tour guide.

'What you should do, as soon as you're in, is tek cabbie's number. That way he'll know not to cheat 'un,' she informed Vanessa loudly, after the cabbie had gone out of his way to help with Felicity's baggage.

'I'm sure this gentleman has no such intention,' remarked Vanessa equally sonorously, but by then his chin was set rigid and they travelled the whole way on the inside lane.

'What d'you think of this?' Felicity displayed her shiny new passport.

'Very nice,' said Vanessa.

'The photo's not too good. I wanted it done from my left side, but he said it had to be full frontal.'

'I think it's very nice,' said Vanessa again. They were not yet past Marylebone.

By the time the plane started its bumpy descent Vanessa, a childless woman, felt that she would have been well equipped to deliver quads. In fact, as she later confided to her husband, 'I could have grown the bloody things on blotting paper by the time she'd finished.'

There then followed the journey to Tartu by train, during which Felicity remonstrated with the ticket inspector, the man selling peaches from a trolley and three of the four occupants of their compartment who had had the audacity to light up cigarettes. They stared at her with universal incomprehension before returning to their newspapers, and belching forth fresh clouds of smoke.

By the time the train pulled into Tartu Vanessa had made up her mind never, under any circumstances whatsoever, to do anyone a favour again. Her humour was not improved by her husband's recent confirmation that Alice Hemingway had not had so much as a sniff at any of her understudy roles during the tour, and that in his opinion this was a very good thing.

She had not spoken to him since Sunday, before she had found out about Felicity, so could half understand his look of confusion as he bounded down the platform to meet her, and found himself saddled with two holdalls and a bag full of women's magazines before they had even been introduced.

'This is Felicity,' said Vanessa, after the customary peck. 'She's engaged to Romeo.'

'I quite like that name,' Felicity opined. 'If it's a boy.'

The couple exchanged glances.

When they were alone Gareth told Vanessa his news. He had chilled a bottle of champagne for their reunion and was pleased to see that she was looking much more like her old self than when she had first arrived.

Felicity had gone in search of Craig to tell him the good news and introduce him to his offspring (now presumably the size of a peanut). To the amazement of his fellow actors Craig was over the moon. They congregated in the students' bar, shaking their heads over the fate of a man of twenty-two who has been pursued all the way to Estonia to rub the belly of his fiancée.

'It's the end of his career,' remarked Archie Frith, who was running out of notebooks, so fast was copy falling into his lap.

'I've got kids,' said Marcus Lemmon. 'Tons of 'em. It's never held me back.'

'That's because you never lifted a finger to help with them,' retorted Christine. The cast mentally adjusted their bets on the reunion surviving the tour.

Bernice appeared, looking particularly majestic in a purple ensemble trimmed with fox fur. 'Come on, everyone. Time for the rehearsal. And remember, no holds barred. This is for Alice.'

The rehearsal went smoothly enough. Alice, if a little downbeat, brought a lot more intelligence to the part than Jasmine had ever managed. Gareth Paynton watched with some amazement as she moved faultlessly through the speeches, once or twice even giving a glimpse of the talent his wife had sworn she possessed. At the end of the run he breathed several sighs of relief. The rest of the cast had reacted well, too – not simply going through the motions, but giving totally creditable matinee standard performances, which was certainly more than usually happened at understudy rehearsals.

Even Maeve and Jude seemed to have put lids on their normal hysteria, confining it to basic eye-rolling and hunching of the shoulders.

At four o'clock they broke. Bernice hurried over to Alice. 'That was quite quite lovely, dear. You were born to play Juliet. Just born to it.' Whilst knowing that this had yet to be demonstrated, Alice felt indecently cheered by the compliment.

Richmond squeezed her hand. 'Give yourself time, child. It's your play. It doesn't have to be over in twenty minutes.'

Flowers began to pile up in the dressing-room, accompanied by cards and messages from the cast. Alice sat amongst them. Why are they treating me like this? she wondered. After all, Philip's been on twice and no one made all this fuss over him. She looked at her watch. It was ages till the half. She felt a sudden desperate need for fresh air. Looking out of the window she could just see the avenue of silver birches. It's safe now, she thought. Janni's gone. I can forget about what happened. But it was towards the river that she turned.

She walked slowly along beside it, looking neither right nor left. At the spot by the willows she stopped, her heart pounding unnaturally. Why am I doing this? she thought. But it had to be done. Otherwise she would never be free.

Very slowly she bent down and looked in the river. It rippled back at her, black and fathomless. Eighteen inches, she thought. It goes down forever.

'Oh. Hello.' Alice gazed in dismay into the dressing-room.

Jasmine turned. 'Oh, hi, Ali. Look at all these flowers. Aren't they gorgeous? And the cards. This one says, "To the best Juliet in the world". Isn't that sweet?'

Alice swallowed. 'Who's it from?' she asked. Jasmine screwed up her eyes. 'Criag,' she deciphered, then burst out laughing. 'Blimey, you'd think he could spell his own name, wouldn't you?'

She never got an answer for at that moment Felicity Wells,

her maternal instincts some months ahead of her delivery date, came charging through the door, having heard every word on the retrograde Tannoy. 'They're not for yous, anyway,' she screeched. Jasmine took a step back in surprise.

'Who the hell are you?'

'I'm Craig's fiancée, that's who I am. And you're that Jasmine Runfold. 'E's told me all about you. How you can't act and you're a snob and you only got the job 'coz your old man's on t'radio. Well, my Craig's a very fine actor, see. And don't you go talking about him like he's stupid just 'coz he's had trouble with his reading. It's all the better he's got where he has, so there. He's not had private schooling like some.'

Jasmine looked distinctly put out by this. True she had had to have a little extra coaching from time to time but she was blowed if she was going to be yelled at by some brassy blonde from the wilderness.

'Oh, F off!' she said sulkily. She'd had a very trying day. The train had broken down just outside Tallinn. They had sat for an hour while various men in overalls wandered up and down the track shaking their pickaxes and spitting, and when the guard had finally turned up it had been to tell them that a car had broken down on the level crossing and that they would have to continue their journey by bus as the owner refused to let them move it.

Thus much Jasmine gathered from the other occupants of the carriage who, though possessing no more than a smattering of English, were extremely good at charades.

'No go. Pff! Pff!' said one, while his companion made the familiar throat-slitting gesture that seemed to accompany so many activities in that part of the world.

They were shovelled off the train and made to wait in the rain for twenty minutes till a bus could be found to take them on. Jasmine had taken one look at the cranking, lurching vehicle and made a decision. She marched up to the green Mercedes parked bang across the tracks and guarded by four men in leather coats, their arms crossed on their chests. 'Which one of you owns this car?' she demanded. The men remained silent, the rain dripping relentlessly from their Raybans. 'Oh, come on,' Jasmine pouted and stuck her foot on the dashboard. The man beside it stiffened threateningly.

'It's a scrummy car,' she said more softly. The man looked nervous. 'I would sooo like a little ride in it.' She cocked her head and gave him her 'take me, I'm yours' smile. The man glanced at the others. They shrugged. 'When this will be mended you might make a little ride. It is possible.'

'Oh, how scrummy,' said Jasmine, and opening the back door, settled herself to wait for the petrol to arrive.

Unfortunately, as was so often the case, the only petrol available was high-grade tractor fuel and this had made Jasmine's trip home slightly less comfortable than being dragged by her wrists round an amphitheatre. They had finally dropped her a mile from the theatre, having relieved her of her wallet and without making even a feeble attempt to gang rape her. All in all it had been a most unsatisfactory day.

Now here was this ignorant little tart giving her a hard time in her own dressing-room.

'Don't you talk to me like that, you . . . you . . . floozy,' stuttered Felicity.

'I'll talk to you how I like. Now clear out of here. Go and give your lover boy a tweak, why don't you? See if there's anything inside those trousers of his, apart from a week's worth of dirty washing.'

'Don't you dare talk about my Craig like that. He's more of a man than any you'd be likely to come across – and I'm the living proof of it, so there.'

Jasmine's eyebrows rose in astonishment. 'Don't tell me he's your father?'

'Don't be so disgusting. You've a foul mouth for a woman, do you know that?'

'And you've a bloody foul accent so do us all a favour and clear off where you came from and stop bothering us. We've got a play to put on.'

'Them flowers're not for you, anyway,' retorted Felicity.

'How do you know?'

''Coz I helped him choose them, that's how. You weren't meant to be on tonight. It's for that girl what's going to . . .' She caught sight of Alice and clapped her hand to her mouth. 'Oh, sorry, love. I didn't mean anything, honest I didn't.'

Alice stared at her dumbfounded.

'Oh, for God's sake,' snapped Jasmine. 'Here, take your bloody flowers then, and I hope they choke you.' She picked up the bouquet and flung it with all her might at the visitor.

Felicity tottered and nearly fell. 'You mind me, you cat. I'm pregnant, that's what.'

'Really? Does lover boy know?'

'He does and he's right chuffed.'

'Why? Is he friends with the father?'

This was too much for Felicity who flew at Jasmine like a bat out of hell, tearing at her hair, and battering her with her puny little fists.

Jeannie chose this moment to make her customary entry. She sighed resignedly and pattered off, only to be nearly crushed by Craig who had heard the exchange and came tearing down the corridor to rescue his intended from Jasmine's not inconsiderable clutches.

'Break it up, you two,' he yelled, undeterred by the intensity of the encounter. 'Come on, now. That's enough.' He spotted Alice, still standing shell-shocked in the corner. 'Hand us that vase. No, put some water in it first. Like for mad dogs. Quick, Ali, for God's sake! She'll harm the baby, else.'

Alice filled the vase with water. 'Now chuck it at them. Chuck it, I said.'

Alice was not at all sure this would not do even more harm to the baby, but she was too traumatised to make decisions for herself. 'CHUCK IT!' bellowed Craig. Alice chucked.

'Not the whole th—' Craig launched himself at the flying vase, missed, and was struck forcibly on the side of the head. He sank senseless to the ground.

'Oh, my lord! Oh no. Oh no. What's happened to you, Craig? Speak to me, my love. Speak to me. Say something.' Felicity knelt down amidst the flower-strewn debris and cradled her fiancé's head against her belly. Richmond, passing by on his way to the toilet, was moved to remark later that 'the young fair girl was making a very good stab at the part,' in his opinion.

Maeve was first on the scene, quickly followed by Jude and then Sam, who had been trying to sober up Nobby in time for the opening act. 'Oh, good heavens,' squawked Maeve, eyes rolling upward. 'What on earth's been going on?'

'Oh, my darling, speak to me,' sobbed Felicity.

'It's his own fault, if you ask me,' grumbled Jasmine, who was very much afraid some of her hair had come out. 'Anyway, don't look at me like that. It's Ali's fault. She's the one who tried to kill him.'

Maeve gave a tiny sigh and sank down beside him.

'What the hell's going on here?' Gareth Paynton, who up to five minutes ago had been feeling reasonably sanguine, gazed with disbelief at the carnage at his feet. 'Sam . . .' But Sam was already on his way to phone for an ambulance.

At the stage door he encountered Philip carrying a large bunch of Arum lilies. 'Out of my way, Mystic Meg,' Sam mumbled, pushing past him to the phone. He dialled the now familiar number then turned to Philip, who was standing perplexed in the corridor. 'By the way, mate, I'd get my skates on, if I were you. Looks like you're on again tonight.'

Philip's jaw dropped. 'Me? Who? Why?'

'No time to explain. Get on up there. It's a bloody madhouse, no kidding. Bring back the Congo. Go on, what're you waiting for?'

'Nothing.'

'Hospital? *Ja*. Bad. Ouch. Theatre . . . Ya. Pronto, *muchos gracios*.' Sam slammed down the phone.

'You still here? I thought you'd be in costume by now.' He hurried past. Philip followed him gloomily along the corridor.

'Who is it this time?' he yelled half-heartedly at the disappearing figure.

Sam half turned. 'Didn't I say? Romeo.'

Chapter Twenty-Nine

'What do you mean, he won't do it?' Gareth surveyed Sam with the incomprehension of a dictator who has just been told that a gnat refuses to be swatted. 'He must do it. He has no choice. It's in his contract.'

'He don't seem too bothered about that at the moment. He seems in a bit of a way.'

'Not him as well? What the hell's the matter with this fucking Company?'

Sam eyed him reproachfully and Gareth struggled to control himself. 'I'm sorry, Sam. That was uncalled for. It's just, I'm a little bit harassed at the moment. I've got Craig Penforth unconscious in the infirmary, his girlfriend in hysterics in my office, Maeve Prentice laid out in the green room, Nobby Clarke drunk in the flies, my wife running off all my bath water, Alice Hemingway . . .'

'Craig's come round.'

'Well, if he's come round perhaps he can . . .' Gareth's hopes faded as Sam shook his head.

'He thinks he's in *Casualty* at the moment. I don't think it's quite sunk in.'

Gareth's shoulders drooped. 'To top it all Jaz is raging round the theatre saying no half-baked understudy's taking over from her on the final show. What's she doing back, for Christ's sake? She's never been on time for anything in her life. Why does she have to start now? And then you tell me Phil Carter's refusing to play Romeo.' He fumbled in a drawer and removed a half bottle of whisky. Absently he untwisted the cap and drank deep, before offering it to Sam.

'No thanks, guv. I need to keep a clear head for tonight.'

Gareth looked visibly stung. 'Yes, that's right. You keep a clear head. Don't worry about me. I'll never work again after this fiasco, do you know that? That bastard Berrell's probably having me unfrocked at this very moment, or whatever they do if you're chucked out of Equity.'

'What do you want to do about young Phil?'

'Do? What can I do? You get back to him, Sam, and tell him if he doesn't fucking well honour his contract, and fucking well get into that costume and fucking well give the performance of his fucking life . . .' Gareth's hands flapped around helplessly '. . . then he'll never work for me again. And that is my final word.'

Sam nodded, thinking that if that was the best Gareth could come up with, it was probably just as well. 'I'll see what I can do.'

'Yes, do that, would you, Sam? Thanks, old friend.' Gareth ferreted for his whisky. 'You're sure you wouldn't like a . . . ? No, quite right. Clear head. Right. Jolly good. Cheers.'

Sam strode down the corridor. He's got to know sooner or later, was running through his mind. Looked like it was going to be sooner.

He found Philip in the men's dressing-room, arms folded across his chest, warding off the assorted pleas and threats of his fellow cast members.

'Come on, Phil. Do it for Craig. You owe him that much at least.'

Philip shifted in his seat.

'You're letting us all down. Not just yourself.'

'You're chicken. That's it, isn't it? You're just a fucking understudy, and that's all you'll ever be.' Philip half rose to punch Clive Barry for this, but changed his mind and sank back.

'I'm sorry,' he muttered. 'I can't. That's all there is to it.'

'Why not, for Christ's sake? Just tell us that.'

'Because it's all such a sham. Dressing up, pretending to

be other people. I don't want to do it any more. Enough's enough.'

'Is it because Jaz is back?' asked Hilly. 'Would you have done it for Alice?'

Philip stared at him. 'Alice isn't on?'

Hilly shrugged. 'Not by the looks of it. We thought it was all sorted but now Jasmine's back, seems it's all been a waste of time. Short of a miracle.'

'Well, bloody do one, then,' snapped Archie Frith savagely. Everyone stared at him. 'You're the one who's got the ear of the Almighty. You sort it out.'

Hilly looked devastated. The others shuffled their feet. 'I don't think that's entirely fair, old boy,' said Richmond gruffly. 'We'd all like it to be Alice, for obvious reasons, but if it's not to be, it's not to be. We've done our best.'

Philip scowled from one to the other of them. 'How come you're all so keen for her to play Juliet all of a sudden?' he demanded. They shuffled their feet again and looked away.

Sam Biggins gave one quick rap on the door.

'Come in,' they all yelled. He took a breath and opened it. 'Phil, got a minute, have you? There's something I want to tell you.' He turned to the others. 'Ali's back on, by the way. Jaz has had to go down to the police station. Few questions about who conked young Craig. Apparently the girlfriend's lodged a complaint. Swears blind it was Jaz. Jaz tried to blame Ali, but . . . well, no one's wearing that.' He nodded jerkily, then holding the door open for Philip, led him away to a quiet corner of the theatre.

The others silently set about their preparations for the evening's performance. Somewhere in the distance they heard a cry like an animal in pain.

When Philip returned he was carrying Romeo's costume.

In the women's dressing-room Alice sat staring at the card on the lilies: '*All my love, always. Philip*'.

Bernice tiptoed over to her and adjusted her cloak. 'Nervous?'

She smiled distractedly. 'I suppose so.'

Bernice gave her a hug. 'You'll be brilliant, I know you will.'

Christine Pink winked at her. 'Sock it to them, sweetie.'

Jeannie tottered over with a sprig of heather. 'Just thought it might bring you luck.'

'Thank you,' said Alice. 'I could do with a whole bush.' The women tittered unhappily.

'Quarter of an hour, ladies and gentlemen. This is your quarter of an hour.'

Alice stood up. The other three rose simultaneously.

'I think I might just get a breath of air.'

'Where?' asked Christine, fearful she might be heading for the river.

'Just outside.'

'Would you like me to come with you?' asked Bernice. 'I'm nearly ready.'

'No – thank you, Bernice. I'd just like a minute on my own, if that's all right.'

The actresses exchanged uneasy looks. 'Of course,' said Jeannie, in a rare moment of decision. 'Off you go. We'll see you down there.'

Alice stood outside the stage door. This is it then, she thought, her stomach pumping like a threshing machine. This is my big chance. A star is born. In Estonia where no one speaks the language. I could do it with a Brummie accent. They'd never know. And Philip's playing Romeo. How about that?

She turned to go back in. He was standing in the doorway. She tried to smile, so did he. Neither succeeded.

'There's something I want to say to you,' said Philip unsteadily. His face looked pale under the make-up. Alice nodded.

Philip stared at the ground. 'I've made a mess of so many things in my life and I'm probably about to do the same with this. It doesn't matter, because I don't want to act any more after tonight.'

'What on earth are you talking about?' Alice stopped him.

'This is your big chance. How can you say you want to give up now?'

Philip kicked a stone. It rang hollowly as it ricocheted off the wall. 'That's why. I've spent too much of my life pretending. Telling myself things will be okay if I close my eyes and pretend I'm somewhere else, someone else. There comes a time when it just doesn't work any more. And this is it. I always thought if I could just get a decent part everything would fall into place. And now I have, and it hasn't.'

Alice stared at him. 'I don't understand you.'

Philip smiled but his eyes were empty. 'No, well, as I said, I didn't expect to make a success of this, but I'd just like you to know that I love you, Alice, and I'd give everything I own for it to have been me. Everything.'

She stood perfectly still. 'You know, then?'

'Sam told me.'

'Is that why you bought the lilies?'

'I'd got them already.'

'Why?'

'They were the most expensive flowers they had.'

Alice fiddled with her sleeve. 'You shouldn't have. On an understudy's pay.'

Philip laughed bitterly. 'It's daft, isn't it, being paid for what you do best?'

'What do you mean?'

'Understudying. I've stood in for the real thing from the day I met you, haven't I? And here I am again. Standing in.'

Something inside Alice snapped. 'What do you mean, "stood in"? How do you think it's been for me? You sneer at me for picking the wrong men all the time. Have you any idea what it's like being in love with someone who thinks you'd make a very good sister? Well, stuff you, you slob, and stuff your rotten flowers! They're for funerals, by the way. In case you didn't know.'

'Beginners, please. This is your beginners' call,' boomed the Tannoy in a fit of technical zeal.

Philip's face contorted with horror. 'I didn't know that,' he gasped. 'I just asked for the most expensive. I wanted to get it right for once.'

'Oh, well, you have,' retorted Alice bitterly. 'The end of the affair. Except there never was one, was there?'

'Between you and Janni Viszla? How could there be?'

'No,' said Alice, with more courage than she knew herself capable of, 'between you and me. I'm sorry, Philip. I know these things are best left unsaid, but you started it. Can I just say, it's very nice to know you love me. But it's not quite the way I'd hoped for, so it seems I'll have to learn to live with that.'

'What the hell are you talking about?' He caught hold of her as she tried to pass him.

Alice struggled to get free. 'We're going to be late.'

'Mr Carter and Miss Hemingway to the side of the stage,' called the Tannoy.

'What do you mean, "the way you'd hoped for"?'

'Oh, for God's sake, Philip. Let go of me. We're going to miss our cue.'

'Tell me, or you don't move from here. What were you hoping for?'

'You know.' Alice looked up into his eyes beseechingly. 'Don't make me make it worse. You know as well as I do. You told me that day at your flat. When we were rehearsing. After your father rang.'

'What? *What* did I tell you?'

'Miss Hemingway and Mr Carter to the side of the stage IMMEDIATELY,' came the anguished summons. Sam Biggins appeared at the stage door, white-faced. 'You two,' he shouted, 'get in there and get on that stage or I'm personally going to run the pair of you through.'

They fled.

The last performance of their foreign tour shocked even the most philistine amongst the Millennium Players' audience. The raw intensity of the lovers' passion, the fury of the sword fights, the heart-rending anguish of a love torn apart, the sickening inevitability of a tragedy unfolding relentlessly, remorselessly, before their eyes, stung even the most staid and cynical to a muffled acknowledgement that Shakespeare knew his stuff.

At the end flowers were thrown, handkerchiefs dragged across tear-filled eyes, the stamp of students' feet signalled that the show had finally come together.

In the bar Vanessa squeezed her husband's hand. 'What did I tell you?' Gareth, who had finished the whisky during the interval, smiled blearily and said he had never doubted her word. He had already been round to the dressing-rooms and made a point of congratulating the understudies on their 'magnificent effort', as he was still managing to call it.

A small party had been laid on in a senior lecturer's room on behalf of the British Council, no representative of which could be found to attend. The cast was strangely ruminative as they ate their canapés and sipped the strong sweet wine. A sense that something had come to an end hung over them, and it was more than their trip to Estonia.

Bernice, who usually thrived on these gatherings, sought out Richmond early in the evening and asked if he would mind very much if they went back to their hotel. She was tired, she said, and would like to get on with her packing. For once Richmond made no protest and the two of them slipped quietly away.

Shortly afterwards the party broke up.

Alice, her mind still in turmoil, couldn't face the thought of sleep. Inexorably she homed in on the river path, wandering along without a thought for where she was going. After a while she sat down on the charred stump of a tree.

It was raining slightly, once more blotting out the 'white night' so beloved of her guidebook. She watched, or rather listened, to the water. 'Limpidly lapping' came to mind. She smiled to herself. What a mess. A few weeks out of her life and she'd managed to wreck the whole thing. Surely even she should have been able to spare Philip the burden of her confession? Now they couldn't even be friends. She knew he would say that they could, just as she knew he wouldn't mean it.

A twig cracked behind her. She looked round, half-hoping

it was Janni, escaped and back to finish the job. It was Philip. She turned away.

'I didn't frighten you, did I?' He came and stood behind her, looking out across the water at the lights the other side. Alice said nothing. 'That's Russia over there, you know. That great red glow.'

'Is it?'

'I wouldn't mind going there.' He crouched down beside her. 'Pity Gareth couldn't have arranged that.'

'I thought you were giving up acting.'

Philip grinned ruefully. 'I don't know any more. I can't see me being any happier as an accountant.'

Alice smiled. 'Not if you spend that much on a bunch of flowers.'

'How do you know what I spent?'

'The price tag was still on.'

He shook his head. 'Failed again.'

Alice reached out and touched his arm. To her surprise Philip caught hold of her hand and almost crushed it between his own. 'Oh, Alice.'

She gazed at him in consternation. Tears were rolling down his face. 'Philip, what's the matter? Philip . . . don't cry. What's happened? Tell me. You can tell me. Is it . . .' She sought around for the fair man's name. 'Robert? Has he upset you?'

Philip shook his head distractedly. 'He always upsets me. I can't stand the bastard.'

Alice gazed helplessly. 'You don't mean that.'

'Yes, I do. He's a wrecker. Goes round ruining people's lives. Not that I care any more.'

'But what's happened to upset you? Is it something I've done?'

Philip gave a great hiccupping sob, then pulled back his shoulders in an effort to control himself. 'Sam told me everything,' he said chokily, staring into the darkness.

Alice waited. 'What did he tell you?' she asked gently when it seemed clear he would say no more. Philip heaved an enormous sigh, almost as though he was coming up from underwater. 'He told me you were very ill,' he said quietly, 'and that you don't have very long to live, and that was why it was so important for you to play Juliet. So that . . . so that . . .' He shuddered and dropped his head into his hands.

'So that what?' asked Alice, wondering if she was suffering some sort of drug withdrawal, so out of her body did she feel at that moment.

'So that you'd have something good to remember.' Philip leant forward and rocked to and fro, his whole body shaking with grief. Alice, without thinking, fastened her arms round him and held him as he sobbed. 'But why?' she asked again and again. 'Why did he tell you that?'

Eventually Philip stopped rocking. 'Because I'd said I wouldn't go on and if they had no Romeo they'd have had to cancel the performance. They've all known for ages, Alice. Maeve saw the fax from England, all about it all being up with you and your time . . . running out.' He gave an enormous shuddering sigh. 'It was only me who didn't know. Sam seemed to think you'd tell me yourself when you were ready.' He wiped his eyes. 'When do you think that would have been?'

Alice felt a chill like ice running through her veins. 'Never.'

'Never? Why not? Am I so far down the list? Or did you think I'd make a fool of myself, the way I am now?'

Alice unclasped her arms. She had never felt so alone. 'I'm not dying, Philip. At least, as far as I know I'm not.'

'But the fax . . . "Time running out" . . .'

'Not mine. Jay's. His screenplay's. It was all to do with that stupid film he was trying to finance. Janni and Alexei were supposed to set up a company to attract funds over here or something. They kept asking for money and Jay, of course, couldn't or wouldn't send it. That's what that was about. Not me. I was the last thing on his mind, you can be sure of that.' She felt the energy seeping out of her like a punctured balloon. 'So that was why they all wanted me to go on tonight? Not because they thought I could act. Just because they thought I might like to try.' She gave a bitter laugh. 'Well, that's certainly boosted my confidence.'

She became aware of a curious hiccupping sound. Philip was shaking with uncontrollable laughter.

'I cannot believe this,' he spluttered. 'I cannot believe what you've just told me. That bloody Maeve! And to think anyone believed her. We must all be stark staring mad. So you're all right? You're well? There's nothing wrong with you?' He leapt up and jumped over the log and then back again. Alice ducked.

'There will be if you kick my head in.'

He stopped then grabbed hold of her and twirled her round in the air. Alice clung on for dear life. 'Can you put me down, please? I feel sick.'

'Not till I've had my wicked way with you.'

She thumped him viciously on the shoulder. 'Put me down.'

Philip lowered her to the ground. 'What's the matter? It was only a joke.'

'Obviously.'

'What do you mean? I thought that was what you wanted – from what you said before the show. Did I get that all wrong as well?'

Alice stood still. 'I'm sorry I said what I said before the show, Philip. I shouldn't have. There's no need for you to pretend to feelings you haven't got. I think I deserve better than that.' She turned away. He caught hold of her.

'Tell me what this is about.'

'Let go. I want to go back.'

'You stay here till you tell me.'

'There's nothing to tell.'

'Yes, there *is.*' He shook her quite forcibly. 'You told me tonight you loved me. Are you saying now you didn't mean it?'

Alice closed her eyes. 'Why are you making me go through this? What good will it do?'

'Tell me.'

She opened her eyes again and looked up into his. 'It means I know you're gay, Philip. You told me yourself, if you remember?'

Philip let go of her and stepped back. He looked as though he had been socked on the jaw. 'When did I say that?'

'You know full well. That time your father phoned. You said there were two things he hated – more than semolina pudding.'

Philip frowned in confusion. 'Reds and gays. It's tapioca, actually.'

'And that he had one of each for a son. You can't have forgotten that, surely?'

Philip's arms drooped. He stared at her disbelievingly. All the strength seemed to have gone out of him. 'And you thought I was the gay?'

Alice found she was equally floppy. 'Well, yes.'

Philip's face twisted between dismay and hysteria. 'It's Paul. That's why it's a problem, don't you see? He's married. He's got a kid. A fabulous kid. A fabulous wife. Everything was fine till that . . . till Robert came on the scene.' He sank down on the log. 'At first we thought it was a joke the way they fooled around together, went away for weekends . . . Robert does modelling so it seemed perfectly normal for Paul to take him on a shoot. It was only gradually that we started to notice things. Well, not me so much. Maxine. I could see she didn't think it was funny any more.

'Then one Sunday I went round there. Paul was out and she just broke down. He'd told her everything. He was going to move out – go and stay with Robert – but Maxine couldn't bear it. She said she'd put up with it if he stayed with her, for Danny's sake. Truth is, I think she hoped it was just a phase, that he would come back to her. Or that Robert would see the harm he was doing and clear off out of it. He was her brother, for God's sake. She thought he cared about her. She thought she knew him.' Philip hesitated. 'The same as I thought I knew Paul.'

Alice sat for a moment. 'So what will happen?'

Philip shrugged. 'I don't know. That's why I took this job, if you want to know. I had to get away.'

'But surely no one blamed you for any of it? How could they?'

Philip said nothing. Alice reached out and touched his hand. 'You don't have to tell me anything you don't want to, Philip. I wouldn't blame you if you never spoke to me again the way I've carried on.'

He nodded. 'Still, it's no way to live, is it? All these dark secrets?' He hunched his shoulders tight then let them go. 'Maxine was very unhappy, very lonely when all this came out. I was the only one she could turn to. I suppose it was obvious we'd end up lovers at some point. It was nothing serious, nothing permanent. More like comfort, I suppose.'

'Or revenge,' said Alice softly.

Philip looked at her. 'Maybe. So. Now you know.'

'Is it over?'

'It was over from the minute I saw you.'

Alice smiled a little sadly. 'That sounds like a line from a play.'

Tentatively Philip reached over and took her hand. 'They don't all end badly.'

At about eleven o'clock that evening Jasmine Ruddock was released from the police station, having amply demonstrated that she could not throw a vase full of water at someone without hitting them head-on. She had made friends with the interpreter, a burly young man not unlike the Curator of Antiquities, and the two of them were last seen heading down town to a male strip joint which he had assured her was due to be raided around midnight.

Bernice, Richmond, Alice and Philip sat opposite each other on the train to Aberdeen. During the week since they had returned home a lot of things had happened.

Jasmine Ruddock had been offered the part of anchor girl for a sports programme being filmed in the West Country. Craig Penforth had informed his agent, and hence Gareth Paynton, that he could not leave Felicity to cope with her pregnancy alone while he set off for a further two months touring the Highlands and Islands.

Gareth had fretted miserably over his copy of *Spotlight* in the hunt for replacements till his wife had pointed out quite sensibly that Philip and Alice had proved themselves more than up to the task, and all he really need look for were two beginners to take over as understudies. 'But isn't young thing meant to be . . . ?'

'Be what, my precious?' asked Vanessa, closing the book firmly on a page of Variety Artiste Juveniles.

'Oh, nothing,' muttered Paynton, as he struggled to remember just what Alice had been suffering from. Whatever it was, she seemed to have recovered now. Looking a lot bonnier. Quite an attractive girl, actually. Yes, things were probably best left as they were. He didn't want the Arts Council coming after him about one or two little overspends that had cropped up during the tour.

He patted his inside pocket, where a letter confirming his contract to provide voice-overs for an army recruitment campaign, struck with one Alexei Morkov, a nice man he had met through Madame Skikne, still nestled. Pity he had had to pay quite so much up front to secure the offer, but he was sure he could bury it somewhere in the final reckoning for the tour.

Alice and Philip had spent a week of wild abandon, washing their clothes, spending their pay rises and pawing over the Aberdeen digs list. Now they were on their way.

Bernice, watching the two of them, so obviously in love, thought dreamily of the days Richmond and she had toured together before middle age, whisky and mortgages caught up with them. She nudged her husband.

'Eh? What?' snorted Richmond who had been dozing behind a colour supplement.

'Sorry, my darling. Did I wake you?'

He blinked rapidly and tried to think what she had asked him. 'No. What? I say, have you seen this?' He peered shortsightedly at the magazine. 'Goodness. No. Well, there you are. Who'd have thought it?'

'Thought what?' asked Philip, trying to look interested.

'No. Here it is.' He turned to Bernice. 'You remember that article there was in one of my *Telegraphs* while we were in Tallinn?' Bernice literally froze, as did Alice.

The two women sat speechless while Richmond peered, harrumphed, adjusted his glasses and began to read:

> The theft of a series of valuable religious icons from the Alexander Nevsky cathedral in Tallinn, capital of Estonia, has been solved. Following information gained from a group of criminals, led by Amelia Rikov, an international authority on Eastern European art, who was recently among a number of people charged with fraud and various other crimes believed to relate to the Russian Mafia, the collection was discovered in the home of a Latvian aristocrat who claimed they were family heirlooms, and even produced fake documents in an effort to substantiate his claim.
>
> Fortunately the icons, particularly the tiny central portrait of the Madonna and Child, were too distinctive to escape the sharp eye of the experts called in to verify the finds. They are considered unique amongst the works of the day for the fact that the Madonna is clothed entirely in red, considered at the time of painting to be the colour of the devil.

'Red?' shrieked Bernice, causing everyone in the carriage to spin round. 'RED? Are you sure?'

'That's what it says, my sweet,' said Richmond. 'Why? Is there something odd about that?'

'No,' said Bernice, her own colour returning to normal. 'No, no, of course not. It just struck me as strange, that's all. Did you hear that, Alice dear? The Madonna was red, not . . . another colour at all.'

'Yes,' murmured Alice weakly. 'Yes, I heard.'

Philip glanced down at her and squeezed her hand conspiratorially. 'Still,' he whispered, 'you were right about the cathedral. It was something else by moonlight.' Before Alice could react he leant across to Richmond. 'Could I have a look at that after you, Richmond, please?'

'What? Oh, yes. Have it, dear boy,' muttered Richmond who was already dozing off.

Philip sat back and flipped the pages. 'Look at this, Alice. Just the thing.' She peered over his arm.

'Oh, yes,' she said demurely. 'Garden centres. How lovely.' Then she kicked him under the table.